ROLL OF THE DICE

DURYODHANA'S MAHABHARATA

AJAYA

Epic of the Kaurava Clan

BOOK I

ANAND NEELAKANTAN

PLATINUM PRESS
PREM JUNFICTION

Times
Group
Books

ISBN 978-93-81576-03-8
© Anand Neelakantan, 2015

Layouts: Ajay Shah
Cover: Kunal Kundu
Printing: Thomson Press (India) Limited

First published in India 2015 by

An imprint of
LEADSTART PUBLISHING PVT LTD
Unit 25-26, Building A/1, Near Wadala RTO,
Wadala (E), Mumbai – 400 037, INDIA
T + 91 22 2404 6887
W www.leadstartcorp.com

This edition is reprinted in 2018

Marketed and Distributed by

 A division of
Bennett, Coleman & Co. Ltd.
The Times of India, 10 Daryaganj, New Delhi - 110002
Phone: 011-39843333, Email: tgb@timesgroup.in
www.toibooks.com

To my Aparna,
and our Ananya & Abhinav

ABOUT THE AUTHOR

 I WAS BORN IN A QUAINT little village called Thripoonithura, on the outskirts of Cochin, Kerala. Located east of mainland Ernakulam, across Vembanad Lake, this village had the distinction of being the seat of the Cochin royal family. However, it was more famous for its 100-odd temples, the various classical artists it produced, and its school of music. I remember many an evening listening to the faint rhythm of the chendas coming from the temples, and the notes of the flute escaping over the rugged walls of the music school. However, Gulf money and the rapidly expanding city of Cochin, have wiped away all remaining vestiges of that old-world charm. The village has evolved into the usual, unremarkable, suburban hellhole – clones of which dot India.

Growing up in a village with more temples than was necessary, it was little wonder that mythology fascinated me. Ironically, I was drawn to the anti-heroes. My own life went on... I became an engineer, joined the Indian Oil Corporation, moved to Bangalore, married Aparna, and welcomed my daughter Ananya, and son, Abhinav. However, the voices of yore refused to be silenced in my mind. I felt impelled to narrate the stories of the vanquished and the damned; and give life to those silent heroes who have been overlooked in our uncritical acceptance of conventional renderings of our epics.

This is Anand's second book and follows the outstanding success of his national #1 bestseller, ASURA Tale Of The Vanquished *(Platinum Press 2012).* AJAYA Book II, Rise Of Kali, *is due for release later in 2014.*

Anand can be reached at: mail@asura.co.in

CONTENTS

WHY WRITE ABOUT DURYODHANA?

Many years ago, I witnessed a spectacle many of my readers would not even have heard about, let alone seen. It was a day of grand celebration. Even the hot tropical sun shining above could not diminish the pervading festive spirit. There were more than 100,000 people assembled to watch the procession and pay homage to the presiding deity of the temple. The devotees belonged to all castes and creeds and the fervour they displayed was bewitching to watch. Strangely enough, the majestic festival was in honour of a man I had always believed to have few admirers, if any. The deity at the Malanada Temple in Poruvazhy village, Kerala, is none other than the most reviled villain of Indian mythology – Duryodhana. If the devotees are to be believed, the tradition of this procession goes back centuries to the time of the *Mahabharata* itself.

There is a fascinating story attached to the temple: Duryodhana came to the village in search of the Pandavas in exile. Thirsty, he asked an old woman for water. Impulsively, she gave him the toddy she was carrying. The parched Prince drank it with relish. It was only then that the woman noticed he was a Kshatriya warrior and he could lose his caste by drinking toddy served by an Untouchable Kurathi woman like herself. Horrified by what she had done, she was certain the Kshatriya Prince would punish her with death if she told him the truth. However, not wishing to cheat someone who had trusted her, she confessed her 'crime', risking her life. She waited for certain punishment, but was astonished by Duryodhana's reaction. "Mother," he said, "there is no caste for hunger and thirst. Blessed are you for putting the interests of a thirsty man before your own safety."

The villagers rushed to see this high-born man who was so different from the haughty, upper-caste men who came only to punish them or treat them like worms. The Hastinapura Prince announced he was gifting the surrounding villages to a temple that would be built but have no idol. A Kurava Untouchable would be the Priest. To this day, family members of that old woman's family are the hereditary Priests of the temple, which has no idol. Instead, the presiding deity is Duryodhana. The minor deities are his wife Bhanumati, his mother Gandhari, and his friend Karna. It is generally believed that the spirit of Duryodhana resides here to protect the poor and weak. He answers the prayers of the destitute and those suffering from disease, poverty, or harassment from those stronger than themselves. This deity is the protector of the weak and downtrodden.

My first reaction to the story was one of incredulity. Why would a Prince of Hastinapura, located at the northern-most border of the country, have come all the way to a village at the southern tip of India – a distance of more than 3000 kilometres – thousands of years ago? The answer to my question was like a slap in my face. The villager asked me why the Adi Shankaracharya had travelled so many times from a village in Kerala to Kedarnath or Badrinath, in his short lifespan of 32 years? It made me rush home to revisit the *Mahabharata*, an epic that has inspired countless writers over the centuries. Once I started viewing the Kaurava Prince through the eyes of the villagers of Poruvazhy, a different picture of Duryodhana began to emerge – far removed from the scheming, roaring, arrogant villain of popular television serials and traditional retellings. Instead, here was a brutally honest Prince, brave and self-willed, willing to fight for what he believed in. Duryodhana never believed his Pandava cousins to be of divine origin; and to modern minds, their outlandish claim now sounds chillingly similar to present-day political propaganda used to fool a gullible public.

Duryodhana's personality comes alive when he makes Karna, the King of Anga at a crucial moment in his life, when he is being humiliated because of his caste. The Kaurava Prince challenges orthodoxy by making a Suta a King, and he does so without selfish motives. His treatment of Ekalavya; his refusal to fight for Subhadra; his courage in taking on the Pandavas; and his unwavering faith in his friends; all make him hero material rather than a despicable villain. He never attempts to justify his treatment of Draupadi. His flaws make him human and believable, unlike the protagonists, who wrap themselves in a cloak of *dharma*, miracles, and divinity, to justify their actions. Tomes have been written in praise of the actions of the Pandavas and Krishna. Great works exist about Karna and Draupadi. There are literary masterpieces in vernacular languages about Bhima, Arjuna, and Kunti. However, except for *Orubhanga*, a play in classical Sanskrit by Bhasa, dealing with

Duryodhana's last moments, and *Gadayudha*, by the medieval Kannada poet Ranna, no authors have been sympathetic to the Crown Prince of Hastinapura.

Ajaya is an attempt to view the *Mahabharata* from the side that lost the war. One of the meanings of Duryodhana is 'one who is difficult to conquer', in other words, *Ajaya* (Unconquerable). Though named Suyodhana, the Pandavas used the derogatory 'Dur' to slander him as 'one who does not know how to wield power or arms'. Duryodhana's story includes those of Karna, Aswathama, Ekalavya, Bhishma, Drona, Shakuni, and many others. It is the narrative of the Others – the defeated, insulted, trampled upon – who fought without expecting divine intervention; believing in the justice of their cause. Perhaps *Ajaya* is my belated answer to the villager, who stumped me with his simple question on the humid afternoon when the procession honouring Suyodhana was marching through the green paddy fields of Poruvazhy: *If our Lord Duryodhana was an evil man, why did great men like Bhishma, Drona, Kripa, and the entire army of Krishna, fight the war on his side?*

SELECT CAST OF CHARACTERS

Bhishma: Grand Regent of the Kuru clan and granduncle to both the Pandavas and Kauravas. Also known as Gangadatta Devavrata. Referred to here as the Grand Regent or Bhishma, a name acquired after he took a vow of celibacy and relinquished his claim to the throne as a precondition to his father marrying Satyavathi, a fisherwoman (who had another son, Krishna Dwaipayana Vedavyasa, prior to this marriage).

Vidhura: Youngest of Bhishma's three nephews, he was born of a lowly house cleaner and the sage Vedavyasa. A renowned scholar and a gentleman, but of low caste, he is the Prime Minister of Hastinapura, and the conscience-keeper of the Grand Regent.

Parshavi: Vidhura's wife.

Dhritarashtra: Son of Vedavyasa, he is the legitimate, though blind, King of Hastinapura, and father of the Kauravas. Denied the kingship because of his blindness, Pandu (his albino younger brother), reigns instead. On Pandu's death, Dhritarashtra assumes the kingship nominally, with Bhishma as Grand Regent.

Pandu: Dhritarashtra's younger brother and briefly King of Hastinapura until his premature death. Cursed with impotency, his two wives (Kunti and Madri), are impregnated by sages and gods. There are, however, enough hints in the *Mahabharata* that their five sons were not, in fact, of divine origin. Called the Pandavas, they are recognized as Pandu's sons, though he did not father them. Pandu dies attempting sexual union with Madri, who then commits *sati*, leaving Kunti to care for all five boys.

Kunti: First wife of Pandu and collective mother to the Pandavas, she also has an illegitimate son. Ambitious, ruthless, and self-righteous, she is determined to ensure Yudhishtra succeeds to the throne of Hastinapura.

The Pandavas (five sons of Pandu):

- **Yudhishtra (Dharmaputra):** the eldest, was born to Kunti and fathered by Dharma or Yama, the God of Death. His claim to the throne of Hastinapura rests on the fact that he is considered Pandu's son, has divine lineage, and is older than Crown Prince Suyodhana by a day. The whole *Mahabharata* hinges on this accident of birth.

- **Bhima:** Kunti's next divine progeny is the Crown Prince's archenemy and is renowned for his brute strength as well as his willingness to use it on his brothers' behalf.

- **Arjuna:** Youngest of Kunti's three divine sons, he is a great archer and warrior, and Yudhishtra's only hope of winning against the Kauravas.
- **Nakula & Sahadeva:** Madri's twins, also of divine lineage, play minor roles in the epic as sidekicks to their three older siblings.

Draupadi: The wife shared by all five Pandava brothers. Dhristadyumna is her brother, and Shikandi (a eunuch), an adopted sibling. She is spirited and does not take insults quietly. Fiercely determined, she is perhaps the real 'man' in the Pandava camp.

Gandhari: Princess of Gandhara, Bhishma forcibly carries her off to marry his blind nephew, Dhritarashtra. She voluntary chooses to bind her eyes to share her husband's blindness. She is the mother of Crown Prince Suyodhana and his brothers, the Kauravas. Her brother is Shakuni.

Shakuni: Prince of Gandhara, Queen Gandhari's younger sibling, and maternal uncle to the Kauravas; his only ambition is the destruction of the kingdoms of India in order to avenge himself against Bhishma for sacking Gandhara, killing his father and brothers, and abducting his sister. Skilled at dice and intrigue, he always carries the dice made from the thighbones of his slain father.

The Kauravas: the legitimate scions of the Kuru clan, that holds suzerainty over all the kingdoms north of the Vindhya ranges. Crown Prince Suyodhana and his hundred siblings are determined to hold onto what is rightfully theirs.

- **Suyodhana:** Usually known as Duryodhana (a derogatory term signifying 'one who does not know how to use weapons or power'), is a name given to him by his detractors. The eldest of the Kauravas, and Dhritarashtra and Gandhari's firstborn, he is the legitimate Crown Prince of Hastinapura. This book is about his fight to claim his birthright. He is perhaps the most celebrated villain in Indian mythology, after Ravana of the *Ramayana*. However, here we see him as loyal and generous and sometimes brash and arrogant; his mind is set against the taboos and convoluted arguments of orthodoxy.
- **Sushasana:** Suyodhana's next sibling; more famously known as Dushasana.
- **Sushala:** The only girl child amongst the Kauravas, she is known as Dushala in popular lore; she is also the loving wife of Jayadratha, King of Sindh.

Jayadratha: King of Sindh, he is Suyodhana's brother-in-law and loyal friend.

Aswathama: Suyodhana's close friend and son of Guru Drona, this Brahmin youth refuses to blindly follow tradition. He believes Suyodhana's cause is just and is willing to fight even his illustrious father. He views Arjuna as his arch foe.

Guru Drona: Teacher to both the Pandavas and Kauravas, and Aswathama's father;

he will do anything to make Arjuna the greatest warrior in the world. His love for his disciple is legendary, exceeded only by his love for his son. Orthodox to the core, he believes in the superiority of his caste and that no lower castes should have the privilege of knowledge. The poverty of his early life haunts him.

Ekalavya: A tribal youth who desperately wants to become a warrior; he is ready to give his life to achieve some dignity for his people.

Karna: A low caste Suta and son of a charioteer, he is willing to travel to the Deep South to become a warrior par excellence. Generous, charitable, and exceptionally gifted, he is Suyodhana's answer to Arjuna's challenge. He is spurned for his low birth and insulted by Draupadi, but Suyodhana staunchly stands by him.

Parashurama: Drona, Kripa, and Karna's Guru, friend-turned-foe of the Grand Regent, and the supreme spiritual leader of the Southern Confederate. A fanatical Brahmin and the greatest living warrior of the times, he curses Karna for duping him about his caste. He yearns to defeat Hastinapura and bring all of India under his sway. He rues the peace treaty he signed with the Grand Regent years ago and awaits the opportunity to ignite a great war.

Kripa: A maverick genius as well as a learned Brahmin warrior, he does not believe in caste. He is Drona's brother-in-law (his opposite), and Aswathama's uncle. He believes Suyodhana has a point. A carefree soul without boundaries, he is outspoken to the point of arrogance but kind-hearted beneath his rough exterior. He believes knowledge ought to be shared freely.

Balarama: Leader of the Yadava clan; an idealistic dreamer who wishes to bring prosperity to his people and believes in the equality of all men. He sees the path to progress as lying in farming and trade. A pacifist at heart, he builds an ideal city on the west coast of India, where he puts his ideas into practice. He longs to prove one can rule without compromising one's principles. Elder brother to Krishna and Subhadra, he is also Suyodhana's Guru and mentor, and inspires men like Karna to reach beyond the imposed limitations of their caste.

Krishna: A Yadava Prince who many consider an *avatar* of Vishnu – part of the Hindu Trinity. He believes he has come to this world to save it from evil. He is also Arjuna's brother-in-law and mentor. He sees the Great War as the inevitable conflict required to put all ambiguities to rest, and for *dharma* to be reinstated. His greatest challenges come from men like Jarasandha, Suyodhana, Karna, Ekalavya, and Carvaka.

Subhadra: Suyodhana's first love, and later wife of his greatest foe – Arjuna.

Takshaka: Leader of the rebel Nagas, he wishes for a revolution whereby the

Shudras and Untouchables will become the rulers and the high castes their slaves. He is a fierce warrior and a megalomaniac dictator in the making.

Vasuki: Deposed Naga King; he is old and frail, but desperately wants the kingship back. He believes Takshaka is leading his people to destruction.

Jarasandha: The King of Magadha. In his kingdom, merit rules instead of caste.

General Hiranayadhanus: Father of Ekalavya and Commander-in-Chief of Jarasandha's army, he has risen from the lowliest caste, the Nishadas, by dint of his own merit and the friendship of King Jarasandha.

Mayasura: A great architect and a low caste Asura.

Indra: The last King of the illustrious Deva Empire. Living in penury in the forest, he wants to make a secret weapon for his son, Arjuna, without which he fears his son is doomed.

Dhaumya: An ambitious and unscrupulous Priest, he acts as Parashurama's eyes, ears, and arm, in Hastinapura. His aim is a perfect society where Priests will decree and the rest follow. He is Kunti and Yudhishtra's chief advisor.

Purochana: A corrupt but efficient bureaucrat in league with Shakuni.

Durjaya: A man of the gutters, he rules the dark underworld of Hastinapura. A crime lord, he engineers riots, and is in the pay of the Gandhara Prince, Shakuni.

Krishna [black] **Dwaipayana** [born on an island] **Vedavyasa** [chronicler of the *Veda*s]: A great scholar, and author of the *Mahabharata*, the *Mahabhagavatha* (the longest epic in the world), and eighteen *Puranas*, he also codified and edited the *Veda*s and is considered the patron saint of all writers. Son of Satyavathi (a fisherwoman) and Parashara, he is the Grand Regent's step-brother. He is also the biological father of Pandu, Dhritarashtra and Vidhura, and thus the grandfather of all the main protagonists of the *Mahabharata*.

And finally, the most unimportant characters in the book:

Jara and his blind dog Dharma: A deformed beggar, Jara lives on the dusty streets of India, accompanied by his blind dog, Dharma. Illiterate, ignorant, frail, and dirt poor, he is one of the many who believe in the divinity of Krishna. He is a fervent devotee of the *avatar*. An Untouchable, rejected by all and spurned by most, yet Jara rejoices in the blessings of his beloved God and celebrates life.

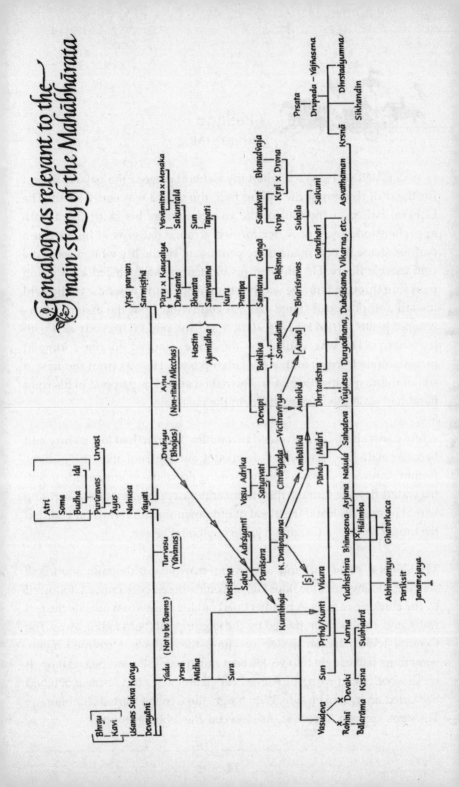

Genealogy as relevant to the main story of the Mahābhārata

Prelude
GANDHARA

IT WAS RAINING HEAVILY when the General entered the palace. Except for the dull rhythm of the falling rain, the palace was eerily silent. The General halted at the foot of the wooden stairs, his heart filled with apprehension. Pools of water formed strange patterns at his feet in a curious shade of red, made more prominent by the lily whiteness of the cold marble floors. He adjusted his battledress and winced as blinding pain shot through him. He was bleeding from many wounds, yet he held his tall and powerful frame erect. A cold wind from the distant snow-covered peaks ruffled his long, dark beard and pierced his body as if with icy shards. He was chilled to the bone, unused to these rugged mountainous terrains and snow-laden passes. He was from the East, a son of the vast Gangetic plains. The naked sword he gripped in his right hand had slain scores of warriors in the past hour.

A few paces apart, his men stood reverently. The rain had lost its fury and become a drizzle. Rainwater dripped from the roof into the gutters, forming eddies of darkness before rushing down the mountainside to join the waters flowing through the distant and dusty plains to the sea, carrying with it human flesh and the blood of unknown warriors who had guarded the mountain city of Gandhara just a few hours before.

The General stood stiff and unmoving, frowning at the faint sounds of sobbing coming from the floor above. Somewhere a cock crowed, followed by the clucking of hens. A peddler cried out his wares from outside the fort walls, and a bullock cart passed by, the jingling of its bells fading away. The General took a tentative step to climb the stairs but stopped again. Something had caught his eye. He bent down painfully and picked it up. It was a wooden cart with a broken wheel – a little boy's toy. A smear of blood had dried on its broken side. With a sigh, the General started climbing up. The steps groaned in protest. As if on cue, the sobbing stopped.

The long verandah ran a considerable distance, vanishing into shadow. It started snowing and the white flakes fell on the wooden benches placed along the corridor, forming strange shapes. The General walked slowly, careful not to step on the dead soldiers. He held the broken toy in his left hand and a curved Indian sword in his right. He hated the snow and the bitter cold of the mountains and longed for the sunny plains of his homeland. He wished only to finish this task and get back to the banks of the Ganga. He paused to listen. There was a rustling of clothing and he sensed somebody waiting for him within. His wounded body tensed. The toy in his hand had become a burden. 'Why did I pick it up?' he wondered. But now he did not now wish to throw it away. With the tip of his sword, he slowly pushed at the half-open door. The General entered the room, his tall and broad silhouette throwing dark shadows into the dim room. Once his eyes had adjusted to the darkness, he saw her; partly veiled by the shadows that cloaked the room. She sat with eyes downcast and her arms wrapped around her knees. She looked tired of waiting for her fate. The warrior's tense muscles relaxed a little as he let out a weary sigh. 'Thank God, no more bloodshed today,' he thought.

An oil lamp in the corner apologetically spread a small circle of dull light. It only served to amplify the darkness beyond the reach of its frail aura. The General turned up the wick and a golden light fell upon the exquisitely beautiful woman. 'My fate is to bring unhappiness to such beautiful creations of divinity,' he thought with sudden anger. He cursed the day he had impulsively taken the oath of celibacy to satisfy his father's lust. It had made almost all the women in his life unhappy and ruined the lives of some. 'Today, I add one more to that unhappy list,' he thought in frustration, and then ruefully chuckled at the irony of fate which deigned that a celibate like himself should hunt women and spill blood for them.

Pushing aside his dark thoughts, the General made an elaborate bow to the lovely woman before him. "Daughter, I am Gangadatta Devavrata, Grand Regent of Hastinapura. You may perhaps have heard the name Bhishma. I have come to seek your hand in marriage for my nephew, Dhritarashtra, Prince of Hastinapura."

In the thick silence that ensued, Bhishma kept his gaze averted from the lovely grey eyes that burned with such fire. In the years to come, Bhishma would always remember those eyes staring into his own, even when they were hidden from the world. The girl let out a wrenching sob that pierced his heart. Collecting herself, she stood up, raised her head, and said with majestic dignity, "Grand Regent Bhishma, I trust Gandhara has not failed in its hospitality towards you. I apologise that my father is not here to greet you himself. I, Gandhari, Princess of Gandhara, welcome you in his name."

Bhishma stood paralysed by the icy chill of her voice. He felt a strange urge to confess everything to her; to justify the acts he had been forced to commit for the sake of his kingdom. He felt small and mean before this young girl who carried herself with such dignity and composure in the face of so much tragedy. Bhishma felt like a brute. He wished his anger would return so that he could take her by her narrow waist and ride off to Hastinapura with her, like a warrior of fable. But he could not; he was a warrior of the old school and a man of chivalry.

"I do not have a choice do I, Sir? When the Regent of Hastinapura decides which maiden is to be stolen as a bride for his nephew, what choice do we, who live on the borders of the great Indian empire, have? Do not perturb yourself... our resistance is at an end. Gandhara has been routed as you intended. I am your captive and shall go with you to become your blind nephew's bride."

Bhishma found he had lost the ability to speak. He looked into the distance, at the snowy slopes of the mountains and thought she could finish him off right now with a quick thrust of a dagger into his back. Yet he did not want to face her and gaze into those grey eyes. Being stabbed by this beautiful woman would be a good way to end his dry life; it was better than knowing such beautiful women existed in the world but all he could do was steal them on behalf of his incompetent or impotent nephews, or whichever fool sat on the throne of Hastinapura. Life had been a series of battles, treachery, politics and intrigue, and he was weary of it – the bloody defence of others – his father, his country, his brothers, his nephews, but never for himself.

He was sick of it all. Yet there was no warrior in the whole of India, no King or Prince, who could challenge the Regent of Hastinapura.

Bhishma walked away, half-expecting Gandhari to stab him and was rather disappointed when she followed meekly. As they reached the verandah, a sudden blast of icy wind hit him and he shuddered. He turned back to see Gandhari looking at the broken toy in his hand. He felt embarrassed, wanting to throw it away or hide it from her gaze. Then he heard a sob. It did not come from the lovely woman before him, but from somewhere within the dark depths of the room where she had sat waiting for him. When Gandhari saw that he had heard the sob, a look of fear and pure hatred crossed her face. Bhishma moved quickly towards the room. Gandhari grabbed at his arm and clawed at his back, trying to stop him. Venting the pent-up anger and frustration of many years, he pushed her back in sudden fury and entered the room. Gandhari fell but was up and after him in a trice, trying to slow him down, scratching him with her long nails and biting – to no effect.

The sobs came from under the bed. The tall warrior bent down, his sword held before him to block an unexpected thrust from a sharp weapon that could slash his face. A small hand reached for the toy cart and then disappeared in a flash. But Bhishma caught the small hand and pulled hard. It was a little boy, barely five years old. Bhishma carried him into the light of the verandah to observe him. The boy was covered in blood but unhurt except for a wound on his left leg. His large, animal eyes looked at the tough warrior-prince with all the hatred he had gathered in his young life. It was at such moments that Bhishma hated himself. He could face a thousand arrows on the battlefield but the little boy's eyes pierced his armour and reached deep into his heart. His Gurus would have advised him not to spare the boy's life. When one conquered a country, it was prudent to finish off all the males and take the women. It prevented misadventures and future wars of revenge. Bhishma could almost hear his father's voice prompting him to thrust his sword through the tiny heart.

Slowly, very slowly, Bhishma put the boy down. He immediately collapsed onto the floor, unable to stand on his hurt leg. "Who is he?" Bhishma asked Gandhari.

"He is Shakuni, Prince of Gandhara. I know you will kill him. That is the *dharma* of the Kshatriya, is it not? I know all about the code of the warrior. But I beg you not to do it in front of me. He is my little brother...please have mercy..." Gandhari begged.

Bhishma stood up, embarrassed and unable to look at the haughty Princess in distress or the small boy who lay wheezing at his feet. His sword trembled in his hand. He slowly knelt and put down the toy cart near the boy, who grabbed at it, clutching it to his heart. Bhishma felt tears flood his eyes. He was irritated at himself for his weakness and pushed the boy away. Shakuni let out a howl of pain. "I will not kill him. I can see how much you love him. Take him with you to Hastinapura. He shall grow up there as a Prince of the Kurus," Bhishma said, hating himself every moment for giving in.

Gandhari let out a shuddering sigh, relieved at having the life of her young brother saved. Bhishma stood up and looked at them. The wind had become stronger and he shivered in the cold. Gandhari picked up the little boy in her arms, stumbling under his weight. Bhishma reached out and took Shakuni from her. As the Grand Regent lifted him, the boy spat into his face with all the hatred he could muster. Bhishma wiped the bloody saliva with the back of his hand and walked on, his face set like granite.

***

They rode back to the dusty plains of the Ganges, to the palace in the eternal city of elephants, to the famed capital of India – Hastinapura. Shakuni lay limp across the saddle of the mighty warrior as the beautiful Princess of Gandhara galloped behind. Throughout the journey, Bhishma was preoccupied with thoughts of finding a bride for his other nephew, the albino Pandu. Experienced warrior that he was, he would not else have missed the hatred burning in the eyes of the little boy. It was the gravest mistake the Regent of the Kurus made in his long and illustrious life.

1 PRINCE OF THE BLOOD

"I WILL FIND YOU SUYODHANA, and drag you out from whichever rat hole you are hiding in. You coward! *Come out*! I am not blind like your father. I will find and thrash you..." Bhima's booming voice echoed through the corridors of the Hastinapura palace.

The little boy cowered under the massive wooden bed, trembling with fear. The emptiness of the cavernous room oppressed him. Cloaked in the musty darkness under his father's bed, he hoped his tormentor would not find him. He could smell the lingering traces of the faint and musky odour which clung to his father, and wished he would return soon. For the last six months, every day had been like this – being chased by his cousin while he hid under the bed and waited with thumping heart for his enemy to lose interest in him and give up, while he cowered in fear. Though a year younger, Bhima stood a foot taller than the pale and wispy Suyodhana. Bhima took pleasure in being cruel to anyone he considered weak. He was something of a lout. What he lacked in brains he more than made up in sheer physical prowess.

***

Suyodhana knew his fat cousin would be prowling the corridors of the palace looking for him as well as his brother. 'I hope he doesn't get hold of Sushasana,' he prayed. Sushasana was agile and could climb any tree. All the bulky fatso below could do then was throw stones at his agile cousin, who made faces at him. Bhima's aim was so poor that more than once he had broken a window and been reprimanded by their stern Granduncle, Bhishma. Knowing Suyodhana adored Sushala, his sister, Bhima also took great pleasure in making the little girl cry when her brothers were around. Invariably Suyodhana or Sushasana would get into a fight with their fat cousin over this. If none of the elders were around to stop it from becoming bloody, the squabble would develop into a brawl, with the other four brothers of the fat boy joining in.

But it was not Bhima whom Suyodhana hated the most. Of his five Pandava cousins, sons of his dead uncle, Pandu, he most feared Yudhishtra, the eldest. Had not his Uncle Shakuni warned him repeatedly about his pious cousin? While the young boy did not understand the inheritance and political issues Uncle Shakuni kept talking to him about, he hated the sheer hypocrisy of his eldest cousin, who was ten years old, almost the same age as he was. Yudhishtra behaved as if he was the most obedient, god-fearing and innocent boy in the world, but his kicks were often the most vicious in a fight. Suyodhana could understand Bhima's brutishness, but his eldest cousin's aggression confused him. In the presence of their elders, Yudhishtra was always sweet and loving towards his cousins, so his vile behaviour when they were alone baffled all the children.

Many a time, when Mother Kunti or Aunt Gandhari was present, Yudhishtra would affectionately kiss Suyodhana or Sushasana. Not that Gandhari could see. She had chosen to be blind like her husband and so bound her eyes. And that was another thing which confused little Suyodhana. Why would anyone refuse to look upon this beautiful world? Uncle Shakuni had once told him that she did it as a mark of protest against their Granduncle Bhishma, who had forced her to marry a blind man. But those words only served to confuse Suyodhana further. Did that mean his mother did not love his father, Dhritarashtra, the King? He had asked his mother once whether Uncle Shakuni was right; that she had chosen permanent darkness as a mark of protest. But she had just laughed and ruffled his hair affectionately. Gandhari had not answered him. But he had seen a damp patch form on the white silk cloth that covered her eyes. Had she been weeping?

How Suyodhana wished he had been born the child of common people. Uncle Shakuni had also told him that his paternal uncle, Vidhura, was the son of a palace maid and had been fathered by the same man who was the natural father of both King Dhritarashtra and his brother, Pandu.

"So what?" the little boy had asked puzzled. And Shakuni had answered that he would understand when he grew up. This had disappointed

Suyodhana. 'When will I grow up?' he wondered wistfully. Perhaps he would then have enough strength to get even with his tormentor. For now, he was all alone, hiding in the shadows and praying that his large cousin would not find him.

**

"I know you are hiding under your father's bed, you son of a blind fool. I'm coming to kick your thick head..."

'Oh Shiva! He has found me; he will get me now.' Suyodhana's heart thumped in his chest. Silhouetted against the fading light of the setting sun, Bhima's hulking frame cast a long shadow on the opposite wall. Suyodhana could only see his legs, but that was frightening enough. He wanted to cry out but knew nobody would come to his aid. He felt all alone in this cruel world, which was conspiring against him. Another shadow fell against the wall. Was it Bhima's younger brother Arjuna, coming to take part in the fun? Suyodhana crouched deeper into the darkness under the bed.

"Bhima, what are you doing here?" It was an adult's voice. Suyodhana peeped out carefully. Who was it? The setting sun emblazoned everything behind the doorframe in red and gold and this person stood like an unmoving black shadow.

Bhima's head turned in surprise at this interference. Suyodhana saw anger flash across his cousin's face.

"Why are you always after me? I will tell my mother." Though Bhima had raised his voice, there was some doubt in it. Suyodhana began creeping out from his hiding place.

"I saw you chasing the little Prince and I know you mean mischief. So I came after you."

"But we were just playing..."

"I do not call that playing."

"Uncle Vidhura, what are you doing here? You know these places are forbidden to people like you." Bhima had regained his confidence and decided that attack was his best defence. He knew well how much that underhanded jibe would hurt his uncle.

Suyodhana saw his uncle's shoulders stoop. 'Should I go back under the bed?' he wondered.

Vidhura looked around, as if to ascertain no one was near and then moved closer to Bhima, who took a few steps back. "Let us decide this before Lord Bhishma."

"I'm sorry Uncle, really sorry! I will go away." Bhima threw a hate-filled glance towards Suyodhana and walked out of the room with an elaborate show of avoiding any bodily contact with Vidhura.

Suyodhana felt a rush of gratitude towards his uncle. He ran forward and hugged the tall, dark figure. For a moment, Vidhura was taken aback. Then he pushed his nephew away gently. Suyodhana looked at his uncle, hurt showing on his young face.

"Prince Suyodhana, you know you should not do that. You cannot touch me, especially after you have already had your bath and should be getting ready for evening prayers."

"But you are my Uncle!" cried the young Prince. He wanted to add that his uncle had just saved him from his worst enemy.

When Vidhura spoke, the little boy could feel the pain that lay hidden within his simple words. "Nevertheless, you should not, my boy." The dark and handsome man stood gazing into the dusk.

"But why not?"

"Enough! I should not be here." Vidhura began to walk away.

Suyodhana ran after his uncle and pulled at his arm. Vidhura hastily pulled away.

"But tell me why."

"You will not understand now, Suyodhana, but when you are older, you will. Now let me go." Vidhura turned and walked quickly down the long corridor.

Suyodhana watched his uncle go, sadness and confusion clamouring in his mind and heart. The sun had set and darkness had spread its mantle over Hastinapura. The boy stood there, his body trembling with emotion. As he turned to go back to his father's room, he yearned to grow up quickly so he could find answers to the questions that troubled his mind and which all the elders evaded. Then he remembered the pain in his uncle's eyes. Perhaps being grown up was not such a good thing after all.

***

Suyodhana felt a desperate need to talk to his Uncle Shakuni about Bhima. Perhaps he was in the *sabha*. How Suyodhana hated his cousins! Uncle Pandu had been dead six months now and his cousins were still receiving condolences and sympathy on their bereavement. That only made them more obnoxious. They had added privileges now, with their mother wielding more power than ever before. Uncle Pandu's second wife, Aunt Madri, had committed *sati* on his pyre and Aunt Kunti had then arrived at the palace, bringing Aunt Madri's twin boys along with her own three sons.

Suyodhana did not relish the thought of going to the *sabha*. He prayed there were no heated debates taking place, as there had been twice in recent months. The first had been when the Grand Regent had decided to make Vidhura, the Prime Minister. Suyodhana had been sitting with his Uncle Shakuni, when the Grand Regent stood up to make that historic announcement.

"Today is a special day for Hastinapura. With the consent of His Highness Dhritarashtra, I appoint the sagacious and learned scholar Vidhura, Prime Minister of Hastinapura." The *sabha* had immediately erupted into an uproar.

"But your Excellency, he is a Shudra; the son of a palace maid!" Dhaumya, a young Priest stood up and shouted over the din. Suyodhana looked up at Shakuni, who sat with a smug smile on his face, gently caressing his knees.

Bhishma raised his hands and the murmurings died away. "*Sri* Dhaumya, must I remind you that like His Highness Dhritarashtra and the deceased King Pandu, Vidhura too, is the grandson of my father Shantanu?"

"But Sir..."

"Must I remind you that the King's grandmother, Satyavathi, was a fisherwoman, who wed my father, a blue-blooded Kshatriya? Must I remind you that when her son Vichitraveera died without an heir to continue the line, the same fisherwoman dared to overrule men like yourself and call upon her other son, the sage Vyasa, to impregnate her widowed daughters-in-law, according to the ancient custom of *niyoga*?"

"Sir, *niyoga* is..."

"Dhaumya, keep your sermons to yourself. Tell me who Krishna Dwaipayana Vyasa is?" The young Priest squirmed at the question. "Why do you feel so embarrassed to speak the truth? Vyasa is the illegitimate son of my stepmother Satyavathi, fathered by the sage Parashara, before her marriage to my father. Vyasa, the son of a fisherwoman, is the father of Dhritarashtra, Pandu, and Vidhura. So which caste does Vidhura belong to?" Bhishma asked with a mischievous smile on his usually stern face.

"Bhishma got him there!" Shakuni whispered into Suyodhana's ears. Suyodhana looked at his uncle for an explanation. Shakuni explained to the young boy that the Grand Regent had beautifully tied Dhaumya into a knot using his own arguments against him. If the young Priest said Vidhura was a Shudra, because of his mother, then the entire Kuru lineage became Shudra, because their grandmother was a fisherwoman. Questioning Vidhura's legitimacy was like questioning the King's lineage.

Dhaumya knew he was beaten. Suyodhana watched him sit down sullenly. The new Prime Minister then took an oath to serve the kingdom until the day of his death.

Though Shakuni had effusively congratulated the new Prime Minister that day, Suyodhana somehow felt that they disliked each other intensely.

Suyodhana vividly remembered the second debate as well. It had all started with his aunt Kunti requesting Bhishma to permit her to attend the *sabha*. When the Grand Regent announced his decision, Dhaumya angrily remarked that it was unprecedented for women to be present in the *sabha*. The orthodox Brahmin quoted various *smritis* regarding widows not being permitted to be seen in public, let alone holding positions of power.

Bhishma placed Vidhura in the forefront of this battle against orthodoxy and the scholar put the learned Brahmins to shame by eloquently quoting the *Vedas* and overwhelming them with examples of women, including widows, playing prominent roles in the country's affairs from ancient times. When logic did not work, the Priests began abusing the man, saying Vidhura did not have the authority to study the *Vedas* and thus there was no question of his quoting scripture. Suyodhana could still feel Vidhura's pain.

Fortunately for the beleaguered Prime Minister, the travelling ascetic and greatest living scholar of the *Vedas*, Krishna Dwaipayana Vyasa, walked into the court that day. Bhishma and even the blind King, rose from their seats to touch the feet of the great man. When Bhishma sought his advice on the ticklish question, the sage quietened the raging war of words with his characteristic humour and wisdom. Considered the final authority on all scriptures, he was in the process of codifying, arranging and recording India's ancient oral literature. He told the Priests that Vidhura was right.

"What right has a Shudra to quote the scriptures? Guru, perhaps you empathise with him because of your special relationship to Vidhura," Dhaumya said, smirking at his supporters.

When Suyodhana asked his uncle what the Priest had meant by that remark, Shakuni told him to keep quiet. But Suyodhana could feel the tension in the air. Shakuni was observing the sage intently.

In response to Dhaumya's barbed comment, Vyasa chuckled. "Why don't you say what you mean, young man? I am a Shudra. Moreover, I was born out of wedlock. I am the illegitimate child of a dark-skinned fisherwoman and the scholarly Brahmin, Parashara, who did not think twice about my caste when imparting knowledge of the scriptures to me."

The Priests stood writhing before him in discomfort.

"I have added to my father's teachings by virtue of the knowledge gained through my travels and discourses with saints and scholars throughout this land. None of these savants ever asked me what my caste was. I have travelled from the Himalayas to the holy city where the three oceans meet, and no scholar asked me which language or dialect I spoke at home. They came from all classes and creeds, and differed in their thoughts, yet they all spoke the universal language of love towards humankind. They lived far from the cities and shunned worldly comforts for the serenity of the forests. They neither clung to power nor claimed supremacy by accident of birth. They did not write *smritis* or believe in them. Yet here you are, using your scholarship and intellect to divide people based on caste, creed and dialect; while the truly great ones only sought the betterment of the whole world. Therein lies the difference. I pray God grant you the wisdom to know the Truth. Should the likes of Parashurama prevail, I foresee bloodshed and war for this holy land of India."

There was perfect silence in the *sabha*. Suyodhana winced in pain as Shakuni's grip tightened on his shoulder. He tried to wriggle away but when he looked at his uncle's face, he suddenly felt afraid. Shakuni was staring at the sage with open hostility. Shakuni looked down at his nephew and his face relaxed as he loosened his grip.

"Kunti may attend the *sabha*," the Grand Regent pronounced to a smattering of applause.

Shakuni stood up to his full, imperious height. "Your Excellency, then what about my sister, Gandhari? Is she too, not qualified to attend the *sabha*?"

Bhishma stared at him for a long time and finally said, "Why not? It is a positive step forward. Like the women of yore, let Gandhari and Kunti bless our *sabha* with their wisdom."

Shakuni sat down, winking at Suyodhana, as the sage Vyasa walked away shaking his head. Suyodhana still rued that day. Now Gandhari no longer had time for her children, preoccupied as she was with countering Kunti's moves. The palace crackled with intrigue and conspiracy between the two powerful women, fighting for the future of their children. Even as a ten-year-old, Suyodhana could feel the tension in the air. The Royal men, however, appeared oblivious to the cold war between the women.

"See how the Priests favour Kunti over your mother," Shakuni had pointed out to him on another occasion. The same Priests had objected to Kunti's presence just a few weeks ago. Shakuni chuckled at Suyodhana's confusion. "Your aunt has endeared herself to those fanatics. She holds more fundamentalist views than even Dhaumya. If you do not watch out young man, one day they are going to throw you and your brothers out into the street like beggars, not to mention your parents."

"But Uncle..." Suyodhana looked up at Shakuni's crooked smile with his innocent dark eyes.

"Do not worry son, I am there to take care of you," Shakuni said, ruffling the boy's hair affectionately.

Now, after his narrow escape from Bhima, he wanted the comfort of Shakuni's presence. Suyodhana walked through the long corridors. Servants were lighting the oil lamps affixed to the walls. He could hear sounds coming from the great hall. He entered the well-lit *sabha*, acknowledging the bows of the guards stationed at the door. Dhritarashtra, King of Hastinapura, sat on a bejewelled throne. His priceless crown reflected golden lights from the crystal chandeliers that hung from the carved ceiling. Near him, in an equally magnificent chair, sat Bhishma, Grand Regent of the Kurus. Shakuni was nowhere to be seen.

Suyodhana watched his Granduncle Bhishma, engrossed in correspondence, intervening only when he felt the assembly needed his advice. Prime Minister Vidhura stood at his side, taking notes. Uncle Vidhura was someone Suyodhana liked, though he did not understand why everyone, including his own parents, treated him with a hint of contempt. Suyodhana tried to attract Gandhari's attention, but it was Bhishma who noticed him, and called him to sit on his lap. Suyodhana considered himself too old to sit on anyone's lap but obliged the old man for a few minutes. He planted a quick, embarrassed kiss on the grandsire's cheek when he insisted, and then hopped down and ran away, the indulgent laughter of the assembly ringing in his burning ears. He wanted to see his Uncle Shakuni.

2 THE TEACHER COMES

SUYODHANA SAW THEM AS THREE dark shadows on the horizon, slowly growing bigger as they approached Hastinapura. It was early and he was dangling from the groaning branch of a mango tree. His brother Sushasana had already climbed higher and was throwing down the ripe mangoes. Their sister, Sushala, was running here and there, trying to collect the mangoes in her outspread skirt. Squirrels chirped angrily at this intrusion.

Though it was early, the summer day was getting hotter and dustier. But like the other children, the three siblings were indifferent to the heat. The ripe smell of sweet mangoes was far more compelling than the travails of summer. Besides, Guru Kripacharya's training class would be starting soon and then it would be difficult to sneak off to the mango groves outside the fort. They had discovered this mango tree at the edge of a cliff quite accidentally the previous evening. Normally, the gluttonous Bhima finished off even the raw mangoes and mercilessly beat up Suyodhana and his siblings if they dared go near the grove. The palace guards usually looked the other way since they knew whom to please and where the real power lay.

Seeing that his five cousins were down by the cliff, Suyodhana felt safe from the goon. He could see them from his vantage point on the branch. The eldest, Yudhishtra, was sitting cross-legged, meditating with a seriousness that belied his youth. Bhima was chasing a mongrel dog. Arjuna was practicing archery, his concentration unwavering as he aimed at his target. With a shudder, the Prince saw that Arjuna was aiming at a nest where a bird was feeding its little ones. Suyodhana wanted to shout out a warning, but before he could, Arjuna had shot his arrow. Fortunately, it just missed its mark. Arjuna stamped his foot in disgust. The twins, Nakula and Sahadeva, were playing with a cloth ball.

The three figures Suyodhana had spotted earlier, turned out to be a Brahmin, his wife, and their son, who looked to be about eight years old. Suyodhana watched the tall, fair Brahmin with the dark flowing beard, approach Arjuna. Behind the Brahmin stood his wife, an emaciated and frail woman, who appeared ready to collapse. The boy with them stood still, his big black eyes filled with wonderment. Bhima moved menacingly towards the little boy, rolling his eyes. The boy's father was talking to Arjuna and did not see it. The boy clutched his mother's hand in fright as the bully grinned, pointing at him. Suyodhana wanted to run down the cliff and fight Bhima. He might not win and Bhima would probably thrash both him and his brother, but at least it would give the frail boy time to escape.

Sushasana had also seen Bhima. Picking up the biggest mango at hand, he stood poised to hurl it from the top of the tree. Suyodhana smiled at the thought of the ripe mango splattering on Bhima's fat face.

The Pandava twins came running excitedly and said something. The wind carried their voices to the top of the cliff and the Prince faintly heard that they had lost their cloth ball in a well. Bhima lost interest in the little Brahmin boy and ran towards the well. Sushasana, who had already let fly the ripe mango at Bhima, saw it miss and land on the ground, and roll towards a bush.

"*Bhai*, you threw away our best mango," whined little Sushala.

"Shut up!" hissed Sushasana, while Suyodhana smiled down at his pouting sister.

Meanwhile, Yudhishtra had uncoiled himself from his meditative pose and was speaking reverently to the Brahmin, bowing and touching his feet and behaving in the obsequious manner Suyodhana had come to despise in his eldest cousin. Bhima was leaning over the low wall of the well while the twins pointed to their ball floating in the water far below.

"Suyodhana, I wish I could tip fatso over the wall," said Sushasana wistfully and Suyodhana almost laughed aloud.

Yudhishtra led the Brahmin towards the well, with Arjuna following with his bow held firmly in his hand. The frail woman trailed behind. Two soldiers stood on guard at the gate of the fort; their faces mirror images of boredom. The Brahmin peered into the well and then slung down the bow he was carrying over his shoulder. He took an arrow from his quiver and tied the end of his *angavasthra* to its blunt end. Then he uncoiled the rope, which bound his belongings and tied it to the end of the *angavasthra*. He leaned precariously over the well wall, and taking careful aim, shot the arrow into the dark depths. From the cheers of the Pandava brothers, Suyodhana could tell the Brahmin had found his mark.

Suyodhana looked at his brother, who was watching the scene with astonishment. It was quite a feat to shoot a ball bobbing on the water thirty feet down a dark well. The Brahmin pulled out the ball, detached it from the sharp tip of his arrow, and placed it into the outstretched hands of Sahadeva, the youngest Pandava. Arjuna fell at the Brahmin's feet but was lifted up with a tenderness bordering on devotion.

Suyodhana could see the Brahmin consulting his five cousins about something. Yudhishtra was pointing excitedly towards the palace. Bhima stood there wearing the look of someone trying hard to understand what was going on. Suyodhana's eyes wandered away to rest on the small Brahmin boy, who lingered a few feet away from his parents. The boy looked around and his eyes locked onto the ripe yellow mango gleaming in the sun. He gazed longingly at the fruit and then darted towards it. He was about to touch it when a small dark figure jumped out from behind a bush and in a swift movement, grabbed the mango from the sand, leapt over the startled boy, and ran off as if his life depended on it. The stupefied boy gave chase. The intruder was looking back as he ran and so did not see the looming figure of Bhima standing in his path. It was only at the last moment that he turned to see the huge Pandava staring menacingly at him. Bhima stood in combat position, and just as the boy reached him, he threw a deadly punch at the boy's head. The boy ducked and in one fluid moment, without breaking stride, swooped down and pulled hard at Bhima's legs. Bhima fell flat on his face.

Suyodhana and Sushasana could not control themselves any longer. They laughed aloud, clutching their bellies, while Sushala joined in, clapping her little hands excitedly and jumping up and down.

The Brahmin turned and saw the urchin in the midst of the Princes, holding the disputed mango. His own son was a few feet away, bawling with all his might, to attract even more attention since he discovered the others were somehow interested in his loss. The five Princes closed in on the helpless urchin, led by the tall Brahmin.

"Guards!" the Brahmin yelled at the figures near the gate.

The two bored soldiers reluctantly got up from their reclining positions and lumbered towards the group. The hot sun was now scorching every blade of grass and the soldiers silently cursed the stranger for making them leave the shade. The urchin stood trembling with fear as the Princes and the Brahmin glowered at him. Bhima had a murderous look in his eyes and was still smarting from the humiliating fall he had taken. As the wind had turned, Suyodhana and his siblings could clearly hear the conversation.

Bhima moved towards the urchin, but the Brahmin immediately said, "Do not touch him and pollute yourself". Bhima looked confused and turned towards the Brahmin, who asked the urchin, "Which caste do you belong to?"

When the boy realized the Brahmin had asked him the question, he lowered his head. How was it, he wondered, that before anyone even asked him his name, they asked about his caste? He mumbled something that did not carry to the Kaurava Princes in their tree.

"What! A Nishada so close to the main fort gate of Hastinapura! An Untouchable walking on the royal highway? Is this how the King runs his kingdom? What can one expect of a blind man? It is no wonder such transgressions of *dharma* happen here." The Brahmin turned to the eldest Pandava. "What is the punishment meted out to rascals who commit such violations in the kingdom of the Kurus?"

The Pandavas appeared embarrassed and did not know what to say. The boys looked at each other. "I can break his head," volunteered Bhima, still smarting from the fall he had taken at the hands of the Nishada urchin half his size.

"Quiet!" The colour drained from Bhima's face. Turning to Yudhishtra the Brahmin said, "You are going to be the next King. You say how we should deal with this rascal. Let me see what my brother-in-law, Kripa, has taught you."

Yudhishtra tensed, trying to remember the correct answer. 'Kripa's brother-in-law? Was this Drona? So this was the famous *guru* whose arrival we all awaited.'

Eyes wide with surprise, Suyodhana quickly slid down the slope towards the commotion as his siblings followed. Something Drona had said to Yudhishtra jarred Suyodhana's mind: 'next King'. 'How can Yudhishtra be the next King of Hastinapura? I am the eldest son of the reigning King, Dhritarashtra,' wondered the young Prince. 'Uncle Pandu ruled on my father's behalf because of his blindness. That does not mean Pandu's son becomes the next ruler of Hastinapura when the time comes.' This was precisely the kind of conspiracy his Uncle Shakuni had warned him against.

Seeing Suyodhana and his siblings approach, the gaunt and fair Brahmin boy looked at them with apprehension and moved closer to his mother. Suyodhana looked at the boy's finely etched face. Curly hair fell to his shoulders and his curved mouth and aquiline nose spoke of innocence and inner beauty. The Kaurava Prince smiled at him in passing.

"Aswathama, come here," called the Brahmin and the boy moved towards his father apprehensively. "What punishment is proper for this rascal?"

Before Aswathama could answer, the dark boy took to his heels, losing the mango on the way. He nimbly jumped over the diminutive Aswathama and ran towards the jungle like a monkey, escaping his captors.

Aswathama ran to pick up the fallen mango from the sand, but before he could touch it, his father stopped him. "Get that boy!"

No one moved. Suyodhana watched the dark boy vanish into a flurry of waving foliage, which became still in a moment. The guards took off in reluctant pursuit of the Nishada who had polluted the royal highway and dared to steal from the royal grounds. Suyodhana knew the guards did not usually take such minor transgressions seriously as the poor always flocked to the palace gates and foraged for leftovers. Except when royalty was present on the highway, the caste rules were not strictly applied. It was too hot to pursue a small boy for such a silly crime and not worth the effort. The guards made a great show of searching for him and prayed the Brahmin would go away and leave them in peace to complete their game of dice. However, the Brahmin would not let them be. He stood in the blazing sun, waiting for the incompetent guards of Hastinapura to capture the culprit.

"What a surprise, brother!" The booming voice of Kripa, the Princes' teacher, broke the spell. Immediately, all the Princes bowed to their Master. Kripa turned towards them saying, "Have you nothing better to do than play in the hot sun? Have you finished the homework I gave you yesterday?"

"Yes Guruji," cried Arjuna, while Suyodhana cursed himself silently for having forgotten.

"You boys go and revise yesterday's lessons. I will take my brother-in-law to Bhishma. So, how was the journey? Hey! Aswathama, you have grown. You are almost as tall as me now." Kripa tried to catch the small boy who was hiding behind his mother.

"Kripa, don't touch him! He touched a Nishada boy," said Drona.

"What? All that is nonsense, Drona." Kripa grabbed the squealing Aswathama by his waist and threw him up into the air.

Kripi, the boy's mother, stood beaming, thankful that her brother had broken the tense scene. Her husband was still watching the guards but Kripa had started walking towards the palace with little Aswathama perched on his broad shoulders. The Pandava Princes and Kripi followed in his wake. Reluctantly, Drona turned, making a mental note of the loose way in which things were run in the largest empire of India. He would have a word with the Regent of the Kurus about such blatant violations of the caste rules. 'No wonder the rain gods are angry and have refused to shower their blessing on this land for the last two years,' he thought.

As the group vanished behind the safety of the fort gates, the little boy perched on the broad shoulders of Guru Kripa, turned back to look at Suyodhana and his siblings, who were counting their haul of mangoes. He smiled at them and Suyodhana grinned back. Neither had any inkling of what life had in store for them.

***

The Nishada boy, who had vanished into the bushes earlier, now darted back to pick up the discarded and forgotten mango. Sushasana grabbed him by his narrow waist but let go when Suyodhana came forward. 'Does he expect me to fall at his feet?' the Nishada boy wondered when he saw Suyodhana. He struggled to hold back his tears, trying to garner as much dignity as possible in his tattered clothes. Suyodhana picked up the mango and offered it to the boy. The urchin was stunned; then he extended a hand to grab the precious fruit. 'Why are you looking so surprised Prince? But then, what do you know about hunger?' the Nishada thought, as he tore into the fruit like a wild animal. Suyodhana pulled his little sister towards him and took the mangoes she was carrying in her skirt. Ignoring the girl's protests, the Prince dropped all the fruits in front of the Nishada and stood back.

Hunger had forced the boy to enter the royal grounds to find food for his starving family. His aunt had been afraid the guards would catch him. Stealing was something he had never contemplated in their better days but when poverty caught up with morality, the lines between the acceptable and unacceptable somehow vanished. He knew that his aunt would be watching the unfolding scene, hidden behind a bush, along with his cousins. They had not eaten for two days. When he had told her of his plan, she had protested just a little. Now he regretted the impulsive thought, sure the Hastinapura guards would drag him to the dreaded prison cells near the Khandiva forest.

"The mangoes are for you," the young Prince said.

The boy stood confused for a moment and then grabbed the mangoes with alacrity, before the Prince could change his mind. His hands could hold only a few and Suyodhana moved to pick up the ones that fell from the urchin's desperate grasp. The Nishada boy held the mangoes close to his chest as the Prince piled on the fallen ones.

"Now go before they see you," Suyodhana said, pointing to the guards, engrossed in their game of dice.

The boy ran towards his aunt, who was watching with baited breath. As the boy was about to enter the jungle, Suyodhana called out to him. The boy's heart lurched. Was the Prince calling to take back his gift? His eyes filled with tears of anger and frustration.

The Nishada stopped in his tracks. When he turned, the Prince was smiling and waving at him. "Hey, what is your name?"

The sun was blazing overhead. The earth beneath his feet seemed to be melting in the fierce heat. He took a deep breath and shouted back, "Ekalavya". Wondering at his own audacity, he ran into the safety of the jungle without waiting to hear what the Prince was trying to say.

***

As the class dragged on through the hot afternoon, Suyodhana sat thinking of Ekalavya's hungry and tired face; and the poverty that had made him dare trespass into the royal grounds. Shutting out the sounds of an enthusiastic Arjuna trying hard to impress his new Guru with his command over the scriptures, Suyodhana's mind remained on the poor Nishada boy. 'Perhaps I ought to learn more about him and his people,' the Prince thought as he caught the eye of a beaming Aswathama, sitting near his father. The boys exchanged grins as their eyes communicated in the silent way only boys of their age can, about how boring the class was.

"Suyodhana, stop your day-dreaming and listen!" The angry voice of Guru Drona broke the monotony of the class and pulled the young Prince back to the dry world of scriptures and holy books and away from life and his dreams.

Arjuna and Yudhishtra were competing with each other to recite the *Veda*s. Suyodhana tried to keep himself awake. Outside, the earth lay soaked in the red of the setting sun and far away from the palace, a tired, black Nishada woman and her five boys slept contentedly after breaking their long fast. A few feet from them, another little boy sat nibbling the mango seeds the Nishadas had thrown away.

3 CHILD OF THE FOREST

EKALAVYA DID NOT KNOW WHY the Kaurava Prince had behaved the way he had. It had been a reckless mission to get into the royal grounds to steal mangoes, but hunger had ripped away his fear. He had been prepared for a lashing by the guards if he was caught, what he had not expected was the strange behaviour of the young Prince in his expensive silken clothes. There had to be a catch somewhere. No high-born person behaved that way. It was as strange as expecting a lion to be meek and eat grass. He asked his aunt whether the mangoes were poisoned. He had been afraid to touch them since they had been given to him so freely but his starved cousins grabbed the fruit from his hands; so he forgot all about poison and princes in the immediate need to fight them for the luscious fruit. His aunt intervened, giving the best fruit to her children. Ekalavya got a not-so-ripe one. The favouritism was nothing new to him but it still hurt. He was determined not to cry over such things. He was ten years old now and almost a man. Men did not cry over silly things.

From the time Ekalavya could remember, they have been walking across India – his aunt, her five sons, and he. It was nothing new to people like them. He had no recollection of ever having a mother and his father existed only in the fantastic tales his aunt sometimes told him. His mother had died the day he was born. Distressed, his father had gone away, leaving little Ekalavya in his brother's charge. Sometimes, she would talk about his father, saying he was a Prince or a King somewhere in the East, and one day he would rescue them all from poverty, but on most occasions, she cursed him for having abandoned his son. She often reminded Ekalavya that he was nothing better than an orphan.

Ekalavya had the faint memory of a man who would carry him when he was only as high as his thigh. This man was the uncle his father had left him with. He now lay buried somewhere in the deep jungles of central

India. He had been caught stealing eggs from a farm and was beaten to death. Whenever they went hungry, and that was quite often, his aunt called out her husband's name. She wailed that had he been alive, they would have all lived like princes. Ekalavya was old enough to know that was not true. He had seen so many others like themselves, living in the shadows of a great civilization, meek before their superiors, while ferociously competitive and cruel to their fellow unfortunates.

Ekalavya could tolerate his cousins but there was another small boy who kept trailing after them. He was even dirtier than they were and had bad teeth and festering sores on his legs. His ribs stood clearly outlined under his stretched and cracked black skin; while his belly button protruded from his bulging stomach like a mushroom. The family often chased him away but he never gave up. Ekalavya's aunt even threw stones at the creature but like a mangy dog, the dirty boy followed them, trying to pick up leftovers and begging for food. He darted away from the pelted stones, only to reappear. Sometimes his aunt felt pity for the boy and offered the urchin whatever they could spare. He grabbed it with both hands and gnawed like a hungry beast of the forest. However, that was rare for they hardly had enough to ease their own hunger.

Nevertheless, the boy kept trailing them. He had found them in the village where Ekalavya's uncle had been thrashed to death. Another man had been caught stealing at the same time and he too, met the same fate. Ekalavya's aunt found the little boy crying near the inert body of his father. Despite her own grief, she had felt pity for the helpless little one and since she was in no mood to eat that day, she had given him her share of food – a mistake she regretted the moment she had handed over the scraps. Now, like a curse, the boy followed them. Some days they would get lucky when some merchant would feed the poor as an offering to the gods to keep him prosperous. Ekalavya noticed that at such times his aunt became generous and offered the boy something more than mere leftovers. She would also talk to him kindly. It was during one of those rare conversations that Ekalavya learnt his name – Jara.

Now, Ekalavya turned away from Jara's hungry gaze. He knew the boy was waiting for him to finish his mango so he could suck at the seed

Ekalavya would throw away. Finally, when he was sure there was nothing left Ekalavya threw the seed away. He despised the creature who stooped so low as to eat the leftovers of a Nishada but he also despised himself for being cruel to the hungry boy. The boy showed no fighting spirit. He was a dog. Ekalavya spat on the ground in disgust. 'Our lives are like those mango seeds; chewed, sucked clean and spat out,' he thought bitterly.

Ekalavya could hear the boy rummaging for the mango seed. He felt a sudden rush of tears when he heard Jara's joyous yelp. Like a rat, Jara sat and nibbled at the seed that had already been picked clean. Deep in his heart, Ekalavya wanted to kill the Prince who had so patronizingly given him the mangoes. It pained him that he was dependent on the generosity of princes and merchants. He looked at his own spidery limbs. 'I am a man now,' he thought. 'I should be able to provide for my family.' He was a Nishada and had any of the older males of his family been alive, he would have been taught the skills of a hunter; but they had travelled far away from the hills of Vindhya, where their tribe lived. Ekalavya stared at the sleeping faces of his aunt and five cousins and felt a wave of pity and helplessness.

Ekalavya had hidden one plump mango in his waistcloth, to eat after his aunt and cousins went to sleep. It was the best one and he knew that if his aunt had seen it, she would have given it to her sons. He wanted to eat it alone. Jara's eyes glistened in anticipation. The moon had risen over the low shrub-covered hills, bathing the earth in silver. Ekalavya looked at Jara. He considered throwing the mango to him but it was too good to be wasted. He plunged his teeth into the smooth fruit and sucked. Jara gulped. Disgusted, Ekalavya threw the half-eaten fruit to the waiting boy, who grabbed it.

As Ekalavya stood up, he heard the sound of hoofs. Far away, among the thorny shrubs, he could see the silhouettes of mounted men. Nagas! Ekalavya stood dumb with terror, rooted to the earth. The Nagas were the most dreaded of all tribes and they were moving towards the palace under cover of darkness. He could see the horses' dark manes glistening in the moonlight. His aunt stirred in her sleep and let out a sigh. Ekalavya could see a tall, dark figure leading the pack. Moonlight caressed his body, turning him into an eerie figure in silver. Jara was still sucking the mango noisily and Ekalavya was afraid the Nagas would hear and come to investigate.

But the Nagas were in no mood to stop for street urchins. The leader was whispering to his followers and with a burst of activity they shot towards the palace. Ekalavya started running behind them, with Jara close behind. He knew what he was doing was sheer madness, yet he wanted to see where the Nagas were going. In a corner of his mind, Ekalavya wished they would take over Hastinapura and treat the nobles inside with the same contempt they had meted out to Untouchables like him, but these were impossible dreams. Hastinapura was too strong and a rag-tag group of Nagas were never going to take over the formidable city. Yet their leader, Takshaka, kept mounting terror attacks on the great cities of India. Takshaka! Ekalavya now recognized the young Naga leader. *He* was leading the covert terror attack on Hastinapura. Ekalavya felt thrilled to witness it. He ran with all the speed his spindly legs could muster and like a puppy, Jara tried to keep pace with him.

The night was so silent that the pounding hoofs sounded like the drumbeats of war. Ekalavya thought it was foolish of the Nagas to make so much noise while attacking one of the most powerful capitals of the world. The Hastinapura guards would chew up these twenty-four men in minutes. Even a boy of ten could understand the folly of their plan. Were they that stupid? Ekalavya wanted Takshaka to win at any cost. Many innocents in the fort would die today. No, they were not innocent. They were not people like him. They were inhuman and treated people like him with contempt, or pity at best. Ten years as an Untouchable Nishada had taught him more about life and human nature than what many older men learnt who were fortunate enough to be born into the right caste.

Ekalavya could understand the hatred and contempt of the nobles. He bore the same hatred towards them. He had the same contempt for creatures like Jara, who belonged to the even more despised lower castes below the Nishadas. Perhaps, if the Nagas took over, things would be different – or perhaps not. Yet there was satisfaction in seeing the high and mighty fall. 'Oh Shiva!' prayed Ekalavya. 'Let Takshaka win today.' But the face of Prince Suyodhana haunted him. Why had the Prince shown him kindness? The high-born were not expected to be kind. It was all so confusing. 'Perhaps the Prince wanted me to do something for him; such high ones are never kind to us,' he thought. But what could a Prince of Hastinapura want from an Untouchable Nishada boy? 'Let them all burn in the fire. They are all the same. If Takshaka wins today, we can watch the palace burn and crumble.'

Lost in his thoughts, Ekalavya had not noticed Takshaka and four other warriors move away from the main body of the attackers. The main force clashed with the soldiers guarding the front gate. The bells of the fort began tolling in alarm. Amidst the clangour of bells, neighing of horses, and clashing of swords, Takshaka and his men moved through the shadows below the fort wall. Ekalavya watched as hundreds of Kuru soldiers clambered down rope ladders from the towering fort walls and engaged the Nagas in combat. The twenty Nagas were hopelessly outnumbered as they fought the Hastinapura soldiers.

It was only when Jara tugged at his hand and pointed to the left of the fort gate that Ekalavya saw it. There was a rope ladder hanging down and Takshaka and his four soldiers were climbing up the fort wall rapidly. As they reached the top, the moon, which had gone into hiding behind the clouds, suddenly emerged and Ekalavya caught sight of a dark figure on top of the wall. This person was helping the Naga leader enter the fort. Ekalavya felt a deep thrill. Takshaka was taking on the might of Hastinapura head on. He felt a desperate need to see his hero in action. Somehow, he had to get in and see what was happening. Jara tried to stop him but Ekalavya pushed the little boy away and ran on. Jara hesitated for a moment and then shrugged and followed suit.

***

Ekalavya quickly climbed up the rope ladder. A few hundred feet to the right, the battle raged on. Jara tried hard to keep pace with the agile boy. Ekalavya could see the four Nagas and their informant, running towards the palace, keeping to the shadows. Hearing something behind him,

Ekalavya turned to see Jara trying to climb the last few rungs of the ladder, which were too high for him. Cursing, he bent down and hauled Jara up.

"Why did you come?" Ekalavya hissed at the little boy but received only a foolish grin in answer. Cursing again, he ran along the wall, but the Nagas had vanished. Where had they gone? Who was the traitor who had helped them get in? It was becoming quieter outside. Had the battle ended? As usual, the sheer numbers of Hastinapura would have crushed the valour of the Nagas. They knew it was a suicidal mission yet they had been willing to lay down their lives to create a diversion to allow their leader to get into the fort. Ekalavya's admiration for the dreaded Nagas increased as he thought of the one-sided battle. But where had the Naga leader vanished? 'If only this idiot Jara had not delayed me, I could have kept up with them. I will take care of the fool later,' he promised himself.

Suddenly, he saw them again. They had left the safety of the shadows and were running towards the palace. The guards were lighting more and more torches, but the side from which the Nagas were approaching, was still in shadow. They had almost made it when a boy in his early teens stopped them. Takshaka tried to fight his way past him but the boy held the Naga leader back; ducking the slashing sword while trying to thrust his own into the Naga's gleaming body. A door opened on the first floor of the fort and an older man ran towards the commotion, shouting at the brave teenager to turn back. Ekalavya stood fascinated, watching the unfolding drama. One of the Nagas kicked the man as he neared and he fell like a log. The teenager held on, despite the cuts he had received. Meanwhile, the man who had helped the Nagas enter the fort crept away into the darkness. No one other than Ekalavya and Jara saw him vanish from the scene as soldiers came running in from all sides.

A tall muscular figure pushed the teenager away and engaged the Naga leader in fierce combat. Ekalavya recognized the Brahmin Guru who had caught him that morning. He prayed for Takshaka to win. Arrows flew thick and fast. They had already claimed two of the Naga warriors but as the soldiers recognized the Guru, they stopped shooting, lest one of them pierce the heart of the Brahmin warrior. Takshaka and the other surviving

Nagas struggled in desperate combat with the Guru. A few Kuru soldiers rushed to help him but he waved them away contemptuously. He was more than enough for these barbarians. With amazing swordsmanship and agility, Drona held off three Naga warriors, including Takshaka. His sword found its mark more than once and Takshaka was soon fighting with his back to the wall.

Ekalavya saw the tall figure of Bhishma, Grand Regent of the Kurus, appear on a balcony of the palace. He was barking orders and Ekalavya could see soldiers running in from all sides with their swords drawn. Hearing the commotion, Drona looked back and shouted that he did not need any help. That was enough for Takshaka. In the split second Drona's attention wavered, Takshaka ran towards the hanging rope and swung himself over the fort wall. Drona roared in rage and tried to get hold of the fleeing Naga leader but the two surviving Naga warriors held him back for a few precious minutes. Drona cut off their heads without even breaking stride and almost caught Takshaka. His sword missed Takshaka's right foot by inches. The Guru grunted in frustration. Guards shot arrows at the fleeing Naga leader as he ran along the fort wall, desperately trying to find his waiting horse. A couple of arrows found their mark and Ekalavya saw Takshaka trying to pull them out from his thigh and shoulder without breaking his run. Drona too, ran along the fort wall, gracefully leaping over the bodies of the fallen while chasing the fleeing Naga.

Ekalavya wanted to see Takshaka escape but with growing admiration, he watched Drona's amazing prowess. How could a man fight that well? What grace and nimbleness! What power and technique! 'I want to fight like that,' Ekalavya thought passionately, just as he heard a scream. A lead-tipped arrow had pierced the Guru's left foot and he had tumbled off the wall landing below with a sickening thud. Guards ran towards the prone figure. Takshaka ran on. He gave a low whistle and Ekalavya heard a horse neighing and galloping towards his master.

"Get him, get him..." Drona tried to stand. In one hand, he held the arrow he had pulled from his leg and the wet, bloody tip glinted in the moonlight.

As the guards rushed towards Takshaka, he disappeared around a corner of the wall. "Chase him... he is getting away you fools," shouted Drona.

The fort gates opened below and scores of mounted soldiers rushed out, galloping in hot pursuit of the Naga leader.

Drona limped back into the fort, disgusted at the way things had turned out. Bhishma stood with his hands behind his back, his face impassive. The breeze ruffled his long salt and pepper beard. The hint of a frown appeared on his broad forehead. An uncomfortable Vidhura stood beside him. When Drona saw the tall figure of Bhishma, he was taken aback for a moment. He looked around at the lifeless bodies of the palace guards and then at the Grand Regent's proud face.

"The soldiers here are incompetent, my Lord. The Naga leader got away because they do not have professional training. They shot me instead of that rascal." There was a tone of accusation in Drona's voice but Vidhura understood the Guru was trying to defend himself for the terrorist leader's escape.

Bhishma looked the Guru squarely in the face. Drona looked away. Finally, the Grand Regent spoke. "It will be more prudent for you to stick to training the Princes. Leave the security of the palace to the professionals. I admire your swordsmanship but not your eagerness to prove your heroism. Vidhura, show the Guru to his chambers. He needs to rest."

Drona's fair face reddened in anger and embarrassment. Vidhura avoided his eyes. Drona burned with humiliation. His employer had insulted him and the fact that he had done so in front of a Shudra, made it almost unbearable. He longed to retort but feared the consequences. He needed the job. Until this employment, he had led a tough life. The thought of roaming from village to village, from kingdom to kingdom, in search of another job, made him shudder. He had gone through all that misery. Poverty had been his constant companion from as early as he could remember. He had a family to feed. The warrior in him wanted to challenge the arrogant Bhishma to a duel. Perhaps the veteran warrior would defeat him. After all, the Grand Sire inspired fear and awe in his opponents. It was even thought honourable to die at his hands. Drona had dreamt of such a death in his youth. It was how warriors wished to die, with honour intact and head held high. Then Aswathama's innocent face rose up in his mind's eye. His son deserved a better life than he had. 'For his sake I must swallow my pride. That is the fate of every father.'

He turned to Vidhura saying, "I need no escort." Drona hurried past him to his chamber.

Vidhura stood back, understanding Drona's pain and so refusing to respond to the Guru's insult. Vidhura gazed at the vanishing form of the Guru, his shoulders stooped. Bhishma could be scathing at times.

"Report to me once they catch Takshaka, though I think it is most unlikely." Bhishma sighed and walked away.

It was then that Vidhura saw a young boy tugging at an unconscious man. He walked over to him and asked, "Is he hurt?"

The boy looked up at the well-dressed person in surprise. "I do not know, Swami."

"You are the fearless one who tried to stop Takshaka, are you not? What is your name, son?" Vidhura asked.

"I am Vasusena, Swami, and this is my father, Athiratha, the charioteer. I am also known as Karna. Swami, please help me to carry my father to our hut. My mother will be worried."

Without a word, Vidhura lifted the prone man's shoulders while Karna tried to lift his legs but the man was too heavy for the boy.

"I think we should help," Jara said to Ekalavya from where they stood in the shadows. Before he could be stopped, Jara ran out.

Ekalavya cursed the idiot. 'Ruined! Now we will be caught and thrashed. That fool Jara!' he muttered viciously. There was no choice. He had to pull back the idiot and run before somebody found them. He chased after Jara, trying to catch the little boy by his hair. The sound attracted the guards and they raised the alarm. Hearing the noise, Karna and Vidhura looked up and saw two Nishada boys running towards them. Before they could recover from their surprise, Jara had reached the prone man and started to lift him. Ekalavya stopped a few feet away, panting.

"Swami, we came to help," said Jara, looking at Vidhura with his wide eyes.

The Prime Minister of the Kurus burst out laughing seeing Jara's frail form. The soldiers had closed in and caught hold of the struggling Ekalavya, but Vidhura raised his hand. "Leave him... these are my nephews from the village."

Ekalavya was even more surprised than the soldiers, who reluctantly released their grip on his shoulders. They bowed and departed. Without a word, Ekalavya joined them in carrying the unconscious man to his hut, located at the lowest level of the fort, near the stables.

A woman stood at the entrance. "My mother, Radha," said Karna.

They gently laid the man on the lone cane cot in the sparsely furnished hut. Vidhura asked the woman for some water, a few Tulsi leaves, and some kitchen herbs. Jara and Ekalavya stood in a corner, afraid to move, unsure how the Minister would react. Ekalavya was confused about why he had saved them from the soldiers. His eyes roamed about the small but tidy hut. These people lived in poverty, yet he was jealous of them. They were lucky; they had a roof over their heads. The faces of his aunt and cousins sleeping in the open came to mind and he felt bitterness well up in his heart.

The woman fussed around her husband while the Minister administered his brew to the dry lips of the injured man. After a while, he stirred and woke. His wife smiled through her tears and Vidhura stood up to leave. Radha protested saying they could not leave without eating something. She thanked Vidhura profusely for saving her husband's life. The Prime Minister explained it had been a minor injury and there was no threat to her husband's life. The charioteer too, joined his wife in pleading with the Minister to eat something in their humble home. Finally, Vidhura consented. He could not deny them this small pleasure without hurting them. He looked at the man and said with admiration, "Your son is courageous. If he was to be trained in arms, he would be an asset to Hastinapura."

"Swami, we are poor Sutas. Who will instruct our son? I am teaching him my own profession and shall make him the best charioteer in the country. But learning archery is beyond our caste status and means."

Ekalavya saw the Suta boy keep his eye fixed to the ground, not wanting anyone to see his shame. 'If he can be a warrior, I can be one too,' he thought fiercely. He turned to see Jara looking at the boiling pot, his eyes pleading for something to eat.

Vidhura remained silent for a long time. "Hmm… let me see, Athiratha. I do not know whether it will work but I will try. The Acharya is a good man and a great teacher. Your boy has done a great service to the country tonight by stopping Takshaka's attack. I will request him to accept your boy as his pupil. But he is conservative and may object to teaching a... I will ask his Excellency Bhishma to put in a word. Maybe... let me see..."

There was doubt in Vidhura's voice but Athiratha was ecstatic. This was the Prime Minister of the country speaking and the charioteer had every reason to be happy. His son's future would now be secure.

Ekalavya was burning with jealousy. How easy things were for some people. He wanted to ask the Prime Minister whether he would consider his case as well but the gap in social status between him and Karna was so great that he did not dare. He bit his lip and stood burning with envy, angry at the fates, which had ordained his birth in the lowest of castes.

'Who needs a Guru? The world is my Guru,' thought Ekalavya. 'I can be a better archer than that lucky bastard.' He wanted to run away from the sickening happiness pervading the humble hut. Jara tugged at his fingers. Irritated, Ekalavya snapped at him to remain quiet. Jara made the universal gesture of hunger. It was the only thought he ever had. At any moment, the Prime Minister could change his mind and then there would be hell to pay. The kindness Ekalavya had experienced from Prince Suyodhana and this important man was unsettling. He remained tense and silent.

Radha had seen Jara's hungry look. She put three plantain leaves on the clean floor and invited her guests to sit down and eat. Vidhura declined, saying it was not his habit to eat so early and that he had not performed his morning ablutions yet. Ekalavya wanted to eat everything Radha served. He was as hungry as a dog. Except for the mango, he had not eaten anything, but he did not want to show these strangers that he was hungry. So he ate slowly, refusing a second helping. Jara stuffed himself with whatever Radha offered and stood up reluctantly when he found there was no more food coming his way. He licked his fingers, savouring the last lingering taste. Ekalavya felt disgusted by the mess Jara had left. As they washed their hands in the backyard, Ekalavya saw Jara beaming with satisfaction. Before he could lash out at his smugness, Vidhura called them in to bid farewell to Athiratha and his family.

***

"Who are you and how did you enter the fort?" There was no smile on Vidhura's face now.

Ekalavya shuddered. Finally, the man was showing his true colours. He felt strangely comforted that the expected pattern of behaviour from a social superior had reasserted itself. "We are Nishadas; we were sheltering in the jungle nearby. We saw Takshaka and his gang riding towards the fort." The moment he said it, Ekalavya knew he had made a terrible mistake.

"How do you know his name is Takshaka?" The Prime Minister's immobile face appeared to be carved in stone.

"Oh, everybody in the forest knows," Jara told him. "He comes to the forest and gives us food sometimes. He said he is going to kill all of you one day and then this palace will be for Nishadas and other forest dwellers like the Nagas and Kiratas."

Ekalavya shuddered at Jara's casual words, sure this was the end of their lives. Vidhura remained silent for a while as Ekalavya's legs started trembling.

Finally Vidhura spoke. "If you keep watch on what Takshaka is doing and report back to me, you will be rewarded."

"Will we get food?" Jara asked, his eyes gleaming.

"You will get food and more. For now, keep this." Vidhura threw two copper coins at them.

"What are these?" Jara asked, never having seen or used money.

"Ask your brother. He will tell you how to exchange them for food. There will be more if you report to me about Takshaka."

Ekalavya averted his gaze as Vidhura's dark eyes bored into him. He wished Jara would keep his mouth shut but that did not happen.

"We saw a man like you... in fine dress... he threw down a rope for Takshaka to enter the palace..." Jara stopped when he saw Ekalavya glaring at him.

"*Who*? Who was it? Tell me!" Vidhura's eyes flashed with anger.

"We do not know his name, Swami. But if we saw him again, we could identify him," Ekalavya quickly added before Jara could say something that would land them in trouble. He tried to keep calm and wondered when this man would let them go.

"Hmm... you may go now," said Vidhura quietly.

Ekalavya grabbed Jara's hand and walked towards the palace gates. He could feel Vidhura's eyes on his back. The guards stopped them to ask whether they were really the Prime Minister's relatives. Before Ekalavya could open his mouth, Jara denied it. Once the guards were sure they were out of Vidhura's sight, they searched the boys and found the copper coin in Jara's fist, and took it. When Jara protested saying the Swami had given it to him, they thrashed him. Ekalavya did not wait for a beating. He threw the other coin down in contempt at their feet and got some satisfaction in seeing the guard bending low, almost touching his feet, to get at it. The other guard saw the derisive smile and slapped Ekalavya across the face.

***

Vidhura was a worried man. He could arrange an identity parade and have the boys point out the traitor but that would alert the spy that his cover had been blown. If it were someone important, it would be hard to nail him on the testimony of two Nishada boys. It was better to wait. He had to find the traitor before he could do any more damage. As he turned, Vidhura saw the profile of a tall man standing on one of the balconies of the first floor of the palace. He was facing West, his head bowed as if in prayer. In a land where everyone worshipped facing the rising sun in the East, it seemed strange that someone was praying facing West. Vidhura waited to see who it was. The man took a long time but when he turned, the rays of the morning sun fell on his face. Vidhura shuddered; it was Shakuni, the Prince of Gandhara. Their eyes met and Vidhura could feel the malevolent energy of those black eyes even from a distance. 'I think I have found the man,' thought Vidhura. But there was no proof. He would have to wait.

***

In the balcony above, Prince Shakuni reiterated the promise he had made to himself when he was barely five years old and Lord Bhishma had laid claim to his ancient land, Gandhara, and crushed it; and then carried off his sister like some common chattel, to be married off to a blind fool who was but a puppet king. Shakuni looked longingly towards the west, where his beloved country lay. Like every other day, he bowed his head and reiterated his vow to destroy India. Yesterday's operation had failed but he would try again. Despite her crooked and confusing caste system, India had her strengths. It was difficult for an outsider to conquer and destroy her. This task had to be carried out by the people of the country itself. Takshaka was only one piece in this game of dice. There were others he was in the process of meticulously placing. The most important one was inside the palace. Shakuni smiled to himself as he moved towards Prince Suyodhana's chamber. It was time for class.

4 The Charioter's Son

KARNA HAD ONCE EXPRESSED HIS SECRET DESIRE to become an archer, to his parents. His father had been silent for many days after. His mother had broached the subject to his father several times in the next few weeks but this had elicited only grunts in reply. Karna had waited, his heart thumping in his chest, praying to Lord Shiva that his father would consent. Then one day, Athiratha asked him to accompany him to the temple. They were not permitted to enter the inner sanctum of the temple as they belonged to one of the lower castes, but were fortunate enough to be allowed access to the outer compound to pray. Acharya Kripa was sitting on an elevated platform under a huge Banyan tree, arguing with his friends. A game of dice was in full flow and the Acharya was on the verge of beating one of his friends when father and son approached him.

Athiratha had taken off his *angavastra* from his shoulder and tied it around his waist as a mark of respect. He stood a few feet from the Acharya, his eyes fixed to the ground in the deferential manner of a Suta who wished to speak to a Brahmin. Karna waited anxiously behind his father. Kripa stopped his arguments and looked at Athiratha in surprise. What was a charioteer doing here?

"Swami, I have a humble request..."

"I am broke as an earthen pot. I do not have any money to lend you. If I had, I would have enjoyed a few more mugs of wine in the tavern." The Acharya broke into boisterous laughter.

Karna knew Kripa was a maverick Brahmin, who did not care for social and ethical norms. Now that Acharya Drona had come, there were murmurs in the palace that Kripa, for all his learning and skill with arms, would be fired as the Princes' tutor. Kripa behaved as if he had not a care in the world. He could be seen in the tavern from early morning, laughing with his cronies, when other members of his caste were busy with prayers and ablution. The conservative Brahmin community viewed his genius as a threat to their cloistered existence. The other problem was that he was far better versed in the scriptures than any of them; and he was always looking for an argument or fight, with anyone who dared to challenge him. They had no answers to his questions about the scriptures and he deliberately mocked the rigid caste rules by openly flouting them and then quoting the *Vedas* and *Upanishads* to justify his actions. Karna knew his father nursed the faint hope that this maverick would help them.

"Swami, I do not seek alms. This is my son, Karna. He desires to be a warrior and learn from you."

"Aha! He wants to be a warrior." Kripa jumped down from the platform he had been perched on and rushed towards Karna. He stopped inches short of Karna's face and peered into his eyes. Karna recoiled instinctively and retreated a few feet. He was afraid of accidentally touching the Brahmin and breaking the caste taboos. Karna could see his father's shocked face. Kripa had already broken the caste rules by coming so near. The Priest at the temple was watching the scene from the gate, a deepening frown on his face. Kripa pushed the boy and Karna staggered back. Then he grabbed Karna by his long hair and lifted him with one hand. He slapped Karna across the face and punched him in the stomach with his strong left hand. Karna winced in pain but refused to cry out.

"Swami... Swami... do not beat him," Athiratha implored.

"Fool! You think this is a beating? Your boy has courage. With proper training, he can be a good warrior. He can withstand pain." Kripa dropped Karna; then swiftly and gracefully jumped back onto the platform. He sat down, his fingers caressing his flowing black beard.

"Will you teach him, Swami?" Athiratha could barely hold back his tears of joy.

"Why not?" A mischievous smile played on Kripa's thick lips.

"He is a Suta... I mean we are of the Shudra *varna*, Swami."

"He may be Naga, Nishada, or Mlecha. Why should that concern me? He will be a good warrior." Kripa looked at Karna, who was beaming with pride and joy.

"When should he come, Swami?" asked Athiratha, his head bowed over his folded hands.

"As soon as you can arrange 1000 gold coins," Kripa replied, his face impassive.

"Swami..." Athiratha could not believe his ears! Even if he served the Hastinapura government until he was 60 years old, he would not earn 1000 gold coins. "We are poor, Swami..."

"That is not my fault, dear friend. I do not care what caste your son is. I care for money. Wine is expensive and so are all the other good things in life. My gambling skills are inferior to my skill in arms. When you can pay, send your son and I shall make him the best warrior in India. Otherwise, he can learn to be a charioteer like you."

"But Swami..."

"Fool! I do not have the whole day to waste in speaking to you. My friends are getting impatient. Come with the money and we shall talk." Kripa turned his back to them and resumed his game of dice.

Father and son stood in silence. Not a word passed between them. The sun had climbed high in the sky and dust swirled in the hot wind from the plains. The Priest had gone into the temple with a rich merchant who had come with offerings. Karna could not face his father. The slap and punch he had received from Kripa had begun to hurt. It would have been better if he had refused to teach a Shudra. Karna turned away in shame.

Athiratha put a hand on Karna's shoulder. When the boy looked up, he saw his father's eyes glistening with unshed tears. At that moment, Karna hated himself. Why could he not be like the other boys of his caste and age? A warrior! And he the son of a charioteer. Karna vowed to learn his caste job and try to become the best charioteer in the land, and make his father proud.

"Karna, do not worry. We will find a way. At least he did not refuse to teach you saying you are of inferior caste. I can sell the chariot and our hut may fetch a few hundred coins. I will find some other work. We will find a way."

"I do not want to be a warrior, father. Let us forget about it. It was but a stupid dream."

"Karna... listen to me..."

"I no longer wish to be a warrior, father. Teach me how to drive the chariot. Do not say you will sell the chariot and house for my sake." Karna trembled with anger and shame.

Passing pedestrians stopped to look at them. Hearing the commotion, Kripa turned. Karna's heart missed a beat. Perhaps it had been one of the Acharya's practical jokes and he would now call them and say he had asked for the 1000 gold coins in jest and that Karna could join his classes the next day.

"Go away, you scoundrels. What a ruckus you make! By Nandi, one cannot even play a game of dice without being distracted by idiots screaming their heads off." Kripa threw in a few choice expletives for good measure.

The temple bell clanged as father and son started back towards their hut. The occasional cawing of the crows and the laughter and shouts from Kripa's group, was carried to them on the oppressive air as they walked forlornly through the dusty streets. Once they reached home, Karna went to the well in the backyard without a word. He looked at the wavering reflection of his handsome face in the dark waters deep below. For a moment he was tempted to jump in and finish everything. Then he heard his mother's sobs and his father's broken voice, and he gritted his teeth. 'I have a duty to serve my parents,' he thought. It broke his heart to think he would be nothing but a common charioteer all his life. If not for the love he bore his parents, he would have taken refuge in the dark waters of the well that day.

***

Until Vidhura said he would recommend Karna to Acharya Drona, father and son had never again spoken of the incident with Kripa. Karna had lost all hope of ever becoming a warrior and reconciled himself to a life of servitude. Now, fresh hope sprouted a tiny shoot in his mind. Finally, Lord Shiva had shown mercy towards a poor Suta boy.

Karna was up well before dawn to complete his morning ablutions. He could hardly contain his excitement. He paced up and down in the small mud verandah, waiting for his father to emerge. Even the harsh cawing of crows was like music to his ears. A few early risers were hurrying to the river *ghat* and the breeze carried the fragrance of jasmine and the faint tinkling of temple bells in the distance. Radha came out first and handed Karna a cup of milk. He drank it impatiently and put down the brass tumbler with a clang on the floor. Then she fussed with his hair and earrings.

"Where is my father?" Karna asked, trying to get away from the affectionate attentions of his mother. He saw his mother smile and knew she would be running to tell the neighbours about their good fortune the moment they had stepped out of the hut. At last his father emerged from his prayer room. Karna jumped down from the veranda and ran into the street.

"Karna, do not be so impatient. Have you prayed?"

Karna felt irritated. He had done all that early in the morning but the last thing he wanted right now was an argument with his father. He stopped and looked up at the sky turning saffron in the east. A glorious sun shone down benevolently. Karna closed his eyes as if to capture the beautiful sight and hold it firmly in his mind. No words of prayer came to him. His emotions were so intense that he was thankful for the absence of words. He felt one with the shining sun. It caressed him with its all-pervading touch and he felt soothed, contented and happy. When Athiratha's hand fell on his shoulder, Karna reluctantly came out of his trance. He smiled and began walking quickly towards the palace. Athiratha looked back at his wife standing in front of their hut, with tears in her eyes. He turned away lest she see the tears brimming in his own. Karna was already many paces ahead and Athiratha walked quickly to catch up with his energetic son. They went past the temple and the Banyan tree, where once again Kripa and his friends were absorbed in their game of dice. Acharya Kripa called out to Athiratha, but the charioteer and his son did not have time to listen as they hurried past – the loud laughter of the decadent Brahmin ringing in their ears.

The guards stopped them at the inner gate of the fort. They stated their purpose. The captain of the guards looked at them suspiciously before sending a soldier to the palace with a message. After a while, the messenger returned to say Vidhura was in conference with Lord Bhishma. They were asked to wait. They waited outside the gate until the sun grew impossibly hot and their shadows shortened into dark pools around their feet. Each passing moment filled them with anxiety. Every time a soldier came from the palace, their hearts beat faster. When they had almost given up hope, thinking the Prime Minister had forgotten his words, the call came. The guard pointed to Vidhura, standing in a corner of the palace gardens. They could hear the faint clash of swords, with Drona barking instructions.

Vidhura smiled at them, apologising for the delay. Karna could not decide whether he was a phony or a truly great man, to be so humble. They crossed the inner and outer fort gates together and entered the palace orchards. As they neared the training grounds, Karna saw that Prince Suyodhana and his brother Sushasana were on their knees in a corner, their heads hanging in shame. Drona was occupied in correcting the stance and aim of Arjuna, the middle Pandava Prince. A small Brahmin boy, who resembled Drona, was collecting the arrows shot by the Princes, while a hefty boy practiced with a mace. The other boys watched Arjuna as he drew his bowstring. The arrow missed the target by a whisker and Drona shook his head in irritation. But Karna was impressed by the boy's proficiency. He shot like a seasoned warrior and it had only been a few weeks since Drona had started his training. 'Perhaps I will be able to shoot like that one day,' thought the son of the charioteer.

"Guru–," Vidhura called out to Drona respectfully.

For a long minute, the Guru did not acknowledge their presence. When he turned, Karna flinched at his expression. Instinctively he knew what was coming.

"Yes, Prime Minister. What can I do for you?" Drona silenced his students with a gesture.

"This is Karna." Vidhura pulled the boy from behind his father. "Son of my friend, Athiratha."

"I am in the middle of a class, Prime Minister."

"Guru, Karna wishes to learn from you..."

Karna could sense the lack of confidence in the Prime Minister's voice. Drona remained silent for a long time and Karna's heart almost stopped beating. He clenched his fists.

"I train the Royal Family, Prime Minister," Drona said finally.

"Yesterday, this boy did a great service to our kingdom. I promised..."

"Prime Minister, I have to reiterate that these classes are only for the Princes." Drona looked away, crossing his hands over his chest.

"I have spoken to His Excellency Bhishma. He has said that if you agree, he does not have any problem with this boy's inclusion. In fact, he said Hastinapura needs all the warriors it can get."

"Honourable Prime Minister, I did not wish to say this but alas you force the words from my mouth. Ask him which caste he belongs to."

"But how does it..."

"I understand your sympathies as you too, belong to these people. He is a Suta, a lowly charioteer caste. I am a Brahmin. Yet you expect me to teach him?"

Vidhura's face flushed with shame and embarrassment. In the court hierarchy, he was far above Guru Drona but he lacked the confidence to confront someone who was his superior by caste. Karna did not want to hear the rest of the argument. He knew it was over. His father held him still but Karna could not control his tears.

Drona turned to Vidhura defiantly. "Do not think you can come here and push me into taking a low-caste boy as my student. As Prime Minister, you can discharge me from my job. If you order it, I will take my wife and son and leave Hastinapura. I may starve or get a job in another kingdom where they respect Brahmins and do not force them to act against their faith. Starvation is better than taking orders from a Shudra. Do whatever you and Lord Bhishma wish, but I will not teach a low-caste."

Prince Suyodhana stood up from his kneeling position. Drona saw it. "You fool! Do you think you can act impudently in my class? Do as you were ordered." Suyodhana sank back onto his knees.

"Drona, you have insulted the country and the Crown Prince by your words! There are limits..." Vidhura drew his sword.

"Are you threatening me, you low-caste? A Shudra Prime Minister, a blind King, and an arrogant Crown Prince! No wonder a Suta wants to become a warrior. Next, a Nishada will apply to become my student!"

Karna felt greater pain for the Prime Minister than for himself. He could see Vidhura was trying to control his anger.

"You will hear from Lord Bhishma." Vidhura bowed deeply to Drona, emphasizing the courtesy.

The mocking bow was worse than a blow. "You... you... how dare you insult a Brahmin? Let me see whether Hastinapura has ears for the cry of a Brahmin or only listens to the complaints of a Shudra. Now get out of the training ground. This place is for Kshatriyas and not people like you. Take the chariot driver and your equals from here. I will answer to the Regent of the Kurus."

Without another word, Vidhura walked away. Karna followed him, his head bowed. Only Athiratha lingered a moment, before finally walking away with a heavy heart.

***

Drona did not want to face the poor chariot driver. He knew the boy had the makings of a great warrior. He had seen him defend the fort the night of Takshaka's raid. Unfortunately, he belonged to the wrong caste. As a human, Drona could sympathize with a father who wished to fulfil his son's ambitions. But his own Guru, Parashurama, had trained him to believe in the purity and sanctity of caste and he did not dare break those rules. He was unlike his brother-in-law, Kripa, whom he both detested and feared. Kripa was a greater scholar and perhaps a better warrior than he was, but he was an unreliable maverick. Kripa found pleasure in deliberately breaking the rules. Drona could not afford to do so. 'I have a son to bring up,' thought Drona, looking at Aswathama, his eyes alight with affection. But Aswathama's eyes were fixed upon the charioteer's son walking away. 'My boy was so sweet until he met that rascal, Suyodhana. He spoilt my boy,' thought the Guru with deep resentment. But Hastinapura paid its employees well. And now there was the worry whether Vidhura would poison the Regent's mind and have him thrown out. Would he be impoverished again? What would happen to his son? And all because of a stupid charioteer who dreamt beyond his position?

Suyodhana reminded Drona of his brother-in-law, Kripa, except that the lad had greater willpower. The boy questioned everything. His doubts were mostly unanswerable. He made Drona feel inadequate. So Drona reacted with the viciousness that only teachers are capable of towards students they do not like. He thought the boy arrogant and attacked him where he knew it would hurt the most – comparing his skill and intelligence to the Pandavas'; and belittling him whenever he could. He wanted to crush the boy's rebellious spirit and mellow him so he would fit into society. Drona knew instinctively that such spirit in a powerful person could only bring about disaster. If the wild forces in the boy were not tamed, he could shake the country and impose his will on it. As a teacher, Drona considered it his duty to mould his students to fit into society. Teaching was not about making rebels who would challenge and change the established order. He was sure that ultimately everybody, including the Gods and god men, conspired to pull down such rebels and crush them into the dust. That was what the history of this country had taught him. The rise and fall of men like Ravana, Bali, and Mahabali, were incontrovertible proof of this. Society was *sanathana*, eternal and unchanging. Rebels and reformers had only one place to go in such a country, and the Gods took on *avatars* to grind such rebels into the dust. That was *dharma* – to protect which, they took human birth.

Drona beat Suyodhana at the slightest provocation and meted out insulting punishments. On the days when even this did not move the stubborn Prince to tears, he would use the ultimate punishment – call him and his brothers sons of *Andha*, like-father-like-sons, unable to see right from wrong. That silenced the Prince for the day, while the five Pandavas laughed at the Guru's comments about their cousins. Drona thought morosely that he was not the only one crushing the dangerous spirit in the boy, and currying favour. After him, his son Aswathama would inherit his post of Raja Guru and advisor to a future generation of Princes. There would be no place for Shudra usurpers like Vidhura in that beautiful world.

When he saw Aswathama talking to Suyodhana, Drona lost his temper and thrashed his son until his own hands ached. He vented all the pent-up anger over his poverty, his confrontation with Vidhura, his fears and complexes, on Aswathama's small body. He pushed the bawling boy towards the Pandavas, forcing him to sit next to Arjuna, his favourite student. Arjuna hid a smile at the plight of the Guru's son. And while the Guru was shouting at Suyodhana, Bhima managed to pinch Aswathama twice and call him a sissy. The boy cried louder, only to be beaten by his father again.

From the thick green foliage of the mango trees, two pairs of dark eyes watched this drama unfold. While the Guru was beating his son, Jara asked Ekalavya, "You think he will teach you now? He was not even ready to teach a boy like Karna. We are Nishadas, far below Sutas."

"Shut up, you fool! You talk too much. I am going to learn from him. One can learn as much by sitting here as by being there, like poor Suyodhana. We will watch what he teaches Arjuna and learn. No one, not even Drona, is going to stop me learning from him. And one day I will surprise him by defeating his favourite, Arjuna." Ekalavya turned to kick Jara, who was laughing at these audacious dreams.

***

"You are late again." Parshavi placed a simple meal before her husband and sat down.

Vidhura merely smiled at her and began eating reluctantly. "Enough," he finally said, refusing a second helping and standing up. "Are the boys asleep?" he asked, as he wiped his hands dry on the towel Parshavi handed him.

"You are asking as if it is something uncommon. You do not even come home but sleep in your office so many nights. When you do come home, it is almost time for you to go back. Why are you working like this?"

"Parshavi, you do not know the pressure we are under. I feel sorry for Bhishma. The old man is carrying the burden of the entire country on his tired shoulders. It is my duty…"

"Don't you have any duty towards your family? Should I remind the great scholar about your duty towards your sons? You are the Prime Minister but just see how we live. We do not even have a house to call our own. You do not wish us to have any servants. You use the chariot only on official duty. You could save time by using it instead of walking all the way to your office and back and spend that time with us. You seem to enjoy poverty. We are the laughing stock of our neighbours. Even junior government officials live better than we do. You are the King's brother, yet see how we live. Is Bhishma unaware of this?"

"We have had this conversation many times, Parshavi." Vidhura hurried to the room where his twin sons slept. He sat near them, quietly watching their faces.

"We should think about them. The times are uncertain. Our boys are good students but will they have jobs when they grow up? All the positions are reserved for Brahmins. I am afraid for their future."

"Parshavi, trust in God. We have not wronged anyone. Trust in the goodness of people. Worrying too much about the future shows your lack of faith in God."

"Then why are you and Bhishma so worried about the future of the country? Why not leave it to God?" Parshavi regretted the retort as soon as she uttered it. Her husband was sensitive about his country. She watched as he rose and moved to their bedroom without a word.

When she finished her chores and entered the room, he was lying with his face to the wall. She sat on the edge of the bed, searching for the right words to melt the ice between them.

He suddenly turned and said, "I sometimes wonder whether all the hard work I put in is of any use."

She gripped his hand. "What has happened?"

"Nothing really. I only wanted to do something good for a poor boy and was insulted by the Guru and lost face. Ultimately everything boils down to caste in this country."

She knew when to remain silent. She sat listening to his deep breathing. It was almost dawn.

"We will build our own house. You are right. When we are gone, the boys should have at least a roof over their heads." The words were almost inaudible.

Parshavi did not say anything. She had heard about the house they would build many times before. She did not wish to argue with her husband again. Instead, she quietly slipped under the quilt and put her hand on his chest. She could feel his heart thumping under her fingers as she slipped into a disturbed sleep.

***

Karna sat in a corner of his hut, staring into the darkness. He was not dreaming of challenging Arjuna one day. He was thinking of the best way to end his miserable, worthless, Suta life.

5 The Maverick Brahmin

KRIPA CURSED THE MOSQUITOES BOTHERING HIM. He had once again lost money while gambling and did not want to go home and see Kripi's face. As on many other nights, he decided to sleep under the Banyan tree. He knew his sister would be waiting for him even though his hours had become more and more erratic. It was a mistake to have married her to Drona, Kripa thought. It was not that he hated his brother-in-law, but he resented the unsolicited advice Drona was so fond of giving him, and his all-knowing attitude. It was a hot and humid night. A starless and damp sky spread over him like a wet umbrella. The crickets were creating an infernal racket, with the frogs joining in. He could smell rain and hear the river swelling. If it rained he would be forced to go home. Kripa did not relish the thought at all.

The first drops of rain fell on the expectant earth. What was that noise? Was it a splash? Some idiot had jumped into the river and was drowning. By Nandi, why could the rascal not have chosen some other time to die, preferably when he was not around? Kripa ran towards the water and saw a dark head bobbing up and down in the swiftly flowing current. The last thing he wanted to do was jump into the river at this ungodly hour. The fool was sure to die anyway. Kripa was a strong swimmer but was unsure whether he would be able to drag the idiot back to shore. With a resigned shrug, he slapped his thighs and jumped into the river.

Kripa gasped as the water swallowed him, surprised at the strength of the current. It was colder than he had expected and the river seemed to pull him into her dark womb with a million hands. The rain had turned into a squall and now pelted down with brutal force. Where the hell was he or she? Then Kripa saw him, 300 yards away, bobbing up and down in the water. The damn fellow was probably dead already. Kripa uttered a few choice expletives and started swimming towards the drowning figure, using his great strength. After what seemed like a lifetime, he managed to grab the drowning man's hair and began swimming back. Exhausted, he dragged the comatose figure onto the bank, a mile from the temple *ghat*. He wanted to kick and scream at the fool but the fellow was unconscious. After catching his breath, Kripa began pressing his quarry's stomach to expel the water he had most certainly swallowed. After an agony of waiting, Kripa was about to give up when the sodden and drenched body stirred into consciousness.

"Who the hell are you, you fool?" Kripa slapped the sodden face and heard a sob.

"Forgive me."

Kripa was surprised. The voice had not yet broken; it was that of a boy, not some drunken reveller as he had expected. Kripa felt sorry for the woebegone figure before him. How much unhappiness must the boy have endured in his short life to compel him to take such an extreme step?

"What happened to you, son? Why are you trying to end your life?" Kripa's hand dropped onto the boy's head while he tried to identify the face.

"Swami, I am a wretched low-caste, a Suta, a charioteer's son, and no one wishes to teach me anything."

Suta! It was the son of that chariot driver, Athiratha. He remembered the day they had come to him and how he had treated them. 'Did I not try to make amends? Did I not call out to them as they passed today, to say I accepted their request? But they were in too much of a hurry to hear me out.' Kripa tried to justify his actions but knew he had behaved like a rogue. There was no denying that. He looked down at the wretched boy and said, "I forget your name but I remember you and your father coming to me. I am Kripa."

"Acharya Kripa? Swami, why did you save me? Why did you risk your life for a worthless Suta?"

"Tell me your name."

"Guru, I was named Vasusena, but am known to all as Karna."

"Karna, you fool! Listen to me. Do not keep repeating you are low-born and such rubbish. No one is low or high. If you accept you are low-born, the world will be happy to concede that to you."

"But I am a charioteer's son."

"You are ignorant. Listen and learn to keep your mouth shut. That will serve you well in life. I will tell you this only once, for I am giving this advice free of cost. I ought to charge you for it but I owe you something now. You allowed me to save you from death and that has made me feel good about myself. For a change, I will teach you something free. Now, tell me what made you jump into the river at this hour?"

The rain had slackened a little and Karna sat without moving, staring at the river that hid so much.

"I know what you are thinking. You are blaming me for what is happening to you. You feel I am heartless and the world is cruel. You are cursing yourself for being born poor. You are lamenting the fact that you have a mere chariot driver as a parent. You look at your dilapidated hut and think how nice it would be to have been born into a rich home."

"Swami, I did not..." Karna did not want to look at the Brahmin's face. The river offered more solace.

"There is nothing wrong with such thoughts. They will make you strive harder in life and motivate you to achieve your dreams, provided you know how to channel your frustration and anger. Life is a gamble. You do not know how the dice will fall. But once they have, how you move the pieces is in your hands. It is mere chance that you were not born a Kshatriya or Brahmin. You could have been born a Nishada or Naga, and then your Suta home would have looked like a palace. The die has been cast and you cannot do anything about it. But you can choose to be a Brahmin or Kshatriya or Nishada or anything you want."

Kripa smiled at Karna's confusion. "Look at me when I speak. You are wondering how is it possible to be something else. Society has taught fools like you to believe in the chance of birth. The Priests have told you that if you are born a Brahmin, only then can you *be* a Brahmin. If your parents are Pariah, you will be a slave forever to all the other castes. It is all too easy to fool the people of our country."

"But... the *Veda*s say..."

"The *Veda*s do not say any such nonsense. The majority of our people have not even read the *Veda*s. Tell me, who is a Brahmin?"

"You are... Acharya Kripa..."

"If we go strictly by the *Veda*s, a Brahmin is one who has sought and found *brahma*; one who has found God within himself, in his thoughts, gained through knowledge. Do Drona or I look like we have found God? I cannot even find the way to my house on most days! A Kshatriya is supposed to be one who has found God in action, by doing his duty. A Vaishya is one who has found God in trade, by creating wealth; and a Shudra is one who has found God in love, by serving society. It has nothing to do with where or to whom anyone is born. You could be the Shudra son of a Brahmin father or vice versa. Whatever the silly Priests say, nowhere in any of our scriptures is it written that any one way of finding God is better than all the others. They do not even say that finding God is better than not doing so. The *Vedic* mind wonders about the mysteries of creation and the universe, but it does not speak in the voice of absolute truth. The *Veda*s merely hold the wonder of Man regarding the universe in which he lives."

"Guru, what you say must be true, but what about the society in which we live?"

"The *Vedas* are clear about society. For society to have balance, all four *varnas* are required. Knowledge, thought, direction, action, power, leadership, wealth, money, art, love – are like the organs of the body. One cannot say only one is important. That is why it is said the four *varnas* are the four parts of Brahma. You may have heard pseudo-Brahmins boasting of how they emerged from Brahma's head; the Kshatriyas from his arms; the Vaishyas from his thighs." Kripa paused and smiled at Karna. "And..."

"And Shudras like me originated from the feet of God," Karna said, looking straight at the Brahmin.

"Feeling glum about it, are we Karna?" laughed Kripa, lifting an eyebrow in his own inimitable style. "Our scriptures used this allegory to show that each *varna* is equally important. But see what is happening now. The head is claiming that only it is important. How stupid! Without the heart, the head is dead. Without hands, the body cannot act, and without thighs, the legs will not remain connected to the body or move. Now the head is claiming that it does not need the legs! The head has become rotten with no exercise. Instead, it has ordered the heart to cut off the blood supply to the legs. Hence, society is incapable of going anywhere. The arms just flay and occasionally beat each other. Sometimes they clap and make loud noises, but it means nothing. The head produces some *smritis*, useless philosophical speculations and rituals, but nothing else. It has stopped producing anything useful for humanity. The thighs too, do not get the protection of the arms, which are fighting each other; nor do they receive knowledge from the head or movement from the legs. They stay in one place and just grow fat and ugly, choking the blood flow to the feet. This is the picture of our society today. The head, the Brahmins, are saying they do not need the feet, the Shudras. Where will they go without feet? They will simply remain where they are and rot."

"But Guru, our country has produced great thinkers. If what you say is true, how…"

"Karna, you speak of the past, but what about the present? The barbarian people of the West are progressing quickly and we have lost our advantage.

If we continue to deny the benefits of education to the majority of our people by claiming the false authority of the scriptures, one day we will find the barbarians ruling us. The people, whom we now contemptuously call *Mlechas*, will swarm across our country, attacking us from the borders of Gandhara or the southern coast. But they will find only the hollow shell of our civilization left. The core has already rotted. They will only need to give a slight push and the shell will collapse. Then they will rule us, all the fools; Brahmin, Kshatriya, Vaishya and Shudra alike, and crush us underfoot. I am sure our frogs-in-the-well will say that it is all written in our scriptures and it is but the advent of the next eon, *Kali Yuga*, or some such nonsense." Kripa stopped speaking and gazed at the cloud-enveloped sky in silence.

"But Swami, it is only by doing one's *kula dharma* that one can achieve *moksha*." Karna had forgotten the rain, agog at the Acharya's words. It was rare indeed for an adult to speak to him about such serious subjects.

"That is another misinterpretation. What is *moksha*? It is finding happiness in life. Nothing more, nothing less. The rest is pure speculation. You should meet my friend, Carvaka. He will explain these things better than I can. If you think you can find happiness in life only by becoming a warrior, then that is what you should strive for. There should not be an iota of doubt in your mind. No guru or scripture can stop you if you are determined to fight for your goals."

Kripa smiled at Karna. 'Does the boy have it in him?' the Guru wondered.

"But nobody will teach me because of my caste..." Karna spoke the only unshakable truth he knew.

"Aha, Vasusena Karna! I hear accusation against me in your tone. But I did not refuse you because of your caste. I asked for my fee and you were not ready to pay. It is not that I care for money. The six feet of soil under the Banyan tree and the slice of sky that peeps through its branches are more than enough for me. But never forget – everything in life has a price. Come to me tomorrow with whatever money you have and I will still teach you to become the finest warrior in India."

"But my father does not have that kind of money..." Karna's heart raced in his chest.

"Bring what you have but remember, like everything else in life, the education you receive will be proportionate to the price you are ready to pay. So what price are you willing to pay, Karna?"

'Here is the test,' thought Kripa.

"I can work for you."

"*Ha ha...* what work can a boy like you do for me? It seems you are not ready to pay any price for your education. You may think I am cruel but I am frank and I have no hidden agenda. There are people who will offer you many things and demand nothing in return. Fear them the most, for they are the ones who will take the things that are most precious to you and then their demands will come at a time when it is most inconvenient to you. In the end, you will find that my offer is the cheapest and least harmful. People like you do not like to learn from men like me. You learn only when the toughest of gurus – life – decides to teach you its harsh lessons. Since you are not willing to bankrupt your father and have nothing useful to offer me, I will give you something equally useless. Come in the morning with whatever small change you have and I will teach you how to behave like a Brahmin."

"But I do not want to become a *Priest*." Karna jumped up in indignation.

"Listen, you young fool! Do you know who the greatest living warrior in India is? It is neither Drona, nor the great Regent of the Kurus nor I. In a land far to the south, lives a clan of Brahmins. Thousands of years ago, perhaps it is just an old wives' tale, Mahabali, the great Asura Emperor, ruled from sea to sea. Vamana Vishnu defeated him and established Brahmin rule. Later, the great Asura King, Ravana, overran this empire and threw out these groups. When Ravana fell in battle, thanks to the treason of his brother, Vibhishana, the Brahmins reassembled. Under the patronage of the same Vibhishana, the land from Gokarna to Kanyakumari came under their rule. From that time on, for a thousand years, they have ruled the land of the Asuras with an iron hand, reducing the Asura chieftains to mere puppets while imposing the most inhumane caste system ever imagined. You think being born a Suta is a disadvantage? You should see the plight of the pariahs in Parashuramakhestra. Then you will understand what disadvantaged really means. It is a beautiful land but like many beautiful things in this world, it is also deadly poisonous."

"Parashurama! But he is the enemy of Hastinapura! How can I...?"

"Karna, when you want to learn, learn from the best Guru. Bhargava Parashurama, the leader of the Southern Confederate is the most formidable warrior in India today. The Parashuramas, from the dawn of our history, have been reckless warriors. They have conducted raid upon raid on the northern kingdoms, to impose their religion and law. If not for Sri Rama, who defeated them once, they would have eliminated all the Kshatriyas from the plains of the Ganga and Yamuna. Their last raid was under the guise of getting the Kashi Princess, Amba, married to Bhishma. It ended in the present truce. But Bhargava almost overran the whole of Uttarajanapada then. They have been a constant threat to all the rulers of India for a thousand years. For them, our caste system is not rigid enough and our religion not pure enough. He was my Guru and Drona's too. He teaches only Brahmins or the Princes of the Southern Confederate." Kripa saw the shocked expression on Karna's young face and chuckled.

"I am neither a Brahmin nor a Kshatriya, how can I..."

"I will teach you how to behave like a Brahmin so you can undertake the trip to his land and learn from our greatest living master. The best thing is that he does not charge money. Since you prefer to save that ramshackle horse and cart of your father and avoid paying *me*. But I warn you; you will end by paying him a heavy price, which has nothing to do with money. However, I am not concerned with all that. You deserve nothing better."

"But will it not be a deception?"

"What Bhargava is doing is deception. His version of the scriptures is so narrow that if my friend Carvaka hears it, he will have a heart attack. Son, one day or the other, he or one of his disciples is going to overrun the entire country and impose their rule on us. Our society is so rotten that I have this dream often. Perhaps one day we will find a Prince who will take pity on the plight of Man and walk away from his palace to live under a tree to seek enlightenment. Perhaps he will give society some respite from self-destruction. However, Bhargava's disciples are sure to travel to the four corners of India, either with the sword of the warrior or the staff of the mendicant. They will thus destroy all the humanness achieved by benevolent Princes and bring eternal doom."

"Swami, I thought Takshaka was the greater threat," Karna said.

Kripa smiled in delight at the boy's perceptiveness and intelligence. "Son, Takshaka and Bhargava are two sides of the same coin. We, the common people, will be caught between such mad men. The Bhargavas and Takshakas do not die, they reincarnate with different names in different times. When such an attack comes, Hastinapura will need all its warriors, irrespective of their origin. What you do, you will be doing for us all. Come to me at dawn and let us start with the *Gayatri mantra*. Let me see whether I can make a Brahmin of a Suta." Kripa walked away, leaving a drenched Karna alone near the swiftly flowing river.

Karna stood for a long time, conflicting emotions gusting through him like the wind on a stormy night. When the sky turned grey in the east, he ran home to wash and change. He hugged his surprised mother, who was watering the Tulsi plant in the courtyard, and rushed out to the river with a dry cloth. Today he was going to be a Brahmin, and after a few days, perhaps a Kshatriya. He could be whatever he desired. The words of his Guru were imprinted on his mind. The world stood open with so many possibilities for the young boy.

"AND WHAT IS THIS RASCAL'S CRIME TODAY?" Bhishma asked Vidhura, without taking his stern gaze from Suyodhana.

Before Vidhura could reply, Kunti stormed into the room, accompanied by Dhaumya and a few other Priests. Vidhura could see Bhishma was annoyed by this unceremonious interruption. He should have warned the Grand Regent. Vidhura knew the Priests, under Dhaumya's leadership, had gone to Kunti. What he had not expected was that Kunti would accompany them to see Bhishma.

Dhaumya opened his bundle of complaints against Kripa. Bhishma listened to them in growing impatience. Finally, he responded that it was a free country; that everyone had the right to believe what they wished to; and to preach it as well. If a great scholar like Vyasa appreciated young men like Kripa and Carvaka, he, Bhishma, was too humble a man to judge otherwise. The Priests could, of course, go to Kripa and show him the scriptural authenticity of what they preached, such as caste, idol worship, rituals, Brahmin worship and so on, and convince him about the correctness of their arguments.

At this masterly disposition, a smile tugged at Vidhura's lips and this infuriated Kunti further. "*Pitamaha*, the men you name are destroying our *dharma*."

Bhishma turned his steady gaze on Kunti. "Daughter, our *dharma* is *sanathana*. They cannot destroy it. No man can. They are merely redefining it to suit our times. *Dharma* keeps evolving to suit the needs of people in different ages. Some may even say it is our own Priests who are destroying *dharma*, by stifling it and misinterpreting our scriptures. However, I am not a scholar like Vyasa, Kripa, or even Carvaka. I am only a warrior. With my limited knowledge and common sense, I agree with Kripa… though perhaps not with Carvaka. This is my personal belief. I do not impose it on anyone else. You too, have the right to believe whatever you wish. I will not allow anyone to trample on your rights. If Kripa stops people from giving donations to Priests through logical discourse, I have nothing to say for you too can go out and convince people to ignore Kripa and ensure they come to you instead. That is between you and Kripa. Come to me if Kripa stops people from going to the temple forcibly. Then he will know that Hastinapura's soldiers and jails exist for a reason. This applies to all of you. If someone hurts Kripa or Carvaka, the same rules apply."

"But *Pitamaha*…" Kunti began to protest. Vidhura quickly began arranging the palm leaves on Bhishma's table. He did not want her to see his smile. He knew what was coming.

"Kunti, do not waste your time and mine with such frivolous matters. You have five children to rear. If you are interested in politics, why not help your brother-in-law with governance? This is not an easy country to rule, even for a sighted man."

Kunti and the gaggle of Priests walked out in anger.

Bhishma looked at Suyodhana, standing to one side with his eyes on the ground, trying to hide his anger and shame. "Son, the truth always prevails. Look it in the face."

Vidhura had dragged Suyodhana to Bhishma just a little while earlier. The second Pandava Prince, Bhima, had broken the right hand of the Kuru Prince, Vikarna. The boy had dared to call Bhima 'Fatso' and paid the price. Vikarna's howls of pain had brought Suyodhana and Sushasana onto the scene. This had resulted in a fistfight in which Bhima thrashed them both. Later, Suyodhana and Sushasana had hidden in the dark and caught Bhima unawares. They could have murdered Bhima had Vidhura not come upon them and dragged them to Bhishma. Kunti had dragged away her son.

Now, Bhishma turned his attention towards his grandnephews. "What brings you all here?"

"Had I not stopped Prince Suyodhana, we would have been trying him for the murder of his cousin, Bhima," Vidhura said, looking sternly at his shamefaced nephew.

"*Pitamaha*, we were playing and did not mean…"

"Suyodhana, you are old enough now to understand who your enemies are and who your friends. What is this about trying to beat Bhima to death?"

Suyodhana turned pale and stood shivering with fear before the Grand Regent. "Answer me!" commanded Bhishma in a voice that brooked no defiance.

"*Pitamaha*, it was just fun. We were talking…" Suyodhana stopped, unable to continue before Bhishma's unwavering gaze.

"You were plotting murder for *fun*? Bhima is your cousin. Both of you are equal in my eyes. It is good to have competitive spirit as Kshatriyas, but not murderous rage."

"Swami, they taunt and torture us and my little sister all the time. They are cruel to the servants. They are selfish; they call my father *Andha*…"

Bhishma remained unmoved by this outburst. "That is no reason to attack someone while hiding in the dark. If you are a Kshatriya, be a man and fight. Grow up to be strong in mind and body."

Suyodhana stood silent, hanging his head in humiliation. He felt aggrieved with both Bhishma and Vidhura. Did he not have the right to get even with Bhima?

"Listen, Suyodhana." Bhishma's voice had lost its edge and there was a hint of kindness now. "One day, you will rule this country. You need to know your enemies and your friends. I have reports that you are slipping in your lessons again and keep daydreaming in class. Drona is full of complaints about your behaviour. Stop roaming the streets, talking to all and sundry. Behave like a Prince. You have no reason to go to the houses of outcastes and Untouchables. You are a Kshatriya. Behave like one. Show some respect for the Brahmins and learned ones. Stop going about with Carvaka and Kripa. They have ideas that may not help you. A King should listen to all, but not be swayed by extremes. Take Drona and Carvaka's advice with respect and then act according to what is good for the country and society. Not all things spoken are true. The Truth changes. Wisdom lies in understanding this. Only then can you be a good ruler."

"But Swami, there is so much misery out there. You have ruled with wisdom; then why do so many people live like pigs in our kingdom?"

Vidhura almost lost his breath. Suyodhana's audacity was galling. Even after so many years of working with Bhishma, he would never have had the courage to ask that question.

Bhishma stared at Suyodhana for a long time. Slowly, a smile lit the old man's face. "My son, you will get hurt one day with such talk. You think I made this society? I only inherited it. I am doing my *karma*, my duty as a Kshatriya, and that is to rule with fairness. I have no utopian dreams of changing the world in a day. Can you plant a sapling and expect it to grow into a tree overnight? You have to water it, nurture it, give it sunlight, rain, and manure, and then slowly, it will grow. Oppression, discrimination and privileges for a few, are as old as civilization. The caste system was well entrenched centuries before my birth. I cannot topple it in a day, nor am I a social reformer. I merely ensure that the poor and those oppressed by birth do not suffer even more. I can ensure power does not go to the heads of the elite. Your father is the King, but my tired shoulders have borne the burden of rule for many long years. Do you think it is an easy job? Ruling is not what your father or your aunt Kunti, think it is. They have seen only the benefits of power. The responsibilities have been borne by me.

"When your blood is young, you dream impossible dreams like ending poverty and misery. But dreams have a nasty habit of getting entangled in life and making a mess. Right now, you are a student and your duty is to learn. Keep dreaming but plant your feet firmly on the ground. Do not be swayed by Carvaka, Drona, or Kripa. Stay away from Shakuni. If someone calls you a blind man's son, forgive him. They say such things because they cannot get even in any other way. Take it as a compliment. Now go and attend to everything Drona teaches you." With a curt nod, Bhishma dismissed him.

Bhishma stood looking out of the window. Far away, across the green fields and villages that dotted the banks of the river, he could see the faint outline of mountains. A dust storm was gathering in the west where the desert lay; shrouded in mysteries and myth. Vidhura watched the deepening creases in the old man's forehead with concern. Ruling this kingdom was getting wearisome for both of them. The petty squabbling and infighting, the constant bickering among his nephews and kin, made them both sad. The country was crumbling from within.

Bhishma turned to the Prime Minister and asked with a hint of humour, "Vidhura, my son, why are you so glum?"

"Sir, Shakuni is spoiling the boys. If we do not send him back to Gandhara, he will destroy our country."

"You are giving him too much credit. What can his puny little kingdom in the mountains do to this mighty land? No, I am more worried about the internal dangers that threaten us. We bought peace with Parashurama at great cost but I am regretting it now. We did not have a choice then, did we? It was either that or breaking my vow of celibacy and marrying the King of Kashi's eldest daughter... what was her name?" Bhishma's gaze returned to the world outside the window.

Vidhura knew it was prudent to remain silent. On most days, the Regent's conversation touched upon those turbulent days of his life. Bhishma had conquered the ancient kingdom of Kashi and carried off the three beautiful princesses, Amba, Ambika, and Ambalika, to Hastinapura, as brides for his stepbrother, Vichitraveera. However, Amba was already in love with the Prince of Shalva. When Bhishma heard this, he allowed her to return. But the Prince of Shalva's pride had been hurt when he had been compelled to fight Bhishma to save the Princess from abduction and had been defeated in humiliating fashion. He spurned Amba on her return. She travelled back to Hastinapura to beg the celibate Bhishma to marry her instead. Bound by the vow of celibacy made to his dead father, Bhishma refused the Kashi Princess.

The story had been told many times by the Grand Regent and others. Vidhura often felt he had actually witnessed the incidents though they had happened before he was born. Vidhura could visualize the distraught face of the dove-eyed Princess of Kashi, begging the adamant Bhishma to marry her. Then, seeing that neither her curses nor her heartfelt pleas had any effect on the Regent of the Kurus, she had left for her father's palace, only to find herself rejected there as well. It was then that Parashurama's spies found her and the plot to invade the Great Plains was hatched by the Southern Confederate.

"I should not have agreed to the truce." Vidhura had lost count of the number of times he had heard Bhishma's lament. "The evil of caste is spreading its tentacles in this holy land and I am ashamed that I did not fight Bhargava Parashurama to the last. He and his nasty band of soldiers have ruined our country. How do the once proud Asuras tolerate him? How did those ancient kingdoms fall into the grip of the Brahmins? The Asuras are the same people who once proclaimed the equality of all men under Mahabali and produced the proud and brilliant Ravana. It never ceases to surprise me what defeat can do to people. History is a bitter teacher. Not even the great Rama could have envisaged the misery he was inflicting upon the poor of the South when he defeated the last Asura Empire under Ravana. He did us all a great disservice when he left the South to Vibhishana and the Parashurama clan. Had Rama ruled directly, perhaps he could have stemmed the evil. Just see what centuries of subjugation have brought them to now."

Vidhura averted his eyes. He wanted to comment that it was no better here in Hastinapura. He still smarted from the insult Guru Drona had meted out to him when he had recommended the son of the charioteer.

Bhishma looked into his Prime Minister's eyes and smiled. "I know what you are thinking. That it is as bad here as there. But you have not seen the world. I am sorry I have to say this to make my point. You are my nephew, but still you are a Shudra, since your mother was a house cleaner. Here you are taunted for your caste, irrespective of your talent and knowledge. Kunti and her Brahmin advisers resent you. So you think life is tough for you. *Ha*... had you been in one of those kingdoms where Parashurama's writ rules, you would be living far from the capital city, untouchable, unapproachable, illiterate, ignorant, and no better than a pig. That is caste for you; not suffering these little taunts from jealous people. If my capital were Muzaris or Madurai, instead of Hastinapura, I would now be washing my palace with cow dung and urine to cleanse the ground polluted by your footsteps. Parashurama and his followers are unhappy we do not follow their version of the scriptures and impose such laws on our people."

Vidhura flushed at the Grand Regent's words. It was embarrassing to be reminded of his origins. Had he not worked hard to learn the scriptures, the *Upanishads*, the sciences of mathematics, astronomy, astrology, as well as music – all that could be learnt? Had he not served his motherland with devotion and dedication? Was he not loyal to the proud man before him? Even the Grand Regent of the Kurus bestowed his kindness as a favour to a poor Shudra boy. His talent and intelligence did not count. Perhaps his presence helped Bhishma feel broadminded. Vidhura thought he was like a prize dog – intelligent and handsome, but a dog nevertheless. At such times, Vidhura hated his job and his master with equal loathing.

"The war we waged with the Southern Confederate under Bhargava Parashurama was not about my rejection of the Princess of Kashi, though that rascal cleverly used the issue as propaganda. Parashurama neutralized our allies using the issue. We had to fight in the treacherous jungles of the Vindhyas. I shudder to think how cheaply human life was lost there. The brutal pogrom Parashurama unleashed claimed the lives of so many

Nagas, Nishadas, Kiratas and Vanaras, who had lived peacefully in those jungles from time immemorial. They were expendable as they belonged to untouchable, unapproachable, dirty and polluted castes. What choice did I have? He would have exterminated them all. There was no alternative but to agree to his conditions. I had no choice..."

A sandstorm was gathering on the far horizon. Vidhura could feel it in the air. 'You could have married Amba and called Parashurama's bluff,' he thought, but did not dare say it.

"I could never have married that girl. I earned the name Bhishma only after taking my oath of celibacy. Else, I would have been a mere Gangadatta. I owe everything to my *brahmacharya*. No, I did not have a choice. The truce was made and I allowed Parashurama's schools of learning and his guild of Brahmins into our kingdom. And see where we are now. Caste practices that had been fading made a great comeback. You know, there were murmurs when my father married a fisherwoman, but nobody ran around calling her names. Not that she would have tolerated such nonsense. I have never seen any woman as strong willed as my stepmother Satyavathi. She was a great lady. It might shock Parashurama, but the fact is that the entire Kuru race originated in the womb of a fisherwoman. A King marrying a mere fisherman's daughter! Can we imagine that now? Times have changed for the worse and I played a part in it. That is what grieves me every day."

A dry breeze ruffled the silk curtains and carried some fine desert dust into the room. The sounds of boys playing filtered into the room from the gardens below.

"Maybe I should have sacrificed a few more Nishada and Naga lives and continued the war. But I thought I was supporting the cause of the poor and that a truce would end the misery of the tribes who lived on the fringes of our kingdom. I wanted Bhargava to take his warrior hoards back and leave us in peace. I thought I was saving the tribes from total annihilation at the hands of Parashurama's army. After the truce, Bhargava was true to his word and went back to his kingdom on the southwestern coast but he left a legacy of bitterness that still haunts us. He gave birth to the evil called Takshaka."

Takshaka's name dragged Vidhura back from his own stream of thought. "The attack by Takshaka... I have my suspicions. I think I know who helped him into the fort that night, Sir."

But Bhishma continued to stand at the window, staring towards the faraway mountains and the river snaking through the wheat fields. The sun was descending into the western horizon. As happened all too often, Vidhura had missed lunch. Work pressure was mounting day by day and there was no respite from the responsibilities Bhishma piled on him. "I think it was Prince Shakuni who aided Takshaka in that daredevil night raid."

Bhishma turned towards him. "What makes you think so? Shakuni? That no-account? I cannot believe it."

Vidhura did not have proof for now and cursed himself for having blurted out the name, knowing the tongue-lashing that would inevitably follow. "I saw him praying facing West." Vidhura stopped, flinching at Bhishma's look of astonishment.

"You saw Shakuni pray facing West and concluded he is a traitor? So the mark of patriotism is to pray facing East? A traitor is someone who prays facing West? Is this your theory? This is a free country and people can pray facing in any direction. Some even do so upside down, like the naked *sadhu*s or some of the Aghoris. Others choose not to pray at all, like Carvaka. Do you consider them traitors as well? I expected a little more logic from you, Vidhura."

"It is not just that. I saw him help a fallen Naga soldier that night and did not like the expression on his face." Vidhura saw amusement in the old man's face. All his insecurities raised their heads like a many-hooded cobra. He cursed himself for making a fool of himself. "I have a hunch he was behind it."

Bhishma moved towards his loyal subordinate and put an arm around his shoulders. "Vidhura, my boy, I think you really need a break. You have started hallucinating. Have you ever tried to understand who Takshaka is and what he stands for?"

"He is a terrorist."

"They use terror, but they are not terrorists. The rebellion led by the Nagas is a reaction to our failure to protect the weak and downtrodden. Takshaka is a creation of that failure. The State's duty is to protect the weak from being oppressed by the strong. When the State fails to do so, the weak will rebel. In a way, the truce I made with Parashurama led inevitably to the rise of Takshaka. He is the mirror opposite of Parashurama."

"Swami... that does not..."

"That does not sound right, Vidhura? Think! What does Parashurama want? Complete Brahmin hegemony and his interpretation of our holy scriptures to prevail. He wants to be the absolute power centre. Parashurama's clan has been waging war against all other castes, and the Kshatriyas in particular, for a thousand years, to establish a perfect kingdom for the Brahmins. All of South India resented the evil of caste. But now it is more entrenched there than in the great plains of the North where it originated. Due to the enlightened rule of my father, Shantanu, and my stepmother, Satyavathi, and the efforts of sages like Vyasa, our kingdom has slowly been getting back its humane face. Whereas in Dakshinajanapada, things have gone from bad to worse. Countries wax and wane in culture, enlightenment, thought and prosperity. Parashurama has ruined the great kingdoms of the South and now they are mere backwaters compared to our own kingdom."

"But what has that to do with the rise of Takshaka and his warriors?"

"Takshaka is nothing but a Naga Parashurama. He too, wants a perfect world where the oppressed becomes the oppressor. All his talk about equality is mere eyewash. If he wins, he will be just another tyrant, like Parashurama. Then the hunted will be the Brahmins, Kshatriyas and Vaishyas, and even other Shudras, who the Nagas think are not downtrodden enough. In fact, it will be far worse than Parashurama taking over, since not all Brahmins accept his narrow ideology. The likes of Kripa and Carvaka among the Brahmins, may rebel and die as martyrs if Parashurama succeeds. In the case of Takshaka, no such opposition exists, except for the might of Hastinapura. It is easier to fool and brainwash a poor Nishada or Naga, who has barely anything to eat and almost nothing to lose, by offering a brave new world. It is easy to get such people to die for his cause, because the people Takshaka has chosen as his tools, are those we abandoned to starve long ago. We have appropriated their farmlands, driven them away from their forests, and chased them out of our royal footpaths, so now they have nowhere to go but into the embrace of the Naga leader. Since none of our Brahmin teachers is prepared to instruct anyone other than Brahmins or Kshatriyas, we are creating legions of illiterate and ignorant folk who will be ready to die for Takshaka's cause. When our schools fail to teach our children what they should know, other schools take their place and teach different lessons, which we may not like. We are building our own funeral pyre."

Vidhura stood silent, thinking that the kind of education he himself had received would now be impossible for any Shudra boy. Things had changed so much for the worse in this land. No one with the baggage of low caste, like him, could aspire to be even a clerk in government service, let alone the Prime Minister of Hastinapura. Merit no longer counted. Every position was based on caste.

"What happened to that brave boy, Vidhura?"

Vidhura's anger and resentment flooded back as Bhishma reminded him of Karna. He still smarted from Drona's insult. "The Guru refused him, saying he was a Suta, not Brahmin or Kshatriya."

"That I know, but I have also heard he is now studying under Kripa."

"Yes, but I do not think Kripa is teaching the boy about arms."

"Yes, that is what appears strange. I cannot understand that Brahmin. Why is he teaching Karna rituals that only a Brahmin should know? The country will lose a great warrior if the boy becomes a Priest. Given his origins, I do not think any temple will give him a job. They will not allow him anywhere near. So what is Kripa doing?"

"Swami, if you could speak to Guru Drona..."

"Vidhura, the Guru is adamant. I do not want a situation where he disobeys my orders. He is a great teacher and warrior. If he disobeys me, I will have to sack him and he might end up with one of our enemy kingdoms. He is a disciple of Parashurama and if he goes back to him, it will be disastrous for us. I will bet on a seasoned warrior like Drona over an untrained boy like Karna. So many boys show early promise and then turn out to be nobodies. Why should we take the risk of losing Drona? It is unfortunate that in our system there is no place for people like Karna. But when is life fair?"

'This conversation is going nowhere,' thought Vidhura. 'Everyone toes the line eventually.' Even Bhishma, whom he respected, was conservative within. He did not dare challenge the Brahmin Guru openly and risk a riot. Perhaps there was practical wisdom in avoiding open confrontation but it still hurt.

"What should I do about Shakuni?"

"Watch him. Nobody is above suspicion, including you and me. The mind is a dangerous thing and can change at any time. Keep a close watch on Shakuni, and on Kripa and Karna. Learn what mischief that imperious Brahmin is up to. One day, I am going to lock him and his friend Carvaka up as mad men. Irritating the Priests by teaching a Suta boy the *Gayatri mantra*! If he wants to do that, why need he do it in full view of the Priests? I will now have to expend a great deal of time talking to Kunti, who will keep appearing with her sycophants every other day, to complain about Kripa."

Vidhura bowed and turned to leave, when Bhishma's voice stopped him. "Amba... *ah*, I remember her name now... Amba... the poor girl was sacrificed to Parashurama's beliefs and my vow. She took refuge in Panchala and died there in misery. It was so sad. I wonder how her son is doing."

Vidhura remained silent. He found it hard to suppress an ironic smile that Bhishma had finally remembered the Kashi Princess's name. He had heard the tale many times before and had learnt to stand by quietly, with a blank face, while Bhishma closed his eyes, lost in his own world. Vidhura bowed and took his leave. He was feeling hungry and walked towards his chamber where the cooks would have sent his food separately. He remembered he had forgotten to warn Bhishma about another threat looming ahead. His spies had informed him that the son of the spurned Amba was growing up fast and developing into a formidable warrior. Amba had eventually committed suicide after struggling with depression for many years. But she had filled her son's mind with hatred against Bhishma. Amba had taken refuge in the palace of King Dhrupada of Panchala and given birth to her son there. In the truce, when great men like Parashurama and Bhishma traded concessions, having sacrificed thousands of lives, the woman who had been the ostensible cause of the war, was conveniently forgotten. Parashurama got what he wanted and Bhishma avoided breaking his vow of celibacy by not marrying the Princess who was later found to have been made pregnant by her lover. She spent a miserable decade at Panchala, cursing Bhishma and her fate. When she finally ended her life by jumping over the balustrade of the staircase and falling to the cold marble lobby where fountains rose in rainbow arcs, her son decided to extract revenge for her life and death.

It was not another enemy being added to Bhishma's long list of foes, which worried the Prime Minister. It was the fact that the son who had been adopted by King Dhrupada of Panchala and been bought up as a Prince, was no son at all. He was a eunuch named Shikandi, and he had vowed to be the death of Bhishma one day. There could be no greater insult to the illustrious Commander of the Kuru armies than to be challenged by a eunuch. Vidhura did not know how to break the news to the great warrior.

7 THE LESSON

SUYODHANA WAS WATCHING DRONA, fear and anger battling for supremacy within. He hated these classes and wanted to be out in the forest, roaming about and watching the birds and butterflies. Every day of the past four years had been torture. His enduring memory was of sitting glassy-eyed, feeling like an idiot, while Drona heaped abuse upon him. Initially, Suyodhana had asked his teacher about various things. Kripa, who had instructed the Princes before Drona, had always been ready to answer any question with a smile. But everything changed when Drona came.

The best times were when the travelling ascetic, Carvaka, visited Kripa. The evenings spent with them were magical. Suyodhana and Aswathama would sit in rapt attention, enjoying the wit and banter of the two men who constantly argued in a friendly manner while the river flowed swiftly behind them. Crows returning to roost would fill the trees above. Men and women would be hurrying back from the day's work, some leading cattle, some with baskets balanced on their heads, while others rode bullock carts towards their villages. Devotees would be walking to the temple, where the Priests would be chanting *mantras* and praising the Gods. Beggars would be waiting at the temple steps, acting more miserable than they were to coax alms from the devotees who had brought offerings for the Gods and Priests. Vendors of jasmine, sweets and boiled nuts, would weave through the milling crowds, selling their wares. Life did not care about the theories the two Gurus were bickering about. Life moved on, irrespective of philosophy, despite the Gods and the thoughts of men. But that did not take away from the enjoyment the boys felt on listening to the old masters argue with each other. Suyodhana, Aswathama, and even the less intelligent Sushasana, learnt more from such wonderful evenings than from Drona's many classes.

***

A whack on the head rudely jolted Suyodhana out of his reverie. His classmates' laughter scorched his ears.

"So you oaf, what is the answer?" Drona barked.

Suyodhana had not even heard the question. He looked helplessly at his friend, Aswathama. But the boy did not meet the Prince's pleading eyes. He sat with his gaze fixed on the ground. For a moment, Suyodhana thought his friend was ashamed of his father's behaviour. Then he saw his lips pressed together, trying to suppress his mirth. What was so funny? "I did not hear the question, Swami." This evoked more laughter.

"I know you are dumb and like your father, blind to right and wrong. But are you deaf as well?" Drona smiled but the Guru's eyes betrayed the malice he felt. More laughter followed as Suyodhana stood alone, stung by the insults and hurt by the unfairness of it all.

"You keep hanging around those good-for-nothing Brahmins, Kripa and Carvaka. You make fun of the Priests and spend your time under the Banyan tree those rascals have made their den. You have spoilt my son too. You roam the streets without caring for the taboos or about pollution; touching everyone, eating with Shudras and playing with children from the slums. Do you know that your friend Kripa is teaching that son of a Suta to be a Brahmin? Rama... Rama... I think the *Kali Yuga* is near. Sutas learning the *Gayatri* and Shudras studying to be literate! People like Kripa and Carvaka, who were fortunate enough to be born Brahmins, are throwing away their good *karma* by teaching everyone to read the *Vedas*. What is the world coming to? And you, Prince Suyodhana... no, I should call you Duryodhana, for that is what you are – one who does not know how to handle arms, is clumsy-footed, a nitwit... You bring only shame on your ancient line and on Hastinapura, Prince."

An awed hush followed these words. But Suyodhana looked straight back at his Guru. "Swami, I do not find any reason to be ashamed. I have done what my heart says."

"Duryodhana, if everyone did only what he pleased, society would soon collapse. That is why there are rules. That is why taboos exist. It is what the scriptures have ordained. It is our *dharma*." Drona walked up and down, delivering the speech he had rehearsed a hundred times in his mind.

Suyodhana's heart sank. He resented the vicious nickname that many relished calling the sons of Dhritarashtra. Though the Princes' names all started with the auspicious prefix *Su*, they were referred to with the inauspicious prefix *Du* behind their backs, right from their childhood. Suyodhana became Duryodhana, Sushasana was Dushasana, Sushala was called Dushala, and so on. The Guru's taunts had ensured the inauspicious names became fixtures.

"Do I have to wait till the end of the world to get an answer from you? Can anyone else answer?" Drona turned towards the Pandavas, who eagerly raised their hands.

"You, Yudhishtra, my son, what is the answer?"

Yudhishtra began quoting from the scriptures with consummate ease while Drona listened raptly. Suyodhana heard nothing. He was sick of always being on the receiving end of Drona's ire. He wanted to be out there listening to Kripa and Carvaka. He longed for the throbbing life of the streets. What use had he for these long-forgotten chants and useless rituals?

The class stood up and moved from the clearing towards the jungle. Aswathama tugged at Suyodhana's hand but Suyodhana only glared at him. He had not forgotten the stifled laughter of the Guru's son when his father was insulting him.

"Hey, please forget it Suyodhana. I did not mean it." Aswathama tried to put a hand on the Prince's shoulder, but Suyodhana shrugged it off and walked on.

Drona was walking quickly towards the forest with the Pandavas enthusiastically following him. Suyodhana searched for Sushasana, but could not find him amongst the screaming and running boys. Dust swirled everywhere and the sun was getting hotter.

"My father is not as bad as you think," said Aswathama from behind him.

"As if I care." Suyodhana walked faster, trying to escape the Guru's son but he knew he was incapable of holding a grudge against his best friend. His only friend. Suyodhana stopped abruptly. "What is the Guru up to?" He could feel the tension easing out of Aswathama who came to stand beside him.

"It could be one of his practical lessons." The two boys looked at each other in dismay. They dreaded such lessons as there would be constant comparisons with the Pandavas. Arjuna was developing into an ace archer. However hard they tried, no other student could match his skill. Drona, who was stingy in praising his son, was effusive when it came to Arjuna.

By the time Suyodhana and Aswathama got to them, the other boys were already seated on the ground and the Guru was preparing a new test. The boys' chattering and the afternoon heat made Suyodhana feel drained but there was no escaping until the lesson ended. He looked around and saw something move in the jungle. The bush on the far side of the clearing shook in an unnatural way. The trembling of the leaves did not follow the flow of the breeze. He stared for a long time, waiting for whatever was hiding behind the bush to move again. Dragonflies buzzed around, alighting on the grass and then scurrying away in alarm. Another movement caught Suyodhana's eye. Was it a Naga warrior hiding there, waiting to ambush them? Aswathama whispered to Suyodhana to pay attention to what his father was doing and the Prince tore his gaze away from the bush.

The Guru was standing inside a small circle he had drawn. "Silence!" Drona raised his hands. The hum of voices died away. "I am going to conduct an important test today. Who will volunteer?"

Nobody moved. All the boys suddenly found the ground below their feet very interesting and sat with their eyes fixed downwards.

"No one... no one volunteers to go first. Fine, then I will have to pick." Drona's eyes scanned the class. Every boy prayed the Guru would spare him. "Aswathama." There was a collective sigh of relief as the nervous Aswathama stood up. "Come here and stand in this circle. Do not forget to bring your bow and arrows."

Suyodhana nodded reassuringly as Aswathama slowly picked up his bow and quiver and walked into the circle drawn by his father.

"Look there," Drona said, pointing to a distant mango tree. "What do you see?"

Was there a catch? Aswathama's heart thumped in his ribcage. What was there to see other than a mango tree?

"It is a mango tree."

"If you befriend a blind man's son, what else will you see? Get back to your seat."

Aswathama sat down, trying not to look at Suyodhana.

Suyodhana was burning with anger. Why did the Guru drag his blind father into everything? Was it his fault that he was blind? Was it not Lord Shiva's will? Now what was the Guru pointing at? Had he seen the bush that was possibly hiding a Naga warrior? Suyodhana tried to concentrate on the mango tree. What was so special about it?

"Bhima."

The enormous Pandava walked with his characteristic elephantine gait to reach the circle. Drona raised an eyebrow in question.

"I see a few ripe mangoes in the tree," Bhima said. The boys laughed aloud.

"My little Prince is hungry I believe." Bhima blushed like a coy bride at the Guru's words. "Please take your place, my son."

Suyodhana tried hard to see what was so special about the mango tree, as one by one, all his cousins and brothers were called. No one was able to answer to the Guru's satisfaction. Finally, Suyodhana heard Drona call his name. He stood and walked towards the circle. As he neared, he saw them – two parrots sitting on the topmost branch of the tree. It was spring and love was in the air. Lost in their lust and love, the birds were oblivious to the danger that awaited them. As he saw them, the horror of what the Guru was asking struck Suyodhana.

"What do you see there?"

"I see love."

"What are you? A poet? Draw your bow and tell me what you see there."

"Swami, I see life. I see two souls, united in love. I see bliss in their eyes and hear celebration in their voices. I see the blue sky spread like a canopy above them. I feel the breeze that ruffles their feathers. I smell the fragrance of ripe mangoes…"

Smack! Suyodhana felt his cheek burn. He staggered and almost fell. It took a moment for him to realise Drona had struck him. "You fool! You good-for-nothing rascal! Are you making fun of me? You think, because you are a Prince, you can taunt a poor Brahmin? I am trying to make you into a warrior and you talk like a woman. Get out of my sight!"

Suyodhana walked back with his head hung in shame. The unkind words stung. He had intended no insult to his teacher.

"A woman!" Bhima called out, and all the boys laughed.

Suyodhana wanted to take on fatso, but before he could move, Drona called the last boy. "Arjuna."

The middle Pandava Prince stood up and walked to the centre. Drona beamed at his favourite student as Arjuna touched his Guru's feet before entering the circle. Sushasana muttered a curse and a few boys from the Kaurava camp snickered. Drona glared at them and silence descended. He turned to Arjuna, who was standing with his bowstring taut. The setting sun kissed the tip of his arrow, making it glow blood red. "Tell me, son. What do you see there?"

"I see the eye of a bird, which is my target."

"*Sabash*! Bravo my son. Shoot!"

"No..." Suyodhana shouted, but Arjuna's arrow was swift. It pierced the bird's eye and brain and lifted the little body a few feet into the air before plunging to the ground with its impaled prey.

The Pandavas clapped at this impressive feat of archery. Drona shed tears of joy and hugged his favourite pupil. The distressed cries of the dead bird's mate filled the sky. It circled the tree over and over again and then dropped down beside its fallen love. It screeched in an agony of loss; tapping its dead mate with its beak. But there were no eyes to see the bird's misery, other than that of a blind man's son. Drona made a speech praising Arjuna's marksmanship, his dedication, and his eye for seeing only the target. He said that the most important qualities of a warrior were unflinching aim, the determination to achieve victory at any cost, and seeing only what was essential. The *dharma* of a warrior was to shoot where his superiors told him to, not to question why.

Suyodhana heard none of it. He walked towards the fallen bird, ignoring the angry calls from his Guru. As he neared, the bird's mate looked at him suspiciously and screeched, perhaps cursing him. Suyodhana could not control his tears. The little creature seemed to sense the teenager's distress. With the wisdom that nature gives those who are unspoilt by thoughts of right or wrong, the small bird sensed the human meant no harm, and sat mourning its love, killed by the warriors of *dharma*. The Prince of Hastinapura knelt a few feet away, his heart heavy. The breeze ruffled the feathers of the dead bird. The Prince paused, hoping life remained, but death does not return what it has claimed. The bird understood the ultimate truth first and stopped its cries. But the Prince was just a fool who had not studied the scriptures enough to know that death is just like changing clothes and that the soul never dies. He sat hoping against hope that the little bird would stir and he could take it home and nurse it back to health. Behind him, a jubilant teacher and his favourite students returned to the palace. The lesson of *dharma* had been strongly instilled; at least in the minds of the Pandavas.

As Suyodhana reached out to touch the dead bird, the sound of running feet startled him. Two dark-skinned boys ran out from behind a bush and grabbed the dead bird. "Hey!" Suyodhana yelled at the vanishing figures of two Nishada boys. He drew his sword but hesitated for a moment, glancing back at his cousins and brothers, walking towards the palace. It was dangerous to follow the Nishadas. The forest was infested with Naga warriors and the Crown Prince of Hastinapura falling into their hands would be a disaster. It was foolish and reckless. But the agonized cries of the parrot hovering above its dead mate, made the Prince follow. 'To hell with security,' he thought, as he plunged into the darkness of the jungle.

***

Trees towered hundreds of feet over Suyodhana and cut off the fading sunlight. The eerie chirping of crickets and the croaking of toads added to his unease. The thieves were nowhere to be seen. They had vanished into the dark maze of creepers and vines. After a while, the Prince realized he had lost his way and cursed himself for his own madness in following them. He moved aimlessly forward, hacking at the thick undergrowth; sometimes finding his way by listening to the cries of the grieving parrot. By the time he stumbled upon a small clearing, it was dark and the bird had accepted its loss and flown away into the night.

A small fire burned in the clearing and a woman with seven children of varying ages, sat around it. The dancing flames cast a ghostly light onto their dark faces. Over the flames, the dead bird was being roasted as the children waited expectantly. Suyodhana was shocked. What bestiality! What cruelty! What sort of devils would do this? He wanted to drag them to Hastinapura and punish them. But before he could act, a hand on his shoulder restrained him. Startled, Suyodhana turned back. "Aswathama!"

Hearing his voice, the eldest boy turned towards them. Aswathama quickly pushed Suyodhana down behind the bushes and motioned to him to remain silent. The Nishada boy looked in their direction for a few seconds more and then got up to see whether the bird had cooked. He began cutting it up and distributing it to the others.

"Ekalavya, give me a bigger piece, I found it," a small boy cried.

"Jara, you scoundrel! You have such a big stomach." Cursing, Ekalavya took a minuscule portion more and thrust it at the complaining boy. Jara grabbed it, attacking it like a hungry dog.

Suyodhana watched in horror as the Nishada family ate with relish. As they were licking their hands clean, the woman said to Ekalavya, "It is good that your hunting skills have improved. This was a small bird but it was better than nothing. The boys were famished. Tomorrow, try for bigger game."

"But he did not..." A savage kick from Ekalavya ensured Jara's silence.

"What a beast!" Suyodhana hissed from his hiding place.

"Do not judge them, Prince. Did you not hear the woman? They have not eaten for days. Hunger makes people do these things. For Arjuna, it was just a target; for you it was love and beauty; for them it is food."

Suyodhana was silent for a long time. He finally stood up as the Nishada family fell asleep and the fire died down. Aswathama stood up too. They had to find their way back. With Aswathama beside him, Suyodhana did not feel the uneasiness that had affected him earlier. Moonlight dappled the forest floor, shining through the gaps in the forest canopy. As the two boys competed to step on the moonlit patches on their way home, Suyodhana said, "The condition of these tribes in our kingdom is so sad. It is a shame that so many people have nothing to eat. The way the Untouchables live, is pathetic. Why is there so much injustice in the world? Why does Uncle Bhishma do nothing about it? I hate the stupid taboos and caste rules."

"Suyodhana, does poverty knock at the door and ask for your caste before entering your home? Can you imagine how poor we were, before my father got this job? I had never seen milk in my life before we came here. Once, my friends tricked me by giving me batter to drink. I drank it thinking that was what milk tasted like. True, the condition of the lower castes is bad, but there is great poverty in every caste. A few people have wealth, power and privilege. The majority suffers."

"I hate it all."

"So change it my friend. After all, one day you are going to be King. I hope you retain the same fervour then. Power corrupts even the most principled."

"I will change the entire system when I become King. I will... hey who is that? Do you see?"

A lone figure was walking towards them. The boys quickly hid behind a tree. Clouds had covered the moon and it was too dark to see the face of the person approaching. As he neared them, the two boys jumped out with their swords drawn and cried, "Halt!"

In a trice, the other had drawn his sword as well. At that moment, the moon broke free from the grip of the clouds. "Hey! Aren't you that charioteer's son?" Suyodhana was surprised to find him there.

"Prince! You are right, I am Vasusena Karna, and my father owes his employment as charioteer to the kindness of your father. I am the son of Athiratha and Radha."

"What brings you here at this odd hour?"

"I... I... I am on a pilgrimage to the holy places in the South."

"Pilgrimage! Are you old enough to go on a pilgrimage? And where are you headed to in the South?"

"Oh... to Rameswaram, Gokarna, Muzaris, Madurai, Sree Sailam, Kalahasthi... My Guru has advised me to travel," replied Karna, gazing at the boys steadily.

"It is rather strange that Guru Kripa advised you to go on a pilgrimage. But best of luck, my friend. Come and see me when you return," Suyodhana said.

Karna bowed. Without looking back, the charioteer's son walked away. His destination was far away and his journey was long. Parashurama's kingdom was located at the southwestern tip of India and it took six months' arduous travel over hot deserts, imposing mountains, and raging rivers, to reach it. Many dangerous tribes like the Yakshas, Kiratas, Nishadas, Nagas, Gandharvas and Vanaras, dwelt in the thick jungles on the way. It was an expedition of extreme peril for a teenager to undertake alone. But seeing him walk away with determined steps, Suyodhana felt nothing in this world could have stopped Karna. The Crown Prince of Hastinapura and Aswathama watched him vanish into the trees.

"Aswathama, I have a feeling he will be back. He is not going to be a Priest. I can see it in the way he carries himself – so proud, so confident. This is one of Kripa's practical jokes. Mark my words, that boy is going to come back and nothing will be the same again."

"Keep dreaming, my friend," laughed Aswathama. "Now, let's get some exercise. Let's see if a Prince's legs are as strong as those of a poor Brahmin boy." Aswathama sprinted off towards the distant palace, hooting and howling; frightening the sleeping birds, which exploded in wild cries above them. Suyodhana gave chase, smiling broadly.

BY WINTER, KARNA HAD CROSSED the desert and reached the ancient and holy city of Prabhasa, along with a party of merchants. The training Kripa had given him on Brahmin rituals stood Karna in good stead and the doors of inns and temples magically opened to him. The sacred thread he wore was a ticket to perpetual free meals. Rich merchants and Princes bowed before him. He was uneasy with the duplicity and was often tempted to cry out that he was a mere Suta, not an exalted Brahmin as they thought, but food was scarce and nobody would have given him a job had he spoken the truth. He had to reach Parashuramakhestra. Had Kripa not told him that a Brahmin is one who seeks knowledge and not merely one who is born into a Brahmin family? Since he was indeed in search of knowledge, there was nothing wrong in calling himself a Brahmin. The son of a charioteer reminded himself of his teacher's words to calm his burning conscience.

Karna halted in Prabhasa for a few weeks and watched a tribe of migrating cowherds from the Yamuna plains. They were the Yadavas, fleeing their ancient kingdom of Mathura, following an invasion by the powerful monarch of Magadha, Jarasandha. The Yadavas had camped near Prabhasa, close to the ancient temple of Somanatha, and were now planning to move on. Karna was invited along with a group of other Brahmins, to a feast the Yadava leader was hosting at the temple. He hesitated to go, afraid someone would discover he was an imposter. If it became known he was a Suta and had dared to dine with his betters, death would surely follow. However, he could find no way of refusing the invitation without sounding churlish, so he was compelled to go along.

Karna tried to make himself as inconspicuous as possible as the Yadavas came to wash the Brahmins' feet. The soiled water was considered holy and sprinkled on the crowd that had come to watch. The Brahmins were then invited into a hall where plantain leaves had been laid out to serve the feast. As Karna chanted the *mantra* along with hundreds of Brahmins, before touching the food, he caught sight of a dark young man, a few years older than himself. With a peacock feather tucked into his curly hair and a garland of marigolds around his neck, he had the look of a handsome dandy. The yellow robes, the bamboo flute tucked conspicuously into the sash at his waist, and the easy, confident way he carried himself, added to the man's charisma. Karna felt uneasy in his presence. It was as though he could hide nothing from this dark young man who exuded such raw energy. Karna felt he was in the presence of someone dangerous but he seemed to be the only person in the room to be so affected. The young man was all charm, sweetness and wit, and people hung on his every word; laughing uproariously at his jokes. 'Perhaps I feel guilty because I have a secret to hide,' thought Karna. He prayed for this ordeal to end.

"Why are you sweating, my friend?" The old Brahmin, who had been Karna's travelling companion for some time now, was sitting next to him. He fanned Karna with his *angavastra* and touched his forehead to check for fever.

"It is nothing, Swami," Karna replied quickly, feeling guilty about the old man's kindness. He watched with concern as the dark young man began walking towards them. Karna stopped eating. He could feel his heart thumping furiously in his chest.

When the young man was just a few feet away and Karna was convinced his cover had been blown, a booming voice filled the room. "*Namaskara*, learned men! We are honoured by your presence."

Every eye turned towards the towering man standing at the entrance with folded hands. He was dressed in white. The broad shoulders rippled with muscle. His straight hair had been combed into a tight knot to the right of his forehead. He exuded power, authority and elegance. But more than anything, it was his smile that set him apart from every other man in the room. There was more kindness and benevolence in those eyes that twinkled with amusement than Karna had ever seen in anyone.

"Krishna, what are you doing here? Come, help me serve our guests." The dark young man moved towards the newcomer, smiling quizzically but his eyes never left Karna, whose appetite had vanished long ago. He stood up now, abandoning his meal. As he went out to wash his hands, he found Krishna standing next to him, his arms folded across his chest, a smile on his face. Karna stopped in his tracks. Suddenly his fear fell away. His cover had been blown and he was prepared to face the consequences.

"Who are you, brother?" Krishna asked sweetly.

"Vasusena Karna."

"Hmm, and which caste are you?"

Karna said nothing but he wanted to scream, 'How does it matter?' He felt the familiar frustration welling up. All his efforts had been in vain. All the travails, the hard work, all those mornings he had stood shivering in the cold waters of the Ganga, as Kripa taught him the *Gayatri Mantra* and the *Vedas*; it had all been for nothing. He had the wrong surname and it did not matter that he had the talent and willingness to work harder than anybody else.

Just as Karna was about to answer that he was a mere Suta, he heard the by now familiar, boisterous voice say, "Krishna, there you are, standing around chatting, while everyone is waiting to hear my dear brother play the flute. Please allow me the honour of entertaining this learned Brahmin."

"But Balarama *bhaiya*..."

Before Krishna could object any further, Balarama caught Karna by the hand and started walking away. Karna struggled to keep pace with the Yadava leader, who said over his shoulder, "Krishna, go and do what you are good at and leave governing to the head of the Yadava Council, my boy."

***

Krishna stood for a few moments more, shaking his head in amusement as his brother dragged the young Brahmin towards his chamber. Did Balarama know what he was doing? 'Such upstarts will destroy society and the country,' Krishna thought sadly. 'These emotional men and women, led by their senses and not by logic, bring disaster upon everyone. Society remains stable because there is a place for everyone and everything in *chaturvarna*.'

Krishna failed to understand why men like Kripa and Carvaka were against one of the most efficient systems developed for a stable society. In *chaturvarna*, each person knew his *kula* and *dharma*, and hence his path in life. A man born as a charioteer got the best possible training to become one and excel in that profession. He learnt the trade from childhood. He did not have to fear any competition and his livelihood was assured. So was it with other professions, be it trade, the Priesthood, or medicine. Men and women did not waste precious years of their lives learning skills that were of no use to them. Instead, they became experts in their *kula dharma*.

What was the alternative? Everybody learning whatever they liked and competing with each other to survive, like animals? Such societies could only collapse. *Chaturvarna* had been developed by Lord Vishnu himself as the Preserver of social order. 'Why do I always dream that I was born into this world to preserve order? Perhaps I am Vishnu's *avatar*; the one sages have long predicted will appear.' Krishna smiled at the thought. '"I am Vishnu, Preserver of the Universe," had a nice ring to it. Why not? I have come to preserve *dharma* in the world. How good our pastoral life was when we followed *kula dharma*. Ah Radha! My first love. Where are you now?' Krishna almost said the words aloud, and then shook his head, a mocking smile on his lips. 'Am I getting emotional? Never! *Stithapranja* is the aim of the ideal man – to remain calm in all circumstances, all the time – in birth, death, love, war or peace. Live in the world like a drop of water on a lotus petal, thinking only about doing one's duty, irrespective of the results, and not getting bothered about success or failure. That is the meaning of life!'

It was unfortunate that some men had to die in the cause of *dharma*. Some of them were good men, but misguided. Krishna thought about the Crown Prince of Hastinapura. Suyodhana was a large-hearted fool who was destabilizing society. The young 'Brahmin' he had met today was another example of misguided youth. Krishna smiled to himself thinking that the foolish boy had not hoodwinked him for even a minute. He knew. Karna should have been content to have become the best Suta; instead, he wanted to be something else, and he was going to cause a great deal of trouble. Such a waste. Bhishma too, was a truly noble man, but again, misguided. If he wanted to fight the system, he should fight for the equality of the *varnas*, instead of mixing the castes. That could only lead to chaos. His own brother Balarama was doing everything possible to harm the established order by moving the Yadavas away from their *kula dharma* of cow herding towards agriculture and trade. It was going to end in catastrophe. 'War might be the only answer,' Krishna pondered sorrowfully. War would bring death and destruction, but there was little choice. 'Life! Death! They were but two sides of the same coin. Is there anything called Death? Does the Soul die? Surely, the Soul is eternal – without beginning or end. *Atma*! My slice of the Universal Soul, the Supreme *Paramatama*.'

Life was nothing but the animated manifestation of the supreme soul. Death was its transformation to the inanimate. The soul remains, just the forms change, as per the rhythm of the universe. The dance of energy, from inanimate to animate, from death to life and life to death. This is the eternal cycle! How does it matter if a few people die or live in this vast universe: the timeless, beginingless, endless infinity that always was and always will be? Does it care if someone lives or dies? Then why are men so afraid of death and war? As there is a rhythm in the universe, there should be a rhythm for society, for life. Men like Suyodhana were creating disharmony, like misbeats in the *tala*. This young man was going to be another headache. It is sad, yet a few had to die. A war, an all-consuming war would be required. That is my burden, thought Krishna, may be my duty, my *dharma* and I have to do it without worrying about the consequences.

'Where are you running to, Karna? Ultimately you will have to face me.' Krishna chuckled at the thought.

"Krishna, the *sabha* is waiting for you." A Yadava elder came to him and touched his shoulder.

Krishna smiled, pulled his flute from his sash, and walked towards the *sabha*. As he entered, the entire assembly rose in applause. He stood before them and smiled at the percussionists who were acknowledging him by tapping their *mrudanga*. Soon, the magic of his music carried the entire *sabha* to another world, where there was only beauty and love. The real world stood still, in rapturous attention.

***

Meanwhile, a trembling Karna stood before the seated Yadava leader. He had decided to fight if the powerful man before him ordered his death for impersonating a Brahmin. Faintly, he could hear music and tried to shut it out.

"Sit down, my friend," said Balarama, gesturing with one hand.

Karna was surprised at the kindness in his voice. 'Perhaps he is not as observant as his younger brother and has not seen through my deception.' Then Karna shook his head, not wishing to continue the pretence. "Swami, I am not what you think. I am a lowly Suta, not a Brahmin. I belong to one of the lower *jatis* of the Shudras, hardly above Pariahs and other Untouchables."

"Oh! Who is a Suta? And why is he lower than a Brahmin and higher than a Pariah? I am only an ignorant farmer. Please educate me."

Karna heard the smile in Balarama's question. It made him angry. He should never have agreed to this farce. He ought to have stayed in Hastinapura and helped his father. Better still, he should have ended his life in the Ganga; if only Kripa had not been so hell bent on saving him. This was all Kripa's idea of a practical joke. "My father is a Suta charioteer and the Pariahs are..." The loathsomeness of what he had said struck him then. That such words could escape his mouth showed that he too, was not free of caste prejudice.

Balarama enjoyed the spectacle of the proud young man squirming at his own words. "You may have thought ill of the Brahmins until you realized that you too, are capable of uttering the same words you accuse others of. You have travelled in the company of Brahmins. How disgusting have you found them to be as individuals?"

Karna remained silent, feeling more ashamed with every passing minute. He remembered the old Brahmin who had been his companion for most of the journey; who treated him like a son. He was one of the most learned men Karna had met and commanded the respect of all. The septuagenarian had once trekked for three hours to find a physician when Karna had fallen ill. 'Perhaps he would not have done it had he known I was a Suta and not a Brahmin at all,' thought Karna bitterly.

"I am sure you would have found in that group some men of noble character, some charlatans, and the majority who just follow whatever the collective is doing, without questioning anything. There is nothing special about that. Take any group of people and you will find the same thing. Remember, they too, are victims of the system. The people who meekly follow caste rules are really the people who are afraid of breaking them. They are cowardly, not cruel. They deserve understanding rather than derision. The future is in the hands of young men like you, who must lead the change. Our country deserves a better system. You are neither above the poor Pariah nor below any Brahmin, Kshatriya, Vaishya, or any *jati* or *varna*. You are what you think you are. I had hoped Kripa would have taught you that by now."

Karna was shocked to hear his Guru's name. Balarama laughed. "Why are you so shocked? He and I are old friends. He wrote to me about you as soon as you left Hastinapura. In fact, your Guru has gone a step further to ensure you are not caught. Knowing you are not well versed with certain rituals, he entrusted you to the care of one of the most learned Brahmins in the group. The old man who has been travelling with you and even acted as your nurse once, is your protector and guide at Kripa's request."

Karna burned with shame at the uncharitable thoughts he had harboured about the old man. He had known all along that Karna was a Suta, yet he had not shown any sign of the prejudice and aversion Karna had come to associate with his caste superiors.

"Karna, remember one thing in life. Never associate any evil with a group. Hate their sins, but not the people. Be generous. Keep giving and the world will return those favours manifold. I know young men of your age do not enjoy receiving advice from older people like me, so I will not bore you further. Since you are going to Muzaris, why not take a ride in one of my ships? It will carry you swiftly to your destination. It will be fun and a great adventure for someone your age. Yes, I know I am asking you to break the taboo the Priests have decreed. If everyone who travelled by sea lost their caste, it would be the best thing to happen to us. Our civilization produced great adventurers and sailors in days gone by. I want to bring those glorious days back. That is why I have chosen to build my dream city of Dwaraka by the sea. What was once the glory of the Asuras of the South, I want to bring to all of India. I will build cities all along the Eastern and Western coasts of this vast land and connect them with large ports on our mighty rivers."

Balarama walked up and down like a man possessed. Karna watched in fascination as the enigmatic leader of the Yadavas spelt out his vision not only for his own clan, but also for the whole of India. "I want to open the world to my people. They should not remain ignorant cattle-herders, led by selfish Priests, stuck with ancient rituals and meaningless mumbo-jumbo. You will have observed that rulers roam about wearing weapons of their choice – they are leaders because they have the power to hurt, kill and maim. It is the fear of the sword, which earns them respect. I too, used to command respect with my mace when I was younger but as wisdom slowly seeped into my head, I have come to believe that true leadership means earning respect through my deeds. So I have abandoned the mace and now carry a plough. It is not just an agricultural implement. I carry it as a symbol of progress. I wish for agriculture to flourish, trade to boom. It is a dream I share with people like Kripa, Bhishma, Vidhura and Carvaka. Do not look so surprised, my boy. We all share the same dream, only our methods differ. The dream of wiping out hunger from this land and giving dignity to people, who live like animals, may not turn into reality in our lifetimes, but why should we worry when there are young men like you, who are bold enough to travel thousands of miles in search of knowledge?"

Karna felt a sob choking his throat. Nobody had ever put so much faith in this poor Suta boy or spoken to him as an equal. It was exhilarating. Perhaps he could be a great warrior. It had just been a selfish dream but now, it seemed to have gained greater purpose. Becoming a warrior would not simply be an escape from poverty; it would also be a journey of self-discovery, an adventure – a cause far greater than petty ambition. The dream was now his destiny.

"Karna, when you reach the land of Parashurama, you will find many things that will fill you with anger and contempt. You will see a proud race living like dogs under meaningless taboos, bound by caste hierarchy. Do not become agitated and do something rash and foolish. Remember that you are there for a purpose. There is no warrior in the whole of India, including Bhishma and Drona, who can match Parashurama's skill. Learn whatever you can from him. One day the time will come to use that skill for a greater cause. Do not hesitate to say you are a Brahmin when Parashurama asks."

Balarama's final words brought Karna back to reality. How would he answer Parashurama when asked the dreaded question? He had never uttered an untruth in all his young life. Now he had to lie to achieve his aim. Was it not like stealing?

"Karna, do not feel embarrassed when he asks about your caste. Look into his eyes and answer boldly that you are a Brahmin. He will ask in his own narrow way but you will answer with the truth that lives in our holy books. You are a seeker of knowledge, a Brahmin in the purest sense. You are more Brahmin than Parashurama. Once you become a warrior and work for society, you will become a Kshatriya, protector of the weak. When you bring prosperity to your people through your work, you will become a Vaishya. When you bring happiness to people through your love, compassion and service, you will be a Shudra. You will be all *varnas* and more – you will be a humane being. Nothing is greater than that."

The curtains fluttered in a gentle breeze that carried the salty taste of the sea. Voices could be heard from outside, ordering labourers to load cargo. Karna bowed and touched the feet of the Yadava leader. Balarama blessed his protégé, took a pouch of gold coins from his waist, and gave it to him. "This will help you with your expenses. My first ship with cargo will be leaving any time now. I wanted to launch it from this holy town of Prabhasa. Look, the sails are unfurling now. Let the compassionate eyes of Lord Somanatha always follow you. Karna, I wish all that is best in life for you. I have to see to some details of merchandise now, but we will meet in circumstances that are more leisurely one day. By then, my young friend, you will be the best warrior in India. Remember, you carry our dreams with you. When you achieve your goal, do not forget what you owe to each blade of grass of this land. God bless you."

Karna watched Balarama turn away, trying to hide his deep emotion. The Yadava leader walked past the Suta boy in a blur. Karna felt inspired; his self-doubts had vanished. What Kripa had not been able to do in ten months of teaching, Balarama had achieved in ten minutes. Karna was no longer the same boy who had entered the Yadava chamber burdened by the guilt of his deception. Now he was a young man with a vision of his destiny. No taboo was going to stop him. No man was going to stand in his way. But as he walked out into the bright afternoon, Karna found the dark form of Krishna standing in his way.

"Who are you?" Krishna asked.

Karna smiled. "I am nobody, my Lord."

"Clever! But give me a straight answer. Who are you?"

"I am everybody," said Karna, laughing aloud and gently pushing Balarama's brother out of his way.

Krishna wanted to stop him, but caught sight of his brother standing a few feet away, looking at them. He remained silent as Karna walked away.

Labourers had pushed the ship into the water and now it gently rose and fell on the waves. The sails were being tested when Karna went on board. The Captain ordered his humble baggage to be placed in a corner of the deck. For a long time Karna sat watching the glistening tower of the Somanatha temple rising into the sky, and the sprawling city of Prabhasa. As the sea turned saffron in the setting sun and the air resounded with the cries of seagulls, Karna felt the ship creak and move. The anchor was raised and a line of rowers pulled hard to take the ship towards the high seas. As the sails unfurled to catch the wind and the ship swayed before steadying, Karna clutched the railing to stabilise himself. He watched the temple towers glimmer in the sun while the sea spread its red-tinted mantle in the west.

"South ahoy!" someone cried and the ship turned and gathered speed.

With his dark mane flying in the wind and the evening star rising in the heavens above, Karna stood in silence, fighting hope and fear. In travelling by sea, he had lost his caste. Karna felt strangely elated. The last rays of the sun caressed his strong body as if in blessing and then sank into the watery depths. Swaying in the wind and moving to the rhythm of the oarsmen's song, the ship carried the young man and his burden of destiny to the dangerous land of the Gods.

9 THE BEAST

THE FOREST SLOWLY AWOKE TO THE chattering of birds. Jara was reluctant to leave his soft bed of grass. It was so cosy lying in the shade of the trees and watching the mist slowly rise from a shy earth. Shafts of sunlight pierced holes in the forest canopy. Monkeys had begun their clever antics high in the trees. They jumped from branch to branch, screeching at each other for no apparent reason. From the corner of his eye, Jara saw Ekalavya was occupied in making a bow. Curiosity overcame laziness and he bounded up. He ran to Ekalavya and took out an arrow from the quiver.

"Don't touch it, you ass!" shouted Ekalavya, without even raising his head. He was busy polishing the bow. It had begun to gleam in the sunlight.

"Hey, are you serious about becoming an archer?" Jara did not receive a reply. 'If Ekalavya learns archery, we will have more to eat,' he thought as he touched the sharp tip of the arrow with a finger.

"Ouch!" Jara howled, looking at the stone that had hit him hard. The stone Ekalavya had thrown had found its mark on Jara's knee and was rolling off a few feet away.

"I told you not to touch it." Ekalavya pointed one unwavering finger at the whimpering urchin.

It was not the usual banter Jara was used to from the older boy. Ekalavya had somehow gained more power and authority overnight. He watched Ekalavya string the bow and test it by twanging the string twice. Then, with a great air of importance, he took an arrow, examined its straightness by closing one eye and sighting down the tip, and then drew the bow and took aim. He had drawn a circle on the trunk of a huge tree that was almost fifteen feet in diameter. Jara waited with bated breath. After what seemed an eternity, Ekalavya shot the arrow. It swished through the air. Jara looked at the fig tree but there was no arrow embedded in the trunk. Ekalavya had missed the mark and even managed to miss the huge tree! Jara howled with laughter, doing a somersault in amusement. Ekalavya kicked at the boy but Jara dodged him and continued laughing. Jara knew Ekalavya had lost his power over him. He was no longer intimidated by Ekalavya. He was just another nondescript urchin – plain and ordinary. Jara ran off enthusiastically to find the arrow. He shouted in glee when he found it a good ten feet to the right of the tree. It had not even pierced the earth. In fact, it had hit nothing and was lying docile, just another piece of dry wood with a sharp tip.

Jara knew he was making Ekalavya angry with his constant jeering but it was fun. He waited until Ekalavya almost caught him and then dashed away to climb up a banyan tree. Jara sat on a high branch, swinging his spindly legs and screaming at Ekalavya like a monkey. Ekalavya tried shooting arrows at him, but they did not reach high enough. This increased Jara's merriment and he started throwing twigs at his tormentor. A few found their mark and enraged Ekalavya further. Jara could climb dizzyingly high and even jump from tree to tree like an ape. He knew the older boy could not touch him. Finally, Ekalavya gave up the chase and started towards Hastinapura instead. Jara clambered down and began following Ekalavya at a discreet distance.

After an hour of walking, they reached the open ground where Drona was teaching the Princes. Ekalavya hid behind a bush to watch. Then he noticed Jara hiding behind a nearby bush and uttered a silent curse. Jara waved at him and put out his tongue, irritating Ekalavya further. Jara was glad they had come to the same place where they got the parrot. Perhaps the bearded man would ask one of the Princes to shoot a deer today. If they could steal it, as they had the bird, they would not have to worry about food for days.

After hours of observation, Ekalavya discovered he had been doing it all wrong. His grip, his stance, and even the way he held his head while taking aim, were all wrong. He made a mental note of how the Princes did it. The Guru was sweet to a handsome teenager who shot arrows with surprising agility and skill – the same boy who had shot the parrot through its eye and so provided their meal. 'I will be better than him,' vowed Ekalavya. He was tempted to go and ask the Guru whether he would teach him as well. What was so wrong in trying? He had heard rumours that Kripa was training the Suta boy. Of course, Sutas were many notches above Nishadas in the caste hierarchy, but why not try it? 'If he insults me, what will I do?' Ekalavya wondered. Conflicting thoughts tortured the young Nishada boy. He was afraid of rejection, but the ambition that burned in his mind was too strong to ignore. By the evening, he had decided to take the chance.

As Ekalavya approached Drona, the evening sun was slowly setting behind the distant mountains. The boys sat in rows. Drona was reciting a *mantra*. The boys repeated it with waning enthusiasm. Ekalavya found his courage draining away with each step. He wanted to run back and hide in the bushes but it was too late. He heard footsteps behind him and knew that blasted urchin had followed him. As they drew near, Drona looked at the Untouchables in surprise and shock. Ekalavya heard the chanting stop as all eyes turned towards them. Drona stood like a statue carved from stone, mentally measuring the distance between them to avoid pollution as per the *smritis*. He stood with his arms crossed over his muscular chest, his eyebrows raised. Ekalavya shuddered. He considered touching Drona's feet as he had seen the Princes do every day and tentatively took a step forward.

"Stop!"

Ekalavya froze at Drona's command. 'Why did I come?' he wondered.

"Why are you here?"

Ekalavya seemed to have lost all power of speech. "Swami, I... I... wish to be your student," he somehow managed.

"I have seen you somewhere before. Wait, are you not the Nishada boy who stole the mangoes when I first came to this lawless land?" the Guru asked.

Ekalavya just wanted to turn and run. He should not have come. This was no place for Untouchables like him.

The Guru of the Royals peered down at the cowering Nishada boy. Turning to Suyodhana, Drona hissed, "See what your father has done. He has allowed such worms to rise up and demand education from Brahmins. See how this country has been ruined. I knew it would come to this. I warned the Grand Regent of the Kurus long ago. Making a Shudra the Prime Minister; allowing all sorts of freedom to people who do not deserve it. Disgusting! First, the Suta boy wanted to be my student, with the Prime Minister actually recommending his case. Now even Untouchables want to be archers. The rise of the *Kali Yuga* is imminent. If this is the case now, what atrocities will occur when you become the ruler of this land, Prince? Not that you ever will be."

Suyodhana's eyes lit with anger but before he could respond, Drona turned towards the Nishada boy, who was still standing with his head hanging in shame.

Ekalavya could sense Jara laughing behind him. He saw Prince Suyodhana looking at the urchin in curiosity. Drona too, looked at the pathetic figure. The boy had sores on his feet and his dark, curly hair had matted into a dirty coil. With his spindly legs, protruding belly, and rashes all over his skin, he was a disgusting object in the eyes of the fastidious Guru. Ekalavya's heart skipped a beat as he watched his face.

"You dirty devil! How dare you come and pollute this place?"

Ekalavya thought at first that the Guru was addressing him. It took him a few moments to realize the Guru's anger was directed at Jara, standing behind him with a stupid grin on his face. 'Oh Shiva! Why did the nitwit follow me and spoil my chances? If he had not come, the Guru would not have been so angry.'

Jara tried to stand still but an overwhelming urge to scratch overcame him. Disregarding the holy presence of a pious Brahmin and the Princes in their resplendent garb, the slum dog's nails scratched patterns on his body. Jara tried to compensate with a buck-toothed smile.

"Get out of here!" shouted Drona, his chest heaving with anger as laughter rose from the ranks of his students. Many of the Princes found this little monkey amusing and one of the Kaurava Princes whistled softly. Suyodhana, Sushasana, and Aswathama, were all laughing. Bhima shared his Kaurava cousins' amusement but caught the eye of his elder brother and stopped himself just in time. He imitated the serious expression his brothers wore and tried to look sufficiently enraged at the insult the two Untouchables were offering the strict Guru.

"Silence!" Drona directed his anger towards the Kauravas. As the hilarity died down, Drona turned his ire on the two Untouchables. Jara instinctively read Drona's mind and backed away. The foolish grin had gone from his face and an expression of concern replaced it. Drona took a few steps towards Ekalavya. "Boy." Drona's voice had lost its harsh edge. Ekalavya looked up in surprise. Perhaps Lord Shiva had showered his blessings upon him finally, thought the Nishada, while Jara took a few more steps backwards. "I cannot be your teacher. The State employs me to teach the Princes. I cannot take a Nishada as a student. Go back to the forest, live with your people, and do your *dharma*. I have nothing to offer you."

Ekalavya's heart sank and his gaze dropped to the ground in defeat.

"But I can give you some sound advice," Drona continued. Advice was cheap and everyone gave it freely to others. Ekalavya looked up to see Drona staring at Jara, who took a few more steps backwards. "Who is that evil-looking boy?"

Ekalavya glanced at Jara with hatred and contempt. "He is an orphan and has stuck with us like a pest for some time now."

"*Hmm*, I thought so. He is too dark to be even a Nishada. What is his caste?"

Ekalavya wondered where this conversation was going. He had never thought about Jara's caste. "I do not know," he mumbled.

"What caste are you?" Drona repeated, this time to Jara, who blinked a few times. He did not know. Nobody had told him. Nobody had ever asked. "Boy," Drona said to Ekalavya, "beware of this casteless fellow. He is evil. He will bring you bad luck. Get rid of him. You at least have a caste. It may be a low one, but you still have something. You have your caste *dharma*. He has nothing. No values moor him to life and he will stoop to anything. He is no better than an animal. Look at his evil face. As long as he is with you, you will have no luck in life. Now go back to the forest and live a fulfilling life befitting your caste. Be a good Nishada and perhaps in the next life you will be born into a higher caste. Gradually, through many lives and by following your caste *dharma* diligently, you will become a Brahmin in one of your rebirths. The Gods have ordained that you spend this life as a Nishada. Accept what has been ordained. Do not ruin it by associating with low people like that boy and fall further." So saying, Drona turned on his heel and the Princes followed him back home.

The sun had almost disappeared behind the blue hills to the north and twilight was spreading its quiet mantle across the world, ending another day. Ekalavya felt the eyes of the Prince who had given him the mangoes, boring into him. But he did not want to meet those eyes; he felt that his whole world had ended.

***

From a distance, Suyodhana watched the Nishada boy and whispered to his friend, "Your father's behaviour was despicable to say the least." Aswathama's heart sank when his best friend pointed out the obvious.

"I do not know why he behaves like that, Suyodhana. At home, he is a strict father but I always feel the love he has for me. He is a different man then. He treats my mother with love and affection. He knows she secretly gives some of his hard-earned money to her brother, Kripa, who either gambles it away or gives it to his friend, Carvaka, who works among the poor in the slums of Hastinapura. Sometimes, he does beat me mercilessly but in the dead of night, when he thinks I am asleep, he comes and kisses me tenderly and I feel he will break my heart with his love. He is a difficult man to understand. He left his childhood home and all our relatives to give us a better life here. His Guru, Parashurama, warned him that nothing good would come of associating with Kshatriyas and that he would be betraying his Brahmin lineage by teaching the Kuru Princes the science of arms. He is a man torn between his beliefs and his basic good nature, Suyodhana. I hope that one day his nature will get the better of his education and he will reject the philosophy of Bhargava Parashurama for good."

Sushasana had been listening to his brother's conversation with the Guru's son. He laughed in blatant mockery and said, "You sissy Brahmin boy, all your justifications for your father's behaviour will not change our opinion of him. He is a nut, a crazy man with fanatical ideas and he will do anything to win Arjuna's favour. All his affection for you is just put on. Sometimes I wonder if you are his son or that blasted Pandava is. Good natured, *bah*!"

"If you do not keep your ugly mouth shut, you glutton, I will knock your dirty, yellow teeth in," Aswathama shouted back, trying to punch Sushasana in the face. He would have succeeded had Suyodhana not intervened.

"Come home now," Drona turned back to shout at his son, far behind.

As the three teenagers reluctantly walked on, Aswathama decided to confront his father about his behaviour towards the poor Nishada as soon as he got home, even at the risk of facing that monumental temper.

***

A star-sprinkled sky spread over the vast landscape. The lights of the palace lit the southern sky with a golden glow. A jungle fowl shrieked from the darkness of the woods, as if to call the son of the forest home. As the figures of the chattering students became specks of darkness in the distance, Ekalavya stirred. His heart was filled with anger and hatred. Jara was responsible for everything. He was the harbinger of bad luck, the casteless, dirty, smelly rat! 'The Guru is right. It was when this evil fellow first showed his face that I lost my parents. When this rascal set foot in my family, my uncle died and left my aunt with six mouths to feed. It was because of him that the Guru rejected me. Look at his ugly face; look at his dirty and unwashed body; look at the dirty nails and the puss oozing from the sores on his legs. Anyone can understand why he brings bad luck."

It was unfortunate that Jara decided to make fun of Ekalavya's predicament just at that moment. He howled like a monkey, finding merriment in the Nishada boy's broken dreams. "*Ha ha ha*... I told you so! It serves you right. You did not listen to me. You thought he would accept your ugly face when he had refused even that Suta boy with a rich and important man's recommendation. What a joke!"

Jara yelled as the first stone hit his nose. The surprised cry soon turned into screams of terror as more and more stones found their mark. Jara clutched his bleeding nose and ran. Ekalavya chased after him. With a final leap, he caught hold of the terrified, black urchin. He beat and kicked Jara with all the anger and frustration he felt and only stopped when he could not bear the pain in his own limbs. He left the profusely bleeding boy to die like a street dog and sought asylum in the darkness of the jungle.

The skies darkened with clouds and it started to rain. Still the boy did not stir. Rain pounded the red earth for a few hours and then became an impotent drizzle just before dawn. When the sky turned a dull grey in the east, the bundle of ill luck whimpered and rose up on all fours. Somewhere in the womb of the forest, a wild beast howled, mourning the passing of the night. The stray dogs of Hastinapura answered, their cries echoing on all sides. Jara stood up on his weak legs. Blood mixed with water to form a dirty puddle at his feet. He looked at his battered body and an animal cry rose in his throat. He howled again. This time, from a distance, perhaps from the woods, the hills, or the narrow pathways of the city, something answered. In that moment, the little boy died and a beast was born. There was only Jara and his hunger, nothing else mattered. No taboos, no scriptures, no caste rules were going to stand between him and his hunger. No God was going to keep him from surviving. Sheer animal instinct powered the beast.

Jara looked at the jungle, which held the secret armies of the Nagas, where he knew his hero Takshaka was preparing to take on the might of Hastinapura one day. He thought of the men and women who were willing to die for the glory of their cause under the charismatic leader. Then he looked at the sprawling capital with its majestic palaces and dark slums, where men and women like him did whatever they had to, to survive. Fate was offering him two choices – a glorious death and heroism under Takshaka or mundane survival in the teeming slums of Hastinapura. As the first rays of the sun touched the wet earth and the forest burst into a cacophony of birdsong, Jara made his choice. He chose mundane survival over spectacular death and began walking towards Hastinapura.

***

Ekalavya returned to the training ground early the next morning. He was feeling depressed and guilty about his behaviour towards Jara. He found the spot where he had left Jara for dead, but the boy had gone. Ekalavya sat on the grass wondering what might have happened to the idiot. As the morning matured, he saw Drona in the distance, leading the Princes to the ground. Ekalavya ran for cover in the woods and disappeared. From his hiding place, he watched the training, thinking this was another way of acquiring the knowledge he desired.

That was the beginning. From that day on, he hid in the woods and learnt by observation. After the classes were over and the Princes had left for their comfortable dwellings, the son of the forest practised what he had seen. After a few months of dedicated hard work, he found he could hit targets as easily as Arjuna. When an arrow was shot with skill, it did not ask whether the hands that held the bow were those of an Untouchable or a Prince. They pierced their targets without prejudice. The daily practice at night gave the Nishada an advantage over his royal competitor – it made him an expert at shooting in the darkness. Ekalavya was like one possessed. He barely managed a few hours' sleep before dawn.

The days were spent assimilating knowledge and endlessly practising what he saw. At first, he missed Jara's companionship but soon got over it. After a year had passed, it was as if Jara had never existed. Jara's disappearance coincided with Ekalavya's luck turning. With no one to mock or tell him that it was impossible for an Untouchable to become a great warrior, Ekalavya's natural confidence reasserted itself and he soon became a formidable hunter. Food was plentiful as he could hunt game with skill and stealth and his family did not face hunger again for a long time.

***

Purochana, the Chief Inspector of City Hygiene, pressed a scarf over his nose. The stench was unbearable. He had left the palace with its cloying smell of incense, and now entered a world of filth, where the streets coiled in on themselves like leeches; the open drains overflowed, and the narrow pavements served as garbage dumps. Purochana knew this world was far removed from what the Hastinapura rulers wished to believe about their kingdom. The other Hastinapura, of luxurious villas, broad, tree-shaded avenues, golden temples, swanky shops that sold diamonds and silks, and noblemen and beautiful women, could well have existed on another planet. This was the dark underbelly of India's cities, where the majority lived. The other was just a charade, as hollow and fake as the promises made by the rulers to the ruled.

People, carts, vendors, pigs, cows, goats and horses, all jostled for space. The streets had a life of their own, pushing, pulling, screeching, blaring, and dodging. They pulsed to their own rhythm. Purochana wiped the sweat from his face and waited to catch his breath, leaning on the stump of a lamppost that had been broken years before he was even born. Rats scurried over his feet and he leapt back in horror. A dirty urchin grinned at his discomfiture and a street dog barked at him. He resumed his walk, dodging carts and pushing the scarred hands of beggars away. Cursing the rude vendors who thrust their fares in his face, he moved along, using his shoulders and hands to swim through the crowd. He averted his gaze from a couple of men who were urinating against a wall with eyes closed. A few steps away, people fought for the hot savouries being fried in days-old oil.

Purochana had walked these streets many times, but they always confused him. He could not stop to ask anyone the way. Today's mission was dangerous. He paused again, trying to recall the direction he had to take. Somewhere to the left, a temple bell chimed and the faint sounds of chanting floated towards him. No, it was not that way. He turned right and continued walking, cutting across the market where clerks, servants, porters, artisans, cart drivers, masons, potters, gardeners, and many others filled the streets from dawn to dusk, haggling over prices and winning or losing their insignificant daily battles. Purochana owed his job to these people. Without them, the well-kept streets of central Hastinapura would have turned into filthy thoroughfares. The manicured gardens and large homes would have ceased to exist.

On the rare occasions he was invited to the parties of the rich, he had heard the elegant ladies complaining about their city and Government servants. *Why doesn't the Government demolish the slums? They are an affront to the eyes.* He had heard that comment from a lady who kept caressing the string of diamonds around her neck. He had been tempted to retort, 'You bitch, without those slums, how would your chariot driver or gardener survive on the meagre wages you pay them? If the slums vanished, would you even have a maid?'

But he had not uttered a word, simply nodding his head in sympathy. He could not risk talking back to the wives of influential men. The men were worse. They spoke of various methods of eradicating this blemish from their land and wondered why the Government did not have the wisdom they displayed after two pitchers of wine. He chuckled at the thought of all the people who hated their country in private and cursed Bhishma or the King, and sometimes even the foreign woman who was their Queen, for dragging down their great civilization. At the same time, they defended the greatness of their country and religion against the criticism of outsiders; with a fanaticism that bordered on insanity. They were easily offended by the wide-eyed wonder foreigners exhibited at the teeming poverty and the glittering riches of this ancient land. They wondered why those materialistic and cultureless barbarians did not restrict their attention to the exquisitely beautiful temples and palaces. Everyone knew foreigners had little by way of family values, besides being immoral and unclean. The people of Hastinapura did not need a certificate of greatness from them. Nevertheless, it irked the elite that these foreigners did not see the inherent spirituality in their music and art or understand the scientific basis of every ritual and superstition. Why did they insist on going about the stinking slums and talking about the Shudras who lived there? Why did they even care?

The people of Hastinapura were not alone in harbouring such lofty thoughts. The clothing, language and accents changed, but the ideas of the elite and comfortably rich, remained the same everywhere – whether in Kashi, Kanchipuram, Muzaris, or Dwaraka. Irrespective of what foreigners thought, the diversity of India was merely peripheral. Her core retained a surprising unity of thought and deed. Purochana laughed aloud. There was a world even grimier than this, the bureaucrat thought. An invisible world, akin to what one sees when one lifts a heavy stone in the garden. Life teems under it, indifferent to its surroundings. Vermin, worms, leeches and ants, all thrive there. Mostly they are harmless creatures, which emerge in the dead of night to find sustenance. Occasionally, there is a scorpion amongst them, with a poisonous sting in its tail.

Shakuni's instructions had been clear. Purochana was to meet one such scorpion, who had a lethal sting. The name once sent shock waves through those who heard it. Both in the dusty streets of Hastinapura as well as in the opulent homes of the rich – the name Durjaya was a conversation stopper. He was capable of hushing voices without even being present. Excitement and fear peppered small talk. Durjaya had once lorded over the kingdom of human vermin. A tyrant, he ruled an empire of beggars, prostitutes and petty thieves in the invisible underworld of Hastinapura. Crime was his weapon and misery his shield. An ambitious man, he soon found that the illicit brewing of arrack, controlling a gang of pickpockets and petty thieves, skimming from professional beggars, and a prostitution racket, yielded only so much. He aspired to bigger things in life. A few years ago, the special guards of Hastinapura had almost crushed his empire of darkness. Durjaya had grown back to strength in the chaotic time of Hastinapura fighting a bloody war with the Southern Confederate. However, once the peace treaty had been signed with Parashurama, Bhishma turned his attention back to the kingdom and times had become tough for men like him once again. Bhishma had personally camped in the dirty streets of the city and decimated the crime lord's empire. Durjaya had crawled into hiding, and waited in darkness for the wheel to turn.

Purochana's mission was to bring the scorpion out and give more power to his sting. Was this the house? The fat man hesitated, adjusting his headgear and drawing himself up to his full height. He checked the dagger hidden in the folds of his waistcloth. Not that it would do him any good if the crime lord decided to do away with him. For a fleeting moment, the image of his bloated body caught in the reeds beside the Ganga, flashed through his mind. He pushed away such inauspicious thoughts. He had to play it cool. He softly tapped at the dilapidated door. It creaked open reluctantly. He could see eyes staring at him. Purochana had to breathe through his mouth in order to shut out the stink that escaped through the partly open door. "I am Purochana, Chief Inspector of City Hygiene," he said officiously.

The door shut with a bang. The entire building shook with the impact. Purochana stood in the street, unsure of what to do. As he was about to turn away, the door opened again and the crooked hand of a leper held out some money. He had won the first round. The fool was afraid enough to offer him a bribe. Keeping his face grave, Purochana took the money, as if bestowing a favour. "Tell Durjaya that his luck is about to change. I want to see him." The door closed again but this time Purochana was sure he would be invited inside soon. He was right.

When he saw Durjaya in the flesh, Purochana was disappointed. The man looked small and ordinary, with a soft moustache and dark hair. He had expected a raving villain. The fat official looked at the pathetic condition of the crime lord's dwelling – the cobwebs, broken chairs, torn carpet. A musty smell pervaded everything. Purochana smiled. This was going to be easier than he had thought.

"I have an offer you will not be able to resist," he said pompously and waited.

Durjaya continued to sit with a blank expression on his face. Purochana's heart skipped a beat. It had been a mistake to look into those glassy eyes. He wanted to get out and go back to his office. That foreigner and his blasted plans!

"Tell me about the offer," the scorpion said simply.

Purochana forgot what he had come to say. "Hmmm… you must pray facing West, you and all your supporters…" Purochana cursed himself. That bit was to come last. He saw Durjaya's eyes expand in disbelief. Before he could be thrown out, Purochana pulled himself together and sat down. He deliberately crossed his legs and kept his hands in his lap so they would not shake. He no longer felt like a supplicant.

"Do you wish to build back your empire? Do you want a stake in smuggling arms and drugs from Gandhara and selling them to the Nagas? Do you want to become the most feared man in the country again, Durjaya?" Purochana watched for any change of expression in the crime lord's face.

Slowly a smile cracked Durjaya's lips. "Are you drunk or just insane? How can a mere city inspector help me to do all these things? Take your bribe and get lost." Durjaya stood up from his broken chair.

Purochana stood up too and as Durjaya walked away, he said, "You are being too hasty, Durjaya. Have you never heard of Shakuni?"

That stopped Durjaya in his tracks. "The Prince of Gandhara?" Durjaya asked in surprise.

Purochana's fear fell away. Durjaya ordered wine and a boy came with a pitcher. Purochana discussed the details as the two men matched each other glass for glass. The boy came many times with snacks and more drinks.

"I have seen him somewhere," Purochana said fuzzily, looking at the serving boy.

"I give employment to people the Government rejects. I am a seller of dreams." Durjaya's speech was remarkably clear still. "You bloody Government servants do not care about them. I give people instant justice, whereas you take years to settle even one case. You deny education to poor boys and I keep such boys from dying. Idiots like this boy Jara, come in hordes from the dark hinterland to this city of riches, dreaming of the day they will return to their villages in a golden chariot. Every bastard wants to go home with a train of servants and be the envy of the fools who have not dared leave the village. I play on their dreams," Durjaya laughed.

"What about girls?" Purochana asked hopefully.

"*Ha ha*... girls! They are different. This is a city of dreams, my friend. People come here to live their dreams. Girls run away from poverty to the glitter of Hastinapura, the city of art, dance and poetry. What beautiful bullshit! They come here dreaming of becoming courtesans in the palaces of the princes or rich merchants. Only handfuls achieve their dream. The rest end up with gangs like us, or on the streets, pedalling their only asset. When they become old, they become beggars. One day they fall down and die. I have uses for dreamers of either sex, Purochana. I had many of them in my gang before that cursed Shudra, Vidhura, let loose his police on me."

"Everything will change now, my friend," Purochana said, pleased by the glitter in the crime lord's eyes.

"Yes, you have brought me luck. Let us drink to your health."

As the crime lord lost himself in drink, Purochana kept looking at the small boy who flitted in and out of the room.

10 NAGAS

ONE DAY, EKALAVYA'S HUNTING HAD taken him deep into the forest to an area he had never ventured before. A dull moon glowed over the forest canopy and made leafy mosaic patterns on the ground. As he reached a mountain stream, Ekalavya heard a low whistle. He was instantly alert. It sounded suspiciously like an alarm or a signal. He hid behind a tree and listened, but nothing moved. Ekalavya waited anxiously. Though he could detect no movement, all his instincts signalled danger. He sensed a presence nearby. Something or somebody evil was watching him. He could feel it in every nerve. He waited for whoever was hiding in the deep shadows to make the first move but not a leaf stirred.

'Perhaps I am unnecessarily jumpy,' thought Ekalavya, and decided to move from his hiding place. But his body did not react as quickly as his instincts. Taking two steps forward, he found himself in a trap, hanging upside down ten feet from the ground. As he tried to free his legs, he saw scores of men surround him with flaming torches.

A dark middle-aged man approached and peered into his eyes. The man had a pockmarked face and an ugly scar on his forehead. He had only one eye and walked with a limp. "Welcome to the world of the Nagas," he said with a smile that showed a huge gap in his pointed front teeth, which looked like fangs. The long thin face and the glassy left eye gave him the appearance of a serpent. "Cut him down," the man commanded.

Ekalavya shuddered. This was the end; he thought and braced himself to be pierced with a sword. One of the men cut the ropes that held him upside down and Ekalavya fell on his face. He heard laughter as he tried to get up. Pain seared through his body. There was blood on his face. Strong hands lifted him. When he tried to writhe free, they merely laughed. Torches flickered and shadows danced around them, making grotesque patterns in the small clearing. The men walked to a stream and threw Ekalavya in. The water felt icy cold on his burning skin. When they pulled him out, he gave up the struggle and walked on between his captors up a steep hill. One of the men cleared the undergrowth with a sharp scythe while the rest followed him in single file.

No one spoke. The silence was getting on Ekalavya's nerves. "Who are you?" he finally gathered the courage to ask.

"The King of Hastinapura," replied the one-eyed leader. His companions laughed uproariously. "Well, I am only half-blind, so I am only half a King." Despite his fear, Ekalavya found himself smiling in amusement. "Son, I am the dreaded Kaliya. You may have heard stories about me. I was defeated by Krishna. Many sing about his valour in defeating a thousand-hooded snake. I am that snake."

They kept walking until Ekalavya saw a clearing ahead. His heart leapt when he saw Takshaka, with a dozen warriors in fierce Naga costume standing around him. An old man sat close to the fire. There were many thatched huts around. Women sat in a group, talking animatedly, some rocking babies. Infants cried and children ran around screaming and shouting. Some young men were singing and dancing, trying to impress the young girls who sat in another group. Other men were brewing hooch and roasting meat. It did not look like the dreaded rebel camp of Takshaka.

Takshaka stood up when he saw the group approach. Kaliya bowed. Ekalavya stood still, undecided whether to bow to Takshaka or not. Finally, he bowed and a smile flickered on the handsome face of the Naga leader. "Oh Shankara! Whom do we have here? Ekalavya, welcome to the humble abode of the Nagas."

The old man near the fire looked up at Ekalavya and then quickly looked away again, shaking his head. Takshaka smiled and stepped forward to hug Ekalavya, who stood stiffly.

"Why have you brought me here?" Ekalavya's tone betrayed more irritation than fear.

"Because this is where you belong. Welcome home, Ekalavya." Takshaka's smile broadened into a grin.

A few of the children found the newcomer more interesting than their games and stood around him in open curiosity. A few brave ones even managed to pinch Ekalavya and giggle at his embarrassment and irritation.

"So, was he difficult to catch, Kaliya? You have been trailing him for how many days... fifteen... twenty?"

Kaliya stared at Ekalavya. "It has been more than a month, Takshaka. He is a natural warrior, always alert. It was difficult for us to remain hidden. He nearly found us a couple of times. His marksmanship is impressive and his perception of his surroundings good. He can be trained to become a great warrior." The old man sitting near the fire looked up in mild curiosity.

"Can someone tell me why I have been dragged to this place?" Ekalavya was close to losing his temper but the sharpness of his tone did not have any impact on the group. A few snickered and somebody shoved the Nishada from behind.

"All in good time, comrade, all in its own time! Have patience. You are here for a purpose. I have great plans for you. I have seen your skill with the bow. Moreover, you are one of us. We are fighting for a great cause. Strong, young men like you will take the revolution forward." Takshaka caught the eye of the old man and abruptly stopped his rhetoric. "Aswasena!" he called. A young man stepped forward and bowed. "Ekalavya, this is Aswasena. He will take care of your needs for now and maybe in future too."

Their conversation was interrupted by a commotion at the periphery of the village. Naga warriors were dragging in a group of people bound with ropes. The entire village thronged around to witness the spectacle. Except for one or two, who looked a little better off, the captives belonged to the striving lower middle class. They were unimaginative, petty, hardworking, honest city folk – the rulers of boredom and monotony, tyrants in their humble homes but meek and submissive outside. There was a look of pure terror in their eyes. The villagers were shoving them, the women competing with each other to pull the hair of their unfortunate counterparts, while the children gleefully punched the captives. Mangy dogs ran with the crowd, barking, snapping and adding to the cacophony. Someone grabbed a baby from the arms of a captured woman and for some time the infant was tossed around by the mob. The agonized screams of the terrified mother drove the crowd into frenzy.

Takshaka and Aswasena ran towards the mob. As Ekalavya was about to follow, the old man near the fire caught him by the wrist. "Escape now! This is a dangerous place. That man is mad and he has made our people insane. If you do not get out now, you will never be able to do so in future. Get out and run before you too, get sucked into this."

Ekalavya looked in surprise at the old man. He had lost most of his teeth and possessed a few tufts of white hair on his head. He looked frail but it was not the weakness of age but weariness with life. "Sir, who are you? Why do you want to stop me from joining Takshaka?" Ekalavya asked.

"Son, do not play with fire. Leave before hatred poisons your mind and rage makes you blind. The world is not such a bad place as Takshaka makes it out to be. Neither is it going to be heaven when he becomes King. You are young. Do not get swayed by peddlers of impossible dreams. Get out now!"

"Who are you, Sir?" Ekalavya asked again but the old man remained silent.

The mob had been brought under control and the prisoners moved to the centre of the village. Takshaka sat on a makeshift platform made of bamboo while the captives stood tied together in a huddle a few feet away. It looked like some sort of trial. The villagers sat on their haunches all around. A few excited ones continued to shout abuse. Aswasena, the young Naga who was to be Ekalavya's guide, came running towards him through the crowd.

Once again the old man hissed, "Don't you have any sense, you fool? Run now! Run or your life will never be the same again."

Ekalavya did not know what to do. A part of his mind told him to follow the advice of the old man, but minute by minute, curiosity was getting the better of sense.

Aswasena stopped near Ekalavya, panting with exertion and excitement. "Come, the leader wishes you to witness the trial of the traitors."

Ekalavya hesitated for a moment, looking at the old man who sat shaking his head in despair, and decided to ignore him. Perhaps the man was insane, thought the Nishada, as he followed the young Naga to witness the trial. "Who is that old man, Aswasena?" he asked his companion.

"Oh, do not mind him. He is mad. He was once the King of the Nagas. His name is Vasuki. He was the fool who frittered away our inheritance and lost our kingdom. He keeps rambling on about peace and such. Our leader has been generous in sparing his life. He holds the mad Vasuki up as an example of what Nagas will become if we are not willing to fight for the cause. The man is a joke. Do not take his ramblings seriously."

They had reached the place where the trial was to be held. Takshaka motioned Ekalavya to take a seat on the wooden log where some men were already sitting. They moved a little to allow Ekalavya to take his place. Kaliya stood with his naked sword resting on his right shoulder, smiling. Ekalavya shuddered at the look of glee in the Naga's eyes.

A middle-aged man stepped out of the mob and suddenly a hush fell. He bowed to Takshaka and the group of men sitting to Ekalavya's right. "Honourable People's Court, we have here the traitors who betrayed our great cause. We are here to decide their punishment. On the far right, we have the man who has done the greatest harm to our cause. Honourable Court, behold Shivarama Charana, the renegade Brahmin of Suryanagara village, a suburb of Hastinapura."

An old man was shoved forward. Tall and lean, he held his head high with pride. There was no look of fear in his eyes as he gazed at Takshaka with contempt.

"Bow to the People's Court," barked one of the guards. When the old man showed no inclination to do so, the guard hit him with the hilt of his sword. The man still stood, unflinching, not even bothering to wipe the blood flowing from his forehead.

"This man, instead of following his caste profession, led an immoral life till he was sixty. He inherited huge tracts of farmland, which his ancestors had cheated from the Nagas a few generations before. He has always been cruel to his workers, abusing them. His labourers escaped from his tyranny and formed our first band of soldiers under our honourable leader, Nahusha. This crooked man understood we were winning so for the last fifteen years he has acted as though he is the most benevolent man on earth. He has conspired with the evil Balarama of the Yadava clan to start training centres for various crafts in his village. He is trying to take the people away from the cause by enticing them into crafts and trade. The government has made substantial grants to him, which further proves the conspiracy.

"Another strange fact, yet not so strange if we understand the true nature of our enemies, is that the man gives equal importance to different men. The list of people involved in undermining the people's war is truly astounding. It includes Balarama, the man who acts like a saint; Bhishma, the arrogant Kuru Regent; the crazy Brahmin, Kripa; the atheist, Carvaka; renegade Nagas, and so on. The strange list is long. Our prisoner has done all this despite stiff opposition from his caste members. It proves he has no principles or ethics. It is also a lesson to us. Our enemies will stoop to any level and form unlikely alliances to defeat the cause of the common people."

It took a moment for Ekalavya to register that the man had stopped speaking. He was stunned by the convoluted logic of the argument. Yet there was no trace of surprise around him. The old Brahmin still stood with his head held high, contempt written across his craggy face. The only other prosperous-looking man among the captives began sobbing, his plump body shaking with agitation. Other men and women began to wail, though Ekalavya was certain they had not understood the longwinded speech. For that matter, he doubted whether many of the rebels understood what the war was about.

Takshaka rose from his seat and began pacing. People looked at him expectantly. The murmuring soon rose to a crescendo but just before it turned unruly, Takshaka raised his hands and the crowd went silent. "This man is an enemy of our people. One by one, we will capture and eliminate all such enemies. Our war is the people's war, against discrimination in the name of religion, wealth, race, language, skin colour or caste. You may think that this old man gave education to a few poor people; gave some money to set up clinics where they distributed medicines; and started schools that taught a few to make petty crafts; and so he is a good man. That is because you do not understand the true nature of things.

"Such enemies undermine our cause. The education he provided talks about *varna* and *jati*; he wants to instil such ideas into the minds of our people so they will always be slaves to men like him. He started hospitals so his labourers would be healthy and work hard to make money for him. He started training centres to have free workers who would fill his coffers by selling to fat merchants. Who bought their first produce? The fat merchant who is standing there weeping. Who bought goods from him? Balarama. Then he sold them to foreigners for more money. Brahmins have prohibited sea travel. Yet these men have revived it. They are willing to break the strictest taboos for money. Look at what Balarama is doing. He is building a golden city near the sea. He and his people will live in ivory towers while people like us, the tillers of the soil and the sons of the forest, will languish in poverty. When they eat sweet dishes from silver plates, we will be eating the dry roots of trees. When they dress in silks, our women will have only tatters to cover their shame. They will have opulent palaces and soft beds to sleep in and we will have stinking caves and hard rocks upon which to rest our tired heads."

Takshaka paused to enjoy the impact he was making on the people around him. They were getting more and more agitated. He continued. "But who made them rich? Who made those palaces and gardens, the chariots, the walkways and broad roads, the exquisitely carved temples? People like us. Our sweat and blood made the luxuries they enjoy. Remember, every activity you do strengthens the hands of our enemies. They will use every coin you add to their coffers to exploit you. My fellow Nagas, Vanaras, Yakshas, Kinnaras, Gandharvas and Asuras – the war has just begun!"

Ekalavya could sense the crowd growing angry as Takshaka spoke. Finally, he paused dramatically and raised his voice to shout, "*Should we allow these bastards to keep us as slaves?*"

"*Noooooo…*" the crowd answered in one voice.

"*Should our sisters go naked; our babies go hungry and our people become homeless, while these exploiters, these rich swine, wallow in luxury?*"

"*Noooo…*"

"What should we do with these traitors?" Takshaka's voice dipped, it was as soft as silk. But the next moment he yelled, "*Comrades, what should we do with these traitors now?*"

"*Kill them! Kill them!*" the crowd roared back. The chant of 'Kill them! Kill them!' rose to a crescendo.

Takshaka turned to the accused. "The People's Court has judged and spoken. Their will shall be done."

The wailing that rose from the hapless men and women could not dampen the frenzy of the crowd. They shoved the old Brahmin to his knees. Kaliya lifted his sword while the man mumbled some prayers. In one clean sweep, Kaliya severed the old man's head and blood spurted from the headless body. The severed head bounced onto the ground as if still alive and came to rest near Ekalavya's feet. He recoiled in horror. The lifeless eyes of the old man stared at the Nishada. Those eyes would haunt him for a long time. The man's body jerked spasmodically until someone stamped on it.

"Victory to the people's revolution," cried Kaliya.

A thousand voices answered. One by one, the jeering crowd pushed each captive forward and Kaliya and his band of soldiers cut them down mercilessly. Finally, the fat merchant was the only one left. Kaliya pushed him forward for execution. He begged for mercy, offering everything he owned to Takshaka, in exchange for his life. Takshaka stopped the merchant's execution at the last moment and the crowd fell silent. "Comrades, he is offering the wealth he has cheated from our poor. Should we spare him and take his wealth?"

"*Nooo...*" yelled the crowd. But there was a hint of doubt in their voices.

A lone voice cried out, "Yes!" Every head turned to see who had spoken.

"*Yes*?" Takshaka asked. "*Yes? Who wants that tainted money? Who said yes? Come forward.* I want to congratulate the man."

The crowd went silent with fear. No one moved. Kaliya stood confused as murmurs bubbled from the mob like a cauldron. Then Takshaka spoke. "Our war needs weapons, men and supplies. Who will provide these? The ones who have exploited our people for their trade, who else? These traders and businessmen will fund our war against their own people. We will use their money to fight. We will hold this rascal captive for ransom. We will use and bleed him and *then* the People's Court will execute its judgement, when he becomes a pauper like us. Take him away. The Court is dismissed."

Takshaka jumped down from the platform. Kaliya's men dragged away the kicking and screaming merchant and locked him inside a hut. In passing, Takshaka patted Ekalavya on the shoulder and smiled but Ekalavya could not smile back. The violence had shocked him. His romantic hero Takshaka was dead and a devil had risen in his place.

As Ekalavya was about to follow the Naga leader, a frail voice called out to him. He turned to find the old Naga King, Vasuki, standing a few feet away, holding onto a staff to support his frail body. "Son, I hope you have learnt your lesson. Escape! This place will make you into a demon. Escape now. Listen to an old man's advice."

A boy, who was barely twelve, kicked the staff out of Vasuki's hands and the old man stumbled and fell. The boy ran away laughing. Ekalavya helped the frail man up and handed the staff to him again. "Escape," the man mumbled again.

Someone cried out, "Hey Ekalavya! What are you doing with that mad man? Come, the leader is asking for you."

'Mad man! He seems to be the only sane one in the whole village,' thought Ekalavya. He hesitated a moment. The person who had called him was talking to someone else and not looking at him. Ekalavya looked around, took a deep breath and ran.

"Hey you..." someone yelled. Ekalavya could hear the villagers running in pursuit. He ran in the opposite direction to Takshaka's camp, crashing into the jungle, rolling on the ground, getting up, stumbling on rocks, and getting up again. He ran for dear life as arrows zinged perilously close and plunged into the tree trunks with sickening thuds. He could hear the barking of dogs as they closed in on him. Ekalavya ran as fast as he could, ignoring the blood flowing from his many cuts and the weakness in his legs, which trembled with fear. He ran over a ridge and suddenly the terrain sloped downwards. Only a few feet separated him from the Ganga. The river rushed through a ravine, frothing and lashing at the rocks that tried to restrain it. Ekalavya had only a few seconds to choose. Behind him lay sure death with the Naga warriors closing in; while ahead lay some hope of living. The river looked dangerous in the pale moonlight with massive rocks that protruded everywhere like panthers waiting to pounce upon their prey. Ekalavya tried to gather the courage to jump into the waters a hundred feet below. Somewhere above the hills, thunder clapped.

As Ekalavya ran towards the edge of the cliff, two fierce warriors leapt from an overhanging tree and blocked his path. The sharp edges of their swords glistened in the moonlight as they advanced cautiously. Ekalavya dodged the first swipe of their swords but lost his balance and fell to the ground. An arrow swished past. It would have punctured his chest had he not fallen. Another arrow landed uncomfortably close to his shoulder. One of the Naga warriors thrust his sword towards Ekalavya's throat. The sharp tip missed by an inch and pierced the earth. It gave the Nishada time to roll a few feet, grab a stone and throw it at the face of his assailant. As the Naga warrior fell with a grunt of pain, an arrow nicked Ekalavya's left shoulder as it winged past. He scrambled up and ran towards the cliff, arrows flying around him. The sky was getting ever darker with the approaching thunderstorm. The roar of the river grew louder as flashes of lightning illuminated the jungle like day. Ekalavya could see more and more dark faces approaching.

The second Naga warrior attacked him from the rear. His sword found its mark as it pierced Ekalavya's thigh. Ekalavya went down with a cry. As he rolled over, he was shocked to find the Naga warrior jumping high in the air. He descended with surprising velocity, his sword pointing straight at Ekalavya's chest. It might have been survival instinct or pure luck but Ekalavya raised his injured leg and kicked the attacking Naga with all the strength born of desperation. The Naga had expected Ekalavya to roll and dodge but not to make an offensive attack in his injured condition. The kick caught him between the legs and propelled him over the cliff. The warrior disappeared into the abyss, his terrified scream fading away.

More arrows where falling around him and Ekalavya could hear the shouts of approaching Naga warriors above the roar of the river. He struggled up and limped to cover the few feet, ignoring the pain shooting from his thigh. He tried to leap but could not. The first Naga, who had recovered from the stone-throw, lunged to grab Ekalavya. For a precious second, the Naga and the Nishada hung over the cliff. As other Naga warriors approached, Ekalavya knew it was now or never. Pressing his injured leg again the face of the rock and screaming in pain and terror, he hurled himself into the embrace of the Ganga. The Naga followed, as he had not let go. Together they fell into the roaring waters of the river. Scores of angry Naga faces arrived a few seconds later to peer down at the flaying figures of the fugitive and his captor, hurtling down the cliff. Providence saved Ekalavya's life as he fell into the raging waters. His companion hit a protruding rock that killed him instantly. The Ganga accepted the son of the forest into her bosom.

***

It was raining heavily when the trembling soldiers informed Takshaka of Ekalavya's escape. The Naga leader received the news without emotion. A surprised Kaliya asked Takshaka why he was not concerned. He had been so insistent about tracking and bringing the boy to the rebel camp. Takshaka smiled enigmatically and said, "Ekalavya is still young and trusts the world too much. He will come back Kaliya, with greater anger, once he sees what kind of world he is living in."

Kaliya did not understand but shrugged his shoulders in resignation. Strategy was Takshaka's area. His duty was just to implement it. But he hoped the young man, whom he had come to like, had somehow survived the roaring river.

11 In The Shadows

SHAKUNI STOOD FRETTING AT THE ENTRANCE of the Queen's chamber. He hated these meetings with his sister, Gandhari; though she was like his mother and had doted upon him since infancy. He vividly remembered their journey from the stark mountains of Gandhara to the sweltering plains of Hastinapura. For most of the way, Bhishma, Grand Regent of the Kurus, had carried him across his saddle while his exquisitely beautiful sister rode silently behind. Bhishma had tried to make him laugh by telling him stories about short-tempered ascetics and funny celestial creatures. He had obliged the old man with a few unaffected laughs. Even at the age of five, deceit came naturally to him and not many saw past his smile.

Bhishma had doted upon him, repentant about what he had done to Gandhara and its people. Shakuni had won the affection of the gruff old patriarch with his sweet ways and skill at arms. The old man had trained the young Gandhara Prince himself. Shakuni was intelligent, skilled, and a quick learner. He had won the affections of many of the palace staff with his affable manners and propensity for small gifts. He could handle anyone, except his sister. It did not matter that she had chosen to be blind like her husband. She still saw through him, the silken band covering her eyes notwithstanding. She could strip his soul naked with just a tilt of her head.

A servant came out of the Queen's chamber, bowed to Shakuni, and informed him he could enter. As he stepped in, the fragrance of sandalwood seemed to suffocate him. The opulence of the room brought back all the ugly memories of his childhood. He cleared his throat to announce his presence and wondered for the umpteenth time why his sister had chosen voluntary blindness. Was it for spite or love? It had been a forced marriage, thrust upon a hapless Princess by a powerful man. 'Bhishma! One day, I will get back at you,' thought Shakuni. Far away to the West, the plains stretched as far as the eyes could see and then vanished into the misty outline of the distant hills. 'Beyond that lies my land,' mused Shakuni, saying a silent prayer.

"Sit, Shakuni."

Shakuni seated himself, unable to think of the right words. He wondered at the commanding presence his sister had and let out a sigh. She was the most powerful woman in the entire sub-continent and the real power behind the blind King. Even the Grand Regent rarely overturned her decisions. She was the only person who could talk back to the powerful old man without sounding rude. She was assertive in a quiet sort of way. She doted on her eldest son, Suyodhana. It was an open secret that she fought her own battles with her sister-in-law, Kunti, who had been plotting behind Gandhari's back to get her own son, Yudhishtra, installed as Crown Prince.

"I will come straight to the point, brother," Gandhari said quietly, as Shakuni grew more nervous. Whenever she addressed him as 'brother', he knew it meant trouble. "Stay away from my sons, Shakuni." Gandhari's blindfolded eyes turned towards her brother.

Shakuni stood up and walked towards a window. He did not wish to sit facing her bound eyes. He caressed the dice he always carried. They rubbed against each other and Gandhari flinched, hearing the unmistakable sound of bone hitting bone.

"I am just being a good uncle to them, sister," Shakuni said, still eyeing the western horizon. The sky was a pandemonium of colours as the sun set in a haze of dust. How cool and pleasant it would be in Gandhara, Shakuni thought wistfully. He wanted to get the meeting over with. It was getting late for his prayers.

"Why don't you go back and take the Governor's post at Gandhara? The Grand Regent has reiterated the offer. You will be the *de-facto* King and have total autonomy. Why are you still hanging around here?"

Shakuni was silent for a long time. Then he turned and threw the dice forcefully onto a nearby table. They rolled and stopped with the six points upwards. A perfect twelve! Shakuni grunted with the satisfaction of a master.

"Throw away the dice. They will bring ruin!" Gandhari snapped, inclining her head towards the sound.

"You want me to throw away the dice? Have you forgotten, Gandhari? You know these are no ordinary dice. They were made from the thighbone of our slain father. Fortunately, our people bury the dead and do not burn them like logs, as do the uncivilized people of your adopted country. Our father's soul lives in these dice. They obey my command. See, I call 'Four!' and they fall in perfect fours. I call 'Eight' and there it is. Observe their magic. And you want me to throw them away? Are you afraid? Have you forgotten everything? Why, you used to tell me when I was young that this blasted country should be destroyed as they destroyed our beloved Gandhara."

"Shakuni, it was a long time ago. I was young and full of spite towards the people of Hastinapura. Now this is my country, my land and my people. My husband rules here and tomorrow my son, Suyodhana, will be King. Please go back and rule our ancestral land. Do not spoil my sons here."

"Spoil? Why would I spoil my own nephews? Do you not know that Kunti is planning to install Yudhishtra as Crown Prince? Where will your sons go then? Where will you and your blind husband go?"

"Kunti, *ha*! What can a poor widow do to me? Everyone knows her sons are not the real sons of Pandu. They do not have any claim to the throne. Pandu was impotent. She had those sons by other men. What claim do such bastard sons have on the throne of Hastinapura? Do not try your manipulations with me, brother. I will not fall for your low tricks."

Shakuni picked up the dice from the table and caressed them. "How innocent you are, sister. Why is Kunti so respectful to the Brahmins and

Priests? Why does she lead their delegations to Bhishma and Vidhura? She is playing a dangerous game. She will pull the rug from beneath your feet before you know it. Why was Kripa fired from his job and the orthodox Drona assigned the position of Raj Guru? Have you seen how Drona fawns over the Pandavas? Do you not see Parashurama's hand pulling the strings and controlling events? What is Dhaumya doing here? Why are they so close to the cunning Yadava Prince, Krishna? How naïve you are, my dear."

Gandhari remained silent. The hint of a smile played on her lips. When Shakuni finished speaking, she slowly stood up and moved close to him. "Look at me," she said. Shakuni reluctantly turned around to face her. He averted his gaze from her bound eyes and looked down. "I can deal with Kunti myself but do not complicate matters. Are you hatching one of your devious plots again? My son will be the ruler of India in his own right. I do not want any blemish on his reputation. Keep your schemes, intrigues and those blasted dice, which you claim to be made from our father's thigh, away from my sons. I do not care about the past. I am more concerned with my sons and my husband. This country has accepted me as its daughter-in-law. Go back to Gandhara today. Am I making myself clear, brother, or do you want me to repeat it?"

Shakuni did not say anything. He turned his back on his sister and faced the setting sun. Gandhari raised her voice and asked him again, "Will you assure me that you will leave for Gandhara today, Shakuni?"

"I will discuss it with Bhishma and let you know."

Gandhari snorted. "Bhishma… *huh*… I know what *he* will say. He dotes on you and lives in the delusion that he wronged you in your childhood. He will say you can stay on in Hastinapura for as long as you wish."

"Then I will not have a choice, sister. If the Grand Regent himself wishes it so…" Shakuni walked towards the door, a smile quirking the corners of his thin mouth.

"I warn you again, Shakuni. Stay away from my children, or else you will pay for it!" Gandhari cried out to his retreating form.

'Why just me, sister? I will make the whole of India pay for the wrongs done to Gandhara,' Shakuni muttered softly to himself as he walked out. In the corridor, he came face to face with the Prime Minister. "*Aha*, so Shudras may now enter the Queen's chamber? This country is progressing quickly," Shakuni mocked.

Vidhura simply stared at the Gandharan Prince and Shakuni finally averted his eyes. Vidhura did not wish to dignify Shakuni's remark with an answer. Shakuni walked away without looking back. Vidhura gazed after him for a few moments; his forehead furrowed with worry, and then decided to follow. The corridors were lit with torches that spewed black smoke, making the air hazy. Vidhura could see Shakuni walking at a brisk pace, his tall and wiry figure entering the circles of light and darkness in quick succession. He wore leather footwear that made no sound. Vidhura cursed his own choice of footwear, made of the traditional wood, which made a tremendous clatter as he walked along. He bent and quietly removed his slippers and then hurried down the corridor on his bare feet to catch up with Shakuni.

Shakuni gently tapped on Suyodhana's door and entered without waiting for permission. Vidhura moved to the door to listen. He prayed that no servant or guard would come along. It would have been awkward to explain why he was eavesdropping, not that anyone would ask for an explanation from the Prime Minister. Nevertheless, it would give another morsel to the gossipmongers to say what else could one expect from Vidhura.

***

Suyodhana rose as he saw his uncle enter his chamber. Sushasana and Sushala were sitting on the bed and they too stood up in respect. Shakuni pinched Sushala's rosy cheeks and commented that she was growing into a beauty like her mother. The young girl blushed and ran out of the room. She was startled to see Vidhura standing outside, but went away without uttering a word. Vidhura cursed his luck again.

"Hmm, I feel a sense of despondency in this room. What has happened to my nephews?" Shakuni asked quietly, sitting down in the cushioned chair near the bed.

"We are fed up with Bhima. One day I am going to murder him," spat out Suyodhana.

"What has happened? That fatso has a sharp tongue, a thick head and strong arms – a dangerous combination," Shakuni said, amused.

"Guru Drona insulted Suyodhana again today, calling him an idiot. We hate his classes. The Guru uses his tongue only to praise Arjuna or Bhima on their valour, Yudhishtra on his knowledge, and Nakula and Sahadeva for their intelligence. The rest of us are nitwits. We are fed up," Sushasana complained.

"Is it just because Drona called you idiots that you are sulking like women?" Shakuni mocked, knowing Suyodhana would flare up.

"Uncle, there are enough people around to call us names and mock at our blind parents without you joining them."

"I think you got licked by Bhima again, nephew." Shakuni twisted the knife another turn.

Suyodhana gritted his teeth. He kicked over a vase of flowers in frustration. It shattered into pieces on the marble floor. Shakuni laughed aloud. "Did he call you the 'son of the blind King'? Did he mock my sister and brother-in-law's helplessness?"

Suyodhana did not reply. Sushasana answered instead. "They do so all the time. Even Guru Drona. Whenever we forget some scriptures or make a mistake, he asks his favourite Pandavas to demonstrate their superior intellect. Then he says 'what more can be expected from the children of the blind?' It is cruel. He keeps saying that the only hope for our country lies in Yudhishtra becoming King."

"Nephews, has anyone told you that those who mock you so much are not your real cousins?"

Suyodhana turned to face his uncle, his eyes wide with surprise. "What do you mean, not our real cousins?" Sushasana too, came to stand close to Shakuni.

"They are bastards!" Shakuni burst into laughter. "Don't stare at me like fools. It is common knowledge that your Uncle Pandu was impotent. Your aunt took lovers to beget sons, at your uncle's insistence. Do you remember your Aunt Madri, who committed *sati* on Pandu's pyre? Well, Pandu forced even her to beget children with other men, and Nakula and Sahadeva are those children. Yudhishtra is the child of some Brahmin; Arjuna of some petty Prince of the Indra clan; and Bhima is the son of a forest dweller. In other words, all your cousins are bastards."

Shakuni paused to see the impact he was making on the two boys. They looked shocked, as if hit by lightning but slowly a smile spread across Sushasana's face. Suyodhana shook his head, as if trying to deny what he had heard. "Suyodhana, it is even worse than you think. There are unconfirmed rumours that your aunt Kunti had an affair with a Prince of the Suryavansha clan in her teens. She gave birth to a son but abandoned the child, fearing scandal. Some say she killed the child after he was born. Others think he is growing up somewhere with foster parents. In fact, I am searching for the boy – he would be a couple of years older than you, if he survived."

"Uncle, Suyodhana is not hearing you," Sushasana cried. Grabbing his brother's shoulders, he screamed with joy. "Suyodhana, don't you see what this means? Yudhishtra has no claim on the throne of Hastinapura. He is just a bastard son, born out of wedlock; the son of a wayward woman."

Shakuni laughed, slapping his thighs. Suyodhana watched them both in silence.

Outside the room, Vidhura shook his head in despair. He was aware of the rumours about Kunti, but he had never judged people by his own moral standards. For him, morality was a personal thing and what Kunti and her husband had done was irrelevant. The thought had never entered Vidhura's mind that Yudhishtra had a claim to the throne of Hastinapura. He was the son of the younger Prince, Pandu. Suyodhana was the eldest son of the reigning ruler, Dhritarashtra. It was accepted that Suyodhana would succeed his father. When Shakuni said that Yudhishtra could not claim the throne because he was a bastard, it had hit Vidhura like a bolt. Why had he been oblivious to the palace intrigue thickening around him? This meant more trouble. He had not paid attention to people like Drona and the Priests and the nobles close to Kunti, who aired their wishes openly regarding Yudhishtra succeeding Dhritarashtra. Now all the unrelated conversations and innocuous comments made by certain nobles; the elaborate courtesy shown by Yudhishtra to all the Priests; and other minor things, which he had attached no importance to earlier, fell into a pattern. Someone powerful and intelligent was moving his pieces with skill. Was Parashurama controlling the strings of this dangerous game? Immersed in his thoughts, Vidhura almost missed Aswathama entering Suyodhana's chamber. He hoped the son of Drona had not seen him.

Aswathama was met with loud exclamations of jubilation and surprise by his friends. But Shakuni frowned when he saw Drona's son. He had not accounted for Aswathama being present and cursed under his breath. Time was running out. He did not have a choice, so he pressed on. Keeping a wary eye on Aswathama, Shakuni said, "Suyodhana, next time Bhima calls you the son of the blind King, you know how to answer back."

Suyodhana remained silent but Sushasana chuckled. "Uncle, my brother is afraid of Bhima's brute strength. Every time either of us has fought him, he has trounced us."

Suyodhana's eyes flashed in anger but Shakuni smiled. Aswathama remained impassive but his eyes bored into Shakuni. "Son, I know you are not strong enough to challenge Bhima. But there are other methods of getting rid of him." He lowered his voice to a whisper. "A few years ago, I told you how we got rid of our enemies in Gandhara. When your opponent is strong, it is not valour that will win the battle, but intelligence." Suyodhana looked startled.

Listening to the conspiracy being hatched by the Gandhara Prince, Vidhura was tempted to enter the room and break up the party. But he needed to know how Suyodhana would react. Suyodhana paced the room, his head down, clenching and unclenching his fists.

Finally, Suyodhana raised his head and met his friend's eyes. Aswathama shook his head imperceptibly and Suyodhana acknowledged it with a nod. "Uncle Shakuni, I cannot agree to such tactics. I am a Kshatriya, a warrior. I may not be an expert with my sword or bow, but that is my fault and I am striving hard to improve my skills. My Guru's open dislike has not made my learning easy. I feel my confidence draining away the moment I see Bhima. I hate the way he and his brothers treat us and others weaker than themselves. But I cannot agree to any unfair means to defeat them. One day, with hard work and practice, I *will* become a better warrior than Bhima. Until then, Lord Shankara has willed that I must endure Bhima's tyranny. I consider it a prod from the Lord to strive harder. Please do not tell me to poison my cousin, however evil he may be."

Vidhura breathed a sigh of relief. He heard Shakuni arguing with Suyodhana and decided that the time for intervention had arrived. He entered and stood in the doorway, his hands crossed over his chest. Suyodhana and Sushasana looked startled to see Vidhura in their room. If Shakuni and Aswathama were shocked as well, their faces did not betray it. A small smile played at the corners of Shakuni's mouth, while Aswathama simply acknowledged Vidhura's presence with a formal folding of his hands and a bow. Vidhura accepted the greeting with a nod of his head and moved towards the Crown Prince. "May I know what this party is for?"

But it was Shakuni who answered. "When we decide to have low-castes at our parties, we shall send you an invitation."

"We can discuss that with the Grand Regent at the Court tomorrow. Perhaps Lord Bhishma can throw some light on the propriety of a Shudra joining a party of nobles plotting murder," Vidhura answered without looking at Shakuni. His eyes bored into Suyodhana, who stared at his own feet.

"Get out of this place to where you belong. This is the chamber of the Crown Prince of Hastinapura. Do not pollute this place," Shakuni said, moving closer to Vidhura.

Vidhura calmly turned towards Shakuni and said, "I think that is my line to you, *Mlecha* – get out of my country to where you belong. This is the chamber of the Crown Prince of Hastinapura. Do not pollute this holy land with your presence."

Shakuni looked at Suyodhana and Sushasana, but they would not meet his eyes, so he smiled at Vidhura and said, "Sir, it was just a joke. Why take it so seriously? Pardon us. We did not mean anything by it."

Aswathama laughed aloud and then stopped as Vidhura glared at him. Shakuni walked away without another word. A deafening silence ensued. None of those who remained in the room observed Shakuni carrying away a white silk shawl belonging to Suyodhana. The young Prince was fond of soft silk and was known to wear beautiful, white shawls. Vidhura felt pity stir in his heart for the Crown Prince. He wanted to put a comforting arm around Suyodhana's broad shoulders, but decided against it. He remembered Shakuni's taunt about his low status and something pulled him back from touching the Prince. He was also a little peeved that none of these high-born boys had bothered to defend him against Shakuni's bigotry. "You should be ashamed…" he began.

Aswathama interrupted him. "Sir, there is nothing for us to be ashamed of. Suyodhana answered Shakuni with nobility. He has been true to his heart and said that he will not stoop to treachery, even though the Pandavas have been harassing the entire Kaurava clan since anyone can remember. If someone has to be ashamed, it should be the Pandava brothers and the coterie of Priests and god men who are determined to ruin this country for their petty gains. Everybody in the street knows that the Pandavas should have no place in this palace. They are as alien to this place as you or I. You owe your position to your abilities and I to the Prince's friendship. But the Pandavas owe their places only to the contrived manipulations of a few Priests and a cunning mother."

Vidhura did not reply. Nobody spoke. A night bird kept calling at regular intervals from the garden. Its forlorn cry helped only to thicken the uneasy silence. Finally, Vidhura said, "Suyodhana, we will meet Lord Bhishma tomorrow. It is not to accuse you of anything but I think some advice from the Grand Regent will help. I would like all three of you to be present at Lord Bhishma's receiving chamber in the morning."

Aswathama tried to protest but Suyodhana stopped him with a gesture. "Uncle Vidhura, I will be there and so will these two. It is always a pleasure to listen to Lord Bhishma." Suyodhana bowed to his uncle.

A rush of affection for the Prince overwhelmed the Prime Minister of the Kurus and his hand touched Suyodhana's bowed head in benediction. Vidhura caught Aswathama's look of surprise and blushed. Hiding his embarrassment, he said in a gruff voice, "Young men, the night is passing and sleep will do us all good. Good night."

Vidhura left Suyodhana's chamber and stood alone in the corridor for a long time. He was afraid for the Prince. He was afraid that the nobility of character he displayed now would wither away in time. The pressure on Suyodhana was going to be tremendous. Inch by inch, the conservatives were gaining space and it was going to be a long-drawn war. The enigmatic enemy, Parashurama, was a master strategist and his invisible grip on society was tightening.

The night bird that had been calling in the palace garden sounded close to the palace now. Its mate answered from somewhere nearby. It might have been a cry of passion but the sound stoked the sleeping fears in Vidhura's mind. He had a premonition that evil awaited in the dark, ready to pounce on him. The bird's cry was an omen. He shivered and looked around to see if anything was amiss. The night was dark and cloudy. The lamps that created islands of gentle light in the sea of shadows had begun to splutter and die. Vidhura was a worried man. His concerns were weaving a tangle in his mind. He could not see anything out of place nor could his ears pick up any unusual sounds. 'Perhaps I am getting old, or as Bhishma is fond of saying, the pressure of work is getting on my nerves,' Vidhura thought, sighing in weariness. 'Today also, work is going to keep me away from home. When will I get some time to spend with my family? My sons will be waiting for me, yet this is my fate, to toil hard and feel guilty for not spending enough time with them.' He sighed to himself, trying to push away the image of his wife and two little sons. Immersed in thought, he turned left and walked along the long, pillared corridor that ran around the palace. Had he turned right instead of left that night, the history of India would perhaps have been different.

***

It took another hour for Aswathama to leave for his home, located more than fifteen minutes' walk from the main palace. Sushasana too, lingered before retiring to his own chamber. A few moments later, the shadow of a thick stone pillar split and a fat man stepped into the dim pool of light thrown by a flickering torch. He had a surprisingly thin face for such a bulky body and was almost bald. The pockmarked face had trapped a frown five decades before and had held onto it firmly ever since. His shoes of soft leather did not make any sound as he walked in the opposite direction to Vidhura. He was careful not to step into the small islands of light thrown by the torches at intervals along the corridor or make any noise to awaken the dozing guards. He belonged to the world of shadows.

He paused near one of the smaller rooms in the west wing of the palace. He did not have to wait for long. The door quietly opened and the Prince of Gandhara peered out. With a curt nod, Shakuni invited the fat man in. There was an oil lamp and a few palm leaf manuscripts strewn on a small table in the corner. Shakuni took a leaf from the pile and handed it over to the man. "Purochana..." Shakuni's voice was muffled but he stopped short when he saw the expression on the fat man's face. He realised his mistake. Names were prohibited in this deadly game of espionage and intrigue. 'What the hell,' he thought, 'Purochana is only a paid servant and I am the master.' But as Shakuni gazed into Purochana's cold eyes, he felt a chill. 'I have to be more careful in future,' he thought.

"That Brahmin boy and Sushasana, showed no signs of retiring for the night and were hanging around in the Prince's chamber," Purochana said as he took the palm script from Shakuni's hand. Though a scowl was a permanent feature of the fat man's face, when he finished reading the message, the trace of a smile appeared on his lips. The message was for Takshaka and simply said: *The package will be delivered tonight.*

"Tell him to strictly follow my instructions and not get greedy and hatch some stupid plans."

"He will not take orders from you, foreigner," Purochana said, distaste making his voice hard.

"The hell he will not! If he takes my money, he will do what I say."

"Let us hope so." Purochana gave a curt bow and disappeared into his world of shadows. He would have to go past the guards at the gates and it was already late. Men slept deeply in the first three hours after midnight and already the first hour had passed. He had only a few hours before sunrise to make his escape, cross the river, meet Kaliya, and deliver his message, take a bath, and get to office as Inspector of City Hygiene. The Nagas had to be ready when Shakuni delivered his 'package'. Though the plot had been hatched months before, the exact date had not been fixed. Shakuni had waited for the time to be right and today the fruit had ripened. The fight between Bhima and Suyodhana had turned ugly and the big Pandava had easily roughed up Suyodhana.

A few minutes after Purochana left, Shakuni opened his cupboard and took out a bottle of wine. It was an exquisite vintage from Gandhara, prized by the nobility. He also took out a small wooden box and tucked it into the folds of his waistcloth. He peered out to see whether anyone stirred outside. Except for the howling of a dog and the drone of crickets, all was silent. Shakuni was wearing the white silk shawl he had taken from

Suyodhana earlier. He walked quickly towards the north wing of the palace, where he knew Bhima slept. He banged on the door thrice before a red-eyed Bhima opened it.

"What the hell…" the words died on Bhima's lips when he saw the bottle Shakuni dangled before his eyes.

"Please come in…" Bhima said, compelled by the contents of the bottle in his uncle's hand.

"Not in this stuffy room. Such exquisite wine is to be enjoyed in the open air. Come, let us go to the *ghat*s and enjoy this beauty from Gandhara."

"The *ghat*s at this hour?" Bhima looked into the darkness beyond the window with apprehension. It was an odd time to go near the river. All the superstitious fears he had accumulated over the years screamed in his mind.

"Why? Are you afraid of the dark?" Shakuni said with a smile, reading Bhima's thoughts with uncanny accuracy.

Shakuni's words stung Bhima. "Am I a child to be afraid of the dark? Come, let us go," he said, hurrying out of his room.

Shakuni followed, a smile on his lips.

***

Suyodhana did not see anything unusual in class the next morning. He did notice Bhima's absence but his cousin had been irregular of late. If Drona minded such unauthorized absences, he never showed it. It would have been another matter if he or his brothers had attempted any such thing, thought Suyodhana. By evening, there was still no trace of Bhima. Gradually, anxiety gripped the Pandavas. Suyodhana also wondered where the idiot had disappeared. Perhaps he was lying stoned somewhere. This simple and most plausible explanation was offered by Sushasana. Aswathama did not say anything but looked worried. By evening, Suyodhana found a strange alteration in the way people looked at him. The search for Bhima had become more frantic and soldiers had begun checking the whole city for the missing Pandava Prince.

On the morning of the second day, the Chief of the Royal Guards woke Suyodhana. He did not bow or look him in the eye. Curtly, he said, "Prince, you are arrested on suspicion of murder and the Court has ordered your presence."

"Murder... what murder...?" Suyodhana tried to protest. When he saw the steely eyes of Vidhura behind the Chief of Guards, he knew argument would be futile.

The guards walked the Crown Prince through the glistening corridors of the palace and across courtyards verdant with blooming flowers. Suyodhana felt shamed by the hundreds of eyes that peered at him from as many windows. He wondered what crime he had committed. He was soon to know. He was to be tried for the murder of Bhima.

12 THE TRIAL

WHEN THE GUARDS ENTERED WITH SUYODHANA, the whole court buzzed with angry murmurs. King Dhritarashtra looked pale and anxious while Queen Gandhari's face seemed set in stone. Suyodhana saw only hostile looks all around. He felt anger building in him. What was this about? Being tried for murder? Who murdered whom? Then it struck him. They must have found Bhima dead and he was the prime suspect because of their infamous rivalry. He tried to recollect what he had said to Shakuni two days ago. He looked around and saw the bitter hatred that burned in his cousins' eyes. Arjuna was glowering with rage. 'If it was not for the presence of Bhishma and the other elders, he would take his revenge on me without pausing to ask any questions,' thought Suyodhana.

Kunti stood up and said gravely. "He killed my son. Is there no justice in this country? A poor widow cannot live in your kingdom peacefully. My son was always so sweet, so loving. Just because Prince Suyodhana could not get the better of him in a straight fight, he has resorted to vile methods. My son is dead. My Bhima is dead. Lord Bhishma… do you not see this injustice? Why did Suyodhana… no, he is Duryodhana… kill him? He was so innocent, my son Bhima…"

"Kunti, we will find your son. He is not dead. He is just missing. We do not have any proof that he has been killed. Please control your emotions…"

Kunti interrupted Bhishma's calming words. "*Pitamaha*, it is my son who is dead and if I appear emotional, please bear with me. Please grant us justice and punish the guilty."

Dhaumya, the young Brahmin, stood up. "We should not deny justice to a widow. The curse of a widow is powerful and she has lost her son. Duryodhana has murdered Bhima. When we already know the character of a person, we need not wait for any proof to punish him. Lack of proof should not be a reason for a murderer to escape. Instead, we should look at his past conduct. Duryodhana has always been wayward and stubborn. His Guru will vouch for this."

"Dhaumya," Bhishma said in a voice of ice, "you will address the Prince with courtesy in Court. There is no need to use derogatory nicknames to refer to Prince Suyodhana."

"He *is* Duryodhana," Dhaumya countered angrily.

From the ranks of the Priests and Kunti's sycophants, the chant arose in unison, "Shame on Duryodhana. Duryodhana... Duryodhana..."

Suyodhana stood in the middle of the Court, his heart sinking with the weight of shame, for something he had not done. He wondered what he had done to cause so many people to hate him. True, he had not conformed to their ridiculous ideas of purity of birth and such nonsense but he had never thought they would hate him for just having a different point of view.

"This young man is arrogant; does not follow the rules or taboos of our holy *smritis*; moves around with low-castes and pollutes the palace. He is argumentative, opinionated and adamant in his foolish ideas. He finds pleasure in questioning the holy books. With his puny intelligence, he tries to argue with scholars and thinks that he can teach the *pundits*. Before entering the temple, he offers money and food to the dirty beggars who throng and pollute our holy places. Many times, I have received complaints from the Priests of various temples. He laughs at the Priests who say it is a sin to help these beggars. He does not understand that by trying to help the poor, he is interfering with the laws of *karma* and that people are poor or rich, Brahmin or Pariah, by virtue of the *karma* of their previous lives."

"What are you rambling about, Dhaumya?" The entire Court was shocked. Nobody interfered with a Brahmin when he was speaking. Bhishma was getting crankier with age.

"Your Excellency, you must allow me to speak and prove my point." Dhaumya glared at the Grand Regent.

"This is not the temple auditorium. Reserve your sermons for where they belong. This is the Court of Hastinapura. We are here to discuss a serious allegation of murder. The accused is the Crown Prince and we need proof, witnesses, and not your complaints about Suyodhana not kow-towing to your ways of thinking. As far as the Court..."

"As per scriptures, the charac–" Dhaumya was stopped short by Bhishma's searing glare.

"*Sri* Dhaumya, you are a great scholar and we respect your knowledge of the scriptures and the *Veda*s. However, I must make two things clear. The first is that when I am speaking, you will not interrupt. The second is that, with all due respect to what has been written in the *smritis*, this Court will go by the presence or absence of proof. That is how decisions in Court are made. If that is a sin, I am ready to pay the price for my bad *karma* in this life or in any life hereafter. The question is do you have anything to prove Suyodhana killed Bhima? This session is most premature. It has not yet been ascertained that Bhima is dead. He has been missing for two days. He is not a child. He is almost eighteen and boys of that age have minds of their own. He could have just run off to see the world."

Kunti stood up angrily. "Lord Bhishma, why do you speak in this way? I will never get justice. Here, there is neither respect for the scriptures nor value for great scholars like Dhaumya. But why am I surprised? Your heart has become as hard as a rock, Lord Bhishma. You do not know what a mother feels. You have never married nor do you know what children mean to their parents."

There was perfect silence in the Court. Suyodhana could see that many of the women watching from the balcony were wiping their tears. Why did Uncle Vidhura not interfere? Suyodhana tried to catch his eye but the Prime Minister did not look at him. He was observing Shakuni.

Yudhishtra stood up. Bowing in turn to the Court, Dhaumya, Drona, and then the assembly of Brahmins, he requested permission to speak. The Brahmins blessed him. He then bowed to the King and Queen, and Bhishma, who looked irritated at this elaborate show of reverence. The eldest Pandava spoke slowly, in a soft voice. In this way, he ensured everybody listened to him. It was difficult to hear him and everyone in the *sabha* was compelled to concentrate on what he was saying as he projected himself as a humble man without ambition: "I am saddened to see my cousin Suyodhana implicated in the murder of my brother, Bhima. I have always loved my cousin and thought him to be an honourable man. If there was no witness to the ghastly act committed by my cousin, I would have refused to believe him capable of such a crime. But someone did see him. If your Excellency permits, we can present the witness."

Suyodhana lifted his head in surprise. A witness? What was this?

"If you have a witness, present him. What are we waiting for?" Bhishma asked irritably.

"The witness is a... err... he is an Untouchable and cannot enter the palace and *sabha* to testify," Yudhishtra murmured.

"Prince Yudhishtra, I am surprised at you. Why should his caste matter?"

"Swami, his presence will pollute the palace and *sabha*. He is of the lowest of low castes, a Nishada. They are not even allowed in the roads that lead to the palace. So how can he enter here and testify?" Dhaumya said loudly. The group of Priests nodded their heads in agreement.

"If you cannot provide any proof and do not allow your own witness to enter this Court, I will have no choice but to dismiss this case and declare Prince Suyodhana innocent. I cannot..." Bhishma stopped in mid-sentence, looking at Dhaumya in irritation. The Priest had stood up to speak again.

"We have discussed the matter and the learned scholars are of the opinion that the Untouchable may be allowed in as an exceptional case. There are provisions for it in the *shastras*. But the King will have to do penance for this sin. A thousand Brahmins will have to be fed and gifts given to them..."

"The King will do no such thing," Bhishma pronounced, his voice shaking with anger. "If you wish to bring forward a witness, do so without conditions attached..."

Kunti stood up and started walking away. "My sons, there is no point to this. We are never going to get justice here." Her four sons stood up to join her.

Eyes glittering with rage, Bhishma stood up. However, before he could speak, the King spoke in a soft voice. "I agree to the penance. I will do whatever the Brahmins ask. Let the truth come out. If my son has indeed committed murder, I will not spare him."

Bhishma sat down wearily and gestured to the guards to bring in the witness. They dragged in a dark boy of about seventeen. He was small for his age and his ribs showed clearly through his skin. He had curly hair and thick lips. But what arrested the attention of everyone was a horrible disfigurement. The left side of his body and face was burnt and the skin had turned a dull, rippled gold, while the rest of his body remained dark. He looked around the Court in terror. The luxury of his surroundings overwhelmed him. He did not know who the King was but bowed deeply with his eyes lowered.

"Do not be afraid. No will harm you. Answer my questions honestly and you will soon be free to go. What is your name?" asked Bhishma.

"Jara," the boy whispered. A guard prodded him with a stick and hissed in his ear that he should cover his mouth with his hands when he spoke to his superiors. Jara's hand immediately went up over his thick lips. He was shivering with fear.

"Remove your hands, stand up straight and answer me, Jara," Bhishma barked.

Jara dropped his hands and stood up as he had been ordered. There were angry whispers all around but Bhishma ignored them and continued, "Son, what did you see? Explain clearly."

"Swami, two nights ago, I was near the temple that sits on the rock... near the river."

Immediately the court erupted into disorder. Some Priests shouted out asking how a Nishada had dared to go near a temple, while others lamented loudly that *dharma* was wilting and the age of *Kali* was near. Jara looked terrified by the ruckus he had caused.

Bhishma waited for the shouting to die down and then said to Jara, "Do not be afraid. You have done nothing wrong. Why were you there in the first place?"

"I went there for food, Swami. You know that every day the temple feeds thousands of Brahmins. Swami, they do not eat everything served and waste a lot of food. The waste bins overflow with leftover food, really delicious food. I go there on most nights. Sometimes other people like me go too and then there is a fight for the leftovers. Dogs and rats fight for the food too. I am always hungry so when everyone has gone to sleep, I go there to forage for food. That night I was alone, Swami." Jara paused and looked around. Many turned their faces away or covered their mouths to avoid any contamination from the Nishada.

"How disgusting!" Dhaumya commented. Jara gave the man who found him so repulsive, a black-toothed smile.

Bhishma nodded to Jara, gesturing for him to continue. "I saw a very tall and well-built man sitting on the rock near the temple; close to the river... he was with someone wearing a white shawl. They were drinking. After some time, the big man began singing in a horrible voice. He was sitting dangerously close to the edge of the rock and the man in the shawl pushed him into the river with a splash. I was afraid to remain any longer and ran away since I was in a place I was not supposed to be. I was afraid the man with the white shawl would kill me too, if he saw me. The guards caught me, Swami. They saw me running from the temple and thought I was a thief. For the last two days they have thrashed me," Jara finished.

Suyodhana stood in the middle of the *sabha*, looking shocked. He was wearing a white silk shawl like any other day. Hundreds of eyes had already pronounced him guilty. The King had turned pale and Queen Gandhari was gripping her hands together. Bhishma called to Vidhura to consult with him and the Court erupted in frenzied discussion.

Before Vidhura could move, Dhaumya stood up. "Your Excellency, do we need any further proof?"

Bhishma addressed Jara again. "Can you identify the person in the white shawl?"

Jara scanned the crowd slowly. Shakuni went pale with fear. Everything had gone according to plan and Takshaka would return the packet any time now. He had not pushed Bhima into the river to kill the Prince. That would have been too easy. He had been playing for a much higher stake – to seal the enmity between the sons of his sister and their cousins. If the Untouchable identified him, it would upset all his plans. The touch of using Suyodhana's shawl had been a last minute addition to his plan. He had reasoned that any overzealous guard on the alert that night would conclude it was Suyodhana taking a stroll with his cousin and let them be. In fact, he had been counting on one of the guards being witness to 'Suyodhana' and Bhima leaving the palace in the dead of night. But he had not accounted for a witness like Jara.

Jara's eyes rested on Suyodhana and his characteristic white shawl. There was a collective sucking in of breaths in the Court. Bhishma looked at Vidhura, who gravely nodded his head. The entire Court waited expectantly for Bhishma's words. At that moment, there was a commotion at the far end of the hall and every head turned towards the main door. A group of guards was trying to push away the throbbing crowds. But what caught everyone's attention was the huge figure of Bhima amidst the guards, gazing at the assembly with a lopsided grin.

"What the…" Dhaumya stopped the curse that was on the tip of his tongue by biting his lip.

Kunti ran towards her son and hugged him as if she would never let go. Bhima looked pleased and embarrassed at the same time. When the confusion died down, Bhishma spoke again, asking Bhima where he had been.

Bhima looked at the assembly and the hostile eyes all around and winced. His experiences over the last two days had been fantastic but he was not sure whether they were in fact true or part of a drug-induced fantasy. He began talking and the elite assembly listened to the impossible story with a growing sense of wonder, scepticism and finally, amusement. It was evident that Bhima was stoned from the moment he opened his mouth. He spoke of the wonderful world of the Nagas. Two nights ago, a Gandharva had called him in his dreams, to fly over the Ganga. The creature had offered him a special potion, saying it would give him magical powers. Bhima had taken the potion and the Gandharva had pushed him into the river. Bhima had flown over the Ganga for some time and finally fallen into a sea of milk and honey. The Nagas had saved him from the sweet-smelling nectar and taken him to their magical world. He had met the Naga King, Takshaka, who had been a charming host. Bhima had met the most gorgeous women and had a good time. When Bhima began describing his exploits with the Naga women, Bhishma lost his temper and banged his hands on the armrest of his chair. That stopped Bhima's flight of fancy and brought him back to the real world.

He looked around to see the hostile eyes of the Brahmins and wondered what he had done wrong. His brother Yudhishtra was hanging his head in shame, as were Arjuna and his other siblings. Sushasana and Aswathama were grinning, while Suyodhana was looking at him with relief, pity, and revulsion. Kunti was biting her lip nervously. Suddenly Gandhari began to laugh. Dhritarashtra joined in with a chuckle, and then the entire assembly broke into laughter. A smile twitched on Bhishma's lips and grew into a rare smile when he saw Dhaumya's face turn red with embarrassment. Only Vidhura remained grave as he observed Shakuni's reaction. He did not like the look of relief on the Gandhara Prince's face. Vidhura was sure that somewhere in this farce lay the deadly hand of this foreigner.

"My son is tired and traumatized by what he has gone through, *Pitamaha*," Kunti pleaded.

"I agree Kunti. He is not normal," Bhishma said with wry humour. Some of the assembly roared with laughter. Vidhura's grave face lightened at last.

"Swami, Bhima has undergone the trauma of near death and he is afraid of Duryodhana. I am sure we will get the facts if we have this trial tomorrow," Dhaumya broke in.

Vidhura collected the palm leaf strips from every member of the Council of Ministers. Vidhura stamped them with the Royal seal and handed them over to the Grand Regent. Bhishma took his time to read each one. He put eight of them on one side and two on the other. Then he looked up and said, "Sri Dhaumya, what Bhima needs now is some antidote to whatever drug he has taken. The Court does not have time to hear the drug-induced fantasies of a stoned man. There will be no trial tomorrow. I am passing judgement now. His Highness, the King, will take action as he deems fit on the advice I give. The Council of Ministers has voted, eight to two, that Prince Suyodhana is innocent of all charges. The Council advises the Court be dismissed for the day. It shall reconvene tomorrow to discuss matters of State."

"So be it." King Dhritarashtra stood up and assistants rushed to help the blind couple from the dais.

There were angry protests from the Brahmins but Dhaumya kept his cool. He knew when to keep a low profile. He walked over to the Pandavas. A few Brahmins followed the King to remind him about the penance of feeding a thousand Brahmins. The tired King wearily agreed and walked to his chamber with his wife.

***

Sushasana and Aswathama joined Suyodhana and hugged the Prince joyfully. As the Court emptied, Vidhura tapped Suyodhana on the shoulder and informed him that the Grand Regent was waiting for him. The Prince followed Vidhura with a sinking heart, bracing himself for a tongue-lashing from his granduncle. As he entered Bhishma's private chamber, he was surprised to find a guest there. The man looked to be in his late twenties but his composure, confidence and calm, belied such a young age. The way the Grand Regent was treating him told Suyodhana he was in the presence of a remarkable man.

The man stood up with a smile when he saw the Prince. Bhishma too, acknowledged Suyodhana by raising his right hand in blessing. The Prince bowed to the Grand Regent and stood reverently as Vidhura took his place to Bhishma's right. Bhishma smiled and said, "Suyodhana, meet Balarama, Head of the Yadava Council. He is a close friend and a man of great wisdom and distinction. I have called him here for a purpose."

"Sir, you embarrass me with your kind words," Balarama said with a smile that lit the whole room. "Suyodhana, I have heard much about you. I am a mere cowherd and not a King. There are no Kings among the Yadavas. We are a republic and I am the elected Head. I hold my position at the will of my people."

Impulse rather than cold logic always defined Suyodhana's response to people. Now he felt an instant liking for the Yadava leader and beamed at him.

"When Vidhura told me Balarama was passing through Hastinapura on his way to Kashi, I thought I would request his help for you, Suyodhana. Your lack of confidence, your habit of getting into trouble with powerful people, and your constant fights with your cousins, worries me not a little. Drona too, is not fond of you and says you are rebellious and do not show him respect. With Sushasana, I will tolerate such complaints, but not with you. You are going to rule this land one day and such habits are not going to make you a good King," Bhishma said, coming to the point as usual.

Suyodhana felt annoyed at being humiliated before a stranger. But Balarama smiled and said to Bhishma, "Sir, you are too harsh. I first heard about Suyodhana when the travelling singers visited my new city of Dwaraka. They sang about the greatness of Arjuna, the middle Pandava Prince. They narrated the now famous test Guru Drona set his students, asking them what they saw in a parrot on a tree. Everyone found Arjuna's answer admirable – that he saw only the target, the eye of the bird. It was spoken like a true warrior and the bards were full of praise. My brother Krishna declared in our assembly that here at last was a young warrior all of India could admire. But the bards also spoke derisively about Suyodhana's reply – that he saw love in the parrot's eyes and refused to shoot the bird, which Arjuna then shot down so brilliantly. When I heard the story, I thought Arjuna might perhaps be the warrior India wanted, but Suyodhana was the man India needed."

Suyodhana blushed as he looked at this uncommon man. The answer had come naturally to him and he had suffered a great deal of mockery from his peers and elders for his unmanly reply. Though he was sure he would say the same thing if asked again, he also wished the incident to be forgotten.

Bhishma suppressed a smile and said, "Balarama, I do not know what to do with this boy. Sometimes I see myself in him, as I was in my youth. The emotions he expresses, the sympathy he shows, are all qualities I admire. However, I never allowed my heart to rule my head, not even in my teens. The poor will always suffer oppression; what they will not forgive is the patronizing attitude of those better off. I had the wisdom to know that acts of charity would not change anything and that we would have to work slowly to change the system, not toppling it in haste. I despise the caste system but I have always been careful to take a balanced view. This boy is impulsive and incorrigible. He fights with the wrong people for the right reasons and is making powerful enemies. I cannot let it continue... he is growing up to be a kind-hearted fool.

"I leave him in your hands, Balarama. I hope you have a month to spare to make a man of this fool. And let me tell you something else. If Drona had asked me that question, I too might have answered the way Suyodhana did, but I would nevertheless have followed through with a well-shot arrow that would have killed the poor parrot and ended its suffering quickly." With that, Bhishma left the room with faithful Vidhura following behind.

An amused Balarama stood shaking his head. The silence that ensued was embarrassing. The Prince did not know what to say to the smiling stranger. 'I am no fool,' he wanted to protest, but he was not too sure of the truth of such an assertion. He looked away, beyond the casements, at the main street that wound through the bustling bazaars and saw a couple of soldiers driving a black man like a bullock while people moved away in horror. They beat the man with canes so he would walk faster and move off the highway quickly. The poor man was crying in pain and calling piteously, "Krishna... Krishna... save me". Suyodhana saw to his dismay that the people were horrified not by the man's suffering but because they were afraid of the pollution the Untouchable could cause them by accidental contact. Suyodhana recognised the man being treated like a beast of burden – he was the witness who had come to testify against him – Jara.

"It is my brother." Balarama's voice behind him startled Suyodhana. The Yadava leader was gazing at the same sight. Suyodhana looked up at him in surprise. "No, not the poor beggar," Balarama said. "He is praying to my brother, Krishna, who is quite a charmer and has started playing God recently. Many believe he is the *avatar* spoken of in the holy books."

"Do *you* believe it?" Suyodhana asked in surprise, glad the ice had been broken.

"What... my brother being God? *Ha ha*! I believe he loves playing practical jokes. Nevertheless, on another level, I do believe everyone has God within them, so there is no falsehood in claiming Godhood. By the way, is there any truth to Bhishma's complaints about you?"

The directness of the query took Suyodhana aback. His instincts told him to trust this man. All that lay suppressed in his mind burst forth. The Prince told Balarama how he abhorred violence and how it made him an indifferent warrior. He said he did not find glory in harming others. He said that he hated the competitive and combative one-upmanship that society demanded and which Gurus like Drona expected from their students. He spoke passionately about the hatred he felt towards his cousins and how he wished them dead. Though it contradicted his talk of non-violence, Balarama seemed not to notice it. Suyodhana finally ended his tirade and stood in silence.

Balarama did not reply for what seemed an age. Then he said slowly, "Suyodhana, it is your fear that speaks. You mistake it for kindness, abhorrence of violence, etc. You are afraid of the superior skills of your cousins and your own failure. You have a good heart and are intelligent, but that is not enough to survive and succeed in life. The hatred you feel towards your cousins is consuming you. There is no need to hate anyone, however repugnant his acts may be. Hate the deed, not the person. You are right in saying you hate the mindless competition of modern times; the often pathological pursuit of material pleasures at the cost of all humanity; the indifference of the successful classes towards their less fortunate brethren; and the vice-like grip of caste, regionalism, gender bias, violence, fanaticism, corruption, sycophancy, nepotism and terrorism, on the people. One *should* hate these things. But what are you doing about it? People like you sit in their cosy chambers and complain about how things are. You take a token tour of the slums and patronize the poor. Why do you not make a few statements to declare your hatred of these evils and make some noise in public places – to convince yourself and a few other poor souls, that you are indeed a champion of such causes? Are you taking any concrete action to change the system?" Balarama paused and Suyodhana looked even more confused.

"I am not helping you understand am I, Prince? I am not a good speaker or Guru, so I will put it in simple language. I have an aim in my life. It is to make our land prosperous again through agriculture and trade. We have lost the traditions of the Asuras, who were great seafarers. We have lost the traditions of the Nagas – they were farmers who tamed the earth and made the soil yield gold. I want to lead my people away from their primitive existence as a pastoral community or hunter-gathers and take them back to that lost glory. Taboos and religion have shackled us. I strive to break free. You may wonder how a single man can do all this and that is precisely the point. I have a goal that is too big for me. It fills me with a passion to live and achieve. I enjoy every moment of my life and ensure that I take a step forward every second, towards my aim. You should visit the beautiful port city I am building. Dwaraka is my dream! Do you have such a dream? A dream that is bigger than you; that you feel is impossible or even ridiculous to think about?"

Suyodhana was not sure how to answer. Did he have such a dream? His ideas were vague, he acted on impulse and refused to follow everything the Guru said or the scriptures demanded, without questioning it first. But he did not know whether he had an all-consuming passion.

Seeing the confusion in the young Prince's face, Balarama continued, "Suyodhana, you may not be sure whether you have such a dream but it is there, you are just too young to recognize it. I will give you a method to discover the dream hiding in your heart. What makes you passionate, angry, irritated, frustrated, happy and sad at the same time? What makes you feel alive?"

Suyodhana immediately said, "Sir, I felt angry, irritated, happy and sad seeing that young Untouchable they brought to Court today. I was angered by his plight, irritated that he testified against me, happy that he was getting a chance to see what is forbidden to people like him; and sad that he was being manipulated. I feel the same passion when I see our dirty streets and the people living like filthy pigs. I feel angry at the system and traditions that keep them living like that. I feel irritated that they do not wake up and fight. But I admire their resilience. I admire how they still manage to make a living out of nothing. I am frustrated that I cannot do anything about it and saddened to see so many live in misery in my land."

Balarama smiled and touched Suyodhana's shoulder. "It is a beginning. This conversation will not change your life. Nevertheless, you have found a ray of light. Work on it. Your dream of a misery-free society is too big and ridiculous. It will give you a purpose in life. Better men have tried and failed. Every era produces men who dare to dream the impossible. They are not perfect human beings or incarnations of Gods on our poor earth. They are mere mortals and have many faults. Many who tried, failed by a whisker, but that did not take away the sheen of their achievements. I have trained myself to dream. So has Bhishma and Carvaka, the atheist. Our methods are different, yet our aim is the same. Who knows which path is right? Perhaps my path of peace and meditation and belief in a higher power to guide my conscience, is the right one. Perhaps the practicality of Bhishma, who feels change has to be worked slowly and if required, with violence, is right. Maybe Carvaka knows best and there is no God, and human beings have to love and be compassionate towards one other and enjoy life to the hilt. Perhaps we are all wrong. It does not matter. The dream is what counts."

"You talk of peace and non-violence but there is violence everywhere in the world. I too, think non-violence is the right way, but I am faced with violence. Bhima harasses me every day and because I hate arms, I have not acquired enough skill to defend myself," Suyodhana blurted out, immediately regretting his words. What he had said sounded so commonplace next to what Balarama had said with such passion.

Balarama smiled at him. "Let us go outside. Call your brother Sushasana, and Aswathama too. One of His Excellency Bhishma's requests is that I instil an interest in arms in you." Balarama began walking towards the door.

This sudden order mildly irritated Suyodhana. Balarama had not answered his questions. But Sushasana and Aswathama were waiting outside. When Suyodhana introduced them, they immediately bowed to the Yadava leader.

"Go and get the maces, the heavy ones," Balarama ordered. Sushasana quickly ran off in great excitement to get the weapons.

They walked towards the practice grounds as Sushasana and a guard returned with maces of different sizes, a few swords and daggers, and even bows and arrows. Balarama tried every weapon for weight and build, commenting on the superior workmanship of the Hastinapura arms. Then he took up a heavy mace and handed it to Suyodhana. He took one himself and invited Suyodhana to face him. Balarama quickly stripped down to his loincloth and made Suyodhana do the same. Suyodhana observed that the Yadava leader was built like an ox and muscles rippled all over his body. Sushasana and Aswathama sucked in their breath in admiration as Balarama spread his legs and raised the mace in combat position. Then, without warning, he attacked the bewildered Suyodhana.

"Defend yourself fool! Hit back! Move..." Balarama screamed at the confused Prince. Suyodhana tried to remember all the lessons he had learnt from Drona, but Balarama was all over him like a typhoon, raining blows on him mercilessly. In less than a minute, Balarama's strong legs had pinned Suyodhana firmly to the ground. He mockingly raised the mace and brought it gently down on Suyodhana's head. He looked at Aswathama and Sushasana, who obligingly cried out, "*Phut!*" gesturing with their hands to indicate an exploding head. They laughed as an angry Suyodhana squirmed under Balarama's right foot.

Suyodhana looked at them angrily and was about to curse when his heart jumped into his mouth. He was not sure whether it was a hallucination or what he saw was in fact real. He gaped at the beautiful girl standing near Aswathama, laughing at his plight. Did such beauty exist in the world? He observed her perfect teeth, the sparkling eyes and small nose, which tilted slightly upward, her rosy cheeks and perfect body. His heart sank. He was not making a favourable impression on the ground. Her eyes met his and then looked away, shy and embarrassed.

"No wonder you hate violence, Suyodhana! Non-violence is the first defence of the coward," said Balarama, while the others laughed. "Do you know why Bhima beats you every time? Because he fights with passion. His passion might be selfish, maybe he wants to get the better of you or prove he is superior, but still he fights with passion. If you want to get the better of him, fight with even greater passion. The greater the passion, the better you will fight. I will give you a *mantra*. You were telling me what you felt when you saw that poor Untouchable today. Every time you act, imagine his face. Let the face of that poor man remind you of your impossible dream. Before every deed, think about how it will affect that poor man and countless others like him. Fighting for glory is a small passion. Fighting for the voiceless, powerless, ignorant and poor, will put fire in your veins and give your muscles incredible power. Then you will not be alone. The whole Universe will come to your aid. Who can stop you then? Now get up and fight like a man." Balarama lifted his foot from Suyodhana's chest and helped him up. The girl stifled a giggle and Suyodhana blushed. "Now block that!" Balarama lashed out at Suyodhana, who stumbled and fell again.

The girl and his friends were laughing hysterically. Suyodhana felt his blood boil with shame. His eyes met those of the girl and he found himself on fire. Suyodhana parried Balarama's next hit quickly and surprised them both. Balarama smiled and changed tactics. Suyodhana fought with passion, desperate to impress the girl. It took almost five minutes for Balarama to pin him down again and he was panting with the exertion. Sweat glistened on his chiselled body as Suyodhana lay squirming under his powerful foot.

"That was better Suyodhana, though I doubt it was your big dream that was fuelling your passion. Now get up and meet Subhadra, my sister. Subhadra, this is Suyodhana, Crown Prince of Hastinapura. Please spare the poor Prince your pranks." Balarama lifted his foot and affectionately placed a huge hand on his sister's beautiful hair.

'What a position in which to be introduced to the most beautiful girl in the world,' thought Suyodhana ruefully as he rose from his awkward position, trying to smile and look presentable in his loincloth. He felt bashful at being almost naked in front of this girl. The stupid grins of his brother and friend did not help matters at all. Blood had clotted on his shoulder. He wanted to touch his wound but wondered if she would consider it unmanly. He stood gaping at her sparkling eyes as she moved towards him.

Subhadra gently touched his bloodied shoulder and said, "My brother is a brute. See what you have done to the poor Prince."

Suyodhana blushed to the roots of his hair and felt his throat go dry.

"Suyodhana, beware of her. She is a witch. You all go along now. I have important matters to discuss with Bhishma. At the same time tomorrow, we will resume our practice. You two can join in if you want," Balarama told Aswathama and Sushasana, as he got dressed. Then he walked away, leaving the lovely young woman in the company of the three teenagers.

Suyodhana stood awkwardly, his natural shyness struggling with the pleasant sensation in his heart. He did not know how to make small talk. Sushasana grabbed her hand and said, "Beautiful bangles!"

"Don't touch me!" Subhadra snapped. But Suyodhana did not miss the smile that flashed before she hid it.

Sushasana was taken aback for a moment but recovered with his characteristic resilience. He was a master at charming girls and completely unused to rejection. Aswathama had taken up a bow and arrow and was aiming at a distant tree. Suyodhana knew he would hit the target with perfect marksmanship. No girl could remain impervious to such skill. His heart sank. He was no match for his rivals. Hell! He had met her a few minutes ago and here he was considering his brother and best friend his rivals!

"If Sushasana and Aswathama will excuse us, I have a few things to discuss with Prince Suyodhana," Subhadra said coolly and grabbed Suyodhana's hand and started walking away.

Suyodhana took a few steps with her in a daze and then realised he was still in his loincloth. He stopped in embarrassment. Subhadra raised her pretty eyebrows in a question. Suyodhana looked longingly at his pile of clothes and she burst out laughing. Suyodhana ran quickly to get his clothes but Aswathama and Sushasana looked at each other and dived for the pile first. But Suyodhana was quicker as his need was more desperate and he managed to get hold of his *dhoti*, though Aswathama got his shawl.

"Oh, leave them and come with me," said Subhadra with a small shake of her head, completing the young Prince's downfall.

Suyodhana awkwardly put on his *dhoti*, unsure whether to face her while he was regaining his modesty or turn towards his grinning friends. Finally, having tightly secured his *dhoti* so it would not slip off and embarrass him further, he looked towards Subhadra. He heard a soft whistle from Aswathama while Sushasana rolled his eyes. As he followed Subhadra like a man in a trance, he heard his friend commenting to his brother, "Two minutes and he has forgotten his companions. He sucks."

"Fool!" Sushasana said in disgust.

Suyodhana smiled at the hint of jealousy in their voices. He looked at Subhadra's beautiful face and his eyes involuntarily slipped to the shapely breasts that rose like lotuses under the soft silk of her *choli*. He had only seen such beauty as the curve of her flat, smooth stomach with its perfect navel in temple sculptures before. His hungry eyes caressed the soft curves of her buttocks and the long legs that ended in beautiful feet. The long fingers, which grabbed his wrist and the smooth shoulders and flowing tresses, drove him insane. He knew not where to let his eyes linger and caress. He only knew he was incredibly happy. He had never thought first love could be so sweet.

13 DHARMAVEERA

THE AIR WAS HOT AND HUMID but that did not take anything away from the bewitching beauty of the surroundings. To the east, majestic blue mountains kissed the skies and verdant valleys slept in their misty quilt. On a narrow strip of land, myriad colours bloomed, as if nature was celebrating her fecundity. Tall coconut palms stood like sentinels beside the winding rivers and enchanting backwaters. A deep-green sea caressed the sun-kissed beaches, while a gentle breeze played hide-and-seek in the cool shade of gigantic trees. But all this beauty was a farce.

The sprawling and ancient port city of Muzaris was in a festive mood. All the great Asura Kings who ruled lands south of the Vindhya ranges had assembled in this slowly dying city for a great event. This day would decide who would win the coveted title of *Dharmaveera*. The title was given to the champion of martial arts, following a tough competition involving all branches of warfare. Warriors from the Brahmin and Kshatriya communities assembled every six years at the majestic arena on the banks of the river Poorna, to decide who was the mightiest warrior in their midst. Though warriors came to compete from every kingdom in India, the disciples of Parashurama took the title every time.

Parashurama was the master of all the kingdoms south of the Vindhyas. He was not a King, but a kingmaker. All the Asura Kings obeyed his decrees in religious and political matters. It would not have been wrong to say that his family was responsible for all the misery around. Thousands of years ago, members of the Parashurama family had brought the mighty Asura Empire to its knees. After the fall of Mahabali and Ravana, the first Parashurama had crushed the spirit of the once-proud Asura race. Now the Asura Kings cowered before Bhargava Parashurama and his men. Over the years, the Parashuramas had conducted no less than sixty-four raids into kingdoms across India, beheading Kings who did not fall in line. These bloody raids had resulted in the mass murder and annihilation of many races. The Devas, Asuras, Nagas, Gandharvas and many others, had faced Parashurama's tyranny. The present Parashurama and his army of suppliant Asura Kings, in their mission to impose their religion throughout India, had overthrown even Indra of the Deva clan. The last Indra was a weak King who ruled a small principality on the banks of the upper Ganga. The victory had been symbolic of Brahmin might overcoming the Kshatriyas and other castes. Now everyone cowered when Parashurama's name was mentioned. What was important to Bhargava was that he was acknowledged as the best warrior and general in India.

However, it was his fate to be the first of his clan to witness the loosening of the caste system and widespread change. He was proud that his ancestors had brought culture and religion to the immoral South and taught them the value of *chaturvarna* and the *smritis*. However, the irony was that as the South fell under the sway of Parashurama, the North began to slip from his hold. He was intolerant of the wave of reforms sweeping the North. He hated Bhishma, who had once been his friend and classmate. He resented the fact that Bhishma had rejected the doctrines he had been taught as a student by the present Parashurama's father. Bhishma had even dared to make the low-caste Vidhura, Prime Minister of Hastinapura.

Parashurama kept himself informed about the changes taking place in Hastinapura and these caused him sleepless nights. He had sent his best disciple, Kripa, to gain back what the Brahmins were losing because of the reforms but Kripa had proved to be a traitor. Parashurama now nursed the vague hope that Drona would create Kings who would be more willing to listen to the advice of the Priests and show respect for their religion. But he did not trust Drona completely. His spy, Dhaumya, sent him regular reports and of late, these had been worrying him more and more. After Hastinapura, another northern kingdom was slipping from his sphere of influence. The young Yadava leader, Balarama, was turning out to be a bigger headache. He had dared to defy the Priests' decree and restarted trading by sea. Dwaraka was fast replacing Muzaris as the major port of the sub-continent and Parashurama's war machinery was being weakened.

Parashurama had only contempt for the rebel armies of Takshaka, which attracted all the low-castes and poor who had nothing to lose. He knew they could be an irritant, but a bunch of low-caste thugs were no match for the trained might of either Bhishma's Hastinapura or the Southern Confederate.

Though the Pandava brothers were turning out to be receptive to Brahminical ideology, their claim to the throne of Hastinapura was weak. Crown Prince Suyodhana showed every indication of becoming another Bhishma, but with recklessness and rashness thrown in, making him more dangerous. Parashurama privately lamented that the Gods were turning against him and that he would go down in history as the man who lost everything his ancestors had fought so hard to build over generations. It would be tragic to have to surrender his beloved lands into the hands of reformers like Bhishma and Balarama. It did not help that he did not have children. There was no one to continue the lineage. Taking over Hastinapura before all was lost was the key and he desperately needed a game-changer.

All Parashurama's hopes were pinned on the handsome young man standing before him. His face was as radiant as the rising sun. Parashurama's eyes scanned the fair form, broad shoulders, and shining earrings and chest plate he wore. The teenager looked every inch a warrior. How could a poor Brahmin boy from Hastinapura be so warrior-like? 'Perhaps I looked like that in my youth,' Parashurama thought with a private smile. He had trained Kripa, Drona, and many other warriors, but he had never seen one as talented and passionate as this young man. Parashurama's chest swelled with pride when he thought that only the Brahmins could have produced such outstanding men. 'Those reformist idiots should see this specimen of manhood standing before me,' he thought. 'Never again will they say caste hierarchy has no meaning.'

It was the culmination of the eight years of intense training Parashurama had imparted to the young man. He still remembered the day his guards had brought the youngster to the palace. They had found him wandering aimlessly near the dockyard. Seeing that he was a Brahmin, they had brought him to Parashurama, who had assumed from his accent that the boy had walked all the way from the North. The boy said he had come in search of a Guru and shown him a letter of recommendation from Kripa. Parashurama had frowned in distaste when he heard Kripa's name, but he never rejected a Brahmin before a test. He had personally questioned the boy on his knowledge of the *Vedas*, *mantras* and *smritis*. He had been impressed by the depth of his education. The boy lacked skill in arms but had greater courage than he would have expected in a Brahmin. Parashurama had decided to take a chance and allowed him to attend his training classes, which included the ancient Asura martial art form of *Kalari*, along with the newer, scientific developments in arms and techniques from all over the world. This training made his warriors the most feared and formidable in the sub-continent.

Parashurama had been happy with his new find. The boy had surprised him from the first. This Brahmin boy from Hastinapura could be the game-changer he had been looking for. He would train him to support the Pandava Princes Drona was teaching. Bhishma was getting old and if the eldest Pandava, Yudhishtra, could be made King of Hastinapura by some means, and this boy developed as his aide, he Parashurama could once again regain everything he had lost to the Grand Regent. Once again, people would return to their roots and religion and respect caste, even in the North.

"Vasusena, my son, you are ready." Parashurama beamed at Karna, who bowed in deep respect, touching his teacher's feet. "Come, let us go." Parashurama put his hand on Karna's broad shoulders and pressed him to his heart. Then they walked past the bowing guards to the deafening cheers of the frenzied crowd.

Karna blinked, adjusting his vision to the blinding sunlight. He said a silent prayer to Surya, the Sun God, touching the ground with his forefingers before lifting them to his forehead and then bowing to the roaring crowd. Tier upon tier of people cheered from the stands of the majestic arena. The rhythmic beating of the *chenda* drums added to the excitement. The flags of different kingdoms fluttered everywhere. It was the day the young warriors from Parashurama's training school would graduate. The entire populace of the sprawling city of Muzaris, as well as many others from faraway lands, had assembled to witness the spectacular show.

An excited announcer was struggling to be heard above the incredible din. He was calling out the names of the Princes and Brahmin warriors who were going to be part of the display of arms. Karna was thrilled by the thunderous applause that shook the arena when his name was called. He took a seat with a clear view of the platform, which had been built in the centre of the huge ground. Soldiers pranced around on majestic Arabian horses, shouting orders.

Some of the Princes of the Southern Confederate and a few Brahmin warriors dazzled the crowd with their horsemanship. The horses thundered from one end of the ground to the other, gracefully jumping obstacles. Warriors in shining armour clashed with their swords or maces, with surprising speed and agility. One by one, the Kings of the various southern kingdoms entered the arena with troops of musicians and drummers, who would be cheering their own Princes. There were many proud parents among the assembled Kings and Queens.

The reigning Chera King, who ruled Muzaris and the Western coast, fell at Parashurama's feet, asking for his blessing. The mighty Pandyas of Madurai, the majestic Pallavas of Kanchipuram, and other monarchs of the Confederate, followed. The Asura Kings then took their seats, waiting expectantly for their young Princes to demonstrate their prowess. Queens dressed in priceless pearls and diamonds greeted each other with cold civility, secretly praying for the success of their own sons. At the end of the show, Parashurama would bestow the title of *Dharmaveera* – Protector of the Faith, Religion, Brahmins, Cows and *Dharma* – on the best warrior. It was a coveted honour and the warrior who won would become one of the acknowledged leaders of the Southern Confederate.

Parashurama made a short speech about the importance of following tradition and religion. Then he blew his conch to mark the start of the proceedings. Karna walked up to Parashurama, bending gracefully to touch his feet and receive his blessing. Then he took up his arms, checking the arrows for sharpness before placing them in the quiver; testing the temper of his bow as well as his swords and daggers. Satisfied, he took the reins of his favourite horse from the waiting attendant and leapt into the saddle with easy grace. Raising his sword to the crowd, who thundered its applause, he swiftly turned to gallop towards his peers. To his left was his strongest competitor and local favourite – the Chera Prince, Uthayan. To his right was the Prince of Kalahasthi, an expert with the mace. Karna could feel tension knot his stomach. The first competition was horseracing and Karna knew the Prince of Vatapi would be the toughest to beat. He also feared the Brahmin warrior from Kalinga, who, like him, had travelled a long way for this knowledge.

Karna's reaction to the call of the whistle was a little slow. The Princes on his left and right had thundered away by the time his horse leapt forward. The warrior from Kalinga was leading the race, with the Prince of Vatapi trailing him. Blood pounded in Karna's head as he concentrated every nerve and sinew to reach the front. The Prince of Chera kept cutting in on him and blocking his path, and he could smell the sweat of the Gokarna Prince's horse on his left. With just one lap to go, Karna was in fifth position, with the Chera Prince in fourth. The Brahmin warrior from Kalinga had established a comfortable lead by the last round while the Princes of Vatapi, Gokarna, Chera, and Karna, vied for the next spot. However, the Chera Prince was more interested in not letting Karna win than in trying to seal his position. The crowd roiled like an angry sea, rising and falling in waves. Rashly, Karna pulled at the reins of his horse as they reached the last bend, allowing the Prince of Vatapi to shoot forward. The Chera Prince veered to the left, thinking it was Karna who was trying to shoot past. Since the Vatapi Prince had not anticipated Uthayan's move, he crashed into him and the two fell in a tangle of horses and men. Karna jumped over the pile-up and finished just behind the Prince of Gokarna. Prince Uthayan glowered at him with deep hatred.

There were many other contests such as chariot racing, the command and control of elephants, wrestling, archery, hand-to-hand combat, dagger play, combat with sticks and mace, and so on, providing hours of entertainment to the ecstatic crowd. There were many individual champions in various categories but by the end of the day, it was clear that the coveted title of *Dharmaveera* would go to either the Chera Prince or the Brahmin boy from Hastinapura. By evening, it was a tie between the two. Karna had excelled in archery but lost precious points in chariot racing. He ruefully thought that his most pathetic performance had been in his own caste's area of expertise. The Chera Prince had excelled in swordplay, exhibiting impeccable footwork and sleight of arm. The crowd had split into two camps and fistfights broke out between the supporters of Karna and those of Uthayan.

***

Outside the arena, the guards stopped a tired Brahmin who insisted he wanted to speak to Parashurama himself. They looked at his tattered clothes and naked feet; decided he was nobody, and asked him to wait. The Brahmin had travelled a long way. If the news he was carrying from Hastinapura had not been so important, he might have slept for a couple of days in a wayside tavern. Dhaumya had discovered the real identity of Parashurama's favourite. Hence, the information the Brahmin was carrying from Dhaumya, was explosive.

Without Parashurama's knowledge, the Chera King had written to Dhaumya to enquire about Karna's antecedents. His spies had informed him that Karna was the only real competition to his son, Uthayan, for the title of *Dharmaveera*. The King harboured a niggling doubt that the Brahmin boy from Hastinapura was not in fact a Brahmin. He was such a natural warrior; the King had taken him to be a Kshatriya. If only he could prove it, Parashurama would have no choice other than to throw the imposter out. With any luck, the boy could be declared Bhishma's spy. It was the only way to ensure the title for his son. However, the reply to his enquiry had still not been received and the Chera King had no choice but to go ahead with the competition.

Had the guards let the Brahmin messenger from the North into the arena to meet either the Chera King or Parashurama, things could have turned out differently. However, the guards, anxious to see the final combat between the Prince and the Brahmin warrior from Hastinapura, did not have time to waste on such unimportant men. They directed the Brahmin to the feeding house where the government fed Brahmins free, thrice a day, and rushed back to watch the final combat. They were relieved to find the last contest would not be archery, as they had feared, but swordsmanship. They knew Karna to be the best archer around but the local Chera Prince was a master of the sword. The guards joined the section of the crowd who were cheering loudly for their Prince and jeering Karna. The Brahmin crowd, however, was cheering for Karna, much to the irritation of the Chera King. But he wisely held his peace. The King prayed that his messenger would arrive and confirm Karna was a Kshatriya, and Bhishma's spy.

The Master of Ceremonies led the two warriors onto the platform. Karna was regretting his impulsive decision to accept the challenge of the Chera Prince for a final test of skill with swords. He knew he was good but not as good as his opponent. He was in a weak position now. Also, he was an outsider and had the support of only the Brahmins. The local crowd cheered for their Prince. The sword in his hand felt like it weighed a ton while his opponent wielded it as if it was made of lightwood. The Master brought the combatants to the centre, where they bowed, locking their shields and swords with one knee touching the ground. The gong sounded once and the crowd erupted into a pandemonium of whistles, drumbeats and applause. Both warriors jumped away, assessed their opponent and charged. The swords clashed and the iron shields clanged with brutal swiftness. It was a fascinating spectacle as the two masters of swordplay clashed in a whirlwind of thrusts, cuts, blocks, dodges and footwork. They fought like fighting cocks, rising six feet into the air and then falling to the ground, only to bounce back again. The frenzied beat of the drums drove the crowd crazy with excitement.

***

The messenger from Dhaumya sat in the feeding house, eating his first wholesome meal in many days. He heard the frenzied roar of the crowd and wondered what the fuss was about.

***

As the fight with traditional swords proved inconclusive, it was decided to test the combatants' skill with the Asura weapon, *urumi*. This was a fearsome sword and Karna had yet to master it. He shuddered at the smile the Chera Prince wore. The *urumi* was twelve feet long – a thin, flat strip of metal that was worn by seasoned warriors like a belt. In the hands of a skilled warrior, the weapon was deadly. It swished through the air with a mind of its own and could wind itself around an opponent's neck or arm like a python. A deft jerk decapitated the head or amputated the arm. It was a difficult sword to master and even more so to defend against using a shield.

Karna took a deep breath as he was handed the sinuous sword. The routine of bowing was completed quickly as the crowd was getting impatient for a result. Once again, the two warriors clashed, but this time it was more confusing and frightening to watch. The flexible swords swished through the air like silver vipers and locked in the air, searching for the opponent's body. The *urumi*s looked almost alive and there seemed to be four warriors fighting instead of two. Twice, Karna narrowly escaped his hand being sliced off. Once he nearly got the Chera Prince's head. It was no longer a competition; it was deadly combat, with the crowd baying for blood.

In one of those quirks of destiny, Uthayan's *urumi* became entangled in Karna's armour for a moment. The Chera Prince tried desperately to free his sword but that second's reprieve proved enough for Karna. He saw the fear in Uthayan's eyes. The Chera Prince had aimed at Karna's neck, missed by a hair, and the *urumi* caught in Karna's armour instead. Then a calm acceptance of his fate wiped out the fear from Uthayan's eyes. In a similar situation, he would not have hesitated to cut off Karna's head. He waited for Karna's *urumi* to wind around his neck and sever it in an instant. A deathly hush fell on the crowd. The Chera King gazed at the scene in horror. Then Karna's *urumi* swished through the air in a crazy arc and wound itself around Uthayan's *urumi*, not his body. With a jerk, the deadly weapon was prised from the Chera Prince's hand.

The match was over. Karna was the new *Dharmaveera*. The arena erupted in a frenzy of blowing conch shells, rhythmic beatings of *chendas* and wild cheers. Shame flooded the Chera Prince's soul and he looked at the warrior from Hastinapura with deep hatred. He had played hard and lost. Now everyone would forget him. The reward for failure was oblivion. His eyes met his father's but the King looked away. His son had failed him. It would have been preferable if Karna had killed Uthayan in combat. At least he would have died with his head held high, not as someone who owed his life to a Brahmin's generosity. One of his ancestors had impaled himself after winning a war, because of a wound on his back. Though he had led his troops to victory and fought well, the illustrious Chera ancestor had decided that his honour had been compromised by the injury on his back. It meant he had shown fear and turned to run away from his opponent. Now Uthayan owed his life to an insignificant warrior from the North. Wearily the King suppressed his thoughts. Though he felt sorry for his son, he had other duties to attend to. He was playing host to the grand event and could not be found wanting in hospitality to his guests. Even an unintentional slight could lead to a bloody war. The Asuras were a sensitive race who protected their honour from real or perceived slights and fought like fools over trivial issues.

Parashurama hugged his protégé on the stage and led the cheers of *Dharmaveera Karna*. Thousands of voices echoed it in jubilation. The Brahmins were dancing with joy. Here at last was a warrior to challenge the arrogance of the Asura Princes. After Kripa and Drona, who had won the coveted title years ago, no other Brahmin warrior had come close to winning. It was a day for celebration, proving that Brahmins excelled not only in learning and rituals but also in the science of arms. They hugged each other in a delirium of joy, their chests swelling with pride.

***

The Brahmin messenger from Hastinapura was desperate to get inside and meet the King or Parashurama but the guards refused to budge. He waited outside the arena, determined to catch either as they emerged, not knowing that the nobles would be taking a separate route to the palace. The gateway he stood in was for the common populace. The messenger thus waited for many hours and finally decided to remind the guards about his permission to meet the ruler. They had completely forgotten him. They advised him to go to the palace, so the Brahmin walked on. Once again, he was denied permission to enter as the King was holding a banquet. Instead, the messenger was taken to the royal guesthouse to rest. All his protests were in vain. It would be the next morning before Prince Uthayan received the fateful message.

***

The nobles and Kings of the Southern Confederate showered gifts on the new *Dharmaveera*. Slowly the arena emptied. Jubilant Brahmins carried the Guru and his disciple to the palace where the King was holding a banquet in honour of the new *Dharmaveera*. Karna spent a glorious night celebrating with the dignitaries of the Southern Confederate. The Chera King was gracious enough to hide his disappointment at his son's failure and bestowed gifts and titles on Karna. Though the silent Chera Prince excused himself from the banquet at midnight, the party continued into the early hours of the morning. Karna was bone weary by the time he reached his Guru's residence, but willingly obliged when the Guru expressed his desire to sleep in the open air of the garden. Parashurama slept with his head resting on the thighs of the charioteer's son, deeply content at having trained the best Brahmin warrior in the world.

By the time the sun turned the tips of the palm fronds golden, Karna's legs had gone numb. But he would not have dreamed of moving and disturbing the Guru's slumber. He looked at the serene face and wondered why this man carried so much hatred for non-Brahmins. In the last eight years, Karna had come to love and respect Parashurama. He had been overwhelmed by the affection shown to him by the old man and come to know him as a kind-hearted and generous person. Once he was sure the caste rules were being followed, Parashurama ensured that the Kings of the Southern Confederate ruled justly. The man owned no personal wealth and lived like a hermit. He had inherited a palace but he offered it to every destitute Brahmin who crossed his path, while he himself occupied a string cot in a small room. The palace was filled with Brahmins from all across India, who had come to learn from him.

Compared to Hastinapura, the people in the lands that had accepted Parashurama as Guru were far more disciplined. The public utilities of these kingdoms worked better and the level of corruption was low. While the low-castes were treated worse than animals and lived inhuman lives, the administration ensured there were no famines and no one died of hunger. All the important posts were reserved for Brahmins but Parashurama ensured there was no nepotism or corruption. Women were treated like slaves but the streets were safe for them even at night; and the law and order machinery worked. It was a strange mix of ugly and desirable. The initial disgust Karna had felt when he had landed in Muzaris as a teenager, had given way to a grudging respect about many things and a sense of despair over others. Parashurama himself remained an enigma. He was mean, fanatical, conservative, bloodthirsty, dogmatic, generous, scholarly, brave, skilled, kind-hearted, principled, dedicated, and determined – all in one. Even after eight years of close association, Karna was sure of only one thing about the man – that the fanatic Brahmin leader loved him like a son.

Karna looked at the serene face of his Guru and sighed. He was feeling extremely drowsy from the exertions of the previous day's competition, a night of partying, and no sleep. The exhilaration of winning had worn off and dread filled his heart over the deception he had successfully carried out for eight years. Now that he was famous, the probability of his cover being blown was high. He wanted to get out of the Chera kingdom and the South before that happened. He did not know how his Guru would react to the truth.

The birds had started chirping in the trees and Karna wished his Guru would awaken. An overwhelming desire to blurt out the truth possessed him. He could not continue the deception with a man who had treated him like a son. No one, other than his parents, had shown him such kindness. Parashurama had been like a father to him. 'What if I told him the truth?' Karna debated. His Guru would certainly be angry but surely, he would calm down again, Karna reassured himself. 'After all, Parashurama loves me as a person, not for being a Brahmin. Will my being a Suta alter his love for me? How can I hide the truth now that I have decided to leave?'

Karna's mind was in turmoil and he did not notice a wasp enter the folds of his *dhoti*. He became aware of a tickling sensation on his thigh but ignored it, immersed in his worries. When he realized it was a wasp, he tried to capture it in his hands. Suddenly pain shot through his thigh. The wasp had bitten him. Karna gritted his teeth. The pain spread quickly, becoming acute. A low moan escaped his lips but he covered his mouth with his hands and bit his fingers and then his tongue as pain wracked his body. His muscles twitched as he struggled to remain still. He could not disturb his Guru's sleep. His fingers buried themselves in the soil. Karna looked at the sun slowly rising over the distant Blue Mountains and prayed for strength. With every ounce of determination he could muster, the son of the charioteer remained still so his Guru could sleep on. However, his tears were beyond his control.

Parashurama awoke when Karna's tears of pain fell on his face. He sat up and placed his palm on Karna's forehead to check for fever. "What has happened, my son?"

Karna put a hand into the folds of his *dhoti* and grabbed the wasp. He pulled it out, crushing it between his fingers. Then he looked up at his Guru through his tears. Somewhere in the depths of his mind, Karna had expected his Guru to acknowledge his sacrifice, so he was shocked to see the expression on Parashurama's face.

"Who are you?" Parashurama's voice had a dangerous edge.

At that moment, Karna knew his deception had blown up in his face. "I... I..." Karna stammered, not knowing how to tell the truth. Words failed him. The enormity of his deception choked his throat.

"You are not a Brahmin. I am sure of that. No Brahmin could withstand so much pain. You must be a Kshatriya... you scoundrel... you cunning rascal... you have deceived me! You do not belong to our caste. You gained knowledge through deception. You belong to the caste I am a sworn enemy of! Sixty-four times my family has fought the Kshatriyas, and now a Kshatriya dares to steal knowledge from me?" Parashurama thundered.

Karna fell at his Guru's feet. "Swami... forgive me... forgive me... I am not a Kshatriya..." Karna wept, holding onto his Guru's feet.

"Liar! You say you are not a Kshatriya? Who else could bear a wasp's sting for hours without uttering a cry of pain... a Brahmin? You want me to believe that? You think I am a fool? I curse you." Parashurama kicked away Karna's hands.

Karna remained kneeling. "Swami... I am your son... do not curse me... I am not a Kshatriya..."

"Scoundrel! You pile lie upon lie. I curse you – you will forget whatever you have learnt through your deception and lies, at the most critical moment of your life. The knowledge you have cheated from me will be of no use when you need it the most. Be gone from my sight." Parashurama turned away in abhorrence.

"Swami... I am not a Kshatriya. I will go, but I have served you like a son... do not curse me, Swami."

"He is telling the truth. He is not a Kshatriya." Both Parashurama and Karna turned their heads in surprise. The Chera King, Prince Uthayan, and a Brahmin, stood watching them. There was a smile of derision on Uthayan's lips.

Karna closed his eyes in despair. He recognized the Brahmin as a Priest from Hastinapura, one who had objected to Kripa teaching him the scriptures. He knew what was coming. Death beckoned. He stood deep within the Southern Confederate where caste ruled supreme and people died for religion. He had made a fool of the proud Asura Kings by becoming the *Dharmaveera*. A Shudra *Dharmaveera*? All of India would be laughing at the Confederate and at Parashurama, when the news leaked out.

"I know a Kshatriya when I see one," Parashurama said.

The Chera King smiled smugly as the Brahmin messenger moved forward and bowed to Parashurama. "Sir, I am from Hastinapura. I know this young man from his boyhood. I have come to convey the message that this is Vasusena Karna, son of Athiratha and Radha of Hastinapura." The

Brahmin paused for effect and Karna hung his head in shame, fearing the next words the Brahmin would utter.

Parashurama's face flushed in anger. "And his caste?"

The Brahmin looked at the Chera King, who nodded impatiently. "Swami, he is a Suta, the son of a lowly charioteer... a Shudra."

Parashurama stood still. Then his eyes disappeared into their sockets as he fell backwards onto the ground. They all rushed to tend the Guru. Karna knew he would be hunted down like a wild dog. The armies of the conservative Southern Confederate were all in Muzaris. He could choose to die fighting but he was young and Kripa's initial training in common sense took hold. Karna ran for his life.

With everyone's attention on the prostrate Parashurama, no one saw Karna slip away. By the time the Chera Prince noticed his absence, Karna had already reached the docks. Uthayan shouted for his guards, barking instructions to bring the fugitive back to him, dead or alive. Karna saw soldiers rushing towards him from the palace. A ship was unfurling its sail in the harbour. The gangway was being lifted as it started moving. Karna leapt across the widening gap, just managing to scramble aboard.

"Hey! Who the devil are you?" a voice cried out.

Karna saw a tall barbarian with dirty yellow hair, standing at the bow of the ship. His skin was as pale as a ghost's. '*Mlecha*,' thought Karna. From his accent, Karna guessed the barbarian was from *Yavana Desha*. The big man looked at Karna closely. "Hey, aren't you that champion from yesterday's competition? *Dhama*... something...?" he asked in broken Tamil.

"Sir... where is this ship going?" Karna responded in fluent Greek.

"You speak my language? Are you from our lands... no.... You are too dark for that. I am the Captain of this ship. We are carrying pepper and spices."

The Captain waved away the sailors who had appeared to confront the intruder.

Karna watched the Chera soldiers assembling on the beach and Prince Uthayan positioning his archers. The ship was gaining speed in the steady wind. Karna wondered why they had not launched any boats to chase him. Onshore, the Asura soldiers were confused. The young Prince wished to launch the hundred-foot-long snake boats to hunt down the imposter. The snake boats were swift war machines with a hundred men rowing each one. It would have been child's play for a snake boat to overtake a sluggish ship, but Parashurama had decreed the sea could only be crossed at the cost of losing caste. No one was willing to live the life of an Untouchable for the sake of catching a Shudra. The only person who could give them exemption was Parashurama himself and he lay in a coma. Frustrated, the Prince ordered his archers to shoot at the foreign ship. Karna watched the arrows fall well behind and let out a sigh of relief.

"What the hell! Why are they shooting at us? Are they chasing you?" the Captain asked.

Karna took off one of the gold chains he had been given the previous day and he put it into the Greek's hands. "Sir... I am from Hastinapura, and I am of low caste. Please set me down in Prabhasa or Dwaraka, and I will find my way back to my native city from there. Please help me, my life is at stake."

The Captain looked at the tall young man in confusion. Yesterday he had been the local hero and now the same people were shooting at him? Finally, he said, "I can drop you at Dwaraka. We will stop there to pick up cotton. Why would they want to kill you of all people? You were terrific yesterday. You are their champion."

"I am a Shudra, a low-born, and I am not supposed to learn the science of arms. They want to kill me for the crime of learning."

"What! Is learning a crime in your country? You people are so uncivilized!

Young man, I will make you an offer. Come to my country and show half the talent you displayed yesterday. You are a master archer! Come with me and see how you will be honoured for your skill. You can even become Governor of a province if you show talent. Your compatriots want to kill you. Come with me instead."

Karna looked back at the men of the Southern Confederate baying for his blood, from the enchantingly beautiful shores of the Chera kingdom. Blinded by rage and prejudice, they wanted him dead for having learnt a skill, for showing talent and beating them at their own game, merely because he had been born into a low caste. 'This is my India, my land. See how they treat a poor charioteer's son, who dared to dream,' Karna thought bitterly, his eyes blinded by tears. He may have escaped the fanatics of the Confederate for now but what awaited him at home? The news of his deception would soon reach there and people would make fun of the Suta who wanted to be a Kshatriya. What use was knowledge and skill if one did not have the luck to be born to the right parents? It was doubtful whether he would even be employed as a charioteer now. The future looked bleak. 'My country considers me an outcast. All the mighty Kings of south India want me dead.' And now a foreigner, whom he thought of as an uncultured barbarian, was offering him greatness on a platter.

The Captain saw the tears in the young warrior's eyes and gently touched Karna's forearm. "Are you alright, young man?"

Karna turned towards the Greek. "Thank you for your offer. Sir, this is my country, my culture, my religion. For every mad man like those on the beach, there are many noble men in this holy land. Your offer is tempting and my country has treated millions like me unfairly, but I cannot leave her for anything in this world. Among all the Kings who cannot think beyond the narrow confines of caste, there have to be some who recognize talent, do not bother about caste, and treat people as human beings. If not, I will die like the many that have been crushed under the tyranny of a cruel system. But whatever the cost, I will not leave India. My destiny lies here."

Karna looked away towards the shining sun, ashamed of the tears that had started flowing down his handsome face. The Greek Captain shook his head and wondered how such a backward country could produce young men such as this one. And the ship sailed its course towards the shining new city of hope, which Balarama had created with pain and dreams – Dwaraka.

14 GURUDAKSHINA

EKALAVYA SURVIVED THE FALL, though it took him two long months to heal. After his fortuitous escape from the Naga camp, he was careful not to stray too deep into the forest again. Instead, he perched in a tree bordering the training ground of the Royals and from this vantage point watched Guru Drona train his students. Once the Guru left with his disciples for the day, Ekalavya would descend and begin practicing what he had seen. Gradually his skills improved and he became a good hunter. Hunger became a thing of the past for his aunt and the children.

The evening he took a deer to his aunt, they had spoken of many things while the meat roasted over the fire under a star-sprinkled sky. His cousins were growing up and Ekalavya was happy teaching them some of the skills he had acquired. They talked of the lost boy, Jara, and wondered where the idiot could have gone. Ekalavya had already decided to search for Jara and bring him back to the family. They were still poor, but now they could afford to feed one more. Ekalavya's full stomach prompted him to be generous.

With single-minded dedication, the Nishada acquired skills to rival any archer's in the country. He heard rumours about the upcoming passing-out-day competition for the Princes and desperately wished he could participate. He burned to pit his skills against Arjuna. Perhaps he could surprise Drona by beating Arjuna at his own game. The Nishada boy dreamt of the day the Guru would embrace him and say he had made a mistake in not recognizing his talent earlier.

Ekalavya made a statue of Drona in clay and placed it in a small clearing. He began each day by doing obeisance to the statue and then practicing for three hours before going to watch the training at the grounds. In Ekalavya's mind, Drona became the father he had never known. Though he resented the way the Guru had treated him, his admiration for the great warrior bordered on devotion. He was jealous of Arjuna, who seemed to have cornered all his hero's love. Drona fawned on the middle Pandava. The only other person he seemed to care about was his own son, Aswathama. However, of the two, it was evident Arjuna was his favourite. Ekalavya saw that Aswathama lacked Arjuna's confidence and arrogance and his father often belittled him, making unfavourable comparisons when he competed against Arjuna. Aswathama craved his father's praise, but it was given sparingly.

Ekalavya accidentally came upon Prince Suyodhana early one morning. He had arrived at the training ground in hopes of collecting any abandoned arrows, which he could then use for his own practice. He was surprised to find a tall, muscular man and a beautiful girl already there, chatting with the Prince and his two companions. They had arrived even before him and been practicing with the mace. Curious, Ekalavya began arriving at the ground earlier and earlier. For almost a month, the tall man came to coach Suyodhana, Sushasana and Aswathama, in the use of arms. The young girl who accompanied him was a treat for the eyes. Ekalavya's heart beat hurriedly whenever she turned her head to look towards the jungle. He learned the man was Balarama, leader of the Yadavas of Dwaraka, and the girl was his sister, Subhadra.

Ekalavya saw a change in Suyodhana and his companions. Imperceptible at first, it was visible to all by the end of the month. The Crown Prince began holding his own against Bhima in class, as did Sushasana and Aswathama. It was as if they had found a well of strength and courage deep within themselves and were drawing from it at will. To the Guru's surprise, the tide began turning slowly but surely. When Suyodhana first beat Bhima, Ekalavya wanted to whistle in delight from his hiding place. He felt inspired by what Suyodhana had achieved. The Prince was half Bhima's size but it was a treat to watch him take on the mighty Pandava with the mace. Suyodhana was all grace and quickness whereas Bhima was brute strength and power. Bhima attacked like a charging elephant while Suyodhana had the grace of a tiger. Suyodhana began winning the bouts, much to the chagrin of the Pandavas. Life would never be the same for them again.

The day Prince Suyodhana beat Bhima for the first time, always remained clear in Ekalavya's memory. Almost a month had passed and preparations were on for the departure of the Yadava leader. Ekalavya saw Suyodhana with Subhadra, deep in the jungle, their legs immersed in the coolness of a mountain stream, chatting about sweet nothings. Ekalavya burned with jealousy and desire but followed the pair discreetly. He knew how to make himself invisible in the foliage of the forest. He gazed at Subhadra and sighed. Such beauty was beyond his reach. He was merely a Nishada. She and the Prince belonged to a different world. Would he ever have a girl like that to hold in his arms? He looked down at his dark body and then at Subhadra's fair face. It was never going to happen.

Suddenly, the Prince freed himself and stood up. "I'm sorry, my love. What we are doing is not right. I cannot betray my Guru, Balarama." Pain and frustration throbbed in Suyodhana's deep voice.

"What has my brother to do with it?"

"Subhadra, I want to marry you. The honourable thing is to ask your brother for your hand. May I do so, my dear?"

Subhadra's face flushed delicately as her anger vanished. She looked up at the Prince, her eyes shining like stars, and hugged him tight. He kissed her tenderly on the lips.

Hiding in the bush, Ekalavya felt ashamed. He had heard about Kings and Princes snatching girls from the street to quench their lust. But here was a Prince who wished to protect his beloved's honour, even when she was willing to give in.

Subhadra pushed the Prince away. "Suyodhana, I don't know why I feel so afraid. Perhaps I am afraid of my own happiness. I am so happy that I fear nothing will come of our love. I'm afraid of my brother…"

"Why, Subhadra? I do not think Balarama would be against this."

"No, no... I'm not talking about him but my brother Krishna. He hates you."

"He hates me! I have not even seen him. What have I done to earn his hatred, other than loving his beautiful sister?" A smile moulded Suyodhana's fine mouth.

"I do not know. But I have this fear always. He says you are the Evil One who has been born to destroy our country and religion. He has a bunch of Priests and holy men around him who have only bad things to say about you."

"About how evil I am? Look carefully, Subhadra; can you see horns sprouting from my head?" Suyodhana burst out laughing.

"Do not laugh, Prince. You do not know the reputation you are earning in certain circles. I myself came here to see the evil Prince of the stories I had heard – a criminal who nearly murdered his cousin by poisoning him and got away on a technicality, an arrogant man who cares nothing for the Holy Scriptures and disrespects Brahmins. Suyodhana, it goes on and on. Frankly, I was fascinated by such a man and was already half in love with you before we even met. I had this fantasy of loving and reforming you. I was rather disappointed you were not the devil you are made out to be. But you are a fool – that is what you are. You are too idealistic to live in this world. You wear your heart on your sleeve. Why do you break the taboos and rules the learned men have prescribed, Suyodhana?" Subhadra looked at him, love and fear fighting for dominance in her face.

"I do not know, Subhadra. I am a fool. You are right about that. I do not fight with people because I am arrogant and think I know better. I fight with some of them because I do not find anything honourable in them. I have never fought with Kripa, Bhishma, Vyasa or Vidhura; though it is true I cannot stand Dhaumya or his cronies."

"I am afraid of Krishna's reaction to our relationship." Suyodhana did not answer but smiled down at her.

Ekalavya became alert as he heard someone coming towards the small clearing near the stream. He saw Balarama approaching, with Aswathama and Sushasana following. As they entered the clearing, the teenagers could not suppress their chuckles. Subhadra gave a startled cry. It was only then that Suyodhana saw them. Deeply embarrassed, he struggled for words as Balarama stood with his hands crossed over his chest.

Suyodhana looked at his chuckling friends helplessly. "I... I am sorry..." Balarama stood staring at him. "I wish to marry your sister..."

"You are sorry you wish to marry my sister?" Balarama asked with a straight face and everyone burst out laughing. "We are leaving for Kashi today, Suyodhana. We will be back in Dwaraka after the monsoon. Come with your elders to Dwaraka then and we will formalize the engagement."

Suyodhana could not believe his ears and looked around at the happy faces in ecstasy. For a bold girl, the shyness Subhadra now exhibited was rather unsettling. He wanted to grab her and shower her with kisses. For a moment, he wished the others would vanish and leave them alone to celebrate their love.

"For now, concentrate on your studies, Suyodhana. Graduation is only a few months away and I do not want you to make a fool of yourself in front of the people of Hastinapura. I am taking your fiancée with me on my pilgrimage to Kashi, so you will not have any distractions. Subhadra, take your leave of Suyodhana. We will depart this afternoon," Balarama told the young couple.

There was little time for a farewell. She looked up at him with tear-filled eyes and Suyodhana melted. He willed his own tears away, for it was unmanly to cry. He had a hundred things he wished to say to her but no words rose to his lips. Abruptly, Subhadra withdrew her hands from his and walked away. Suyodhana watched the brother and sister walking towards the palace with a sinking heart.

"Enough, lover boy! We have to practice." Aswathama's voice brought Suyodhana down to earth with a thud.

"Was it you who brought Balarama here?" Suyodhana wanted to bang his friends' heads together.

"It was this stupid Brahmin's idea, yes," Sushasana said laughing, while Aswathama grinned sheepishly.

"You fool! You could have caught us…" Suyodhana stopped mid-sentence, realising he had said too much.

"Caught you in what…?" asked Aswathama, winking at Sushasana.

"Reading the *Shiva Purana*, obviously," replied Sushasana. Both youngsters burst into uproarious laughter. Suyodhana could not help grinning.

"You clown! If I had not brought Balarama here, they would have left and you would be roaming about singing sad songs in your croaking voice, yearning for her while she was being married off to some other Prince. I deserve a treat. However, I am not so arrogant that I will deny you my blessings. I will not even mind if you fall at my feet to express your deeply-felt gratitude," Aswathama said nobly.

Suyodhana lunged at him to land a punch on his mocking face. Soon the three friends were laughing, singing, dancing about and making thorough fools of themselves. The jungle echoed with their merriment for a long time after they left. Ekalavya came down to the clearing. He could discern Subhadra's perfume, which still lingered in the air. He could not stand so much happiness. His heart went out to the kind Prince. He hoped that Suyodhana would find happiness with his Yadava Princess. But Ekalavya was a Nishada and he had seen life in all its heart breaking glory at much closer range than the Prince. Suyodhana was a good man and Ekalavya was happy for him. But he knew such joy and real life rarely went together. No self-respecting God would allow a good man to be happy for long. God has relevance only in the unhappiness of good people.

Ekalavya forgot the Prince's love life as another thought gripped him. Balarama had mentioned Graduation. Ekalavya passionately wanted to participate in the event. Perhaps, if he impressed Drona with his prowess, life might take a better turn. He knew it was an impossible wish. He would not be allowed anywhere near the arena, except in the stands as a spectator. Yet, there was nothing wrong in dreaming.

"Gods of the forest! One chance is all I ask," he shouted. His wish echoed around him. He shouted out the words again. And again, the forest replied. When he grew tired of the game, he lay down on the grass and watched the soft clouds racing in the sky. 'My day will come,' he kept reminding himself, as the breeze gently flowed over his wiry frame. He could almost hear the roar of the crowd and the applause. He could see himself bowing modestly before the King. He could imagine his Guru's face glowing with pleasure. As the day wore on, the Nishada's dreams became more colourful and the applause more thunderous. When the shadows of trees became giants and started marching towards the east, he was still lying on the grass staring at the sky. He did not know that life would give him not only a chance, but also a choice, all too soon.

Ekalavya woke to a glorious day. He felt one with nature, alive and fresh. The forest caressed him with its hues of green and soothed his ears with birdsong. Something in his mind told him it was going to be an important day in his life. He jumped into the cool waters of a mountain stream and swam. He sang his heart out and teased a cuckoo – imitating and confusing it. He finished his prayers to his Guru and took up his bow and quiver of arrows.

Ekalavya saw the Princes assembling at the training ground and took up his usual position behind the thick foliage, to watch. They were busy practicing. Their skills had improved considerably. Drona was walking between the youngsters, barking instructions, correcting the grip of one Prince and shouting at another for not keeping his eyes on the target. By afternoon, the group had split into many islands to have lunch. Ekalavya saw four of the Pandavas grouped together in one corner while Suyodhana and his friends wandered away towards the palace. It was siesta time for the Guru. They would reassemble in a couple of hours.

Ekalavya continued to watch Arjuna with envy and amazement. The Pandava Prince was not resting like the others. He kept practicing and shooting his arrows with dexterity. 'I need a chance, just one chance, to prove I can beat him,' thought Ekalavya, his heart heavy in his chest. He looked wistfully at his own bow, made of bamboo, and his arrows of cane. He did not know that his deepest desire was about to come true – with disastrous consequences.

A mangy puppy entered the far end of the ground from the direction of the city. It was on its daily foraging trip. From its protruding ribcage and spindly legs, it was apparent that the dog had little luck with its scavenging. The black puppy, with sores showing through its sparse hair, was an affront to the eyes. It was also a brave answer to the challenges of life. The only thing that stood between death and the little dog was its sheer determination to survive. But this was soon to be challenged. The dog looked suspiciously at the group of young men and paused for a second, its ears twitching as its canine instincts screamed to it to go back into the safety of the jungle. But hunger won out. The dog took a tentative step forward and waited for a chance to dash through the group.

Arjuna saw the puppy and drew his bow, aiming at its right eye. Ekalavya watched anxiously. The puppy was quite far away and he was sure Arjuna would miss. But he was wrong. Despite the distance, the arrow pierced the puppy's right eye with accuracy. For a second there was utter silence. Then the puppy broke into agonized yelps, blood spurting from its blinded right eye as it twitched and rolled on the ground in pain. Every head turned to look at what was happening. In the distance, Suyodhana and his friends looked back in confusion. The Crown Prince realised something was wrong and the gang began walking back.

Ekalavya could not hide his admiration. It was a perfect shot, bang on target. The Pandava Princes gathered to congratulate Arjuna, who stood smiling. A beaming Drona looked at his protégée, pride swelling his chest. Ekalavya saw the happiness on the Guru's face and impulsively decided his time had come. He had waited so long. Arjuna had shot the puppy from almost seventy feet, with perfect aim. If he was to impress these nobles,

Ekalavya would have to do better than that. He was hidden almost a hundred feet away and the puppy was no longer standing still, as it had done for Arjuna. In agony, it was rolling about and running from side to side, then falling onto its back again, trying desperately to dislodge the arrow.

Ekalavya's hands trembled with tension as he drew his crude bow and took aim. He uttered a silent prayer and regained his concentration. Then, with perfect aim, the Nishada shot the struggling puppy. The arrow swished past the Pandava Princes, missing Arjuna's neck by inches, and found its aim with a sickening sound, in the left eye of the puppy. Time stood still as the dark Nishada emerged from hiding. Every eye turned to him. The puppy lay still in a pool of blood. Ekalavya bowed to Drona, waiting for the congratulatory words he was sure would follow. He waited for his Guru's embrace and tears of joy; his confession that it had been an error of judgement to deny him the training he had sought, because of his caste. He waited for all the Princes to applaud, for the great Arjuna himself to touch him and accept him as his equal and friend. He would forgive them all magnanimously and join the Hastinapura army as the first Nishada to break the caste rules, thought Ekalavya exultantly. A bright future and glorious career awaited him, its doors wide open and beckoning.

"Guru, this Nishada has insulted me," Arjuna shouted.

Ekalavya raised his bowed head in shock and surprise. Drona stood silent, immersed in his own thoughts. He saw Suyodhana and his son were tending the injured puppy. Surprisingly, it was not dead and stirred when the Crown Prince touched it. Aswathama was trying to hold it still. 'Fool!' thought Drona. 'When will he understand that it is impure to touch such dirty creatures as dogs? As a Brahmin, he must keep away from them.'

"Guru... Guru... witness this injustice!"

Arjuna's cries brought him back to the problem at hand. As a warrior and teacher, the Nishada's skill had impressed Drona. He wondered how the Nishada could possibly have learnt to shoot that well. Who could be his Guru?

"Who is your Guru, son?" Drona could not conceal his admiration though he wished to sound stern.

Arjuna noticed it too and pressed his lips tightly together in anger. "You are my Guru. I owe everything I have learned to you," Ekalavya said.

"Guru… he lies," Arjuna shouted. "It is unfair. You have cheated us. You promised my mother in front of all the Brahmins and Pundit Dhaumya, that you would make me the best archer in the world. Have you forgotten? You have eaten the salt of Hastinapura but have betrayed us by teaching an Untouchable greater skill than the Princes of the kingdom."

Drona stood still; shocked into silence by the words of the student he loved the most.

"Forgive him, Arjuna. He may have needed the extra money. Do not talk so rudely to our Guru." Yudhishtra said smoothly.

The words stung the proud Guru more than Arjuna's outrage. They were questioning his integrity. 'I have many faults, but dishonesty is not one of them,' thought Drona. "You scoundrel! When did I teach you? You liar!" he yelled at the shocked Nishada.

"Swami, you did not teach me directly. I learnt by watching you train the Princes." Despite his best efforts, tears flooded Ekalavya's eyes.

The Guru stood watching the trembling Untouchable with pity and horror, his mind raging with conflicting emotions. The warrior in him wanted to hug the boy and declare to the world that he had found the most talented archer of all. The human inside him wanted to celebrate the achievement of a poor Nishada against all odds. But caste prejudice choked such foolish thoughts and he felt inexplicable hatred towards the Untouchable who had put him in such a fix.

"A thief! What more can we expect from his kind?" muttered someone.

"He is lying, Guru." Arjuna was still trembling with jealous rage. "Not even Kshatriyas can become so skilled just by watching someone practice. And he wants us to believe that he, a mere Nishada, is smarter than all of us?"

"Perhaps he is even smarter than Aswathama," Yudhishtra said.

That put an end to all conflict in the Guru's mind. He too did not believe anyone could acquire such skill by observation alone. His son Aswathama was good; Arjuna was better; but both of them got sufficient training from him. This dirty, black urchin could not be more intelligent than either the Prince or his own son.

"Son, if what you say is true, it is indeed a remarkable achievement. I feel proud and you have all my blessings," the Guru told Ekalavya.

There was a collective sucking in of air from the Princes. Ekalavya could not believe his ears. At last, all his hard work had paid off. The hours of practice while ignoring hunger and thirst, the countless mornings watching – it had all been worth it just for this moment. He fell at the Guru's feet, his body shivering with emotion. He wanted to kiss the great man's feet but held himself back as he did not wish to pollute the Brahmin. He kissed the black earth instead and felt lucky to be born in this blessed land.

The Nishada's gesture touched a sore spot in the Guru's mind. Drona saw his son nursing the puppy. How would his son manage in this world once he was gone? Despite all his skills, poverty had been Drona's constant companion until he got the job of teaching the Hastinapura Princes. He owed his position to the kindness of Kunti. This job was the only way he could ensure a proper education for his son. And the idiot chose the wrong Prince to befriend. 'My duty is to do what the sons of Kunti want. But this Nishada is also like my son-in-arms,' thought Drona. He cursed himself for feeling admiration and pity for the Untouchable lying prostrate at his feet. Guru Parashurama's angry face flashed into his mind and he moored his wavering thoughts to that solid rock. Everything became clear suddenly. This Nishada was challenging not only his favourite disciple and his son, but also the entire concept of *dharma*. He ought to show no sympathy towards such upstarts. The Guru took a deep breath as he recalled that glorious day when he had won the *Dharmaveera* title all those years ago. Had he not taken a vow that day to protect *dharma*, cows, Brahmins, and the eternal religion? How could he be foolish enough to think of encouraging a Nishada, even for a second?

"As per custom, you must now give me my *gurudakshina*."

Ekalavya scampered up to stand with bowed head. "Command me, Swami," he said. The Nishada's mind rippled with waves of ecstasy. It was official – he was a disciple of the greatest warrior of Hastinapura now. His dream had come true. 'Shankara, oh Lord of the Universe, you are too kind to this Untouchable,' he thought in silent gratitude.

"I want your right thumb as my fee."

A shocked silence followed Drona's words. Even Arjuna flinched when he heard it. Only Bhima looked confused and asked his twin brothers what the cranky Guru was going to do with a thumb.

The world came crashing down upon Ekalavya. His mind and body became numb. He knew it was the end of his dreams. As a lefthander, his right thumb was important. He would never again be able to grip the heavy Indian bow without the thumb of his right hand. The cunning Brahmin had finished the archer in him with one move. Ekalavya stood erect, his head held high. He looked at the faces of the Princes around him and wondered at the privileges of being born into luxury and wealth. Then he gazed at his calloused black hands. A beast cried in the jungle, as if to beckon him back to the world where he belonged. He looked up at Arjuna and saw the Prince avert his gaze. Then Ekalavya took the sharp hunting knife from his waist and bowed to the great Guru one last time. He knelt and firmly spread his right palm on the earth.

Yudhishtra went pale at the thought of what he was about to witness and looked away. Suyodhana turned from the task of tending the puppy to look at the Princes behind him, surprised at their sudden silence. He sensed something horrible was about to happen and ran towards them, leaving the arrows he had extricated from the puppy's eyes, on the ground. Aswathama and Sushasana followed.

Suyodhana saw the flashing arc of the falling blade and shouted out. The razor sharp hunting knife severed Ekalavya's thumb and it fell away. Blood spurted from the open wound, spattering the Guru's white *dhoti*. Drona did not bother to look down; his eyes remained on the setting sun. Suyodhana shouted at the Guru but his fury did not touch Drona. Instead, Bhima shoved the Prince and soon the Pandavas and the Kauravas were fighting like mad dogs around the Guru. Drona could not have cared less. As the black Nishada boy lay prostrate at his feet and his students were busy trying to murder each other, the learned man wracked his brains to scan through the holy books for the words that would tell him he had done the right thing. But all he heard was silence.

Aswathama's angry words finally pierced the Guru's numb mind. As the sun disappeared behind the tall trees, leaving a few idiots to fight over silly things like the broken dreams of an Untouchable, the Guru remained standing with his hands crossed across his broad chest. A dusty black thumb lay at his feet, mocking all his learning and greatness. 'My son, why are you so blind to your father's love? Can you not see that it is all for your future? You may think I did this for Arjuna, but it was really for you, Aswathama.' The Guru's tears finally found release and streamed down his grizzled face.

***

The Nishada slowly awakened to consciousness at the feet of the Brahmin Guru. He had no eyes for the fight the Crown Prince was putting up for him against his cousins. Nor had he ears for the angry words a Brahmin boy was showering on his great father. He had not sought anything extraordinary. All he needed was a little space to grow and a word of recognition from the man he admired, for all his dedication and hard work. He had paid the required fee with shattered ambition, for the knowledge he had stolen. Ekalavya ran into the welcoming arms of the jungle, far from civilized Hastinapura and the holy men who inhabited it. He ran until he was sure he was safe in the embrace of nature and then he collapsed onto the moist earth. The forest was unusually warm and humid and he felt as safe as a baby in the womb. He had not wept when he severed his own thumb and buried his dreams, but now, with the trees as his only witnesses and a crescent moon leering from the sky above, the son of the forest broke into wracking sobs.

Two pairs of eyes, hidden behind the entwined vines of a crooked tree looked at the shaking form of the Nishada. As his agonized sobs grew into animal howls, the two Nagas who had been trailing him for the past few days, rushed through the forest canopy like a couple of monkeys, with a message for Takshaka. Later that night, the Naga leader said to his faithful aide Kaliya that the time for revolution was near. The severed thumb of a black man would spark the fire.

***

The Guru continued standing alone for a long time after everyone else had left. The dark night cloaked him. He did not see Ekalavya leave. Nor did he care when Vidhura, who had come to investigate the ruckus, herded the Princes and the Guru's son, towards the palace after breaking up the fight. Drona merely stood with downcast face, looking at the lifeless thumb of the Untouchable, wondering what he had done.

Had he turned, he would have seen the wounded dog slowly get to its feet and sniff the air as if unable to decide whether it should trust the forest with its lurking beasts or the city. It foolishly continued to believe men were less dangerous than the beasts of the jungle. On tottering feet, it found its way to the teeming streets of Hastinapura. By a miracle, no carriages ran it over. A few hurrying pedestrians did indeed kick it away, but the dog kept walking blindly. When it smelt food, it stopped. A human hand brought the inviting smell close to its muzzle. The dog hesitated, afraid of this sudden kindness. Then hunger overcame fear and it grabbed the food from the dark hand that offered it.

Drona returned home at midnight. He did not see the man asleep on the footpath or the blind puppy lying curled in Jara's arms. Not that he would have cared, but had he bothered to look, he would have seen true happiness in the peaceful face of the homeless man.

15 DHARMA

ARJUNA WOKE WITH A START, SWEATING PROFUSELY. He gazed into the pitch darkness outside. Not even a leaf stirred. He could hear the soft breathing of his brothers and mother. What a nightmare! He quietly opened the door and stood gripping the balustrade of the balcony. However hard he tried to shake off the image of the bloody black finger lying lifeless in the mud, it kept returning to haunt him. What had he done? Why had the Guru done such an unspeakable thing? He tried to recall the Nishada's face but the only thing that came to mind was the severed thumb at the Guru's feet.

"Why are you standing here, Arjuna?" His mother's voice shook him out of his reverie. "Why are you sweating? Do you have a fever?" Kunti approached her son with concern and put a cool hand on his burning brow.

"Mother, I want to ask you something. Is it so important that I should win every time? Is it necessary that I should be the greatest archer?"

"Arjuna, you know we are all alone. We have no one to support us, except perhaps Dhaumya. I am a widow but I want the best for my children. No one can say Kunti has not brought you up well."

"But mother, today I was responsible for a heinous thing. Is it right to deny someone knowledge just because he is of low caste? For a moment, I despised my Guru for what he did. I feel ashamed I was responsible for his action."

"Do not let a Nishada worry you, Arjuna. I heard about the incident from Yudhishtra. Though I may not agree with the way Guru Drona dealt with the Nishada, please do not judge him by this one incident. He has your best interests at heart. Who knows, that Nishada might have become a member of Takshaka's army. It was for everyone's good that Drona did what he did. Everyone has their own *dharma*. As a Kshatriya, your *dharma* is to be a great warrior. As Yudhishtra's brother, your *dharma* is also to help him gain the throne. He has to have your support. Not only him, but..."

"Mother, I know all that. Yet that Nishada's thumb refuses to leave my mind. He was such a fine archer. Better than me. I have begun doubting our definition of *dharma*."

"The path of *dharma* is never going to be easy, son. Tomorrow you may have to raise your hand against your loved ones for its sake. The reward of *dharma* is *dharma* itself."

"Even at the cost of human suffering? Even at the cost of death?"

Kunti sighed. She wondered how to explain something, which she herself did not understand properly. She moved towards her son and lifted his chin. "Arjuna, promise me you will fight for your brother, and for your mother, who has seen only misery in her life. Promise me that you will behave like a Kshatriya and defeat that evil son of Gandhari."

Arjuna remained silent for a long time, while Kunti waited anxiously. Then he said, "I do not know anything about *dharma*. I am not even sure my cousin Suyodhana is evil. But how can I deny my mother anything she asks? Even at the cost of my own happiness, I will do whatever is possible to make my brother King. I only hope when the time comes, my hand will remain steady."

Arjuna did not wait to hear his mother sigh in relief. He disappeared into the darkness. Kunti stood staring at a faint light emanating from a home far away. 'If only Pandu had been older than Dhritarashtra,' she thought wistfully. Then there would have been no confusion regarding Yudhishtra being King. There would have been no need for this cold war with Gandhari. She often wondered who was the more unlucky one, Gandhari or her? 'I have suffered enough. I will not rest till my firstborn becomes Emperor of India,' Kunti thought with grim determination. She felt the old familiar pain for which there was no cure. Firstborn! Where was her firstborn? Perhaps everything would change if he came back. Then there would be no question of who was the elder. Neither Suyodhana nor Yudhishtra would be the legitimate heir. Kunti wondered for the millionth time whether he was alive and how he looked. The faint light in the distance burnt bright for a moment and died. She remained in still silence as darkness enveloped her.

***

In the home where the last light had gone out, a Brahmin lay shivering as fever burned his body. "Kripi, has he come back?"

"Not yet." She had answered the same question many times since her husband had returned.

Suddenly, Drona sat up. "He has come. Open the door, woman."

Kripi rushed to the front door and opened it. Aswathama entered and walked to his room in silence. "Son, come and have your food," Kripi called. But her son slammed the door shut without answering her. Kripi looked at her husband who sat with his eyes fixed on the spot where his son had been. She closed the front door and gently pushed her husband down on the bed. She resumed wiping his forehead with a wet cloth.

"Kripi, shall we go back?" he asked her softly. She did not reply. "I did something today that no human being should have done." Drona turned his head away from his wife and stared at the blank wall.

Kripi rose to light the lamp, but he caught her wrist and made her sit down near him. Drona told her how he had claimed his fee from the poor Nishada. She was shocked, thankful for the darkness that hid her face.

"I did it for him Kripi, and he won't even look at my face. He keeps company with that evil Prince. He has spoilt our boy. He is doomed, that Suyodhana. He has unleashed forces that will consume everything we cherish and destroy the social order. I do not have anything against Nishadas, or anyone for that matter. But our forefathers made rules for a purpose. Everyone should know their place. See what your brother Kripa's preaching has done. See what Bhishma's odd ideas have done to our society. There is no order to anything. Shudras become Prime Ministers and Nishadas aspire to become Kshatriyas. The social order is collapsing."

"We are Brahmins. What is our *dharma*?" Kripi asked.

"To teach, to know the truth, to learn, to think and guide…" Drona stopped mid-sentence and turned angrily towards his wife. "Are you accusing me of not following my caste *dharma*?"

"Ask yourself," Kripi said, as she picked up the bowl with the water and rag cloth, and moved towards the kitchen.

A crescent moon had escaped the clutches of the clouds and sneaked into the dark house. Drona stood up, angered by his wife's words and went into the *puja* room. He saw the idol of the dancing Nataraja shining resplendent in the moonlight. Impulsively, he fell to the floor in obeisance and began reciting the 108 names of Shiva to calm his turbulent mind. When he felt his mind calm and become silent, he slowly raised his head to gaze at his God… and shouted in horror!

Kripi rushed in from the kitchen, toppling vessels and utensils. Aswathama came running, almost colliding with his mother.

"Aswathama, look… look… the Lord has only four fingers…. His thumb is missing. See his face… it is that Nishada… it is he…. What have I done, Kripi?"

Mother and son looked at each other in dismay. They could see the bronze idol of the dancing Shiva they had brought with them from the South. It was perfectly crafted.

"Kripi, can't you see… I have sinned. The Lord came to test me and I failed. I failed as a Guru, as a Brahmin, as a human…. What have I done?" he cried in agony.

There was a sudden banging on the door. Aswathama hurried to open it as Kripi tried to calm her husband.

"What is this ruckus?" Dhaumya and a group of Brahmins entered.

"Come with me, Guru. Let me explain," he said, going to sit near Drona, who was still kneeling on the floor. "Let us discuss this between us so things become clear. It is sad, but you did what was required. Come with me."

Drona finally stood up and nodded at the Priest.

"You are not taking my father anywhere," Aswathama moved to cut off their exit. Dhaumya and Aswathama stood glaring at each other.

"Let him go, son," Kripi told her son. Reluctantly Aswathama turned away. As mother and son watched, Guru Drona walked to the banks of the Ganga with his fellow Brahmins.

***

Jara arrived in Durjaya's dangerous world a few months after he had run away from Ekalavya. He walked the whole night and found himself on the Royal highway. By morning, he was starving and he was desperately in need of rest. The angry stares of strangers did not bother him at first. He was an illiterate, without any knowledge of the *smritis*. He was unaware that he was breaking caste rules by walking through streets forbidden to people like him. As there were guards on the streets and no official rule against Untouchables, no one dared stop him. The Priests knew overt discrimination would invite the wrath of Lord Bhishma himself, so they merely seethed at the sight of an Untouchable polluting the avenues of Hastinapura and waited for the urchin to break a written law.

The opportunity came sooner than they expected. The Priests had underestimated the desperation of the hungry boy. For them, hunger was an abstract concept, *maya*, an illusion, but for Jara it was a harsh reality. The Untouchable walked into the temple. The Priests gasped in horror. Jara did not see Shiva smiling broadly at him, for his eyes was fixed on the sweets piled on a silver platter for the god of stone to eat. The Nishada grabbed the sweets with both hands and then felt a sharp sting on his back. The glowering Head Priest held a whip. The next lash cut open Jara's face. But the boy still would not let go of the sweets. He stuffed the food into his hungry mouth and grabbed more, not bothering to wipe the blood flowing down his cheeks. Someone kicked away the platter and the sweets scattered over the temple floor. It was no longer a divine offering fit for God. It was now filth, polluted by dirty black hands.

Jara fell to the ground, grabbing at the food. The next kick was aimed at his chin. "Bastard! I just bathed and will now have to bathe again," shouted one Priest as he kicked Jara repeatedly. The other Priests kept away as they did not wish to touch either the Untouchable or the angry Priest, who was now polluted by the boy. Jara was sure he was going to die. His only thought was to eat as much as possible before they killed him. When he raised his head to see what was happening, he was astonished to see his assailant go flying through the air, hit the deity, and collapse in a heap. A huge Brahmin was standing nearby. He grabbed the whip from the Head Priest's hand and Jara braced for it to connect with his scrawny body. He closed his eyes in fear. He heard the whip crack and a scream pierced his ears but he did not feel any pain. Slowly, he opened his eyes. He could hardly believe what he was seeing.

"How is it now, you scoundrel? How do you feel? Hitting a small boy, eh? Which scriptures tell you to do that, you dogs?"

The huge Brahmin obviously knew how to use the whip. He swung it with terrific effect and perfect aim. The Priests were running here and there, trying to escape the assault. Jara found that his mad saviour had locked the door of the temple and trapped the Priests inside. Jara and a grinning Shiva were the only witnesses to the assault.

"Kripa, you will rot in hell! You are hurting Brahmins... sin... sin." The Head Priest tried uttering a curse between his agonized cries. He was bleeding all over and purple rashes were breaking out on his paunch and back.

Kripa laughed loudly and kept lashing the hapless Priests. He only stopped when they stopped whining and blabbering. Satisfied, Kripa threw the lash at the Head Priest and said, "If you run to that fool Dhaumya, or that woman Kunti, to complain, I will come again. Next time I will not take so much time, for instead of a whip, I will use my sword. Have you understood, you idiots, or do you want me to say it in poetic Sanskrit?"

The Priests did not dare open their mouths. Kripa saw Jara looking wistfully at the crushed sweets on the ground. He picked the boy up and kicked open the temple doors. He put the boy down only when he reached the Banyan tree he usually sat under. "Are you a fool to take those sweets from the temple?" he asked Jara incredulously.

"I am hungry," Jara stated with touching simplicity.

Kripa felt tears fill his eyes for the first time in many years. "Come, I will buy you food," he said, and crossed the street towards a vendor selling ripe yellow mangoes and home-cooked food.

Jara followed. When they reached the vendor, Kripa searched through the folds of his *dhoti* and cursed. He had no money on him, having lost everything in the previous day's play. He called out to a rich merchant who was passing by, "Hey, can't you see a Brahmin standing here? Why do you not offer me anything?"

The Vaishya looked at Kripa apologetically and fumbled with the strings of his cloth purse, drawing out a few coins. He bowed to the insulted Brahmin and handed over the money. Kripa blessed the merchant, who went away with a pleased expression.

"Don't look at me like that." Kripa winked at the Nishada, handing over some money to the food vendor. "I do not do it often. I earn my food through my own labours. Today I did not have the luxury of showing you that resolve. You are too hungry. Every principle is broken one day or another and if it is for the right cause, there is nothing wrong in that. Your hunger is right enough for me. Perplexed? Do not bother, just eat."

Jara ate silently as Kripa looked at him. Kripa was feeling pleased. He had wanted to beat up the temple Priests for quite some time now and he was grateful the boy had provided him with the opportunity.

Jara marvelled at how easy it was to get food here. You only had to ask and it was given. He also observed that one could exchange coins for food. That night, while Kripa slept, Jara fumbled in the folds of the Brahmin's waistcloth for coins and then ran away to the poorer parts of the city with his loot. He did not feel any remorse or guilt at his action. Thereafter, the coins gave him food and he ate well until they ran out. When he had none left, he started asking people for food but found it was difficult to get them to part with their money. Something else was required to coax them. Kripa had used his sacred thread, but Jara did not have that option. Instead, he began using a knife to threaten people. Sometimes he succeeded, at other times he was beaten up. But he took it all in his stride. It was all part of life. He began earning notoriety in the neighbourhood. Like a fox, he crawled into his hiding place under a small bridge during the day. Nights were for prowling, scavenging and hunting. The beast that was born when Ekalavya thrashed him, was now fully grown and learning to survive in the urban jungle.

Jara never forgot the beating he received from the Priests, so he was particularly vicious when his victims were Brahmins. It was inevitable that his notoriety reached the ears of the lord of the underworld – Durjaya. He had special need of such boys. So Jara was sucked into Durjaya's world with ease. Jara was excited by his new life. No one asked him his caste. There were people here of all castes and creeds and there was a strange equality and honour among them. Money was plentiful and so was food.

There were other gangs sprouting up in other slums of the great city. Often, gang wars broke out between them. The gangs played a deadly cat-and-mouse game in the dark alleys of Hastinapura. The city police sometimes joined in the fun. But the others were small timers. Durjaya knew he owed his strength to the support from across the border and the pleasure of the Gandhara Prince. He was careful not to squander such support. He cultivated competition among his young men and girls, to motivate them in their adventurous life of crime. But Jara would nevertheless have ended life as an unidentified corpse in the gutters of the city soon, had fate not intervened. His destiny was not to be a martyr in a gang war at the age of seventeen. The Gods had other plans for him. They would not let him die so easily and end his suffering so quickly.

Five years had passed since Jara had stolen from Kripa. He was a young man now, full of the vigour of life. He was also an assistant leader in the gang of teenage boys who broke into people's homes in the dead of night and robbed them. A lad in his early twenties called Daya was the leader of their group. Durjaya used a beautiful girl as bait, to create a stiff rivalry between Jara and Daya. She flirted with them both and egged them on to perform daredevil feats. The boys competed with each other in cruelty and crime to please the girl and their boss. Daya seemed to hold the edge and it made Jara burn with jealousy and anger. He wanted to prove himself.

Jara had kept a Brahmin's house under surveillance for the past few days. The house was close to the fort and that added an element of risk. It was both fun and adventurous to loot a house so near the guarded precincts of the fort. The Brahmin seemed to be a singer and many rich people visited him on most days to hear him sing. He did not seem particularly prosperous, but that could have been because he wished to hide his wealth. If he was not wealthy, how could he afford to feed those who visited him? Some days there would be a crowd at his door and on other days, no one. Jara waited for the monsoon as it would be easier to act under the cover of rain. No one would hear his victims scream.

Ten days after the rains broke and the drains of Hastinapura were overflowing, Jara revealed his plan to his gang members. Daya remained unimpressed. He had learnt that real wealth lay not with the Brahmins or Kshatriyas, but the merchant Vaishyas. He had marked a rich silk merchant's mansion as that night's target and did not wish to hear about Jara's harebrained scheme to loot some singer. The girl they both wanted giggled, and Jara threw his wine tumbler to the floor with great violence. He would show them, these grinning nitwits. The gang left together for the city in the dead of night but Jara slipped away when they neared the singer's house. Daya shook his head and continued on his way.

Jara gritted his teeth at the mockery gleaming in his rival's eyes. It was raining heavily when he jumped the small wall that separated the house from the street. Somewhere a dog howled and thunder clapped in the sky. He walked around the house, trying each window and door lightly to gain entry. When he found them all bolted, he decided to clamber onto the thatched roof and jump in. It was a slippery climb in the rain and his progress was slow. Twice, in the lighting, he saw the silhouettes of the guards on the fort walls. He moved towards what he thought was the kitchen and made a hole in the thatch to peer in. He could hear whispers coming from the dining room and see a faint glow of light. Jara cursed. He had expected the household to be sound asleep. He could not wait much longer as the guards might see him. He slowly crawled through the hole in the roof and jumped down, landing softly on all fours.

Krishna, you are the only food we need. Your compassion feeds my hungry stomach and those of my wife and children. How we rejoice in your play, and lose ourselves in your ways, Achyuta, Madhava... Something in the voice of the singer arrested Jara for a moment. He had drawn his knife and could see shadows moving in the room beyond the kitchen.

"Enough of your prayers! The children are hungry and have not eaten anything since yesterday. What use is your Krishna if he cannot even give us food?" A woman's voice rose in irritation and Jara flinched. They had not eaten in two days? And he of all people had come to loot this house? Jara was shocked.

A child, barely four years old, walked into the kitchen. Jara tried to move deeper into the shadows, but the child saw him and giggled. He did not know what to do. He tried to hide the knife he held. Had he not heard about the hunger in the Brahmin's home, the beast in him would not have hesitated to plunge the blade into the soft body of the girl. But he knew what hunger was, he knew its pain. He could not kill anyone who was hungry.

"Bhavani, come here and eat," the woman called. When the little girl did not move, the mother came into the kitchen. She was shocked to find a man with a knife there and stood frozen. Recovering in a flash, she grabbed the little girl and screamed. Outside, the rain lashed down in unmitigated fury, rattling the doors and windows of the old house. The woman ran with Bhavani towards her two boys and threw her protective arms around them all. The boys were twins, younger than Bhavani, about three years old. The woman huddled in a corner with her children, her teeth chattering in fear.

The Brahmin looked up and saw Jara, who tightened his grip on his knife, ready to use it if required. "Krishna, you have come…" he cried. There was no fear in his voice. It was ecstatic, almost rapturous. Jara was perplexed. Had he come to a mad man's house? The Brahmin danced around Jara and fell at his feet. "I knew you would come one day, my Lord, my beloved," he exclaimed joyfully. Then he turned to his wife. "See who has come! Bring the plantain leaf. Give my Krishna food! Woman, what are you doing there? Have you forgotten your duties to our guest?"

Jara stood like a statue, his brain numb. The Brahmin shouted to his wife again. She looked at Jara's knife. He was embarrassed by the hatred in her eyes. He threw the weapon to the floor. The hint of a smile played on her pale lips and he felt ashamed to have barged into her house with the intention of harming them. The Brahmin was still prancing around excitedly, trying to arrange seating and a tumbler of water for his guest. Never in Jara's life had anyone shown such happiness at seeing him. People had kicked, lashed, shouted, stoned, and punched him, but never had anyone considered him a human being, let alone a God. Jara had only the faintest knowledge of Krishna, who was becoming known as a god man. He knew many people had started worshipping him as a miracle worker and an *avatar* of Lord Vishnu. In the slums, people needed magic to escape the mundane harshness of life. Krishna was magic.

"I know your mischief, Krishna. You are acting as if I have not recognized you. Please accept my hospitality and offerings, Lord…" The Brahmin grabbed Jara's hands and made him sit on the floor. He placed the plantain leaf before him and started serving a sticky porridge. "Eat, my Krishna…" the Brahmin urged and then broke into a song of rapture.

The melodious voice soothed the burning mind of the Nishada. The song was about Krishna's compassion, about how the Lord tests his devotees. It was about the hidden Krishna in every soul, in every living and non-living thing, and how he blossoms in love and acts of kindness. The words were about bliss in nothing and infinite happiness in everything. Jara did not possess the knowledge to understand the meaning of the words. It made no sense to his brain but touched his heart, and he broke into sobs. "Swami, I am not your Krishna. I am just an Untouchable," he managed to say between sobs. He expected to be beaten or screamed at. If the Brahmin had done any such thing, the beast that lay dormant in the Nishada's heart would have reached for the knife.

Instead, the Brahmin said softly, "You are neither touchable nor untouchable. You are what you are. You are Brahma, you are Vishnu, and you are Maheshwara. You are my father, my son, my mother, and my brother. You have come to my humble abode to share my food. You are my guest and my God. Please eat, my Krishna." He poured the entire contents of the porridge pot onto the plantain leaf before the Untouchable.

Jara was unable to see clearly through the tears, which flooded his eyes, but he picked up the porridge. It oozed through his fingers. He suddenly felt ravenous and attacked the food, licking the leaf clean.

The mad Brahmin broke into another song. When he finished, he touched his head to the floor in obeisance before Jara and said, "I am blessed, my Lord. First, you came as food in front of a hungry man. Then you have come as a man hungry for food." He turned to his wife and told her to get water for their guest to wash his hands.

The woman put down her sleeping twins on the ground and walked towards the kitchen. As she opened the door, a cold wind rushed in and the lamp flickered. She waited outside with a pitcher of water. Jara looked at the twins and shuddered. They looked emaciated and pale. As he moved outside to wash his hands, little Bhavani followed him. He saw her looking wistfully at the empty porridge pot. With a start he realised he had eaten the family's dinner and they would now go hungry. The woman gave him a derisive smile.

"Mother, I am sorry…" At a loss for words, Jara could not look at her.

"We are used to his insanity," the woman said, her lips twisting in either pain or a glimmer of amusement.

"I thought you were rich. I have seen many wealthy men visiting this house. That is why…" Jara could not complete his words.

"So you came to rob us. If you had just asked him, he would have given you whatever you wanted… not that we have much."

The little girl came to stand near her mother. The woman picked her up and planted kisses on her cheek. The child smiled angelically. "He sees Krishna everywhere. He has talent and sings well. On good days, people flock to hear him and the room is stacked with presents in cash and kind. Anyone else would have become rich by now. But he says the gifts are not his, but his God's, and he has no claim on them. Whatever he earns, he gives away the same day. He considers it an affront to his God to believe in the future and save for it. He says that he who has made us will provide. By the evening, everything is dispersed to whoever comes to our gate. All kinds of lazy men, beggars, saints, noblemen, women, and charlatans, flock here to get their share. He sees his Krishna in every soul and does not care if his family goes hungry. This is my fate – to see my children go hungry while my husband feeds strangers and thieves…" She stopped suddenly.

"Mother, forgive me. I came to loot you." Jara saw the little girl's thumb go into her mouth and the mother tenderly kiss her. The food rumbled in his stomach. He saw that a puddle had formed on the kitchen floor from the dripping hole in the roof through which he had entered. They could hear the Brahmin chanting his God's name from the other room. Jara's eyes met those of the woman. He felt like weeping. "Mother, you will not go hungry tonight. I will come with food," he said, not knowing what else to say. The woman just smiled. The girl had slipped into peaceful slumber.

Jara hesitated a moment longer and then turned on his heel and walked out into the wet night. The streetlights had died long ago in the rain and it was dark and damp in the streets. Except for the gurgling of the storm water drains, the night was silent. He did not know where he could get food at this time of night. He kept wondering what made people so crazy that they gave away everything. Earlier, he was used to men beating him up if he asked for food. Now he had become the person beating others up. The lashes he had suffered from the temple Priest still hurt, at least in his mind. He did not understand the world. Life confused the ignorant Nishada. Could people be so savage, yet so kind at the same time? It was easy and convenient to believe that those who were different were evil. He had developed a deep hatred for all Brahmins after the incident in the temple. But crazy men like the singer tonight, shook the foundations of his hatred and confused him. He kept walking aimlessly.

Jara saw a butcher's shop with a ram tied to the leg of a *charpoy* standing in the thatched verandah in front of it. The shop was closed and the butcher was snoring loudly on the *charpoy*. Here was food! 'I could repay my debt to the mad Brahmin and be done with all these mushy feelings,' thought the Nishada. He felt indebted to the mad man and feared he would lose the ego and hatred he had accumulated over the years. He wanted to return to the world of crime and adventure. Jara untied the ram and walked away. It took him a while to locate the house but he eventually walked through the front gate with a spring in his step. He was the giver now and not a sneaking thief. A strange sensation of happiness filled his heart. The first understanding of the joy of giving entered his dark heart and the Brahmin who gave away everything began to seem less crazy.

Jara knocked on the door and the Brahmin opened it. Jara's dark face lit with joy and pride. He pulled the struggling ram closer to him and said, "Swami, here is a gift. You can eat him for the next few days. I will feed you again after that." Jara looked at the Brahmin's wife for approval but she just shook her head sadly.

"Krishna, you are back. You are so kind to me. Your mischief knows no bounds. Don't test me like this." The Brahmin spoke as if in a trance. He knelt and caressed the ram's face. The animal stood still, as if sensing the kindness in the gesture. Then the Brahmin stood up and walked into the darkness behind the house.

"Mother… won't you accept my gift?" Jara felt anger rising within him. He knew why they would not take his offering. The woman just shook her head and looked at her sleeping children. "Is it because I am an Untouchable that you will not accept my gift?" Jara asked bitterly, tasting the familiar bile in his mouth as he uttered the words. He averted his eyes. He could not face her.

"No, my son," the woman answered softly. "He believes that every living thing has a right to live, until God calls it back to his abode. He cannot approve of killing anything for the sake of food or pleasure. Your present is one more mouth to feed. That is all."

The Brahmin returned with some grass and put it in front of the ram. He looked at the creature eating peacefully. Jara could not stand it anymore. It was killing him. He hated the Brahmin. Unless he was able to repay this debt, he would never escape from this guilt and hatred. He turned and ran wildly into the night.

When he returned once more, with a sack of rice stolen from a shop, the house was burning. Some people were standing in the street, watching. With a primitive yell, the Nishada threw the sack of rice to the ground and ran into the inferno. People were shocked to see a dark man running into the raging flames. Before they could stop him, he had jumped into the burning house. Frantically, he searched for the Brahmin and his family inside. A beam fell and almost pinned Jara beneath. He screamed in rage and tried to get out of the fire raging on all sides. Someone pulled him out and tried to put out the flames licking the right side of his body. They rolled him on the ground and poured water over him. When they were sure he was out of danger, they turned to search for the victims inside the house.

Jara lay on the ground moaning. When they brought out the charred bodies one by one, he could not say a word. They were all dead – little Bhavani, the twins, the woman he had called mother, the crazy Brahmin, and even the ram. He remained frozen and mute, even when they moved him to a public hospital and dressed his wounds, leaving him to live or die in the indifference of the free ward.

It took him six months to recover. The physicians did not know his name and called him Golden Mongoose. The name was puzzling to the dark Nishada until he saw his reflection in a broken piece of mirror someone had thrown into the hospital garbage. By that time, his burns had almost healed. But he was shocked to see his face and body. His left side retained its unblemished, smooth dark skin. His right side was puckered and had a dirty golden hue. With his face partially burned away, his teeth were visible on the right side of his face where the lips had shrunk. He understood at last the reason for his nickname. He looked hideous. But Jara did not cry. His tears had dried long ago. He threw away the mirror with a shrug and walked back to his sickbed. He had no use for reflections.

***

They threw him out of the hospital once they were confident he would survive – if living a beggar's life could be called surviving. He later learnt that Daya and his gang had decided to check what had happened to him on their way back that night and barged into the Brahmin's house while he had gone in search of food. The Brahmin's craziness had driven Daya mad and he had killed the singer in anger. Then he had no choice but to murder everyone in the house, lest there be witnesses to the murder. It sounded so simple and routine. The gang burned down the house before escaping so no proof remained of their deed. Daya had felt regret for a day or two but soon recovered. His imitation of the Brahmin's crazy talk was a hit at their booze parties. Durjaya invited Jara back into the gang through a messenger, but Jara refused. The beast in him had died in the fire. He felt as crazy as the dead Brahmin. It did not matter to him that the Brahmin's God had not saved him from the thugs. He became possessed and a new Jara was born – one who was a total misfit in the world.

When Jara was able to walk a little and had saved some coins earned by begging, he went to see Kripa. He went at night, after the temple had closed, to avoid any angry Priests. He wished to ask Kripa for forgiveness, for stealing his money so long ago. When Jara reached the Banyan tree, Kripa was fast asleep. Jara called to him. When the Guru did not stir, Jara shook his shoulder. Kripa awoke with a curse on his lips; looked at Jara's hideous face, and drew back in alarm. Then recognition dawned and he smiled.

"Swami, I made a grave mistake years ago. Here is the money I stole from you. Forgive me." Jara felt relieved of a great weight.

"*Ha ha*... you did not steal. I stole from a fool by threatening him with my sacred thread. You were smart to steal the money and get away from me. I cursed you for an hour and then I was happy for you. I knew you would survive when I found the money missing. You were suited to this world. Now I am worried. What makes you think you can survive as a saint in this world, unless you make it your business to exploit the gullible and greedy?"

Jara did not answer because he did not understand the import of Kripa's reasoning. But he pleaded with him to take the money until the Brahmin became angry and cursed him to get out and let him sleep. Kripa added some choice expletives about saints and holy men before returning to his slumber.

The same day, Jara witnessed Shakuni pushing Bhima into the river. He was hauled before the *sabha* in Prince Suyodhana's trial for the murder of his cousin. Even though Jara was intimidated by the splendour of the palace, the King, and the regal-looking nobleman who barked at him to stand straight and speak like a man, he was glad he had had a hand in Prince Suyodhana being freed of the charge. He took the beatings he later received from the guards as a test from God. It was all Krishna's *leela*, thought the Nishada, as his frail body lay bruised and broken.

Jara asked many people where Krishna was to be found. Some told him Krishna was a Yadava Prince from Dwaraka, who had become an *avatar* because of his wisdom and ability to create things from thin air. Others said it was all a farce and that Krishna had no such powers, that he was just another Prince playing dirty politics. Jara became angry when he heard these opinions. Krishna was the dead Brahmin's God. He could not have been wrong. With a passion that bordered on insanity, the Untouchable believed in Krishna's infinite compassion and omnipotent power. Every moment was spent in His worship and every act was given as an offering. Soon a new voice was heard amidst the cacophony of the narrow lanes of Hastinapura. The harsh lives of the poor were softened by the sweet voice of Jara singing his God's praises.

It was this Jara that the blind dog took asylum with. Guru Drona passed them, sleeping huddled together, on his way back after claiming the thumb and dreams of another Nishada. The next morning, the dog licked Jara awake. The soft tongue caressing his dirty face felt good. It was a blessing to be alive in this beautiful world. Jara kissed the earth, as was his habit, and thanked Krishna for his mercy and kindness. He sang of His wisdom, His *maya*, His mischief, and His love. The blind dog, its eyes encrusted with dried blood, listened in rapt attention, wagging its tail. A few pedestrians threw coins onto the rag spread before the beggar.

By afternoon, a whim seized Jara. He wanted to name his new pet. He thought of many names, but only one struck him as good enough. He had heard the word used by many holy men. It was used so casually that it had become commonplace. The Untouchable did not know its real meaning, but that did not matter, it was his dog and it was a free country. He could call it whatever he wanted. Jara lifted the blind puppy to the sun and it whined. Like a father at the *naamkaran* ceremony, he placed the puppy in his lap. "Dharma, Dharma, Dharma," Jara whispered three times into the dog's ear.

The ignorant beggar had unwittingly chosen a curious name for the dog blinded by Arjuna and Ekalavya. Dharma, the blind street dog, wagged its tail in happiness as the Untouchable caressed its head affectionately. Around them, life went on without caring a whit, on the streets of India.

THE SHIP REACHED DWARAKA on a misty morning. Karna thanked the Greek Captain, who reiterated his offer to take him to his own country. From the deck where they stood, the golden domes of Balarama's palace and the city's temple spires were clearly visible. Karna smiled at the foreigner and shook his head. A close bond had developed between the Suta and the Yavana. Karna tried to pay for his voyage with some of the money left from the prizes he had won with the *Dharmaveera* title, but the Captain refused, saying he would be betraying the pride of his motherland if he charged a warrior like Karna. A few days before, under a star-sprinkled sky, on a calm sea, with the ship just an insignificant speck in the vast universe, Karna had told the Greek his story of struggle, ambition, achievement, and the curse of his Guru. For some inexplicable reason, it had moved the *mlecha* to tears.

The Captain accompanied Karna to the dockyard and people watched with curiosity as the yellow-haired barbarian and the tall Indian, dressed in barbarian clothes, hugged each other. They knew they would never see each other again and that made the friendship feel more real and eternal. The Captain watched the Indian fall on his knees and kiss the ground and a great hatred for Karna's country filled the Yavana's mind. Despite all its wonderful temples and great cities, India could not withstand an invading power for long if it continued to treat its men and women of talent like dirt just for being born into the wrong caste. The Supervisor of Customs came to meet the Captain, cutting short his fantastic dreams of invading India, and he soon became mired in the complex world of commerce.

Karna had only his bow and quiver of arrows, the whip-like sword *urumi*, which he wore as a belt, and some borrowed clothes from the Captain, as his only possessions. The future looked uncertain and frightening. Perhaps he should try to meet the Yadava leader and ask for employment, he thought, though his heart lay in Hastinapura. He yearned to see his parents and impress his former playmates with the skills he had acquired. He wanted to jump into the cold waters of the Ganga and swim against her powerful currents. It had been unbelievably beautiful floating in the tamely flowing Poorna at Muzaris, when the moon played hide-and-seek behind the coconut palms, and such nights were close to Karna's heart, but he always missed the brute force of the Ganga. The swift-flowing waters from the Himalayas and the reflection of the lights of the many temples and palaces on her banks, was an enchanted world no other river in the world could match. The Ganga had one thing that other rivers could not offer Karna – the flavour of his childhood and the fragrance of nostalgia. He longed for his home.

Karna touched his heart and his fingers rubbed against the smoothness of his armour, bringing back a flood of memories. The armour had been a gift from the King of Kalinga, when he had visited Parashurama. Impressed by Karna's talent, the King had given him the exquisite armour, forged by his best blacksmiths, saying it was a gift from Surya, the patron God of Kalinga. In the ancient Sun Temple, blacksmiths had made the masterpiece, working for seven long years to create the lightest and strongest body armour. Learned Priests then placed it at the feet of the Sun God and worshipped it every day. The armour Karna wore was of unknown antiquity. The tradition was to bestow the armour upon a warrior who would safeguard *dharma* and always be righteous. Every year, during the annual Surya festival, astrologers consulted the stars to determine whom the God was pleased to bestow the armour upon. For many years, the God had been silent and the Priests had put the armour reverently back to the feet of the deity. Such a warrior had yet to be born. Generations of Kalinga Kings fervently wished they would be the ones chosen to present the armour to such a warrior.

The Sun God had blessed the present King of Kalinga, as the stars now pointed to such a warrior. The mighty King had fallen at the feet of the twenty-two-year-old, while Guru Parashurama looked at his most outstanding disciple with pride. The Guru had said the Sun God had blessed the Kalinga King indeed, as Karna was not just a great warrior but also a learned Brahmin. The Court of Muzaris had exploded in applause while Karna squirmed within. The King was reverential and he had insisted Karna bless him every morning until he left the Chera kingdom. Now the King of Kalinga was one of his many foes and wanted his head. How could such a reverential relationship be thus easily broken just because he was a Suta? Was it not defying the wish of his patron God, Surya, wondered Karna in deep sadness.

Immersed in his thoughts, Karna reached the palace gates. He cursed himself for not having purchased some proper clothes. He was still wearing the Captain's borrowed clothes, which itched in many places. The guards looked at him with suspicion and curiosity. They had never seen a fellow countryman wearing such clothes. Karna asked for a palm leaf at the Security Chief's office. Scribbling 'Vasusena' on it, he asked for it to be delivered to the Yadava Chief. He put down two coins as a bribe but the Security Chief laughed and returned them politely. Karna was pleasantly surprised. He waited under the shade of a tamarind tree outside. He looked around and saw the city had prospered greatly in the last eight years. Although he had not been here before, he had heard it had been a wasteland where nothing grew. He had also seen a miniature model of it in Balarama's room, and the passion in the Yadava leader's eyes, which energized everyone around him. He could easily imagine him working hard to raise this city up from nothing. His admiration for Balarama rose still higher.

Dwaraka had an air of freshness and energy. There were shining mansions and swanky shops; curiously shaped chariots, with all manner of decorations and trappings, whizzing past in the streets; teenagers prancing around on horses; and elephants lumbering past carrying noblemen and women, leaving the sweet chimes of bells behind them. The city was completely unlike the mad chaos of Hastinapura or the exotic cosmopolitism of Muzaris. It was not yet the largest city in India but it was definitely on its way. It lacked the art and culture of Kashi or Kanchipuram and the glitter of Mathura, but compensated for it with the vigour of youth. Balarama was working his magic. He had built a city from nothing. He was also showing the world that he could build a city that followed rules – with clean streets, proper drains, hygienic eating-places, tree-lined avenues, and tiled footpaths. Balarama was showing everyone that all this was possible here and now.

A guard broke into Karna's reverie. He bowed low and invited him to follow. Karna was escorted to the entrance of Balarama's chamber, where he hesitated a moment, wondering how the Yadava leader would receive him. Then he took a deep breath and entered. Balarama looked older. His hair had begun to recede, making his forehead look larger. He sat poring over the bundles of manuscripts piled on his table. What struck Karna immediately was the utter simplicity of his white attire. With a white cotton *dhoti* and a shawl thrown loosely over his shoulders as his only adornment, the great leader of the Yadavas looked like any of his people – except for the magnetism that emanated from him like an unseen force. Karna thought that without the gold ornaments, sparkling diamonds or pearl necklaces he had come to associate with the rich Kings of the Southern Confederate, Balarama looked almost naked. Karna stood, waiting patiently for Balarama to raise his head and say something. He felt embarrassed and irritated, but hoped this did not show on his face. He had expected a warmer reception from his mentor.

After what seemed an eon, Balarama raised his head from the pile of work and smiled at Karna, who relaxed a little. "By Shiva, you have grown so tall and handsome! My mind still carried the image of the young boy who stood in front of me years ago and spoke of his dreams. Karna, how happy I am to see you!" Balarama rushed to embrace the stiff young man. "You are still a sentimental rascal. I knew you had come and were standing there waiting for me to say something. I was just seeing whether you had changed. I am happy to see you have not. You still have the emotions of a human being. I was afraid your training would have made you lose your goodness of heart and turned you into a calculating and manipulative man, hungry for worldly success. But your face reflects your goodness and I am happy, Karna."

Karna cursed himself. Did his face really show whatever he thought? Balarama led him to the couch in the corner and sat down without letting loose his grip on Karna's wrist. He touched the armour and said admiringly, "It looks great on you. Such fine workmanship! Where did you get it?"

These words broke through Karna's reticence. He recounted his adventures in the South and talked of the glittering Asura kingdoms and their proud Kings. He spoke of the horrible caste system, which was many times more rigid than in Hastinapura, and the dogmatic men who regulated it. He spoke of the miserable life of the Pariahs and other Untouchables, alongside the life of leisure of the richer classes. He described the great dance forms and magnificent temples, the architecture, engineering skills, and music, of the Southern Confederate, and the lovely lands that had been blessed by nature's bounty. But when he mentioned his enigmatic Guru, Parashurama, he choked. Karna no longer felt like a proud warrior, but a young boy scolded by his father for no fault of his.

Balarama watched Karna and squeezed his shoulder when the young man stopped speaking. He understood the emotions Karna was trying to keep hidden. "What happened then? Were you able to make a good impression on him?" Balarama asked softly.

"I… he… he was like a father to me, until…" Karna stopped short and turned his head away. He stood up and walked to the window. He did not want Balarama to see his tears. 'Am I a woman who cries over such silly things?' he thought. In the garden outside, a beautiful young girl sat on a park bench, singing a melodious song. A few of her friends sat listening with rapt attention as her mellifluous voice caressed the flowers and added a special fragrance to the breeze. Her voice soothed his mind and stirred feelings of some unimaginable pleasure.

"Did he discover who you were?"

Karna turned quickly, his eyes full of the anguish in his soul. He told Balarama his story – from the day he left the shores of Prabhasa as a young boy, to winning the coveted title of *Dharmaveera*. But when he narrated the curse of his Guru, his voice dropped almost to a whisper. "I am a fugitive now, with all the Kings of the Southern Confederate baying for my blood. They want my head for making Parashurama look a fool. I do not know what happened to my Guru. I cheated them and perhaps I deserve to be punished." He smiled at Balarama ruefully.

"I knew something had happened to you since my spies inform me that Guru Parashurama is still unconscious and that a warrior from the North, who was his disciple, did something terrible to him. I had given you up for dead until I got a message from the King of Gokarna." Balarama went to his desk. Taking a palm leaf from it, he handed it to Karna, whose face darkened as he read.

"Karna, I would love to have you stay here, but things are not as they seem in Dwaraka. I am fighting a tough battle with the conservatives here. I have to compromise on certain things to prevent civil war. I fear that one day we Yadavas are going to kill each other and put an end to all I have been working for. Rest today and start early tomorrow for Hastinapura. Bhishma has things under control there I hope. Moreover, Graduation Day for the students of Guru Drona is only a month away, and you can perhaps apply for an Officer's post with Prince Suyodhana. As you know, once graduation is over, the Prince comes of age and gains some independence in taking decisions in the affairs of State. I will write a letter to him, recommending an Officer's post for you... not that you need any recommendation," said Balarama smiling.

Karna looked away to the garden. The girl had left and except for a few butterflies and sparrows, it was empty. His mind was in turmoil. The future looked bleak indeed. The King of Gokarna's message was clear. Karna was a wanted man. The Kings of the northern kingdoms, if they found him, were to capture him dead or alive, and hand him over to the Confederate. Danger lurked everywhere, and like a fool, he was roaming about the streets of Dwaraka, blissfully unaware. An arrow from someone hiding behind a tree or pillar could finish off the Shudra Dharmaveera in an instant.

"*Namaste*, brother."

Karna's stomach knotted on hearing the familiar voice. He turned to see his hated foe standing at the door.

"Yes, Krishna? Have all the arrangements for the *puja* been made?" Balarama tried to sound casual. With his yellow silken *dhoti*, a peacock feather in his curly hair, glittering ornaments all over his body, his flute tucked into his waistband, and a garland of flowers around his neck, Krishna looked divine. There could not have been a greater contrast than the simple white cotton Balarama wore and Krishna's finery. Karna could not help noticing how handsome the younger Yadava Prince looked.

"*Namaste*," Krishna said to Karna with a smile. "I seem to know this young man from somewhere, brother."

"He is Vasusena Karna of Hastinapura, an old friend of mine. You cannot find a better archer in all of India," Balarama replied proudly, while Karna looked bashful at this sudden praise.

"Ah! Now I remember him. He is that Suta boy who went to the South to become a warrior. He may be your friend brother, but his former supporters at the Confederate are now on the lookout for him. What is he doing here? Do you want the Confederate armies to descend upon Dwaraka and reduce our city to dust? Also, I think you forget Prince Arjuna, when you say Vasusena is the greatest archer in the land." Krishna smiled.

Karna burned with anger at the insult. He knew the Yadava Prince was merely trying to provoke him and was waiting for Karna to react. That would have been good enough reason to order his arrest. But Karna stood in silence.

"Krishna, why are you trying to pull his leg? You may be rest assured that I have sufficient influence with the Kings of the South. They would not dare start a war now. We are strong enough to defend our walled city. Please leave us alone now. I will discuss the arrangements for the *puja* later," Balarama said.

Krishna kept smiling at Karna. "As you wish, brother. Do ensure our people are protected from the Confederate armies." He bowed formally to Balarama, folded his hands in farewell to Karna, and walked out of the room. Karna continued to see the frozen smile long after he had gone.

Balarama turned to Karna, a frown between his eyes. "You must leave Dwaraka. Go to Hastinapura, and watch your back. Keep a low profile. There are many forces working around us. Do not underestimate Parashurama's power and reach. It does not matter that he is lying unconscious somewhere in the South. Leave Dwaraka before dawn."

A chill went down Karna's spine when he heard the weariness in the Yadava's voice. He wanted to ask him many things but before he could open his mouth, Balarama called a servant and asked him to show Karna to his chamber. Karna bowed and touched the Yadava leader's feet before taking his leave. His mind was in turmoil. He did not know what the future held. The only thing he was sure of was that danger lurked at every turn. The spies of the Southern Confederate could reach him anytime, anywhere. As he reached the guest chamber, he saw Krishna standing with his arms crossed, at the end of the shadowy corridor. Involuntarily, Karna's hand went to the hidden *urumi* at his waist. Krishna did not miss the Suta's action and his taunting laughter filled the empty corridor. Karna quickly entered the chamber and stood with his back firmly pressed against the closed door, thinking frantically about what to do. He locked the door and sat down on the couch in the corner. For a long time he sat, tensely listening for any footsteps or suspicious movements, until exhaustion finally claimed him and dragged him into a dreamless sleep. The palace remained eerily silent.

A soft knock on the door woke Karna with a start. It was dark. He had slept for a long time. He cautiously opened the door, keeping a firm grip on his sword. A beautiful face looked back at him. Karna's heart skipped a beat. The girl had captivated him with her song that afternoon. He did not know what to do. Should he invite her in? Was it improper to keep her standing outside?

Her red lips parted in a pearly smile at Karna's confusion. "I am Subhadra, your friend's sister," she said, bringing her palms together in greeting. Karna bowed and stepped out. "Prince, I hear you are going to Hastinapura tomorrow. Will you be meeting the Crown Prince there?" There was a hint of bashfulness in her voice.

"Devi, I am no Prince. I am Karna, a charioteer's son. But it is true I am going to my hometown," Karna replied with an amused smile.

"Oh, I thought you too, were a Prince of Hastinapura... never mind, can you pass on a message to Suyodhana?" Subhadra asked, biting her lip at her mistake in using the Crown Prince's name instead of the honorific.

Karna looked at her as she lowered her eyes. He smiled at her flushed cheeks and teased, "It is not easy for commoners like me to meet Princes and Kings."

"Oh you must. Just mention my name and you will get an audience," Subhadra told him blithely. "Tell him I will be there for the Graduation ceremony... and that I miss him."

Karna looked at the twinkling eyes and the curly hair that flowed down to her waist. 'Lucky bastard,' he thought. His mind was fluttering like a trapped butterfly. Someone already had a claim on her and he should forget such thoughts. Karna sighed ruefully. Such was the luck of some people – to be born into a noble house and be loved by a beautiful Princess.

"Sister," Karna addressed Subhadra, and felt immediately relieved by the appellation, "I shall try to pass on the message to His Excellency."

"Thank you," she said, bowing to him. She turned and disappeared into the darkness with a flurry of rustling skirts and chiming anklets.

Karna gently bolted the door. A little of her sweet fragrance had sneaked into the room and his thoughts wandered again as he sat by the open window, looking at a smiling moon floating among the clouds. How beautiful life was! He contemplated Subhadra's message. How was he going to get an audience with the Crown Prince? The innocence of her love was so refreshing. One day, perhaps life would reward him with such a pure love. His thoughts drifted to his humble home and poor parents. He felt guilty that he had not thought about them much in the long years of his absence. There had been a new world to conquer and an exciting life to be lived. They were so far away and he was chasing his dreams. But sitting in a dark room in Dwaraka, the small hut in Hastinapura did not seem so far away to Karna. It could not have been easy for the old couple in his absence. He could understand them better now. Living in the same house, they constantly saw the bed he had slept in, the broken toys he had played with, the dress he had discarded, and would have thought of him every day. Karna missed his father's gentle smile and his mother's cooking, the touch of her hand on his head. He longed for home.

His reverie was broken by the sound of footsteps. A normal man would not have heard them, but Karna was a warrior trained by the best Guru in India and his body sensed danger even before his ear heard the soft sound of feet. Someone was outside! He could feel it. Had someone pushed the door slightly to test its strength? It might have been nothing, perhaps just the wind, but not a leaf stirred outside. Just then, the moon went into hiding behind a dark cloud and there was a sudden chill in the air.

Karna quietly picked up his small bundle, checked his weapons, and listened. 'Am I getting paranoid?' he wondered, as he walked on tiptoe towards the window. Outside, the sky was cloudy. Most of the torches around the palace had died away. Near the fort gate, a flickering torch cast its reluctant light on a couple of dozing guards. Karna weighed his options. This place was dangerous and it was best to get out of Dwaraka before dawn. The journey would be tricky as miles of jungle and desert lay between here and Hastinapura. It was easy to get lost in the intervening arid lands and ruins of ancient cities. He needed a horse. Going on foot was out of the question. Graduation Day for the Princes was nearing and he had a vague plan about how to impress the powerful people and gain employment. Perhaps the Yadava leader would lend him a horse. It was still dark.

This time it was unmistakable. The door rattled and the tip of a knife was inserted through the gap between the door and the doorframe. Someone was trying to move the bolt. Karna's heart thudded in his chest. There could be many warriors waiting for him in the corridor. 'Should I stay and fight or get the hell out of here before it is too late?' Someone kicked the door, but it held. Karna grasped his possessions and jumped out of the window. His assailants would expect him to make a dash for the gate or hide in the garden. He had to outwit them, so he perched just under the window, saving his breath.

A dark face peered out and cursed. "The bloody Suta has escaped!" The speaker kicked over a table and the sound of shattering glass reverberated across the palace.

"Bloody fool! Do you want to wake everyone?" snapped a voice. Silence followed.

They could be coming any moment now. Where were the Royal stables? Was it the faint outline of a roof he could see on the eastern flank? They could catch him any moment. Karna ran across the lawn, half expecting an arrow to pierce his throat. He touched his armour, finding comfort in its heaviness and promise of protection. Karna reached the stables, panting and out of breath. He could see four dark figures moving through the palace gardens, searching every bush and tree. In the faint light of the torch at the gate, their shadows had grown into monsters crawling across the lawn. The horses were restless, sensing the presence of a stranger. If one of them neighed, it would attract the prowling men's attention. Then there would be no option but to fight; to kill or be killed.

There were hundreds of fine horses in the stables. Karna quickly assessed each. Finally, he found the black one he wanted and went up to it, praying it would not neigh. He approached cautiously, speaking gently to calm it down before untying it and walking it out of the stable. The stable guards were sleeping on *charpoys* under the open sky. Karna steered the horse clear of them and began walking towards the gate, careful to keep to the shadow of the thick fort wall. He mounted only when he was sure he had put enough distance between himself and the stables and then trotted towards the gate, telling himself to remain calm.

There were streaks of red in the Eastern sky. The Morning Star shone brightly. Karna kept an eye on his pursuers, who were showing signs of agitation. Suddenly one of them stopped and stared in his direction. Karna halted, hoping that stillness would be less conspicuous than movement. The moon escaped the folds of the dark clouds exactly at that moment. One of the men saw Karna on the horse and clicked his tongue loudly to alert his companions. They turned immediately, saw him, and sprinted in pursuit. Karna galloped towards the gates. He had no idea of how he would make the guards open the massive fort gates before his enemies caught up with him. The wall was too high to jump over. His horse neighed in frustration, finding its path blocked. The guards, who had been dozing, awoke and saw Karna struggling to control his horse. Karna cursed his luck as more guards came running towards him from various parts of the fort. He was trapped!

Karna saw that his four pursuers had quietly slipped away and were no longer part of the posse which now surrounded him with naked swords and lances at the ready. Obviously, they did not want the others to know of their presence. That made them all the more dangerous. Karna knew that even if he somehow managed to talk his way out, he would still have to face those dangerous men later on his long journey to Hastinapura.

The Security Chief arrived. Pointing his sword at Karna, he barked at him to dismount. Karna complied without a word. Resisting would have been foolish. There were hundreds of armed guards around him. He did not know how to explain the possession of a horse from the Royal stables. It would be embarrassing if his host was informed.

"Hey! Aren't you the warrior who sought audience this morning?" the Security Chief asked. Karna looked down. It was shameful to be caught as a common thief. "Do you have any explanation for this, Sir?" the Chief asked politely.

Karna could not think of any answer without being untruthful. The Chief called one of his assistants and said something to him softly. The man bowed and ran towards the palace. Karna knew what that meant and fervently wished the ground would open and swallow him up. The messenger had gone to fetch Balarama.

***

"What is this nonsense, Chief?" The booming voice of the Yadava leader filled the air and the guards immediately bowed respectfully.

"Your Excellency, this man was trying to steal..." began the Chief.

Balarama interrupted him. "Steal! Do you know who he is? This horse is my gift to him. You have now insulted my guest. Chief, people will laugh if they hear of this incident. Is this the way the Yadavas treat their friends and guests? What have you done, Sir?"

The Chief hung his head in shame while Karna looked at Balarama in astonishment. "I apologize for my audacity, Sir. Please forgive your humble servant." The Chief bowed before Karna, burning with shame.

Karna was at loss for words. The man had only been doing his duty and was now being shamed before his subordinates. Anything Karna said would sound incongruous.

"Do not worry Chief," Balarama said, patting the poor man on the shoulder. "You have done your duty well. It is my fault. I should have informed you earlier that our guest would be leaving early. All of you have served Dwaraka well," Balarama said to the guards. Smiles broke out on the previously anxious faces.

"Sir, you are too kind, we do but our duty..." The Chief kept his head bowed but his shoulders were no longer tense.

Karna touched Balarama's feet and whispered that he was sorry for what had happened. The first rays of the sun were nudging the earth from her sleep.

"Beware, Karna! The path you have chosen is not easy. I do not know what has transpired to make you leave in such desperate haste. But danger will always be just one-step behind you. You have dared to challenge centuries-old prejudices and the old India is not going to let you go so easily. May the compassionate blessings of Mahadeva be with you always. Whatever happens, remember one thing – be grateful for what life has offered you and be generous, especially when fortune and luck desert you. Godspeed Karna. I hope Hastinapura will have the eyes to see your ability and not your caste."

As Karna mounted his horse, he heard another voice that instantly filled him with dread. He quickly turned his head and saw Krishna in all his divine glory, standing beside his frowning elder brother. The smile never left Krishna's dark and handsome face when he repeated what he had said earlier, a little more loudly this time, "Hastinapura is very far away, my friend… really far, and the path is perilous and hard. Do you have it in you to make it, Karna?"

Karna felt his anger rise at the taunt but willed himself to keep calm. Saying nothing, he brought his palms together and bowed his head. Turning his horse towards the rising sun, he said a silent prayer. His heart leapt with joy at the prospect of going home. 'Hastinapura is waiting for me,' he thought, closing his eyes for a moment to trap the bliss he felt. He did not think of the dangers that lay ahead. He only felt extreme gratitude for life. And so he left the two Yadava brothers, so different from each other, to fight their own cold wars. He turned north, leaving behind the streets of Dwaraka with the milling crowds who were indifferent to his destiny and pursuits. He would ride through steaming jungles, sweltering deserts, and dry riverbeds, in the coming days. Hastinapura awaited the return of the humble Suta who had dared to dream.

Unknown to him, four soldiers left Dwaraka after him. Their mission was clear: capture the Suta or kill him. A messenger also left for Hastinapura. He was the first of a galloping relay, carrying an urgent message to the Priest Dhaumya, who would receive it much before Karna's arrival; if Karna managed to reach at all. Someone was taking no chances. In similar fashion, other messengers travelled to the important cities of the Southern Confederate. All the messages were identical: *The fly is caught in the trap.*

17 Wanted

HASTINAPURA WAS GETTING READY for the big event. It was the culmination of twelve years of training. The hundred sons of King Dhritarashtra and the five sons of his brother Pandu would show the world they had grown into fine warriors under Guru Drona. Invitations had gone out to the many kingdoms of India – from Gandhara in the West, to Kamarupa in the East, to Kashimira in the North, and Lanka in the South. Many of the invitees were vassal Kings and the invitation constituted an order from the Grand Regent, couched in polite language, to attend the event. Others were friendly States, like Dwaraka and Vanga, and their rulers were present at the grand event as a gesture of goodwill.

It was midnight when Bhishma summoned Vidhura to his chamber. "I am worried about the Southern Confederate. They should not be made to feel insecure by our open display of warriors and arms. Is there any basis for the rumours about Parashurama?" Bhishma did not take his eyes from the pile of palm leaves in front of him.

"The spies say he has yet to regain consciousness. If this is untrue and he is well, it would be risky to invite the wrath of the Confederate." Vidhura waited for Bhishma to lift his gaze from the palm leaves.

"Vidhura, do you imagine I am afraid of war with anyone? The only thing that stops me is my reluctance to break two decades of peace. The Southern Confederate is far away, but Khandiva is nearby. Takshaka has already deposed the last Indra and made him into a puppet. We can expect an attack from his ragtag mob any time." Bhishma placed another palm leaf to his left after reading it.

"Sir, a bigger threat is the worsening law and order situation in the city. Should I flush out that rat, Durjaya? He is using the Gandhara market as a cover for his nefarious activities. It is high time we demolish the market." Vidhura fidgeted, stopping himself from uttering the Gandhara Prince's name.

Bhishma wearily put down the palm leaf he was reading and rubbed his tired eyes. "Vidhura, I have always tried to project a tolerant image towards different races and faiths. I do not want to become a northern version of the Confederate. Demolishing the Gandhara market will be stomping on the rights of the minorities. Durjaya is a petty crook. We can finish him whenever we want. Concentrate on the Nagas and keep a strict watch on the Confederate."

Vidhura wanted to retort that the majority of people like himself, the Shudras and the Untouchables, did not have any rights in Bhishma's tolerant land. But he did not say it aloud and so escaped the wrath of the old man. It would have been an unfair accusation. The Grand Regent had personally vetoed Dhaumya's proposal to reserve all Government posts for Brahmins, only that morning. It was late. Vidhura longed to go home, hug his children, and sleep like a log. He looked outside the window. A lustrous moon bathed the earth in silver light. The peace of the night was misleading.

"What the hell is this?"

Bhishma's question shook Vidhura from his musings. He took the palm leaf from Bhishma's hand and moved to read it in the dim light. The colour drained from his face. "Sir, this is explosive," he said as he handed the message back with a trembling hand.

"*Hmm...* not yet, but it could very well turn out to be. We have to stop him," Bhishma said gravely. He read the message one more time. It was from the Maharaja of Vatapi, a powerful King of the Southern Confederate. A Shudra boy from Hastinapura had betrayed and insulted the Kings of the Southern Confederate by becoming the *Dharmaveera*. The Confederate demanded that Hastinapura capture and hand over the scoundrel to them; failing which, the peace treaty would be considered invalid. It was almost an open declaration of war.

"Watch out for him. Send a few capable men to search. Seal all the roads leading to the city. He must be caught at any cost." Bhishma stood up from his seat and began pacing up and down.

"That would be impossible Sir, with the thousands flowing into the city from all over India to watch the grand ceremony. There will be more than 20,000 people in the arena on the day and many more thousands milling around the *mela* grounds nearby. Nothing like this has happened in two decades and everyone is excited. How can we stop a single man from entering?" Vidhura asked, as he took the message to read.

His hands trembled. Anything untoward happening at the Graduation ceremony was unthinkable. The responsibility was his. "Besides, security arrangements have been beefed up to prevent a possible Naga strike. We do not have the workforce to start a manhunt now. This is apart from the policemen needed to prevent petty mischief like chain snatching and theft, from Durjaya's gang. We are overstretched as it is, Sir." Vidhura was almost pleading now. As an afterthought he added, "Besides, we do not know what he looks like, where he is from, or anything else."

"Vidhura, do not panic. Think with a clear head. If my memory serves, you once took the same boy to Drona, a few years ago. You remember that charioteer... what was his name? His boy wanted to be a warrior and our Guru refused him since he was a Suta."

"Vasusena Karna, Athiratha's son?" Vidhura asked in shock. He had fond memories of the bright and enthusiastic son of the charioteer and still smarted from the insult he had suffered at Drona's hands.

"I believe it is the same boy. I admire his grit and determination. Alas, we live in a petty world. We will have to sacrifice him to avoid a bloody war and loss of life. Capture him alive. I do not want his blood on our hands. His only fault was to be born into the wrong caste. Deliver him to the fanatics of the Southern Confederate and be done with it. I am confident you will find a way to capture him. Just see to it that he does not end up as another Naga rebel. And, of course, keep him away from that crazy Kripa at any cost. We cannot afford any of his pranks right now. Good night, son. Meet me in my chambers early in the morning." The Grand Regent vanished into his private chambers, leaving a worried Vidhura alone.

Vidhura stood in the pale, flickering light of torches that threw haphazardly moving shadows in the corridor, and pushed his tired mind to think clearly. The boy would have grown into a young man by now. How could anyone identify him amongst the thousands who would flock to the city for the ceremony? Vidhura began walking towards his quarters, immersed in thought. Karna would certainly visit his parents. Yes! That was it. He would place guards in disguise near Athiratha's house. But what if Karna thought it better to visit the arena before seeing his parents? No, surveillance of the charioteer's house would not be enough. It would be far better to capture him in the outskirts and send him packing to the South without any fuss. A meeting between Takshaka's men and Karna could prove disastrous.

'Tomorrow I will visit the charioteer's hut along with the Court artist,' Vidhura thought. Perhaps the boy resembled his father. The artist could make a rough portrait of Karna using the father as a model – a younger Athiratha, with more muscle and a well-built body, as they said the young man was a great warrior. He could then send his spies to every nook and corner of the city with copies of the portrait and perhaps they would find him. Better, he would announce a reward for capturing Karna alive and post the pictures around the city. He would merely say Karna was a wanted criminal, and an award of 10,000 gold coins would be sufficient to tempt many to keep a lookout for him. It might just work. Vidhura entered his spartan chamber and gently closed the door. 'Tonight, my family will sleep without me again,' he thought ruefully. It was almost dawn before sleep blessed the harassed Prime Minister of Hastinapura.

***

Another soul was wide-awake with excitement in a distant wing of the palace. Purochana knocked on Shakuni's door a few minutes after Bhishma retired to his chambers. After some time, the bureaucrat left the Gandhara Prince's room, disgruntled. The foreign Prince had not shown much enthusiasm for the news he had brought.

"What good will it do Gandhara if a Suta cocks a snook at the fundamentalists of the Southern Confederate?" he asked Purochana. He grudgingly put a few silver coins into the open palm of the bureaucrat for this bit of useless information.

Purochana left cursing the entire lineage of Gandhara under his breath.

But when he had closed the door securely behind Purochana, Shakuni smiled, wanting to yell with joy. He fished out the dice from his waistband and threw them onto the marble table crying out, "Twelve!" When the dice spun and settled on the same number, he rubbed his hands in glee. Looking at the dice he had chiselled from his slain father's thighbone, he chuckled. "Father, things are moving as you would have wished. I can see blood. I can smell death. India... you are finished... war... the BIG WAR... Bhishma, you bastard... I will show you what a Gandharan can do to your country." Shakuni laughed. He dropped to the ground, bowing to the West, again and again.

After a while, his trance broke and he rushed to his writing table. He had urgent work to do. He hurriedly scribbled a note to Durjaya. If the underworld lord could catch the stupid Suta, he could be held hostage while the tension mounted between Hastinapura and the Confederate. Perhaps he could be smuggled to Gandhara and hidden in one of the caves in the mountains while the Indians fought and destroyed each other in a bloody war. The only thing he had to do was plant a rumour that Hastinapura was shielding Karna – who had insulted all those egoistical fools of the South. Things were moving his way sooner than he had expected.

**

"I have done whatever that bloody foreigner has asked. I have made the city unsafe, ensured no one sleeps peacefully, arranged for plunder and arson. Hell, I have even given instructions to my minions to pray facing West, towards his frigid country. Though I do not care one way or the other about that. But what more does he want?" Durjaya glared at Purochana.

"Durjaya, you have done a good job and the Prince is happy with you. But he asks you to expand your activities to other cities as well, even to those of the Southern Confederate. Can you make every city and town in India unsafe?" Purochana took a sip of the expensive wine he had brought as a gift for the underworld king.

"You want Bhishma on my back again? For the pittance your Prince throws at me, I have delivered well."

"Money is not a constraint. Do you have the capability or should I try some of your rival gangs in the city?"

"Are you threatening me, Purochana?"

"Are you feeling threatened, my friend?"

Durjaya glared at the Inspector of Hygiene with distaste. Purochana took another sip and smiled. "Let me hear what he is offering," Durjaya said finally.

Purochana nodded. After much haggling, the price for bleeding India through a thousand cuts was fixed. As an afterthought, Purochana said, "Is catching a Suta too much to ask of you?"

"Stop talking in riddles and tell me the price. What Suta?"

Purochana took the cloth drawing Vidhura had pasted all over the city and placed it on the table in front of Durjaya.

"*Bah*! For 10,000 coins, you want to me do this? Are you insulting me with petty change now?"

"Fool!" Durjaya winced at the insult. Purochana chuckled to himself. How the equation had changed from his first visit. "Catch him and hold him. If instructions come, smuggle him to Gandhara. You will be rich beyond your wildest dreams."

"Who is this man? Why is he wanted so badly?" asked Durjaya suspiciously.

"He is someone who will change the entire history of this country."

Durjaya stared at Purochana, then at the drawing. Finally, he said, "Tell me the amount."

***

By the next evening, the entire city of Hastinapura was swarming with men looking for Karna. Vidhura's spies and Durjaya's henchmen roamed the streets, scrutinizing the face of every stranger. All prominent corners and junctions had cloth posters with a portrait that resembled the poor charioteer Athiratha in his younger days. The huge bounty on Karna's head was sufficient for many to forget eating and sleeping and join in the hunt for the fugitive instead.

Jara's sleep was disturbed twice. When the night was still young, two police constables came and kicked Dharma the dog into the gutter. They beat the beggar awake and thrust the crude picture of the wanted man in his face. It looked vaguely familiar to Jara, but he shrugged his shoulders and smiled at them, showing his crooked teeth. They cursed him and left, asking him to inform them if he happened to see the man. Jara went back to sleep. The blind dog crawled back to him. In the dead of the night, Durjaya's men woke him again, with a sharp kick to his ribs; showed him the same picture and asked him the same questions. Jara realised something serious was happening.

The thugs went away, giving Jara the same warning the police had. Jara realized who the man was now. It was the charioteer Athiratha, but looking much younger. He and Ekalavya had once visited his house many years ago on the day they had seen Takshaka attacking the Hastinapura fort. His wife had fed them well that night. Jara forgot many things but never acts of kindness, for they were few and far between in his life. He owed the charioteer's family for the food they had given him long ago. They were probably not looking for the charioteer himself but his son, thought Jara. Who would pay so much for a charioteer? If the life of the son was in danger, he ought to do something.

Jara stood up from the footpath he had slept on and began walking towards a tavern on the southern outskirts of the city. There were many paths leading to the city but Jara trusted his instincts. He was sure the fugitive would choose this way. Jara would await his arrival and warn him if possible.

Initially, the tavern owner tried to chase him off, but when he discovered the beggar could sing beautifully about the glories of God, and that travellers stopped to listen to him, he decided to tolerate Jara's presence: It was good for business and the songs the beggar sung were about a compassionate Krishna, and moved tired travellers to tears. Moreover, Jara paid for his food with the coins he earned by singing. The tavern owner could afford that kind of charity. So the beggar sat waiting for his man, singing about his God, with Dharma the blind dog, for company.

***

Unaware of the peril that awaited him, Karna galloped towards Hastinapura. It had been a long and arduous journey. A merchant he met had advised him to travel through the drying bed of the river Saraswati to save time. As Karna rode through the dying river with its ankle-deep water and huge patches of barren sand, he could not help but remember the grand civilizations, which had flourished on its banks thousands of years ago. The history of the grand Asura civilization, with its sprawling cities; and the awe-inspiring stories of the First Indra, who smashed those cities and brought Deva rule to India, flashed through his mind. 'This is where the *Veda*s were born,' he thought. 'These are the banks upon which the ancient sages sat and pondered upon the Universe and the riddle of life.' Where had the heroes gone? Where were Rama, Ravana, Mahabali, Indra, and Bali – the heroes of the Devas, Asuras, Nagas, and the tribes who had inhabited this holy land? Why did such people no longer exist? 'Perhaps I am being harsh about our modern times, since history has a tendency to scatter gold dust over mundane things. Who knows what those heroes were really like in real life? Some may have been tyrants or despots. Myths acquire colour over time. Perhaps Balarama, or even Krishna, will become a hero, or even a God, as time goes by.'

Karna smiled at the thought. Krishna was already considered a God. He was carefully cultivating his image as an *avatar* of Lord Vishnu and everything he did was projected as a miracle. Already, among the cattle herders and lower classes, he was thought a God and they prayed to him. The Krishna path was easy. He asked only for people to believe in him and promised miracles would happen in his devotees' lives. He was an easy God to follow. Balarama offered no miracles other than hard work; no heaven other than the here and now; and no sanctuary other than self-belief. He was a wise man leading a country of fools. 'My country does not deserve Balarama,' Karna thought ruefully.

The clang of an arrow hitting his armour jolted him abruptly from his reverie. He looked around surprised, trying to see where the attack had come from. He stared into the thick shrubs on the left bank of the river and steered his horse towards them. He had whipped out his bow and an arrow gleamed between his rock-steady fingers. He waited for a single move by his unknown enemy to identify his hiding place to finish him off. Not a leaf stirred. But Karna knew enemies were close by. He could sense their presence and feel their eyes watching his every move. He was out in the open and vulnerable – easy prey. His armour had saved him but Karna knew it would just be a matter of time before they aimed at his face and got a lucky hit. Another arrow swished by, perilously close to his ear. It had come from a different angle to the first. It was foolish to wait around for an arrow to pierce his throat.

Karna whirled his horse round quickly and took flight. Suddenly it began raining arrows. He ducked and weaved across dry shrubs and leaped over boulders, urging his horse through puddles of water at a gallop, trying desperately to gather speed. The sun was a ball of fire over his head and the desert sizzled with heat. Karna sped across the heart of the holy river, praying. He had to make it to cover and fight back before an arrow found its mark. He turned his head as he jumped over a thorny shrub and saw them clearly. There were four warriors and they were gaining on him. Karna whipped out his bow again and shot an arrow without slowing his horse. He had aimed at the leading man's head, but the man ducked easily and continued gaining on Karna. Another arrow hit Karna's armour, almost piercing it. He knew he was at a disadvantageous position. He was outnumbered and fleeing from them. His back was towards them and he had lost precious seconds in turning his body to take aim. He had no choice other than to be recklessly brave.

Karna pulled at the reigns of his horse suddenly and it stopped dead in its tracks. He jumped down and shot an arrow, all in one fluid movement. It pierced the eye of one of the warriors, and he fell from his steed. The remaining three did not even pause to look back at their fallen colleague. They had been through enough battles to be indifferent to death. Karna tried to suppress his rising panic as he saw them approaching. He fired the next arrow. This time it caught the right arm of a galloping warrior, who uttered a foul curse as he plucked it from his flesh without caring to look at the wound. The leader shot an arrow that almost got Karna. It missed the Suta's throat by a whisker but pierced the horse's stomach. It neighed and began thrashing around wildly.

As they neared the trapped Suta, the warriors put their bows back and drew out their glistening swords. Karna shot arrow upon arrow at them. He found his mark many times but none of the hits was fatal or sufficient to slow the warriors. Finally, he threw away his bow and arrow and fumbled at his waist. He could see the looming figure of the leader closing in on him as he tried desperately to extricate his sword. The horse had fallen and was thrashing wildly. In the nick of time, Karna pulled his sword free and blocked certain death with inches to spare. Sparks fell over him from the clanging swords as he panted with exertion.

The leader smiled at Karna as the three remaining warriors circled him on their horses. Hardened veterans as they were, Karna's foolhardy resistance was rather amusing. They jumped down from their horses and stood in combat position, swishing their swords gently, taunting the Suta. They had been pursuing Karna for days and were bored with inaction. Hastinapura was only a day's journey away and the spot they had chosen to end the Suta's adventure was the last desolate area. A few leagues further on, villages and small towns peppered the highway to Hastinapura. They had to finish this upstart with no witnesses to link the crime to their master. On their way back, many taverns offering heady brews and beautiful women, awaited them. The leader gestured to one of his companions to end this silly task.

The warrior who moved to kill Karna was arrogant and confident of his own skill. What could a novice barely out of his teens do to a veteran of many battles like him? He had not reckoned on Karna's skill or ferocity while fighting for his life. In a few seconds, the man was bleeding from numerous cuts as the Suta fought like a cornered beast. Things were not looking good for the pursuers. There was no one about to see if three men took on one youngster together, so the leader slyly moved to corner Karna, gesturing to his companions to attack from the other side. A thrust of the sword in the back was what the upstart deserved after all. It did not work out the way the leader had planned. Instead, Karna left him sprawling on the sand with a powerful kick on the shin before he could even use his sword.

"Why are you doing this to me? What wrong have I done to you?" Karna yelled in anger. "Get lost! Do not make me kill you. I am sorry about your friend."

The warriors looked at each other in surprise. The death of their companion had not bothered them at all. Death was a warrior's unfailing friend, but the audacity of a Suta to say to their faces that he would kill them, was unbearable. "Enough of these games," the leader shouted to his two comrades. "Let us teach this bastard a lesson."

The three warriors rushed at Karna with drawn swords, screaming abuse and taunting him about his low caste. Suddenly they halted, looking in amazement at the sizzling, ribbon-like weapon in Karna's right hand. They had never seen anything like it. It wriggled like a snake.

"What is this, you buffoon? Your mother's ribbon?" the leader asked. The others burst into uproarious laughter. The hilarity stopped when the *urumi* wrapped around the leader's neck in the blink of an eye. The blood drained from the leader's face. He knew what it was now. He had never seen the weapon but had heard about it from people who had travelled to Asura territory. It was a vicious thing with a mind of its own. He could feel its sharpness cutting into his neck.

"Let me go on my way and I will not hurt any of you," Karna pleaded again.

The leader could see the logic in the Suta's cry; however, before he could say anything, his foolish companions rushed towards Karna with their swords. His scream of "NO!" was never completed. The holy riverbed of the Saraswati had been soaked with blood since the dawn of civilization. The leader's severed head was just a minor addition to her bloody treasures. His companions soon met the same fate. It was all over before it had really begun.

Then the unexpected happened. A few indifferent crows, a dying river, and some sorry shrubs, were the only witnesses. Bards in the pay of the *avatar*s would have thrived on such a scene and narrated how wise men were right in saying that only people born into the Kshatriya caste could be warriors. How else could one account for the foolish son of a charioteer who sat on the dry riverbed for a long time, feeling guilty about the lives he had taken? And which idiot waited two days in the desert, nursing his wounded horse, instead of thrusting his sword into its heart and ending its misery, as any warrior would have done without blinking an eye? Which warrior sweated away under a blistering sun to give it a burial when it finally died? And which Kshatriya foraged for dry wood to give his slain foes a proper cremation instead of leaving their corpses for the foxes, wolves and vultures? It was a shame the Suta did not know the basics of *dharma*. His duty as a warrior was to kill, not to worry about the consequences. Until he learnt, he would never become a Kshatriya.

Such stupidity delayed Karna by another two days. The horses of his pursuers had escaped into the vastness of the desert and he had to walk the rest of the way. On the third day after his first killings, the charioteer's son resumed his fateful journey towards Hastinapura, without being fully aware of the peril he faced. The city awaited her prey – in her alleys and taverns, at her busy junctions, in shops and in places where more than two people met; they spoke of only one thing: the fate of the Suta upstart. Vidhura, Durjaya, and Dhaumya's men anxiously scanned the face of every new person arriving in the city, discreetly comparing it to what they assumed to be the sketch of Karna. Many enthusiastic young men, drawn by the bounty on his head, formed gangs to patrol the streets at night, stopping every stranger to question him about his credentials. They all waited for a man who looked like the charioteer Athiratha in his youth. They were sure Karna would try sneaking into the city in the dead of night.

On the eve of the grand ceremony, when the pompous parade of the Princes set the streets of Hastinapura alight, Karna entered the city unchallenged. It was an evening in which the crowds were dancing wildly to the beat of booming drums and blaring horns, and drunken men fell over each other on the footpaths. The celebrations on the streets claimed every eye. Two irritated guards, who would rather have been partying in the streets than doing their boring duty at the city gate, stopped Karna for a routine check. They glanced cursorily at his face, comparing it to the sketch of the wanted man. There was no resemblance. So they took their customary bribe and let him in without a second glance.

When Karna entered the tavern beyond the gates and heard the gossip, he finally understood he was a wanted man, with a huge price on his head. Fortunately, no one recognized him but he knew it was only a matter of time before he bumped into someone from his childhood. He lost his appetite. Fear knotted his guts, making him dizzy. He could not touch the food spread on the plantain leaf before him. He paid for the food and folded the leaf. He did not want to leave it untouched. Someone's suspicions could be aroused. Instead, he casually walked out, like the many customers taking food home.

He had to hide somewhere for the night. The next day, he would somehow get into the arena and challenge the Princes. Perhaps they would not even allow him to display his prowess but would arrest or kill him before he even entered. It was also probable he would get only a few moments to demonstrate his skills. The whole of India was hunting for him for not allowing caste to stand in the way of his ambition. He had flouted traditions this holy land held sacred. He was sure he would pay the price. 'Oh Shiva,' prayed Karna, please let me live one more day, so that I can show my people what even a Suta can achieve if given half a chance.'

Karna was about to throw the food into the waste pit when he saw a beggar sitting under a tree. A dog sat resting its head on the beggar's lap. Karna walked over and put the food in front of him. The beggar smiled at Karna gratefully. Something in his eyes tugged at Karna's heart.

"Swami, you are very kind to feed our hunger. You are my Krishna, who has brought me food," the beggar said, folding his hands together to honour Karna.

Krishna's name sent shivers down Karna's spine. His fear returned. Did the beggar know he was a wanted man? Perhaps when the police questioned him later, the beggar would remember his face. He had to get away quickly.

"Swami, this is the second time you have given me food. I recognized you the moment I saw you entering the city. All these people are looking for the wrong face. How can I forget the taste of your mother's cooking? When I was a child, I came to your home with my friend; the night you stopped Takshaka so bravely. Swami, do you remember me?"

Karna remembered him now. He was the Untouchable boy who had come home that night with Prime Minister Vidhura. 'Oh God, he knows me! This is the end,' Karna thought. Ten thousand gold coins would make the beggar rich beyond his dreams and Karna cursed himself for his impulse in giving him food. A group of guards had arrived at the tavern entrance and were checking each traveller. Karna stood helplessly, unable to decide whether to run or stay; in the forlorn hope they would not recognise him.

"Swami, do not be afraid. Lord Krishna will be with you always. Trust me and climb this tree. There is a hole up there, where a man can hide. Quick, climb up now—" Jara urged in an urgent whisper.

Karna ran to the other side of the tree and hastily climbed up, his heart in his mouth. Why were they chasing him like a criminal? He crawled into the hole and held his breath. The dog barked and Karna peered down through the thick canopy. A couple of guards walked over to the beggar and shoved a cloth sketch in his face. Jara mumbled something. The guards began beating him with their sticks. Dharma's barking and the beggar's whimpering made people stop and stare before moving hurriedly away. Karna despised himself for not intervening to stop the guards. 'I must survive till Graduation day,' he reminded himself over and over. The guards finally left, kicking the dog into the gutter, where it lay yelping. When Karna regained his ability to breathe, Jara was chanting Krishna's name.

Karna had felt proud about giving him leftover food. The beggar's gratitude had made him feel big and important. Now, after what Jara had done for him, he felt small. What could have prompted the beggar to give up such a fortune when all he had to do was point a finger upwards? Was it just the little rice he had received or was it something inexplicable that Karna's tired mind could not grasp?

As the night wore on, the crowds in the streets thinned. The tavern finally closed its doors. The sky had exploded into a million stars. Jara hummed a tune. The dog stopped whining and moved closer. Jara's calloused hands caressed the creature's head. The night remained silent, almost in anticipation of something. Jara broke into joyous song. A pleasant breeze ruffled the leaves of the trees, as if keeping time and Karna felt peace descend upon him like a gentle mist. As Jara sang about the mercy and compassion of God, which made life so beautiful; and the kindness of humans, which made it so heavenly to live, the Suta drifted slowly into a dreamless sleep.

18 GRADUATION

WHEN DRONA ENTERED, THE ENTIRE ASSEMBLY rose in respect. Aswathama, who accompanied his father, immediately moved towards Suyodhana, and Drona fumed. The Guru walked over to Kunti, who folded her hands in obeisance. Arjuna fell at his feet, leaving the other Pandava brothers to jostle for the Guru's favour.

Tenderly lifting Arjuna, who was lying prostrate at his feet, Drona looked at the handsome face of the Pandava Prince. What he would not give to have a son like Arjuna. Why could his own son not see the writing on the wall? The future belonged to the Pandavas. It would be wiser to attach himself to the winning side. It was evident in the way the Court had assembled. All the Priests, under Dhaumya, stood with the Pandavas. The only Brahmin standing with the Kauravas was the cranky Kripa, who was a special invitee of the Grand Regent. Perhaps, as Dhaumya sometimes said, Bhishma was showing signs of senility. How else could one account for the presence of Kripa in the Royal Assembly? One had only to look at how the clown was conducting himself now – chatting with the minions serving refreshments, cracking jokes, slapping his juniors in jest, and behaving without any respect for the Court or the great men and women who graced it. Drona could feel the anger emanating from the Brahmins near Kunti. They were fuming at this open flouting of the taboos. Kripa waved casually when he caught Drona's eye and even had the audacity to bow in mock deference. It took all the self-control the Guru had mastered with his yogic practices to keep from exploding with rage.

"Guru, years ago, a poor widow entrusted her boys to you and what noble men you have made them into," Kunti said to Drona, her hands folded in humility and appreciation.

"Devi, the seed of goodness and nobility lay in their hearts. I was merely the occasional shower that helped the seeds to grow. Today, they make us all proud. I was fortunate to have disciples like them," the Guru replied gracefully. He pulled Arjuna towards him and looked at the tall young man smiling at him. Drona felt something tug at his heartstrings. How he wished his son was like this man – what humility, what skill – he truly was the embodiment of perfection. Why did Aswathama always argue against everything written in the Holy Scriptures and befriend a no-gooder like Suyodhana? Arjuna, on the other hand, accepted everything wise men like Dhaumya said, without questioning them, and had the wisdom and humility to know that better men than he had written the scriptures and his duty was merely to follow them.

"You promised me you would make Arjuna the best warrior in the world, Guru. Today is the culmination of all our hopes and prayers. This poor widow will forever be in your debt."

"Devi, have no doubt your sons will surpass all others today. Is there any archer in India who can rival Arjuna? Is there anyone more skilled than Yudhishtra in the use of the lance? Bhima will show you how one can combine strength and skill. That lovable rascal is going to make the arrogant Suyodhana look a fool. Not that Suyodhana is bad with a mace, but who can beat your Bhima? Nakula and Sahadeva are excellent swordsmen. Even I am afraid to oppose them. You have been blessed with good sons and today you will see that my promise has been well kept," Drona said.

When Bhishma entered the *sabha* and saw the young faces looking up at him, pride swelled his heart. Today was an important day in the lives of the Princes. They represented the future of Hastinapura. On his right, Yudhishtra and his brothers stood in glittering splendour. To his left were the sons of Dhritarashtra, led by Crown Prince Suyodhana. The King's personal aide and scribe, Sanjaya, was describing the wonderful scene to the blind Royal couple. Kunti, Dhaumya and Drona stood together, Bhishma acknowledged their greetings. His saw Suyodhana, looking haughty and indifferent to the drama surrounding him, and the Grand Regent could not suppress a smile.

The murmuring in the *sabha* subsided and all eyes turned to Bhishma, standing next to the King. He gazed at the assembly and then addressed the graduating young men, brimming with energy and enthusiasm. "My sons, today is the most important day of your life. Today you leave your childhood behind and become men. You have completed your training under Guru Drona, and each of you is a tribute to him. Today, Hastinapura, and the whole of India, looks at you with hope. You are the future. Our country has faced many struggles and challenges in the past, but it is the youth who will decide the path India will take. We all stand here with optimism in our hearts. One day, Prince Suyodhana will follow his father as King of our ancient land, and I am sure Drona has inculcated in him the wisdom to take on that great responsibility. All of you will occupy important positions as governors, ministers, military chiefs, administrators, and so on. I know you are at an age that resents listening to advice, but unfortunately I am at an age that relishes giving it."

Bhishma paused as everyone laughed. His patrician face broke into a smile. "My first piece of advice is that Graduation Day should not mean the end of your learning. Learning is a continuous process and your training has merely prepared you for that never-ending journey. Learn from everyone, everywhere, and everything. Use every moment to do so. That is the only legacy we leave behind when the Great God of Time, calls us back to his abode. My second piece of advice is, when you are in positions of power, the trappings of power are many and may often hinder you in taking the right decision. When your mind knows not what to do, here is a *mantra* for differentiating between right and wrong: any decision you take will affect some people favourably and others unfavourably. The right decision is always based on the greatest common good and not in favour of one particular group."

Bhishma paused and looked at Dhaumya. The Brahmin stared back coldly at the Grand Regent. "I wish you all success." Bhishma said to the young faces looking up at him, suddenly feeling his own youth returning, ignited by their burning enthusiasm. Bhishma dramatically drew his sword and raised it high. "Sons of the Kuru race, make our country proud. Show the world what fine men are capable of. Your fellow citizens await you in the arena outside. Welcome to the future!"

Bhishma's rich, deep voice boomed over the assembly and electrified the *sabha*. The sounds of conches, drums, horns and bugles sounded in joyous cacophony. The King stood and the guards threw open the huge doors of the *sabha*. The young warriors rushed into the sun.

***

On either side of the Royal highway, thronging crowds cheered enthusiastically as noble men and women, Princes and dignitaries, in glittering chariots, or on armoured elephants and fine horses, rushed towards the arena. As the procession entered the huge stadium, the multitude rose up in waves, like a giant monster waking from slumber. The ear-splitting sounds of drums, conches and whistles reverberated in the air as the dignitaries took their seats. The Princes rode into the arena, waving to the crowd. The Grand Ceremony had begun.

In the stands reserved for the Untouchables and lower castes, among the 20,000 strong crowd, a dark youth sat impassively, without even blinking. The wildly dancing young men around him were annoyed at the way he sat like a stone amidst their revelry. His right hand lay hidden in the folds of his *dhoti*. The physical pain when he had cut off his thumb at his Guru's command had long gone, but the wound in his mind refused to heal. The thumb still had a ghost presence in his hand and Ekalavya felt the pain anew whenever he let his mind dwell on it.

Outside the majestic entrance to the arena, another young man sat among the beggars and petty vendors, waiting for a chance to enter. It would have been easy to walk into the gallery but he needed to carry his weapons in and that created a problem. The security arrangements were thorough. The guards were confiscating any weapons carried by the spectators. Karna knew this was his final chance. He had to get into the arena with his bow and quiver of arrows at any cost. Jara sat contentedly with Dharma, watching the crowds. As a beggar, he was not allowed inside. But he had no complaints. Life was as good in the street as it was inside the arena, where men would compete for glory and prepare for the wars they would fight in the future. Every time a cheer rose from within, Karna tensed. Jara patted him, telling him to trust in God. He would not let him down. After a while, the beggar's constant implorations irritated Karna's already tense mind and he snapped at Jara to keep quiet. Jara smiled at the ambitious young man, but did not forget to place a consoling hand on Karna's shoulder.

Inside the arena, the disciples of Guru Drona held the galleries captivated by their spectacular display of equestrian and martial skills. As each Prince performed, the spectators cheered enthusiastically, while the Guru sat haughtily in his seat, indifferent to the wonder of the crowd. What else did they expect from disciples of Drona? He waited for Bhima to take on Suyodhana, and then the mesmerizing display of archery he was sure Arjuna would put up.

Near Drona, Aswathama sat in despair. His father had prohibited him from bringing along his bow and arrows. When Aswathama had pleaded with his father to allow him to participate in the Grand Ceremony, Drona had shouted that the ceremony was only for the Princes of Hastinapura. Aswathama had retorted that the Guru was choking his own son's talent, but Drona had not given-in. Aswathama had acidly remarked that his father was afraid Arjuna would lose to him. The remark angered Drona, carrying as it did the weight of truth, and he slapped his son. Aswathama left the room disheartened, leaving Drona feeling guilty over what he had done. He kept an eye on his son now and was secretly happy he was sitting near him instead of keeping Suyodhana company.

***

Karna got his chance when the duel between Suyodhana and Bhima began. With the guards busy cheering for one Prince or the other, Karna quietly sneaked into the arena. The stadium was packed to capacity but a villager moved a little to allow Karna to sit down. He looked at Karna's bow and frowned. Karna ignored the stares around him and tried to remain as inconspicuous as possible as he watched the duel between the two Princes.

Bhima towered over Suyodhana by a foot. He was all bulk and muscle and the heavy mace looked like a mere stick in his huge hands. He stood with his legs spread apart in combat position, wielding his mace with ease, taunting Suyodhana and trying to make him angry. Dhaumya was leading a group of Brahmins in cheering for Bhima. The majority of the common people were familiar with the Crown Prince, as he often visited their dwellings and was seen on the streets. They wanted their Prince to win. However, given the disparity in the size of the combatants, there was an uneasy silence. The gallery held more people from the villages and countryside than the city itself, and for them, Bhima was the hero and Suyodhana the arrogant Prince. That was what the bards kept singing about in their villages and they had no reason to disbelieve it. They were too naïve to know that the bards sang in praise of anyone who paid them well. The Truth was both malleable and for sale.

Suyodhana scanned the seats of the dignitaries to find those lovely eyes amongst them. When he saw her, his heart leapt with joy. He raised his mace to her. Subhadra stood up from her seat and waved. When the first blow came from Bhima, Suyodhana realized this was not a demonstration duel. Death danced in Bhima's mace, following Suyodhana's every step. The big Pandava attacked Suyodhana like a mad elephant and the cheering from the nobles grew louder. The poorer sections of the gallery maintained an uneasy silence initially but soon began cheering for Bhima, imitating their social superiors; sure, the Crown Prince would fall. Suyodhana was fighting a losing battle. He felt alone, with the whole world willing his defeat.

Bhima kept attacking with murderous intent. None of the elders interfered to stop it. Everyone anticipated Suyodhana's defeat. Dhaumya's group of Brahmins were delirious with joy. At any moment, Suyodhana would fall and his claim to the throne of Hastinapura would be weakened after such a public defeat, even if he escaped alive. The path of the darling of the conservatives; Yudhishtra, was opening up rapidly. The nobles too, waited for the inevitable fall of the Crown Prince. However, Suyodhana refused to give up. With grit and determination, he fought back. Imperceptibly, the tide began shifting against the Pandava. Suyodhana remembered the advice of his mentor Balarama, about fighting for a bigger cause than individual ego, and his blows started getting deadlier.

Defying the wishes of the holy men, the son of a blind man fought with passion against a man of superior strength and divine lineage. The turn of events was more than the group of Brahmins, who had branded the self-willed Suyodhana as evil incarnate, could digest. They looked at Krishna for solace but there was only the usual smile on the Yadava's handsome face. The cheering began to die down amongst the nobility and the Brahmins. But, from the gallery where the common people sat, the noise picked up and the cheering for Suyodhana soon became deafening. The Priests could not believe their eyes. All their efforts to plant stories about the Crown Prince over the years, was going to waste. They had to do something before the villain became a hero of the masses.

Drona sat watching the scene in horror. He could feel the accusing eyes of Kunti boring into his back. He had failed in his promise.

"Stop it somehow," Dhaumya hissed into Drona's ear.

The Guru hesitated a moment, looking towards Krishna for guidance. Then he stood up and walked towards the ring, commanding the duel to stop. Suyodhana ignored the Guru and continued to press his advantage. "Bhima, throw away your mace!" Drona shouted.

The giant Pandava blinked uncomprehendingly at first. When the command finally dawned on him, he flung away his mace and stood unarmed in front of his angry opponent. Suyodhana's mace stopped a few inches in front of Bhima's skull. Drona had assessed Suyodhana's character correctly. He knew the Crown Prince would never hit a disarmed opponent. The nobles heaved a sigh of relief. Drona chided the Prince for forgetting this was just a friendly duel and not a battlefield. Suyodhana remained silent. He knew it was useless to defend himself. He just kept staring at his Guru, his head held high, until Drona exhausted himself. The entire gallery watched as Bhima went towards his grim faced mother, while Suyodhana walked away, alone.

"Disgusting!" A voice from the Untouchables stand pierced the air. Every eye turned towards Ekalavya. The unthinkable was happening – an Untouchable was airing his opinion aloud regarding a Guru. There were protests from the Brahmins stand and many shouted to the King and the Grand Regent to catch the scoundrel and teach him a lesson for his impudence. Bhishma's face was stony and Dhritarashtra sat immobile in his seat. Kripa's mocking laughter, following the Nishada's comment, did not make things easier for the nobles and Priests. Something significant had to be done; or else, things would spin out of their control.

"Arjuna!" Kunti cried out. The Priests took their cue and began chanting the middle Pandava's name. Suddenly, hope lit their faces. If anybody could change this situation, it was the great archer.

Drona stood up to announce his favourite student. "Citizens of Hastinapura, what you have seen thus far is nothing compared to what you are about to see." Drona paused for effect, looking around. In a thundering voice he announced, "Behold! The greatest archer in the world, ARJUNAA..."

A golden chariot, drawn by the finest horses, entered the stadium and drove around it at great speed. In it, Arjuna stood like a God. He looked so handsome and noble in his expensive silken clothing and glittering jewels, that many young women gazed at him with lust and love. As he sped around below the stand of dignitaries, he shot a number of arrows with great dexterity, each landing at the feet of a nobleman, as an offering. It was the archer's salute, an impossibly impressive feat. He shot an arrow carrying a garland towards the flag of Hastinapura. The arrow whisked past, garlanding the fluttering flag. The crowd rose in thunderous applause. Then Arjuna shot at the targets placed at various distances, with grace and poise. The crowd was enraptured. They had forgotten the duel between Suyodhana and Bhima. Arjuna had saved the day for the nobles.

The proud Guru turned to Kunti. "Devi, I have kept my promise." Before Kunti could express her gratitude, an arrow fell at Drona's feet. Surprised, the Guru looked at his favourite student but the chariot with Arjuna was no longer moving. Another young man stood before the still chariot with drawn bowstring. With surprising quickness of aim, he shot arrow upon arrow, performing the difficult archer's salute. The arrows fell at the feet of the nobles. With an ease and grace that bordered on arrogance, the young man effortlessly mimicked Arjuna's feat.

Arjuna jumped down from his chariot, stung by the challenge, and began shooting at the most distant targets. Unfortunately, for the noble Prince, his challenger began hitting each target before Arjuna could even place his arrow on his bowstring. The mesmerized crowd began cheering the unknown archer. The contrast between the two contestants could not have been starker. Arjuna stood in the magnificent costume of the aristocratic Kshatriya, with glistening gold jewellery and diamond studded headgear, holding his gold-plated bow. He looked like a God just descended from the heavens. His challenger stood in his tattered clothes, bareheaded and barefooted, as if he had just come off the street; a poor bastard of low caste. He could have been any one of the faces in the gallery – an insignificant and irrelevant common man.

Panic gripped the aristocrats once again. Kunti felt faint. The nobles were angered by such a brazen display by a commoner. They turned on the hapless astrologer who had fixed this particular date as auspicious for the Grand Ceremony. The stars seemed to be conspiring against the Princes. Drona walked into the middle once again. He saw Arjuna's hands were shaking and he was making mistakes in his panic. The silken clothes of the greatest archer in the world were soaked with sweat, whereas his challenger stood poised and calm, shooting arrows in an endless flow.

"Stop!" shouted Drona. Both young men dropped their arms. Turning towards him, they bowed. Drona asked the ill-clad young man in a voice dripping with sarcasm, "This ceremony is for Princes. May I know which kingdom your father rules?"

The loud laughter from the stands resounded like thunder in the young warrior's ears. Arjuna breathed a sigh of relief. Before the stranger could answer, an old man came running onto the ground shouting in joy, "Karna! My son! You have come back…" Athiratha rushed to hug the son he had not seen for years, but stopped short when he saw the humiliation on Karna's face. With pain, the old charioteer saw that Karna was ashamed of his father. He wished his son would raise his head and look at him. He prayed that his son would run to him as he had as a little boy. But Karna stood with his eyes fixed to the ground. Like a chastised dog, the old man walked back into the crowd and disappeared.

"A Suta!" Drona laughed aloud.

The stands shook with the laughter of the aristocrats. The smile returned to Arjuna's handsome face as he wiped the sweat from his brow.

Dhaumya smiled at last. This was his domain. He walked into the ground and said clearly, "You low caste filth, why don't you go and clean the stables?" He looked at the stands and joined in the laughter that followed. "Son of a charioteer..." Dhaumya stared at Karna as recognition dawned on him. "Son of Athiratha... You are the man all of India has been hunting for over the past few days. *Ha ha ha*, the long arm of *dharma* has finally caught up with you, Suta. You think you can escape after insulting Guru Parashurama? You are finished."

A murmur of recognition went through the crowd. Prince Shakuni, sitting amongst the dignitaries, cursed himself. The opportunity to bring the Southern Confederate and Hastinapura to war had been lost. Blast that incompetent Durjaya. 'Why do I waste my money on that idiot?' he thought bitterly. Now the Suta would be handed over to the Confederate and the relationship between the two powerful forces would return to the status quo.

Karna knew his story had ended when his father came running towards him. 'Why did he have to do that? I would have gone to him after the event, after the world understood I am a better archer than Arjuna. Now I stand insulted before all because of my foolish father. Little does he know he has signed my death warrant."

A strong hand grasped Karna's wrist. He looked up. It was Crown Prince, Suyodhana. He smiled at the son of the charioteer, and then took his sword from its sheath and raised it to the sky. In a calm and clear voice, he spoke to the crowd. "Are we not ashamed to ask the caste of a warrior? Do we have the tradition of seeking the origin of rivers or brave men? Why should it matter if Karna's father is a charioteer? Or is Prince Arjuna afraid to lose to one better than he?" Suyodhana turned to his cousin. "Arjuna, if you are a man and a warrior, accept the challenge and beat the Suta instead of hiding behind these stupid beliefs."

Drona stopped Suyodhana. "Enough of your arrogance, Prince! You have crossed the bounds of propriety. I am ashamed to call you my disciple."

Suyodhana ignored Drona and continued to stare at Arjuna. In the gallery, Ekalavya held his breath. Arjuna turned helplessly towards Dhaumya, who looked confused. Arjuna then looked at his friend, Krishna, and found the courage to answer his cousin. "Suyodhana, I will not fight a low caste Suta. I am a Prince of Hastinapura," he declared haughtily.

"If you are a Prince, you will fight a King now," retorted Suyodhana. He shouted to the crowd, "My countrymen, you are about to witness something unique." Suyodhana turned towards the Grand Regent and the King. "Your Excellency, Your Highness, with your gracious permission..." Suyodhana addressed the group of Brahmins saying, "What I am about to do is in the exalted traditions of the *Veda*s. I wish to call for a real Brahmin, one who understands the scriptures as they were written."

The entire crowd of Priests stood up and began shouting at the Crown Prince. Kripa ran towards the beleaguered Prince, laughing. Drona could not believe his eyes when his son Aswathama followed Kripa. Karna found himself crushed in Kripa's bear hug. Aswathama smiled at Suyodhana and stood beside him, his strong arms crossed over his broad chest. Dhaumya begged the Grand Regent to stop Suyodhana from insulting the Holy Scriptures and holy men, but Bhishma's face remained expressionless. A nervous Vidhura attempted to pacify the agitated Brahmins, but he was ignored. Shakuni rubbed his palms together in excitement. Things were turning out much better than he had expected. If he played his cards right, he could develop this into something much bigger and more violent than he had hoped. He looked at the holy men, vehemently trying to protect their selfish interests by denying even basic dignity to the majority of the people, and smiled...

Suyodhana raised his voice again. This time he addressed the assembled Kings. "Great Kings of India, most of you have inherited your kingdoms. But here is someone truly deserving of becoming a Kshatriya. Please come forward and strengthen my purpose."

An impenetrable silence followed as the Kings gazed back stonily. No one moved. Then one of them stood up slowly. With deliberate steps, he walked towards Suyodhana. Bowing to the Prince he said, "I am Jayadratha, King of Sindh. You are doing the right thing and can count on my support. It is a privilege to befriend a man like you, if you will accept my hand in friendship."

Suyodhana smiled at his lone supporter among the Kings and grasped the hand held out to him in a firm grip. The crowd waited with baited breath. Karna watched as Suyodhana turned towards the overflowing gallery.

"My countrymen, I have a dream. Perhaps some of you may say it is an impossible dream. Yet, it is beautiful. I see a tomorrow where all barriers will crumble and we will live in a free world. I see a future where we stop asking people about their caste and treat each other as equals. I see my country breaking free of the grip of irrational beliefs and superstitions. I see a tomorrow where there will be no limits placed on what one can achieve. The accident of birth will not stand in the way of achievement.

"This young man is proof that talent knows no caste. There are forces in our society that want to cloister everything, corner every privilege, and treat others like dust under their feet. This man is hunted by the great kingdoms of the South. But what was his crime? He wanted to learn. Now, Parashurama's followers want us to punish a man for daring to dream; to insult him for not being born into a high caste. Is this the right thing to do? Have we ever paused to think what will happen to this land if we keep denying knowledge to everyone? The majority live in ignorance and poverty. A few decide who is pure and who is not. Which are the scriptures these people quote? Why are they afraid to let everyone learn the *Vedas*? Are they afraid that people will then see that most of the taboos and inhuman practises they advise have no sanction in the holy books? Where are these people leading our country? Has the time not come to say – *enough*!"

Suyodhana paused and took a deep breath. The arena waited in anticipation. "As the Crown Prince of Hastinapura, I can only make you one promise. I will not allow Parashurama and his cronies to win in our land. More than that, I wish to see our compatriots of the Southern Confederate free of the clutches of men who destroy our religion and culture in the name of *dharma*. Today, on this day of graduation, I have come of age and this is my promise to you, my beloved people. Every moment of my life, I will strive to wipe out hunger, ignorance and pain. My dreams have the sanction of our holy books. May Lord Mahadeva strengthen my arms. I will strive with my last breath to wipe out the curse of hunger, caste and inequality which is spreading from the Himalayas in the far North to where the three seas meet in the Deep South. This is my dream, my promise, my *dharma*."

There was utter silence from the 20,000-strong crowd. Then an unseen hand seemed to lift them as one body. Their cheers rose towards the heavens as the sun tinted their faces saffron.

As Karna watched the Crown Prince, his eyes filled with tears, Suyodhana made the historic announcement. "My countrymen, after thousands of years, witness the coronation of a King, based only on merit. I give away my inheritance of the prosperous Anga country in the East of our great land, to my friend, Karna. His being a Suta is incidental. From today, he will be known as Anga Raja, in recognition of his merit as a man."

A shocked silence followed before the ranks of the Priests exploded in rage. A few tried to run onto the ground, pulling out hidden daggers, but they were stopped in their tracks by Prince Sushasana. The Kaurava brothers formed a protective ring around the Crown Prince and the stadium erupted into thunderous applause, much to the discomfiture of the conservatives.

"Let the coronation ceremony begin for Anga Raja," Suyodhana ordered.

***

In the stands, Ekalavya stood up with a heavy heart. His ghost thumb twitched as he fought to control his tears. After sacrificing his thumb on the altar of caste, he had cursed the country he had the misfortune to be born in. Now, witnessing Karna's sudden turn of fortune, he felt the bitterness of his loss intensify. 'I could have been in Karna's place had Drona not cheated me of my future,' the Nishada thought. He could not sit and watch Karna become a King, and walked out of the stadium.

As Ekalavya left, Jara saw him and cried out, "Brother…" Lost in a morass of self-pity, the Nishada did not have ears for the beggar. He absently threw the loose change he had towards Jara and without looking at him, continued walking. As the noise from the stadium grew fainter, hope sprouted again in the wounded mind of Ekalavya.

A Prince had dared challenge the system. Perhaps the future would belong to him. Perhaps this country was not as bad as he had imagined if she had given birth to one such as Suyodhana. 'Why should the lack of a thumb stand in the way of my dreams?' the Nishada wondered, and took a fateful decision. He ran to where his bow lay gathering dust. Picking it up gently, he began practising again. Perhaps, even without a thumb, he could best Arjuna.

***

Inside the arena, things were getting out of control as far as the Priests were concerned. Thick clouds had covered the sun and lightning zigzagged across the heavens in crazy patterns. But nothing could silence the chants that rose from 20,000 throats. Dhaumya and his group watched in horror as Kripa and Aswathama flouted the most sacred rules of the *smritis* and did the unthinkable. As the Suta was anointed King and a Kshatriya, which itself was a blatant transgression of the caste rules, Kripa and Aswathama chanted the most sacred of all *mantras* – the *Gayatri* – before all. Did the fools not know it had to be kept secret? That no ears other than those of a Brahmin, could hear it? Did not the *smritis* say that molten lead had to be poured into the ears of Shudras or women who heard it, even accidentally? Who would control that crazy Kripa and the foolish son of Guru Drona, who were even now chanting the sacred *mantra* aloud and urging the crowd to chant it after them? Dhaumya squirmed as the air thundered with the holy *Gayatri mantra* being repeated by thousands of men and women of all castes, creeds and colour.

And so, Karna officially became King of Anga; the first Shudra to be thus elevated in many centuries. With that one bold act, Suyodhana burnt the last bridge connecting him to the conservatives. Dhaumya was determined that the evil that had arisen in the form of Suyodhana, had to be eliminated at any cost. The future of India and the protection of *dharma* depended on it. He looked at Krishna for solace but the Yadava was looking at Kunti.

Krishna watched servants help his aunt leave the arena. He shook his head. Yudhishtra had forfeited a golden opportunity. Suyodhana had outwitted everyone with his masterly move of making the talented Suta his friend. If the eldest Pandava had had any sense, he would have done what Suyodhana had done and gained a formidable warrior as his friend. 'How will I drive any sense into these fools?' he wondered. Why had Kunti fainted? Something did not add up. Krishna watched the coronation of the Suta with a smile. The game was getting tougher and he was loving it. He looked at Subhadra and saw that his sister's eyes were not fixed upon Suyodhana. Those dove-like eyes were brimming with tears at the image of the forgotten Arjuna, standing to one side, ignored by everyone. Slowly a plan started forming in Krishna's mind.

"Suyodhana should not have insulted Arjuna like that. Why did he elevate an unworthy man?" Subhadra asked her brother.

"Let us go," said Krishna, taking his sister's hand.

***

Outside the stadium, Jara fiddled with the copper coins Ekalavya had thrown, thinking sadly that Ekalavya had not even bothered to look at him. He saw a dejected Athiratha walking towards his hut and called out to him. The charioteer did not turn. Immersed in his own worries about how to break the news of their son's return to his wife, he did not hear the beggar's call. How would he tell a mother that her son had become a King, but had not even looked at his father's face? Jara gazed at the fading figure and cried, "Oh Krishna, why do you try the poor and humble in this way?" Jara heard the waves of an unknown chant coming from the stadium. He suddenly felt hungry and handed over a coin to a food vendor, who gave him a banana leaf. Since he was an Untouchable, the food would be served on the leaf, which was placed in a hole in the ground. Jara waited for the food to arrive. Dharma too, sat patiently, occasionally wagging his tail and licking Jara's face. Jara did not mind the rain that had started falling and waited for quite some time before the food vendor finally spooned boiled rice into the hole. Jara closed his eyes to offer his customary thanks to Krishna for the food.

At exactly that moment, a chariot sped past at great speed, splashing dirty water from a puddle. When Jara opened his eyes, he almost cried. The food was splattered with stinking water and no longer edible. He could only see the back of the vanishing chariot and the silhouette of a man with a peacock feather in his hair, and a woman beside him. "Why do you show food to a hungry man, only to take it away? Don't you have any mercy, my Lord?" cried the hungry beggar.

Later, when the crowd emptied out of the stadium, Jara was pleasantly surprised to see Karna riding with the Crown Prince. He wished Karna well, as though a beggar's goodwill mattered in this land of Gods. When he checked to see whether the dirty water had drained from his bowl of rice, he found a trail of ants had invaded his food. He immediately felt guilty about his outburst towards his beloved Krishna. The Lord had known that the hunger of these little creatures was greater than his own. For Him, the ant and Jara were equal. How arrogant of Jara to think Krishna had been cruel to him. It was just his *leela,* and He was merely showing the beggar that he was getting greedy and not caring about his fellow creatures. Had he not dined the previous day? How much harder must it be for these tiny, helpless creatures in the rain, thought Jara. Joyfully, he watched the ants carry away his food.

***

Inside the palace, Dhaumya and the five Pandava brothers huddled together to decide on the future. Drona's household was in turmoil.

Aswathama had walked out of his home to meet Suyodhana after another argument with his father. Jayadratha, Karna, and Sushasana, sat celebrating the great day. Suyodhana kept an eye on the King of Sindh. He had noticed that the King seemed to have a soft corner for his sister Sushala, and his brotherly instincts were on the alert. In another room, Shakuni lay wide awake, his mind working out various schemes to carry forward his mission.

Before leaving after the long day, Vidhura gently asked Bhishma about handing over the fugitive to the Southern Confederate. Bhishma stared at his Prime Minister and then shook his head saying it was no longer possible. When Vidhura expressed fears about a war with the powerful Confederate, Bhishma answered cryptically that some wars were worth fighting. Walking back to his chamber alone, Vidhura smiled to himself at the remark. Such moments made working under the Grand Regent a delight.

***

In the forest, Ekalavya fought pain and fear to practice archery...

In their hut, the aged charioteer consoled his distraught wife, murmuring that her son would surely come to see her the next day, but secretly doubting his own words...

In a chariot speeding towards Dwaraka, a thoughtful Prince held the reins while a Princess remembered Arjuna's dejected face. They travelled on in silence...

In the streets of Hastinapura, a hungry Jara and his blind dog walked along slowly. As his haunting song about a compassionate Krishna, who watched over not only his devotees but the tiniest of God's creations, floated over its dwellings, big and small, the greatest city of India slowly slipped into sleep. Night had fallen on another day in the long history of an ancient nation.

19 REVENGE OF A BRAHMIN

DHRITARASHTRA ANXIOUSLY WAITED FOR HIS SON to appear. He was puzzled by his wife's silence. "Gandhari, I hear the Suta boy is a better archer than Arjuna. What was his name? It was a great thing our son did. It took courage. Suyodhana need never again fear Arjuna with this newcomer and Aswathama to support him. But why is he late? Gandhari, why are you so silent? Are you not proud of your son? How many of us could have done what he did today?"

"They have come," Gandhari answered softly, adjusting the King's headgear and ornaments with practiced fingers before sitting down beside him.

"Your Highness, see who has come to see you," said a familiar voice.

"Ah, Shakuni! Welcome. Where are the boys?" Dhritarashtra turned his head towards the sound.

"Why do you look so serious, sister?" Shakuni asked with a crooked smile, walking towards Gandhari.

"What is it you want here, Shakuni?"

"Gandhari, why are you always so harsh to your brother? Let him celebrate this day with us. But where are the new archer and Suyodhana?"

"I am here, father," Suyodhana replied, walking into the room through the curtained archway with Karna and Aswathama.

"*Aha*, there you are. The man of the moment." The King stood up and embraced his son. "Where is your friend?" Dhritarashtra reached out.

Karna moved forward and touched the King's feet. The King ran his hands down Karna's muscled arms and smiled. "You have the long limbs of a great archer."

"The best in the country, perhaps in the world, Your Highness," Shakuni intervened. "Arjuna notwithstanding."

"Suyodhana, you almost finished Bhima, I hear," Dhritarashtra chuckled. "Well son, you are now a warrior and have the support of those who will not desert you in battle. All your boyhood you have feared your gifted cousins, but you need do so no longer." Dhritarashtra ignored his wife's restraining hand. "Gandhari, I wish to see my son succeed me. I do not want a bastard to sit on the throne of Hastinapura. Is that so wrong?"

"Yudhishtra is the son of Yama, the God of Death," Shakuni said, watching Dhritarashtra's face turn red with anger.

Dhritarashtra tapped the floor angrily with his stick. "No! He is the son of some unknown Brahmin. Gandhari, do not interfere. I am the King and have the right to decide who will follow me. I have suffered enough. Is it my fault I was born blind? Was there any warrior who could defeat me with a mace, blind or otherwise, when I was young? I have a gift for you, Suyodhana. Gandhari, ring the bell."

As the three young men and Shakuni watched, four guards staggered in with a full-length iron statue of a warrior, mace lifted over his head in combat position.

"It looks like someone we all know!" Shakuni exclaimed, admiring the wonderful workmanship despite himself.

"It is for you, Suyodhana. Take it and practise on it," the King said.

"Yes, nephew, practice breaking Bhima's head. Soon the time will come to do it on the real one," said Shakuni.

Gandhari stood up, her hand shaking. "Shakuni, please leave us. How often I have told you…. Go to Gandhara and administer your lands. I do not want you here."

"I will talk to the Grand Regent. If he permits…"

"Shakuni, please leave us now," commanded Gandhari. "I wish to speak with my son."

Karna and Aswathama followed Shakuni out, thankful to escape the embarrassing scene.

When they had left, Gandhari pulled her son to one side and felt his face with her fingers. How she wished she could see his face. How tall he had grown. He was a man now, no longer the little boy who hid under his father's bed. "Why did you do it, my son?" she asked gravely. "Why did you make a Suta a King, and risk losing the support of the nobles? You have made powerful enemies today. They will try everything to stop you from inheriting your father's throne. Why did you do it, Suyodhana?" Gandhari waited for her son to speak, fearing his answer.

"Mother, I did it because it was the right thing to do."

Gandhari turned away, lest he see the dampness spreading over her blindfold. Thankfully, a guard came to say Guru Drona wished to see the Prince in his chambers. She heard him bid farewell to his father, and nodded her head without facing him when he took his leave of her. She stood still by the window until the sound of his footsteps faded away. She was proud to have borne such a noble son, but the mother in her was afraid. She knew that doing the right thing never went unpunished.

***

When Suyodhana entered the Guru's chamber, the Pandava brothers were already there. Their conversation stopped abruptly when they saw him. Suyodhana greeted Drona and his cousins, and stood waiting for the Guru to speak.

Avoiding Suyodhana's eyes, Drona said, "Prince, it is time to pay your *gurudakshina*. By now, you know that I care neither for money nor for land. I am a Brahmin and such material things do not affect me in the least. But years ago, I had a close friend. We were both disciples of Parashurama. He was a rich Prince and I a poor Brahmin. When we finished our studies and parted, he promised to help me in the future if I ever needed it.

"For years, despite winning the coveted *Dharmaveera* title, I was unable to find a job suited to my talents. Poverty and hunger became my constant companions. When some boys in the neighbourhood forced my son Aswathama to drink batter, calling it milk, I decided it was time to go and meet my friend. He had become a King by then. I went to him with a begging bowl. He made me wait for two anxious weeks before granting me an audience. Instead of helping, he insulted me. I will never forget the laughter of the Panchala courtiers when their King mocked my helplessness. Busy with the pleasures of his newly acquired kingship, he treated me contemptuously. He made fun of my threadbare clothes and said that despite my talent, he had always known I would never amount to anything. He patronizingly offered me the post of a junior teacher in a remote village. I lost my cool and challenged my erstwhile friend to a duel. But he said Kings do not duel with beggars.

"Insulted and heartbroken, I left Panchala that day but the fire of revenge still burns in my heart. The King is none other than Dhrupada, King of Panchala. Prince, bring that rogue to me and let me spit in his face. As the Crown Prince of Hastinapura, this is the least you can do for your Guru." Drona looked at Suyodhana.

Suyodhana was at a loss for words. Drona saw his hesitation and said irritably, "I knew you would be reluctant. When have you ever respected your teachers, elders, or Brahmins? Arjuna would do it in a trice, but Yudhishtra said it would be proper to ask you first, as the country's Crown Prince."

Trying hard to suppress his rising anger, Suyodhana replied, "It is improper to wage war against a friendly vassal state without adequate reason. Besides, I cannot possibly undertake such a mission without the permission of either the Grand Regent or the King."

"Proper reason? *Tchaw*! Insulting a Brahmin is not proper reason for you, Prince? You will have the King's permission within the hour. Then you will follow my orders, as is your duty as my disciple. If you fail, which I fear you will, Arjuna will be sent to ruin Dhrupada's cursed land. Go and get ready."

Suyodhana bowed and left the presence of his Guru. Walking towards his chamber, he was a worried man. Aswathama, Sushasana, Jayadratha, and the newly crowned King of Anga, were waiting for him. Karna stood up when he saw the Crown Prince and bowed. The son of the charioteer still felt uneasy being in the company of these aristocrats and his movements were awkward. He did not know whether to show the courtesy due to Kshatriyas and Brahmins by a Suta, and be considered stiff and formal by his new friends, or be cool and unaffected, and risk being called arrogant.

Suyodhana, sensing his dilemma, went to Karna first and made him sit down near him. "We are all friends here, Karna. You can be comfortable with us. In fact, we are honoured to have your friendship. Do not think for a moment that I am bestowing a favour upon you. I regret not being able to do more for such a talented person."

"I have been telling him that he is the only one among us who has earned the respect he has been given, whereas the rest of us were lucky to be born privileged," said Jayadratha, King of Sindh.

"What can I do in return for such undeserved friendship, Your Highness?" Karna said.

"Begin by calling me Suyodhana. Or if you wish, you can use my nickname, Duryodhana, as Dhaumya and his disciples prefer," suggested Suyodhana, amidst laughter.

"That certainly suits you better. You really do not know how to use your weapons well. Otherwise you would have used your mace and smashed Bhima's thick skull that day, Duryodhana..." Aswathama said, adding more merriment.

Suyodhana found his mind eased of its tension. "Listen! We have a problem. The Guru has asked me to attack Panchala and capture Dhrupada, as my *gurudakshina* to him," Suyodhana informed his friends, warily eyeing Aswathama.

The young Brahmin smiled and said, "I know! That is an old grudge my old man holds. Every night he bores us to death by talking about the insult he suffered at Panchala's hands."

"But that's great! I was waiting for some action." Sushasana jumped up from his seat enthusiastically.

"Sit down, you idiot!" Jayadratha pushed aside the younger Kaurava. "Suyodhana, is it worthwhile fighting a battle over a man's personal vendetta? Besides, I do not think the King will give permission to wage war against a friendly vassal state."

"Exactly my thoughts, Jayadratha. Also, I do not want to start a war without the permission of Bhishma or the King."

An uneasy silence followed. A guard knocked on the door, entered, bowed, and gave the Crown Prince a message. Suyodhana dismissed him and read the message. Then he gravely handed it to his friends

"What the hell?" Jayadratha cried out. "How did Guru Drona manage this?"

Sushasana jumped up, grabbed the palm leaf from Jayadratha's hands, and read it aloud. It was an official order from King Dhritarashtra declaring war on Panchala, and appointing Crown Prince Suyodhana Commander-in-Chief of the Hastinapura forces, to lead the attack.

"Suyodhana, this is outrageous. How can the King order an attack on a vassal kingdom without any provocation? I too, am a vassal King. How can I sleep peacefully without worrying about Hastinapura's armies running amok in Sindh, if this is how Hastinapura treats its vassals?" Jayadratha grabbed the palm leaf from Sushasana's hand, read it again and threw it down in anger.

Everyone looked at Aswathama, carefully measuring his reaction. "Hey, do not look at me. I am not answerable for my father's deeds or misdeeds. I suggest we go to Kampilya, capital of Panchala, and sort things out. If Suyodhana does not take up the assignment, Yudhishtra will, and that will be a disaster. Let us see whether Dhrupada is ready to compromise to satisfy my father's ego."

"What he says makes sense," Karna said, watching Suyodhana's face.

A deep silence ensued. Suyodhana began pacing the room, his hands clasped behind his back, his head bent. His friends waited anxiously.

"We do not have a choice. The King has ordered it." Suyodhana said.

Jayadratha went out, slamming the door shut with a bang.

***

By the evening, two divisions of Hastinapura cavalry and three divisions of infantry started towards Kampilya, the Panchala capital; with Suyodhana, Sushasana, Karna, and Aswathama in the lead. Jayadratha refused to participate in the attack and remained in Hastinapura. He had another reason as well. Suyodhana was aware of it. He thought Jayadratha was an honourable man and if his sister Sushala found the King of Sindh attractive, Suyodhana was not averse to sealing the relationship through marriage.

The armies of Hastinapura reached Panchala the next afternoon. Breaking through the feeble defences at the border, they laid siege to the capital. What remained of the Panchala army withdrew into the city fortress to brace for an attack. However, surprising the Commanders, Suyodhana sent a polite request for an audience with the King. It took a whole night of heated debate amongst the Panchala nobles to decide whether to trust the Crown Prince or not. They suspected treachery in such an unusual offer from an invading army. Finally, the eunuch Shikandi, the King's adopted child, volunteered to receive the invaders.

Suyodhana entered the palace unarmed, along with Karna and Aswathama. He had instructed Sushasana to attack and take the fort in case he did not hear from them in a couple of hours. At the entrance, a giant of a man waited to receive them. As they neared, Aswathama's eyes grew round in surprise. Was it a man or a woman? He nudged Karna, who whispered the person was a eunuch. Suyodhana turned and gestured for silence. Shikandi bowed to Suyodhana and they entered a luxuriously furnished hall. The entire Panchala *sabha* rose to receive the Crown Prince of Hastinapura. The King looked rather agitated. A handsome young man stood close to him and kept whispering into his ear. Suyodhana and his friends stood in the middle of the *sabha*.

The King rose from his throne. "We are at your service, Prince Suyodhana. We would have come to Hastinapura had you ordered us to do so. We are your vassals and friends. That should mean something, even to powerful kingdoms like Hastinapura. You give us protection from our enemies and that is why we pay homage. But, if you become our enemy, who will save us smaller kingdoms? Does the Grand Regent know about this or is it your own adventure?" The young man beside the throne put out a restraining hand to prevent the King from saying something undiplomatic and making the situation worse.

"Sir, we come not as invaders but friends," replied Suyodhana. "We have come at the behest of one of your old friends. Guru Drona is still angered at the way you received him long ago."

"Ah Drona!" King Dhrupada exclaimed. "I have long regretted behaving like a boor that day and have repented it every day, every moment. I was young and drunk with power, wine and women. His poverty looked so ridiculous to me. Drona is a man of great talents but he was wallowing in self-pity and misery instead of living life fruitfully. I laughed at him, his poverty, and his situation. I felt so superior that day. Later, when I returned to my senses, it was too late. My old friend had gone. I tried to make amends, but he would not relent. Now he has sent his disciple to ransack my country."

"Sir, we too, wish to avoid unnecessary bloodshed. This is a misunderstanding between old friends. This young man here is Drona's son and..."

Before Suyodhana could finish, King Dhrupada rushed towards Aswathama and embraced him. "Ah, you look exactly like your father when he was your age. I wonder why I did not see it when I first set eyes on you. Your name?"

"Aswathama, Your Highness. And this is Karna, King of Anga."

"I am honoured indeed by your presence, Sir," Dhrupada folded his hands in a *namaste* to Karna.

Suyodhana was pleased by the King's welcome to his friend. He had feared Dhrupada would not treat Karna courteously because of his caste, but the King showed no such signs. He introduced them to Shikandi, the eunuch, whom Dhrupada had adopted long ago; and the young man standing near him – Dhristadyumna, Crown Prince of Panchala.

When the initial ice had been broken, Suyodhana gently broached the terms of Panchala's surrender, without actually using the word. Dhrupada agreed to bear the entire cost of Suyodhana's expedition, give two bullock-carts of gold, precious stones and expensive clothes, fifty horses, and one hundred cows, as gifts for the Guru. Dhrupada appreciated Suyodhana's terming the spoils as the King's gifts to his old friend. It enabled him to save face. Dhrupada also promised to go to Hastinapura and apologize to the Guru soon. He insisted his guests stay another day. The occasion was a special one for Panchala as the Princess Draupadi was turning eighteen. They had all heard of her famed beauty and the young men were more than willing to accept the King's invitation to attend his daughter's coming-of-age celebration. Suyodhana was proud of the way he had handled a tricky situation and was sure the Grand Regent would appreciate it.

That night, the palace glowed with a golden hue from thousands of oil lamps. The young men revelled in the festivities. Folk musicians filled the air with soulful renderings of old love songs, as Suyodhana and Sushasana danced to the wild rhythms of the drummers, much to everyone's amusement. They even dragged in the shy Karna. Soon Aswathama and the Panchala Prince, Dhristadyumna, joined in as well. While the young men danced, Dhristadyumna observed that Karna's movements suddenly became awkward. He followed the King of Anga's gaze and smiled. He understood why his new friend had suddenly become clumsy-footed. A little way away, sat his beautiful sister Draupadi, dazzling in a beautiful costume and sparkling jewels. She looked celestial. Her luminous black eyes roved over Karna's chiselled body. Aswathama too, observed the sudden change in Karna and let out a gurgle of amusement. Sushasana picked up the cue and began exaggerated gestures to the love songs the folk artistes were singing. Suyodhana grinned at his friend.

Dhristadyumna ran over to his sister and dragged her towards the group. "This is Karna, King of Anga," he said, introducing him first. He then named the others.

Draupadi bowed formally to Karna and joined her hands in a *namaste*. Karna looked at her lovely face, dark smooth skin, perfectly shaped red lips, and pearly white teeth, and let out a shaky breath. He had not expected to see her from such a close distance and stood awkwardly, not knowing what to say, his heart beating faster than the roll of the country drums around them. She stared at his face and he felt his skin burning wherever her eyes touched him. The trace of a smile lit her face, making it look even more angelic. Karna found it impossible to drag his eyes away. He kept gazing at her, not knowing what to do; not caring for the comments of his grinning friends. When the silence between them grew awkward, she bowed once more and returned to her seat. Aswathama pulled Karna back to their wild dancing. He tried to regain the joy of a few minutes before, but he could feel her eyes on him and his legs felt wooden.

"Soon there will be a *swayamvara*," Dhristadyumna said quietly in Karna's ear after the party had grown old and the beautiful night had begun greying. "I will ensure you get an invitation, Karna. Come again and win my sister's hand like a true warrior."

"Not while I am here to compete against him," Aswathama butted in.

Sushasana smacked the Brahmin on the head saying, "Fool! You wish to fight Karna? Are you sane?"

***

When they left Kampilya the next day, they were happy beyond words. Aswathama and Sushasana sang the rowdy songs they had learnt the night before, and Karna was lost in his own world where everything looked lovely and had her name written over it. When they passed a derelict village on the way, Karna insisted they stop. The lack of drinking water and the condition of its inhabitants was impossible to witness and then walk away from. Suyodhana ordered his soldiers to dig a well. It delayed them by another four days, but the happiness this act gave them and the villagers, was worth the delay. Aswathama mockingly wrote 'Draupadi's Well' on it when the masons had completed the wall. Karna knew it was useless to chide his happy-go-lucky Brahmin friend. He had no choice but to join in the laughter. Seeing Karna's happiness, Suyodhana was reminded of his own love. He yearned for Subhadra's touch. The thought of her smile was like a soothing caress on his tired body and kept him going until he entered the gates of Hastinapura.

People thronged both sides of the road to hail the victorious Prince. The procession entered the palace gates to cheering and applause. At the top of the flight of steps leading to the palace, Drona stood with his hands on his hips. Beside him stood the Pandavas, and a group of Brahmins, with Dhaumya at their head.

The Crown Prince went to Drona, bowed to his Guru, and said, "Sir, Panchala has been vanquished as per your wishes. The train with gifts is here, as you can see. Dhrupada repents the wrongs he has done you and..."

"Where is Dhrupada?" Drona asked frostily.

"Sir, he surrendered and sent these gifts for you. He will come to seek your pardon in person."

"Enough, Duryodhana! Gifts! *Pshaw*! Who needs his gifts? What are gifts to a Brahmin? I told you I do not care for material things. He insulted me and I wanted you to capture and bring him here, tied in chains, and throw him at my feet. Fool! You have sold the honour of your Guru for a few gold coins. Perhaps the Panchala army even defeated you and you looted some villages on the way back to present me with these 'gifts'. Your delay would thus be explained."

Trembling with rage, Drona rushed to the carts containing the gifts and kicked over a few pots. Coins rolled over the ground. He turned back to Suyodhana, still angry at what he considered the Prince's betrayal. "Since you insisted on taking this Suta and my foolish son with you, what else did you expect? Do any of you know how to even hold a weapon properly, let alone fight with it? You have insulted me. I will show you how warriors who follow the path of *dharma* behave, how disciples who respect their teacher, act. Arjuna!" Drona called. The Pandava Prince came forward and bowed. "Show this coward how to follow simple instructions. Bring me my foe. Make him crawl before me like a worm."

"Your wish is my command, Guru." Arjuna bowed again and blew his conch.

Before Suyodhana could react, hundreds of equestrian guards galloped towards them and took up combat positions. The five Pandavas ran, as if on cue, towards the cavalry and mounted quickly. They thundered past the shocked Suyodhana and his friends. More cavalry joined them and the hundreds turned into thousands as the imperial army of Hastinapura rushed towards unsuspecting Panchala, with Arjuna in the lead.

On either side of the road, the people who had begun dispersing after having cheered Suyodhana's return, regrouped and began cheering Arjuna. Dhaumya had been fanning the flame of patriotism to new heights and everyone was excited about the way their country was dealing with a vassal kingdom. Within hours, Dhaumya had successfully spread rumours that the Panchala army had defeated Suyodhana and that Arjuna was now leading a new army to teach the proud Panchalas a lesson.

Arjuna's army descended on a sleeping Kampilya. Before the unsuspecting Panchalas understood what was happening, Arjuna had smashed the city defences, set the city on fire, and breached the palace fortress. Bhima stayed back in the city to supervise the looting and arson. The battle was soon over. Arjuna entered the King's chamber, woke the sleeping Dhrupada, and arrested him. Yudhishtra captured Dhristadyumna and the eunuch Shikandi. By noon the imperial army had begun marching back with King Dhrupada chained in a cart for all to see. His son Dhristadyumna and Shikandi, were also tied in similar fashion. The victorious procession rushed towards Hastinapura. Behind them, Kampilya lay in ruins, the shops and temples smouldering. Severed limbs and lifeless bodies lay scattered in the streets. The signs of invasion and defeat were written all over the unfortunate land.

By evening, Arjuna's victorious army entered Hastinapura and the people thronged the Royal highway to see the captured Panchala King and heap abuse on him. They hailed Arjuna and his brave brothers, who had accomplished what the Crown Prince had failed to do. The greatest archer in the world had saved the honour of the kingdom and was dragging their enemy through the streets. The citizens felt proud. Some expressed it by rushing to the captured foes and spitting in their faces, others by flinging abuse. A few bold ones managed to punch the captives. The procession swelled with dancing young men, drummers, and a group of Brahmins hailing the victory of *dharma* and shouting slogans in favour of Arjuna and Yudhishtra.

Drona stood on the veranda near the main entrance of the palace. On the grand steps leading to the lawn and garden, stood more Brahmins, holding flowers and scented water. As Arjuna and his brothers dismounted and walked towards their Guru, they chanted holy *mantras* and showered them with petals. Yudhishtra fell at Guru Drona's feet, and then at Dhaumya's.

Choked with emotion, Drona was unable to utter a single word. He hugged Arjuna. "My beloved disciple, what more can a Guru ask?" he kept repeating, as his tears of joy wet Arjuna's broad shoulders.

Dhaumya raised his hands and the drumming stopped. The Brahmins gulped on their unfinished *mantras*. "This is a proud moment in the history of Hastinapura. Today, our boys have proved to the world that our kingdom will not tolerate any insult to Brahmins. Prince Yudhishtra here has taken his first step towards upholding our eternal *dharma*. He is not a mere Prince; he is the embodiment of *dharma*. From today, let him be known as *Dharmaputra* Yudhishtra, Son of Dharma."

Dhaumya raised his hands and the holy *mantras* resumed as the eldest Pandava bowed his head in humility. The crowd gave a huge cheer and someone cried out: *Jaya Jaya Dharmaputra Yudhishtra*. The words echoed from thousands of throats. The drums began beating again. Dowager Kunti came running from her chamber and edged her way towards her sons. She turned to wave to the crowd, who roared back.

"Where is that evil man who dared insult our Guru?" asked Dhaumya.

Arjuna and Bhima rushed to the cart where the bound Dhrupada sat. Bhima grabbed the defeated King of Panchala by the throat, and with Arjuna leading the way, he pulled and shoved him towards Drona. Nakula and Sahadeva dragged Dhristadyumna and Shikandi in similar fashion. The Priests spat on the captives as they passed them on the steps. Bhima threw the Panchala King at Guru Drona's feet.

The Guru laughed loudly, slapping his thigh. As his old classmate and friend fell on his face, the Guru kicked him. The crowd cheered. "*Ha ha...* now who is at whose feet, you arrogant Kshatriya? Who is the supplicant and who the benefactor? You rogue... remember the day I came to you for help and how you treated me? This kick is for your arrogance and this one is for your pride…"

Suyodhana and his friends finally broke through the ranks of the Priests and reached the Guru just as the horns sounded in the familiar blast announcing the arrival of the Grand Regent. The chariot carrying Bhishma and the Prime Minister entered the palace gates and the crowd grew silent. People moved to make way and the Grand Regent ascended the steps quickly. He stopped near the Panchala King, coiled into a foetal position to protect himself from Drona's vicious kicks. Drona paled when he saw Bhishma's rigid face and burning eyes.

The Grand Regent lifted the fallen man and was shocked to see it was Dhrupada, one of their prominent vassal Kings. "Can anyone explain what is going on here?" Bhishma asked, his voice cold with contempt. Everyone trembled in fear. No one wished to face the Grand Regent when he was angry.

Dhaumya knew the responsibility for an explanation had fallen onto his shoulders since Drona showed no inclination to speak. He moved forward. "Your Excellency, this man insulted a Brahmin, and we are meting out just punishment."

"Insulted a *Brahmin*? Do you know who this man is? He is the King of Panchala, and you are treating him like a criminal. Who did he insult and when?" No one dared answer. Bhishma drew his sword and cut the ropes binding the King. He ordered the eunuch and the Prince of Panchala be freed as well. Then he turned to Dhaumya. "Tell me who insulted whom? When and how?"

"Sir, he insulted our Raja Guru Drona."

"When?"

Dhaumya looked at Drona, who finally came forward. "Your Excellency, he insulted me seventeen years ago, when I went to beg for his aid."

"*What*! Guru, is this is a joke? He insulted you seventeen years ago and now you capture him using the Hastinapura army and destroy our relationship with a vassal state? Who ordered the attack on a friendly State without my permission? You have many questions to answer, Drona."

Dhrupada laughed loudly at hearing this, which further provoked the Brahmins. "*Adharma*! *Adharma*! Does the pride of a Brahmin have no value in this land? Shame on Hastinapura," they chorused, gaining courage in the anonymity of the crowd.

Bhishma ignored them and moved menacingly close to Drona. The Guru unsheathed his sword, ready to take on the Grand Regent and become a martyr to *dharma*.

Kunti ran between the two men. "*Pitamaha*, why are you ruining my sons' reputation like this? Is it because they have done what the Crown Prince could not?"

There were many retorts the Grand Regent could have made but he was a gentleman. Kunti was aware he would never address a woman rudely in public or in private. Bhishma shook his head in despair. Grabbing the King of Panchala's hands, he said, "Your Highness, accept my apologies for what has transpired. I have no words to express my regret and sorrow. Please accompany me to the *sabha*. Let me see what I can do to right this wrong committed by Hastinapura."

With a heavy heart, Bhishma walked to the *sabha*, followed by the others. The showdown began. Drona offered his resignation. Bhishma angrily responded saying he would have been fired anyhow. The entire assembly of nobles rose in protest, as an amused Dhrupada and his sons watched how Government was run in Hastinapura, the de-facto capital of India. Prince Suyodhana was summoned and given a public tongue-lashing by the Grand Regent, for forgetting his *raja dharma* in leading their forces against a vassal state without provocation. When the Prince tried to defend himself saying he had orders from King Dhritarashtra, the Grand Regent turned to look at the monarch in disbelief. Bhishma asked the Prince where his common sense had gone, reminding him that he was duty bound to disobey orders if they went against what was right. Suyodhana remained silent. In the depths of his heart, he believed he should have refused to follow the Guru's orders in the first instance. He accepted he had made an error of judgement.

But Drona refused to be cowed. When he found he had the support of the Brahmins, he remained defiant and stubborn, refusing to apologize. The most he would say was that he would consider Dhrupada a friend again, now that he had been paid back in his own coin. The incident was best forgotten.

Bhishma then summoned Prince Yudhishtra, who calmly maintained that he had followed *dharma* and done his duty without worrying about the results. When asked, Arjuna said the same thing. He added, that as a disciple of Drona, his first duty was towards his respected teacher and what was due to him. The nobles received the statements of both Pandava Princes with applause.

Bhishma looked helplessly at Dhrupada. A mocking smile played on the Panchala King's lips. Bhishma knew he looked foolish. He enquired about the gifts the Panchala King had sent Drona, and ordered them returned immediately. Dhaumya interjected to say that gifts given to a Brahmin could not be taken back. However, Drona could distribute them among the Brahmins present since he was an ascetic and did not care for material things. Bhishma exploded in rage, banging his clenched fist on the armrest of his chair. The situation was turning ugly.

Then King Dhrupada stood up to say he would not take back anything he had gifted. The Brahmins accepted his statement with loud cheers and praised the generous King of Panchala. Dhrupada folded his hands and bowed to the Brahmins who had spat on him just a short while ago. They blessed him with long life.

Bhishma felt sickened by the farce playing out before him. He dismissed the *sabha* and walked tiredly back to his chamber. He did not wait to see

Drona approach Dhrupada and hug him. As Bhishma walked past, Shikandi drew an imaginary line across his throat and smirked. Immersed in his own thoughts, the Grand Regent did not see the gesture, but Vidhura saw the hatred in those glassy eyes and shuddered. He placed himself protectively between the eunuch and the Grand Regent, and breathed a sigh of relief when Bhishma was safely past Shikandi. The Grand Regent was tired and heartsick. Hanging his head in defeat, he entered his chambers and waited for Vidhura to close the heavy doors.

***

In the *sabha*, the Panchala King accepted Drona's invitation and everyone proceeded towards the banqueting hall to eat and drink in the name of friendship rediscovered. Suyodhana and his friends were standing near the doorway, animatedly discussing the turn of events, when someone tapped Aswathama on the shoulder. The young Brahmin turned to see the burning eyes of Dhristadyumna staring into his own. With all the venom he could muster, Dhristadyumna hissed, "You untrustworthy Brahmin! For a while, I thought you were my friend. See how you have treated my father. We trusted you and gave you gifts to avoid a war, and you repaid our hospitality by dragging us like criminals in chains through the streets. Mark my words you cowards, you and your great Guru will pay dearly for this. Ask the old nut to check his throat every day. One morning he will have no head."

Aswathama grabbed the Panchala Prince by the throat. "Another word about my father and you are a dead man, you bastard."

Dhristadyumna's hands wrapped themselves round Aswathama's throat in reply. The two young warriors struggled to choke each other to death. Suyodhana and Karna rushed between them, struggling to push the duo apart.

"My apologies, my friend. Let the past remain in the past," Suyodhana said to Dhristadyumna.

In reply, the Panchala Prince spat viciously on the floor and walked away. Aswathama tried to follow him with his sword drawn, but the strong arms of Karna restrained him. Shikandi stood behind them, watching the drama with a leer on his face. Once Dhristadyumna had walked away, the eunuch went up to Suyodhana. In an effeminate manner, Shikandi touched the Crown Prince. "Prince, my brother wants Drona. But whom does this beautiful lady want? Tell me, my handsome Prince. You do not know? How unfortunate. Well, I want your Granduncle. I am in love with the most eligible bachelor in India. Wait till I get Bhishma," Shikandi said in a high-pitched voice, imitating a coy woman. Then he walked away, blowing a kiss towards Suyodhana and caressing Karna's cheek in passing. Karna shuddered at the touch. Suyodhana shook his head in dismay. The circle of hatred was growing bigger and bigger around them.

***

Inside the Grand Regent's chambers, two worried men discussed the future course of action. Bhishma wished Kunti and her sons to leave Hastinapura. He was angry about what had happened in his absence and all Vidhura's attempts to pacify the Grand Regent were in vain. He said, Vidhura did not understand the consequences of Drona's folly; that Hastinapura was fortunate the Southern Confederate was still incapacitated without Parashurama, or else the act of insulting a powerful vassal State would have given them an excellent opportunity to move in. He was sad about the way caste was slowly creeping back into the northern kingdoms and wanted to cut down Dhaumya's influence. Kunti and the Pandavas had become a rallying point for the conservatives and to break this dangerous trend, they had to go.

When the old man's anger had cooled a little, Vidhura put forward his idea. He suggested the Pandavas and their mother could be moved to the village of Varanavata, which was sufficiently far away from the capital. Bhishma agreed and asked the Prime Minister to arrange it. Vidhura reminded him the village was backward and did not have suitable dwellings for the members of the Royal family.

"Spare no expense, Vidhura, else Kunti will be telling everyone I have treated her badly. Build a palace but do it quickly. Who can you get to do the job efficiently?"

"Sir, I have a man in mind. He is efficient and fast, but…"

"But what? Call him and start," Bhishma ordered impatiently.

"Sir, he is very corrupt and…"

"*Bah*! Corrupt… who is not corrupt in this land? Let him skim some money and get fat, but let the work start today. Go on, call him!" Bhishma snapped his fingers.

Vidhura bowed and went to do the Grand Regent's bidding.

***

"I am sure she is behind it, Krishna," Kunti said, handing a tumbler of buttermilk to her nephew. "The King is not that evil. But for *her* manipulations, he would not have asked us to move to Varanavata. Neither would *Pitamaha*. She and her brother are determined to ruin our country."

"Do not blame Gandhari for everything that happens to you, Aunt. About Shakuni though, I agree." Krishna was sitting on the windowsill, his fingers drumming in tune to some song in his head.

"When you sent for me, I came rushing from Dwaraka, fearing something terrible. But it is better for everyone if you and your sons move away for a while. The Grand Regent is right in sending you to Varanavata."

"I smell a conspiracy, Krishna and I am afraid. I have no one to turn to except you. Even Arjuna has fallen out of favour with *Pitamaha* after conquering Panchala. Someone is poisoning *Pitamaha*'s mind; maybe that Vidhura."

"Vidhura is nobody's enemy, nor is he anyone's friend. He is the only man without any selfish interests." Krishna smiled at Kunti.

"Then why does he not tell *Pitamaha* that Arjuna was only doing his duty to his Guru?"

Krishna took a sip from the tumbler and put it back on the sill carefully. He smiled at Kunti and said, "Arjuna always does his duty. That is what I like about him."

"I have not brought up my sons like Gandhari. Duryodhana used to be a sweet child, but just see what he has grown up to become – no respect for his elders, no respect for the scriptures, and no respect for traditions. What can we expect from the sons of a foreign woman?"

"Aunt, strategically, you made a mistake by allowing that Suta boy to drift towards Duryodhana. The Crown Prince has become a hero now. Either that boy should have been captured and handed over to the Confederate or he should have been brought over to our side on the day of the Grand Ceremony. Before I could do anything, Karna had become King of Anga. I never expected Duryodhana to be so cunning. I have to admit it was a master stroke." Krishna looked out of the window. He remained silent for some time, immersed in his thoughts. Then he turned back to face his aunt. "Are you feeling well, Aunt? Why do you look so pale? Are you alright?"

"Nothing... nothing... It is just the weather," Kunti said, fanning her flushed face with a palm fan.

"That Suta is going to be trouble," Krishna said, peering at his aunt intently. Kunti moved to pick up the tumbler, avoiding Krishna's eyes. "Do not worry, Aunt. Nothing will happen to your sons. I will always be there for them. There is no one dearer to me than Arjuna. When the time comes, I will steady his hands. The way Duryodhana is behaving, I am sure we will be dragged into a war soon."

"I hate the idea of war. If only..."

"A war is necessary. Not that I am a warmonger or unaware of its terrible consequences. But the very structure of society is being shaken by Duryodhana and his friends. There is nothing noble about the caste system, yet *chaturvarna* is something that gives our society strength. What Duryodhana proposes will lead to chaos. There will be no specialists left if anyone can become anything. Society will become weak. People will not know what their duties are and there will be unhealthy competition. It will become a dog-eat-dog world. I believe I have been born with a purpose – to preserve our social order."

"Krishna, I do not have the wisdom to understand your thoughts. I can only request you for one thing. My sons and I are alone in the world. Our enemies are powerful. The King and the Queen hate us and Duryodhana will stoop to any level to eliminate us. I want my son to sit on the throne of Hastinapura at any cost. Will you help me achieve that? More importantly, I do not want any of Gandhari's sons to rule while I am alive. I have suffered enough."

Krishna stood up to leave. "I have to leave now, Aunt. I must pay my respects to the Grand Regent and be off to Dwaraka early tomorrow morning. It is better you accept the King's offer and move to Varanavata. I do not rule out the possibility of a conspiracy to get rid of you, but we will find a way out. To fight Duryodhana you need powerful friends. Unfortunately, Arjuna has made Dhrupada an enemy for Guru Drona's sake. Let me see whether something can be done there. I will drop in at Panchala on my way back and try to make amends. Go to Varanavata. Play the game. Be ruthless in your execution. Do not hesitate. Survival is the biggest *dharma*. The scriptures say, nothing is a sin during danger. It is called *apat dharma*. Think and you will find a way out."

"Be with us, Krishna. We do not have anyone else."

"Of course, Aunt. I will be with you and your five sons to the last." Krishna touched his aunt's feet and moved towards the door.

"Krishna, I have… No, it is nothing…"

Krishna bowed and went away. Somehow, Krishna's promise that he would protect her five sons failed to calm Kunti's turbulent mind.

***

A few days later, in the dead of night, the Gandhara Prince woke with a jolt. Someone was gently tapping on his door. Cursing the interruption to his sleep, he fumbled for his dagger, found it, and hid it in the folds of his *dhoti*. He picked up the small lamp from the table and cautiously opened the door. Purochana stood outside. "What the hell?" Shakuni cursed again, thinking the bureaucrat had come to collect his payment.

Purochana walked in and sat down on Shakuni's bed. He pummelled the soft pillows and said, "Nice place you have here, foreigner."

"What do you want, buffoon?" Shakuni asked grumpily.

"*Aha*, spare me that tone, foreigner. You will hug and shower me with kisses when you hear what I have come to say. No cheating, please, like the last time. I want 1000 gold coins and three times that for any action on it, okay foreigner?"

Shakuni instinctively knew it was important. This serpent would not have dared wake him so late at night otherwise. "Agreed," he said and took the coins from a shelf, counted twice, and threw them onto the bed.

Purochana took his time counting the money, while Shakuni fidgeted. Then he told the Gandhara Prince the news. Vidhura had given Purochana the task of building a palace for the Pandavas and the Grand Regent had sanctioned a huge amount from the treasury for its construction. Despite himself, Shakuni let out a yelp of joy. Then an idea struck the Prince like a flash. He explained to Purochana what he wanted done. Purochana replied that building a palace of lac was too risky. But before the new day dawned, Shakuni had settled the deal for 10,000 gold coins. Purochana left for Varanavata to begin work, without even performing his morning ablutions. His fortunes had changed at last.

Bubbling with excitement, Shakuni could not sleep. He took out his dice and threw them onto the table crying, "Six". They spun and came to rest on double threes. He laughed in delight. The dice were rolling nicely. If things went as planned, the Pandavas would be trapped in a highly inflammable palace. But he would ensure they escaped unhurt. He did not want them to die. That would have been far too easy. In that scenario, Suyodhana would ascend the throne in due course and his unfortunate cousins would soon be forgotten. He wanted the Pandavas to escape with the knowledge that their cousins were trying to murder them. The conspiracy to murder the Pandavas had to reach the ears of that fool Vidhura. Shakuni was sure the conscientious Prime Minister would take care of the rest.

As dawn inched across the eastern sky, painting the horizon saffron, Shakuni turned his back on the glorious sight and fell to his knees for his morning prayers. Turning West, he prayed for the glory of his motherland. Things could not have looked better for the foreigner.

20 House Of Lac

VIDHURA SURPRISED PARSHAVI BY sending a messenger to Bhishma, asking for leave. When her husband announced they were going to visit the place where their house was to be built, she could not believe her ears. The boys were excited to have their father with them for the picnic and the humble home of the Prime Minister of Hastinapura was filled with the enthusiastic yells of his ten-year-olds. When they walked to the gate, they were surprised to see Bhishma's official chariot waiting.

"Swami, the Grand Regent has sent this for your use." The charioteer bowed respectfully to the Prime Minister.

Vidhura wanted to protest it was a private trip and not an official one, but knew he could not return the chariot without offending the Grand Regent. Parshavi climbed in, pulling her boys into the luxurious interior. Vidhura hesitated, but his family was already inside, so he climbed in and the chariot moved forward.

Parshavi said to her husband, "Do not look so glum. You are not committing a crime. It is not your official chariot. The Grand Regent knows you well, so he has sent his own." She tried to close her ears to the ruckus created by her sons. When they reached their destination, Parshavi was shocked. "Are we going to build our house in this jungle?" she asked her husband as the boys ran out to jump into the stream nearby. There were hundreds of butterflies fluttering around and cuckoos answered each other somewhere above them. Beyond the excited cries of her boys, she could hear the music of crickets and the chirping of birds. A fragrant breeze ruffled her hair and then fled to play with the leaves.

"Don't you like it?" Vidhura asked.

Parshavi was close to tears. This untamed spot was far from the bustling streets of Hastinapura, from the shops and markets. How was she to run a household if Vidhura shifted them to this jungle? It was all right for a picnic, but...

"I am going to build the house with my own hands." Vidhura was rushing around, eagerly pointing out where the kitchen would be, and where his study.

Parshavi smiled, feigning enthusiasm to indulge him. By the evening, he had involved the boys in his project and it turned out to be one of the most beautiful days in their lives. On the way back, Vidhura kept speaking of their dream house. Parshavi listened without interrupting as the chariot sped along the busy streets of Hastinapura.

After Vidhura had seen the boys fall asleep, something he could rarely do, Parshavi asked him, "Why don't you talk to the town architect and use the palace masons?"

"Parshavi, we are building our home, not a public building. It would be wrong to use my position for personal gain. Besides, I want to build it with my own hands. When it is done, you will be thankful we did not go to any architect."

She knew the house would never be built, not in her lifetime. That was the last time her husband spent the whole day with them. He would sneak away to the jungle whenever he could find some spare time and work on the house; refusing help from his subordinates and advice from the experts. He toiled in the hot sun and freezing cold. The boys accompanied him a few times and then lost interest. Every monsoon the rains would bring down whatever he had built. Vidhura would curse the lack of time, not his skill, and sulk for a few days. Then he would start building the house again. The Prime Minister's never-ending house construction soon became a running joke in Hastinapura.

***

Ekalavya was in a bad mood. His aunt had quarrelled with him again. She had been at her irritating best ever since he had resumed his practice with the bow. He knew she was right in blaming him for ignoring his cousins and her. After the loss of his thumb, he had slowly emerged from his depression and begun taking care of the family by working as a scavenger, the only job open to a low caste like him. He detested the work, which involved cleaning toilets and drains and carrying stinking human waste in baskets on his head and dumping it far from the posh homes of the nobles. He always felt unclean, no matter how many times he bathed. People ran from him as though the mere sight of his dark body was polluting.

Dogs and pigs walked in the streets and no one cared. But the same streets were cleaned with holy dung after Ekalavya walked past. His very footsteps were polluting. He hated his life, his fate, his country, and his job. But he knew it was either this or death by starvation. He had remained resigned to his stinking life until he saw what happened to Karna. It gave him hope that there was a future for people who worked hard and followed their dreams, as long as men like Prince Suyodhana existed. From that day, he was relentless in his pursuit to regain his skill in archery, determined not to let the double handicaps of caste and the lack of a thumb, stand in his way. Soon, hunger crept back into the poor Nishada's home, but the family was powerless to stop the scavenger challenging his fate.

The reason for the morning's tiff was that his aunt wished to leave Hastinapura and migrate to a distant village called Varanavata. Ekalavya wanted to remain in Hastinapura. Here, there was a chance that someday the Crown Prince would notice him and perhaps he too, would become an important person like Karna. What would he do in a backward village like Varanavata, he asked his aunt? She bemoaned the fact that he had stopped caring for his cousins and that she was tired of trying to feed him. He was always playing with his bow and arrow instead of going to work. No one was willing to give her work, even as a house cleaner, since Ekalavya was a scavenger. How was the family to survive if he continued with his insane obsession? She kept punctuating her sorrow by hitting her chest and forehead with her fists.

Ekalavya screamed at her, saying she was trying to live off him. He cruelly added that while he carried rich people's shit, she and her fat children ate and remained idle. He regretted the words as soon as they were spoken, but it was too late. His aunt did not reply. She wiped her tears, tightened the small cloth bundle that contained all their worldly possessions, and cleaned her youngest child as best she could. She did not heed Ekalavya's apologies and pleadings, and walked out of the thatched hut with her children and her pathetic bundle. Ekalavya ran behind her, trying to persuade her to stay, but she said she was going to Varanavata to see if life offered anything better. Ekalavya fell at her feet saying he was sorry.

She gently placed a work worn hand on his head and mumbled a prayer. Then she said to him, "I am not angry with you, Ekalavya. But I realize it is time for us to part. You are a grown man and I have done my duty to my husband's brother. I have my own children to feed. I cannot be a leech, sucking your blood. I did not expect anything when I brought you up. Now, there is nothing I can do to aid you in your ambition, other than pray. May Lord Shiva be with you always. May your dreams come true. If you wish to see your cousins or me, come to Varanavata. I hear the Grand Regent has built a great palace for the righteous Pandavas there, and the place is developing fast. They say the eldest Pandava is now called Dharmaputra Yudhishtra, and that he is the most truthful man in the world. The Pandavas are friends of Krishna, the *avatar* of Lord Vishnu. I am sure Varanavata will be a much better place for us than Hastinapura. This place has been cruel to us. Here everyone treats us like worms. In a place ruled by the Son of Dharma and blessed by the good wishes of Krishna, I am sure there will be some space for a poor Nishada woman and her five sons."

Ekalavya hugged his cousins one by one. The eldest was just a few years younger than Ekalavya. The boy held his head high while saying goodbye to his cousin. But when Ekalavya held the youngest, he broke down in tears. The boy was nearly thirteen and Ekalavya had started training him in archery. The lad showed great promise. His aunt began walking and the elder children reluctantly followed. Ekalavya took a small knife from his waist and handed it over to the young boy, who hesitated a moment, took it and then ran to join the others. The Nishada watched his only relatives in the world become dots on the distant horizon and vanish from his world.

***

The woman and her sons walked for many days before they reached Varanavata. The village was developing into a town, but she was rather disappointed. She had expected a larger place. The only remarkable building was the huge palace, which looked new and luxurious. How big a place did a family of six need, she wondered as she stood gazing at the dome glistening in the sun. She was afraid to walk on the main road. She was sure they would be chased away as unclean.

The youngest boy pulled at her wrist, wanting to have a better look at the palace. "Mother, let us walk on the road. Why are we walking so far from it? I want to see the palace."

"Who do you think you are, son? Are you a Brahmin or a Prince to walk on the main road in broad daylight? We are Untouchables and we will pollute the road."

But the boy would not give up. "How will they know, mother? We are not in Hastinapura now. Nobody knows us here."

"They will know by the colour of our skin, son."

The boy looked down at his dark skin and became silent. It was not something he could change. The woman did not know what to do. They were all hungry. Six days before, they had raided a waste pit near a temple, in the dead of night. There were many leftovers from a feast held for the Brahmins the previous day, by some pious merchant, as insurance against his sins and avarice. The eldest boy had stood with a stick in his hand, pushing away the growling street dogs as his brothers and mother scavenged for food in the pit. They had to hurry, as the Priests would be coming soon to open the temple for morning prayers. If anyone saw them near the holy precincts, there would have been hell to pay. They collected as much of the leftovers as they could. The mother was careful to leave some for the street dogs. She knew the pain of hunger. The food had sustained them for a while, but in the last two days, they had not found anything to eat.

The Nishada family walked past the magnificent palace and reached the river flowing behind it. They stepped into the waters of the Ganga and drank until their bellies almost burst. Fish of many shades swam around their ankles and they soon forgot their hunger. The children's shouts of delight as they chased the fish brought tears to their mother's eyes. For a while, she too forgot the scorching earth behind her and the misery it harboured.

"Mother," someone called.

The woman was shocked to hear herself so addressed. She turned, terrified to see a noble-looking man standing with his palms joined in a *namaste*. She involuntarily moved back, knowing she was closer to him than the caste rules permitted. Her sons climbed out of the water and the youngest ran to her, his face was pale with fear.

"Devi," said the stranger, dressed in fine silk and jewellery, addressing the Untouchable woman in her tattered clothes. "I am Yudhishtra, eldest son of King Pandu. My mother, Kunti Devi, wishes to see you. Will you come to our home with your sons?"

"Swami, I do not think you have understood who we are. We are the lowliest of all castes. How can we pollute your palace with our steps?" the Nishada woman asked.

"Mother," the eldest Pandava said, ignoring the look of surprise on her face at being addressed in this way, "the Lord says that service to the poor is the greatest service of all. Come and bless our home."

The eldest boy shrugged his shoulders and started walking towards the palace. His three brothers followed. They were thrilled at the chance to see a real palace and real Princes. The woman looked at her youngest son, gazing up at her eagerly, and then at the kind expression on the Prince's face, and nodded her assent. The woman followed Yudhishtra, her youngest son beside her. She could not believe her luck and smiled at her boys' excited chatter.

A shepherd, who was standing and watching, moved towards the woman and whispered in her ear, "Don't go woman. It is a trap. Do not trust the high and mighty." Then he turned and walked away.

She stood for a moment, confused, but her sons kept walking. Finally, she shrugged and followed the Son of Dharma. As they neared the palace, the guards bowed respectfully to the Prince. She saw their eyes enlarge in surprise at the group of Untouchables walking into the palace behind the Prince. She could almost hear their silent exclamations and lifted her head with some pride. But as the Prince ascended the steps leading to the main entrance, she hesitated. Should they follow him? What if they touched something and polluted it and they ordered her arrest? Yudhishtra turned and smiled. Behind him, the woman could see the lovely face of Dowager Queen Kunti, standing with her handsome sons. Kunti folded her hands in greeting to the Untouchable woman, and her sons bowed.

Before the Nishada woman could recover from the shock of these nobles bowing to her, Arjuna came running down and caught hold of her eldest son's wrist. She wanted to warn the warrior that her son was a Nishada and he should not touch low castes, but her boy smiled confidently up at the greatest archer in the world and ran up the steps behind him. Her other sons followed. Before she knew it, her children were chatting animatedly with the noble Princes. The woman slowly climbed the steps and stood before Dowager Kunti, her head bowed in respect.

"You have blessed us with your presence Devi, please come inside. We have arranged a chamber for you and your sons." Kunti led her to a room larger than the biggest home the Nishada woman had ever lived in. It had a huge bed and there were bowls of flowers, fruits and delicacies, the likes of which she had never seen. Even though she was starving, there was so much food before her that she thought they would not finish it all even if they lived to be a hundred.

"Devi Kunti, what have I done to deserve so much kindness?" the woman asked through her tears.

An enigmatic smile appeared on Kunti's face. "You are serving a great cause. You and your five sons are serving *dharma*."

"What is *dharma*?" the Untouchable woman asked the mother of five great warriors.

"Perhaps you will not understand it just now but do not worry about it. Eat and rest." Kunti smiled again.

At that moment, the youngest Nishada boy ran into the room. When he saw Kunti, he hesitated a moment and then ran to his mother. She could feel her son shivering in fear and smiled weakly at the noble woman who was frowning at the child's reaction. The Nishada woman wracked her brains to find an excuse for her son's irrational behaviour. But before she could, the room filled with the laughter of her other sons. They ran into the room shouting in merriment, overturning a flower vase here, and breaking some expensive figurines there, as the bulky Bhima chased them. The woman looked fearfully at Kunti and was relieved to see that she too was enjoying the antics of her sons.

The boys saw the delicacies spread on the table and began eating ravenously. Kunti smiled once more and called her huge son to her. Bhima desperately wanted to join his newfound friends in eating the delicacies and sulked over the denied treat. He picked up a few treats, hiding them in the folds of his *dhoti*.

"Sleep well. We will speak tomorrow," Kunti said to the grateful Nishada woman as she left the room.

Bhima looked longingly at the table where the Untouchables were attacking the food like hungry hyenas. Sighing in frustration, he followed his mother out.

She was waiting for him outside. "Throw away those sweets you have taken."

"But mother…" Bhima sheepishly brought forth the hidden sweets.

"Fool! Don't you know they are laced with drugs? How will I ever drive some sense into your head?" Kunti grabbed the sweets from his hands and threw them out of a window.

**

The Nishada woman did not hear the argument between Kunti and her son. She held herself back until they left, then joined her sons in satiating her hunger. There was a faintly bitter taste to the food, but she ignored it. She had tasted worse, having often fed on stinking throwaways during her miserable life. With every bite, she thanked her benefactor, praying to God to give Kunti and her sons' long life and happiness. She did not hear the small click of the latch, locking her and her children into the luxurious room. The lucky Untouchable and her children continued eating, blissfully unaware of having been trapped in this heaven, while downstairs; their benefactors took an important decision regarding *dharma*.

**

"Brother, I feel it is wrong. They are innocent and..." Arjuna was trying to reason with his eldest brother.

Yudhishtra looked at his mother, who shook her head in despair. Bhima sat dreaming about food, not caring for the intense debate going on. He was a lucky man. He did not think too much and did whatever his mother or brothers commanded. The whole debate about *dharma* simply bored him. But Arjuna never gave into anything without an argument. The twins sat to one side, discussing women and wine. Bhima moved towards them, to listen to their far more interesting conversation.

"Arjuna, these Untouchables lead miserable lives. We are doing them a great good by allowing them to die for a worthy cause. They will thus be born as Brahmins in their next life." Yudhishtra tried to maintain his composure while convincing his obdurate brother.

"The youngest is barely thirteen. It is cruel to trap these innocent people like animals, with food as bait," Arjuna retorted.

"Son," Kunti finally said in a tired voice. "We were lucky to get early warning that Duryodhana has hatched a plan to burn us alive here. Had your Uncle Vidhura not warned us, imagine what could have happened! Every moment we remain here is dangerous. We acted on Vidhura's message and checked the walls – they are indeed made of lac and they will catch fire faster than a bundle of dry hay. I always thought Vidhura was against us, but this shows we cannot fathom God's deep and mysterious ways. It was His will that this mother and her five sons arrived to act as decoys for our 'death'. Besides, remember your Gurus teaching you about *Apat dharma*. Nothing is considered wrong if it is in self-preservation. Who are we to question His will? Dhaumya will be waiting for us at the *ghat* with a boat. If we do not act tonight, it may be too late. Tomorrow, Duryodhana's men are planning to torch this palace and roast us alive. But we will outsmart them and do it today."

Arjuna shook his head in disagreement and appealed to Yudhishtra, ignoring his mother's words. "Brother, if we are sure Suyodhana is behind this, let us fight him like Kshatriyas, and defeat him in the accepted manner."

Yudhishtra exchanged glances with his mother. After a long pause, he said in a soft voice, "We have to outwit that evil man and go into hiding until we gain some powerful friends. We cannot go to Hastinapura, as the Grand Regent is not pleased with us. We must do this Arjuna. We do not have a choice. Without six charred bodies as proof of our deaths, Duryodhana's spies will keep hunting us. Let the world think we are dead when they see the unrecognizable bodies of the Nishada woman and her five children. Think only of your duty and do not worry about the consequences. They will die for a great cause, Arjuna. Be proud to be the torchbearer of *dharma*."

"Brother," Sahadeva interrupted, "there will be five bodies but the youngest child is too small. It will give rise to suspicion."

"He is right," Kunti said, regretting not having thought through all the details. "Yudhishtra, how many guards are there?"

"Seven, mother."

"Order a feast for them inside the palace," Kunti said. "There will then be enough bodies to create confusion among the spies."

"That is disgusting! The guards were sent by the Grand Regent for our protection." Arjuna stood up abruptly.

"Arjuna," said Yudhishtra, his patience wearing thin, "what is their primary duty as guards? To protect us from danger. If a situation arises when our lives are under threat, is it not their *dharma* to protect us, even at the cost of their own lives? What is wrong or disgusting about them laying down their lives for us? They will just be doing their duty as per our scriptures; nothing is more sacred than dying while doing one's duty. Such people reach the paradise of Lord Vishnu. In fact, we are helping their souls leave this miserable world and reach Vaikunta."

"But…"

"Arjuna, enough! Do not talk like your cousin Duryodhana," Kunti also stood up, ending the argument.

Arjuna knew he was defeated. He was a mere warrior, whereas his eldest brother was a learned man. He never uttered a lie, and all the Brahmins hailed him as the epitome of virtue and righteousness. Arjuna left the room, confused about the whole concept of *dharma*. Maybe one day someone would explain things to him clearly, so he would not feel the pinch of his conscience in doing what his mother suggested. He could hear the gentle snoring of the Nishada woman from what had once been his chamber. Arjuna stood staring at the Ganga flowing in the distance, trying to ignore his thoughts about a poor mother and her five children who had trusted them. Arjuna struggled with the impossible tangle of right and wrong. His brother and mother's arguments made no sense to him. They only created immense sadness in his confused mind.

The sun slowly sank into the holy waters of the Ganga and the river blushed red like a coy bride at the touch of her partner. As darkness fell over Varanavata and mist enveloped the rushes along the banks of the holy river, a dark figure alighted from the small boat he had been rowing. He looked at the brightly lit palace of the Pandavas in the distance and felt a sense of pride. It looked solid. No one would imagine it to be built of lac. With this project executed, he could now retire. He wanted to leave Hastinapura and migrate to a city where money was respected above other things. Perhaps Heheya, on the West coast, he thought dreamily. He also needed to dump his ugly wife and get a younger one. All the money he had made swindling the Government and the public, had been buried in a secret place. Until now, he had lived the life of enforced penury, imitating the lives of his honest colleagues in Government service. He knew his reputation was not good, but he was careful not to leave behind any proof of his activities. In this way, he had weathered many inquiries conducted by the Prime Minister's men. 'In another week I will retire and lead a wonderful life in the company of lovely damsels, in a sea-facing mansion in Heheya,' Purochana thought.

The Prince of Gandhara was a strange man. He had sponsored the entire building of the palace of lac for the Pandavas. It helped that Purochana could then sell the teak wood the Government had supplied in the black-market, making a fortune. Initially, Purochana thought Shakuni had hatched the plan to finish off the Pandavas and was terrified of the consequences, were his involvement to become known. He had been furious when he learned Shakuni had leaked hints about the palace of lac to that painfully honest Prime Minister. Once Vidhura had worked out there was a conspiracy, he had informed the Pandavas to be vigilant. It took a great deal of money for the Gandhara Prince to pacify the angry bureaucrat and convince him to complete the last step of the operation.

Purochana reassured himself that it would be the last operation he would undertake for that bastard. Shakuni's plan made no sense to him. The foreigner wanted him to lock the palace gates from outside and burn down the palace. Purochana had indignantly retorted that he was no murderer. The Prince then insisted that he open the gates at the right moment and allow the Pandavas to escape! This was not murder, just a prank, the foreigner assured him. Purochana was relieved. Once the deal was negotiated and settled, he began dreaming of his retirement. He could now live a life of luxury. Shakuni also offered him an additional incentive if he agreed to tell the Pandavas that the fire had been part of Suyodhana's conspiracy to get rid of them. Purochana readily agreed, sure, that the Pandavas would be grateful and even reward him for his loyalty.

Purochana planned to burn down the palace in the dead of the following night. For a day, he had to hide somewhere and observe the movements of the Pandavas. He was careful to keep to the shadows as he moved quietly towards the palace. The creepy silence that pervaded the place made him restless and jumpy. There was something sinister in the air. All his instincts screamed danger. He wanted to go back to the boat and row away but the thought of the huge incentive Shakuni had promised made him stand his ground. There were no guards at the entrance, which was strange. The lights had gone out and darkness enveloped the palace like a shroud. A bat flew close to Purochana's head and merged into the blackness of the night as he almost screamed.

Carefully, Purochana walked towards the palace, trying to keep his hands from shaking, silently cursing himself for having agreed to do this reckless mission for the foreigner. As he neared the palace, he could hear bits of conversation escaping from a shuttered window. He paused to listen but could not make sense of what was being said except for someone mentioning the name of the Chief Priest of Hastinapura. Purochana took out his knife and tried to prise open the window a little. He was still trying to do so when he heard a door open. Despite his bulk, he quickly moved back, just in time to see the silhouettes of a woman and four men emerge. They huddled together for a few minutes. Then a fifth man came out, holding a small lamp in his hand. The woman closed the door and checked the latch. She hurried away with four of the men. The man with the lamp waited until they were safely away and then took some rags and spread them around the walls and pillars of the veranda. He poured oil onto the rags from a large vessel he also carried. He stood still for a few seconds, as if in prayer, and then lit the fuel-soaked rags with the flame from his lamp. Turning, he ran towards his companions.

Purochana had forgotten for a moment that the palace he had made was designed to catch fire in an instant and burn down in a matter of minutes. An explosion threw the fat bureaucrat a few feet away, numbing him with shock. Before he knew what had happened, the palace of lac was engulfed in a roaring blaze. In the light of the burning palace, Purochana recognized the Pandavas running towards the river. He could also see a boat approaching the *ghat*. Hell! The Pandavas had escaped and outwitted him. The heat from the fire was tremendous and Purochana moved away, trying to make sense of what was happening. He thought of following the fleeing Pandavas, but his mission was not to kill them. It was better to escape and then claim he had accomplished his mission; get the money from the foreigner, and vanish.

He was about to turn back when a woman's scream of terror froze his feet. He could see people in flames, running inside the burning palace, desperately trying to get out. 'Unlucky bastards,' thought Purochana. He was turning to run when a child's scream changed everything. He was shaken to see a mother desperately trying to push a young boy through a window. Without thinking about the consequences, Purochana ran towards the burning palace instead of away from it.

"Swami, Swami…" the dark-skinned woman screamed out to him, her hair aflame, as she tried to shove her child through the burning window. The child was crying in fear and trying to slash the bars of the window with a small knife. The woman was obviously an Untouchable, but what the hell, a child was in danger and he had to do something, the bureaucrat thought frantically. Ignoring the heat, Purochana ran towards the window. 'Why am I risking my life for a dirty black urchin?' a part of his brain kept screaming. However, something he never even knew existed in him, made him remain rooted to the spot under the window.

Retribution for such acts of compassion is swift and sure and it came in the form of a wall crashing down from the burning palace. It was almost as if somebody high above had pushed it down in anger. It crashed down onto the civil servant, pinning him to the ground. He watched in horrified helplessness as fire engulfed the mother and child. As the flames crawled towards him and began devouring his corpulent body, Purochana thought sadly that not even his wife knew where he had hidden the money from a lifetime of swindling. 'I wasted my life and am now dying for a useless cause,' was his last thought.

***

Far away, a boat lay anchored in the waters of the Ganga. Dhaumya, a couple of his assistants, and Kunti and her five sons, watched the God of Fire devouring the palace. Arjuna sat staring at his feet.

"I feel terrible, but what choice did we have, Guru Dhaumya?" Kunti asked, looking at the burning palace.

Dhaumya turned to her. "Devi, nothing is considered wrong when your own life is in danger. But now you have to be careful. I hope the Great God Agni will have devoured all the bodies beyond recognition. Devi Kunti, it was a masterstroke to get those Nishadas. Leave the rest to me. We will spread the rumour that the Pandavas died in the fire. Keep a low profile until you gain powerful friends. Go to Panchala. There is going to be a *swayamvara* there. The King will be giving away the hand of his daughter to the best archer. Arjuna can easily win the beautiful Princess Draupadi as his wife."

Dhaumya's words did not evoke any response from the gloomy Arjuna. Kunti and the Head Priest exchanged glances while Yudhishtra shook his head in frustration. Somebody had to explain the complexities of *dharma* and *karma* to his naïve brother.

The Priest sat down beside Arjuna. The handsome Prince immediately stood up, rocking the boat. "We trapped them like animals!"

"Prince, you have nothing to fear. Think of them as celestial beings from the court of Indra, who came to earth because of a curse. They were born Untouchables because they had disrespected some Maharishi. But their dying in the cause of *dharma* has now expiated their sins. It is a good story and our fellow citizens will eagerly believe it. We will repeat it in all the temples and soon there will be fools dying to uphold its veracity." Everyone except Arjuna laughed at Dhaumya's words.

"I wonder what disguise we should take on?" Yudhishtra asked the Chief Priest.

Dhaumya replied without hesitation. "Disguise yourselves as Brahmins. You will then get food whenever you want, and respect, even if you don't want it."

As the sun peeped in the Eastern sky, they freed the boat and started rowing towards Panchala. Some way down the river, they passed a ferryboat, overflowing with people. The Pandavas did not see the dark young man sitting on the prow, bound for Varanavata. But the Nishada's eyes never left them.

21 SWAYAMVARA

EKALAVYA DISEMBARKED FROM THE BOAT at the *ghat* and like all the other passengers, his eyes went to the smouldering remains of the palace. He had heard rumours in the ferryboat that the Pandava palace at Varanavata had gone up in flames the previous night and that the Pandavas and their mother had died in the mishap. People were talking excitedly, pointing at the black smoke snaking its way towards heaven, and commenting on the misfortune of the poor Pandavas. Ekalavya followed the group walking towards the charred ruins. He was confused about the identity of the Priest he had seen in the boat they had passed, but he was almost sure the man sitting with bowed head had been Arjuna.

Ekalavya sorely missed his family when they left. He had tried to suppress the urge to visit them by punishing himself with long sessions of gruelling archery practice. But the impish smile of his little nephew kept haunting him. On an impulse, he started towards Varanavata, curious to see how they were faring in the land of the righteous Pandavas.

There was nothing much left of the palace when Ekalavya reached it. The air was foul with the smell of burnt flesh and hair, and there were puddles of dirty water here and there. People stood in groups, covering their noses with their hands to ward off the smell of death. A few guards were directing the *chandalas* in extricating the bodies. Some women screamed and cried out whenever a charred body was carried to the bullock cart waiting a few feet away. People sucked in their breaths as the *chandalas* brought out the body of a woman. Sniffs and sobs punctuated the uneasy silence of death. "Rajamata Kunti," someone murmured. The *chandalas* brought out the bodies of her sons. The crowd pushed and jostled to have a look at the dead Pandavas. Ekalavya thought the bodies looked too small to be those of the well-built Pandavas. But who knew what fire could do?

"Where is Bhima?" a man near Ekalavya wondered aloud. The next corpse to come from the smouldering ruins answered his question. "Bhima," the crowd cried, a hint of pleasure tinting their horror. A few women let out high-pitched wails. The bearers of the fat bureaucrat's charred body puffed and panted, struggling under the dead man's weight. They heaved the body into the cart, pushing it to one side to make room for more bodies. It was then that Ekalavya saw it. Something gleamed on the chest of one of the corpses. A shiver passed through the Nishada's heart and he became numb with grief. He wanted to deny it, but it was unmistakable. With terrified steps, he moved towards the cart in which they had piled the bodies.

Next to the dead Purochana, lay the charred body of Ekalavya's youngest nephew. Even in death, the boy held the knife Ekalavya had given him on parting. The Nishada's tears began to flow when he saw it held securely in those charred fingers. The *chandalas* had not noticed him until Ekalavya tried to pull the body out of the cart. They pushed him away. Whatever valuables the dead bodies carried were theirs by right. It was one of the few incentives for working in this macabre profession. They were already irritated that the bodies of the Princes and the Rajamata had not yielded anything worthwhile. They were not about to allow another Untouchable to rob them of their dues.

When Ekalavya rushed towards his nephew again, one of the *chandalas* hit him with his long stick. Others arrived and they thrashed the Nishada without mercy. Ekalavya was in no mood to fight and their blows were soothing in a way, making him temporarily forget the ache deep in his heart. When they were satisfied the Nishada would not wake up anytime soon, they dragged him like a sack and dumped him under a tree.

The cart carrying the bodies started with a jerk. It rolled on, creaking and squeaking on its journey towards the cremation grounds near the river. The head *chandala* hacked the knife from the corpse. It was a cheap knife but perhaps he could get a mug of country liquor for it, he thought as he tucked it into his waistband.

***

When Ekalavya returned to consciousness, it was late afternoon. The funeral pyres had died down some time ago and the Priests had gone home after a funeral feast hosted by the head of the village. The grief Ekalavya felt was more unbearable than the pain in his limbs. He tried to get up and was surprised to find two strong hands assisting him. He looked up at the dark face of a shepherd, smiling at him. "Aswasena," Ekalavya mumbled, as recognition dawned. His Naga friend from Takshaka's camp hugged him tight.

"I tried to warn her, but she did not listen," Aswasena said to the confused Nishada. "Ekalavya, our people have been watching you ever since you started practicing archery again. The great leader had given up on you after you sacrificed your thumb to please Guru Drona. But your determination to fight back has impressed Takshaka. He keeps talking about you in all his speeches and now you are a hero to all the young Nagas in camp. He wants to meet you. He does not bear any ill will towards you for deserting the cause. He always said you would come back once you learnt there was no future for people like us in this country, unless we overturn the caste system. What happened to you and your family is not unique. For thousands of years our people have suffered injustice. Ekalavya, come with me to Khandiva forest. It is the only way for the downtrodden, the poor, the oppressed; for people like us. For the sake of your murdered family, for your hacked off thumb; for our wretched people, come back to Khandivaprastha."

Ekalavya looked at his friend. "You sound like Takshaka, with your bombastic words and dramatic expressions."

"Will you come?"

Ekalavya looked at his right hand with its four fingers. The ghost thumb itched. The image of his cousin's hand holding a knife flashed through his mind. He stood up, ignoring the pain that shot through his limbs, and stared into the Naga's face. "Yes," he said.

A shout of joy came from Aswasena as he hugged his friend. As night fell, the two friends began their long journey towards the dark jungles of Khandiva.

***

"I do not know whether my heart beats with happiness or fear."

Gandhari could feel the trembling in her husband's cold fingers. The world around them was dark. Vidhura had just paid them a visit. Though the King had tried to appear unmoved before the Prime Minister, the moment he heard him walk away, he had turned towards his wife. She did not say anything, nor did she wish to. She tried to pray but the comforting words eluded her. There was only numbness in her mind.

She had felt Dhritarashtra's silent satisfaction when Vidhura told them the news. But dread had spread through her veins. She wondered whether her husband had understood what the Prime Minister was hinting at. When Vidhura left, his words hanging ominously in the air, Dhritarashtra had asked Gandhari, "Could Suyodhana really do something like that?"

For Dhritarashtra, their firstborn could do no wrong. But Gandhari was not so sure. She moved away from her husband, trying to find the window and catch the softness of the breeze on her face. She could hear his laboured breathing. Poor man! When Bhishma had brought her to this palace so many years ago, she had been shocked to see the man who was to marry her. No wonder Bhishma had been compelled to ransack kingdoms and steal away brides for the Princes of Hastinapura. Gandhari still remembered the horror of seeing Dhritarashtra for the first time and shuddering at his sightless eyes. She had kept an arm around Shakuni as she viewed the splendour around them, trying to protect her brother from evil men. She willed herself to remain unflinching before the gaze of the curious courtiers. She could hear the whispers of the men and women who had assembled to see the exotic gift Bhishma was giving his blind nephew. She could also sense their sympathy and hear their clicking tongues. With a vehemence that bordered on insanity, she had torn a strip from her shawl and tied it over her eyes. From that day, she had shared Dhritarashtra's blindness.

"Daughter, why are you doing this?" Even now, she could clearly hear Bhishma's shocked words. The agony and guilt in his words had given her some satisfaction. It still did after all these years. The images of that day remained vivid. There had been a time when she had shared her brother's dream of destroying the country that had stolen her sight. But it was strange how this dry and dusty land seeped into the mind. The smell of spices, the music of temple bells, the fine dust that seemed to enter every pore of the body in the hot sultry summers, had claimed her heart. The dreams of destruction and revenge had vanished long ago. The man she had shrunk from had become her husband. Was it love or sympathy for an insecure and handicapped man? She was afraid to ask that question of herself. When she had taken the terrible vow to bind her eyes, she had wanted only to hurt Bhishma with that gesture. She had thought she would never forgive him for what he had done to her father and her homeland. Yet, respect for the Grand Regent had crawled into her mind over the years and refused to go away despite her efforts.

"They once cheated me of my inheritance and made my brother Pandu sit on the throne while I stood by like a lackey," Dhritarashtra said, gritting his teeth. "I am blind, I see only darkness... even the crown I wear is a gift from my brother... They gave me my birthright as if bestowing a favour on me, after Pandu died. But I am just a figurehead. Bhishma and Vidhura rule this kingdom."

Gandhari heard him get up and find his mace. She gripped her hands together. She could not bear to think of him as weak and vulnerable. He was the King of Hastinapura, he ruled a kingdom as large as a continent, yet he was afraid of his own shadow. He was deferential to all, polite and soft-spoken, weighing his words before speaking them. But in their private chamber, he was a different man. Gandhari knew what was coming now; she was familiar with that sound. Her husband was venting his frustrations on the iron replica of Bhima. It had been a gift to his firstborn, but Suyodhana had never used it. It now stood in the royal bedchamber. Clang! Dhritarashtra's mace hit the iron mannequin with great force.

"Will you stop this?" Gandhari asked, her voice filled with pain.

There was a pause. Then he resumed hitting the statue with a vengeance, as if to prove to himself that he was a King with some power, at least in his bedroom. Gandhari walked towards him, unafraid of the mace he wielded. He stopped, sensing her presence near him. She prised the mace from his hands and made him sit on the bed. He buried his head on her shoulder in defeat. But Gandhari lifted his face and felt it with her fingers. He was so vulnerable in her hands that she wanted to weep. The women of Gandhara never cried, she reminded herself. How much indignity this man had suffered, she thought, as she stroked her husband's thick hair. It felt like Suyodhana's. Perhaps it had turned grey or even white by now, but it felt and smelt like her son's. In their world, colour did not matter. She tried to imagine what her firstborn looked like now.

"Now our son will get what is rightfully his. He is not blind like us, Gandhari. I cannot say this to anyone else, but you will understand. I feel relieved the Pandavas are dead. I hope it was an accident and not a conspiracy by our son. I do not believe he would do anything like that. Suyodhana has never been cruel. But do you think he did...?"

Gandhari did not say anything. She wanted to believe her husband. Surely, their son would never do anything so ignoble. But what about Shakuni? Poor Kunti! Had she really died? What a horrible death for her and her sons. Had she died or was it just another trick? Gandhari despised her, but somehow she found it hard to believe Kunti had died. Kunti was a survivor. But Vidhura had said Kunti and her five sons had died in the fire that gutted their new palace. Gandhari felt ashamed of the thoughts that haunted her mind. The small bubble of joy that threatened to grow and fill her mind was unsettling. She shook her head, as if to remove such thoughts.

Dhritarashtra was restless. He stood up, pushing Gandhari's hands away, and searched for his mace. Once again, the room echoed to the sound of metal crashing on metal. Gandhari sat on the bed, trying to shut out the hatred emanating from Dhritarashtra's mace. A cold fear began creeping into her body. She could shut out the sights of India, and could close her ears to her husband's frustration, but how would she cope with the dread spreading through every nerve. With utter clarity she knew that Vidhura was all wrong, and her son blameless. She was sure Kunti would come back with her sons and suck them all into something unimaginable. She wanted to see Suyodhana, to keep him nearby. For once, she wanted to see his face instead of feeling it with her fingers. In the world inhabited by Shakuni and Krishna, she knew her son was all alone, fighting a fool's battle. She wanted to hold and protect her son from the world.

***

The news of the Pandavas' deaths spread like wildfire. Dhaumya's men fanned the flames of the rumours that Duryodhana had murdered his cousins. There was anger in the streets and Durjaya's men used it effectively to trigger a few riots. There was widespread destruction of public property, arson and looting. The Crown Prince was heckled in the streets. The Prime Minister went to Varanavata to discover the truth. But Bhishma summoned him back to the capital when the riots started spreading to the villages. Vidhura had to discontinue his house-building. The public execution of some rioters helped bring back sanity and the efficient Prime Minister restored peace and order within a week. Durjaya's men slithered back into their hiding places. They would remain in their sleeper cells until their leader called them to action.

Suyodhana was frustrated at this turn of events. He loved being among the people and often visited the nooks and corners of the kingdom he was destined to rule. The love and affection the common people showed, recharged him. However, things turned for the worse following the rumours of the Pandavas' deaths. He knew people were aware of their mutual antipathy but he could not accept that so many thought he would stoop to the level of causing his cousins' deaths. Once, a mob surrounded him in the street and threw eggs at him. They would have lynched him had a beggar and dog not suddenly appeared on the scene and stood between the angry mob and the Prince, until the guards whisked him away to safety.

After that incident, Bhishma had ordered him not to venture out of the palace. Though almost a year had passed since those dark days, it still hurt when he thought about it. The crowd had screamed, 'Killer

Duryodhana' at the top of their voices. The nickname 'Duryodhana' hurt more than the tag 'killer' did. He missed the company of his friend Karna, who was away in Anga, doing an efficient job of putting his fiefdom in order. Sushasana had formed his own group of friends and the brothers had drifted apart and no longer spent much time together. Sushala, now betrothed to King Jayadratha of Sindh, was floating in her own happy world and no longer came to his room to talk. Aswathama remained the only companion in his enforced confinement. In his loneliness, his yearning for Subhadra became more acute. She had not replied to any of his messages after Graduation Day, and that added to his worries. He had written to Jayadratha, since Sindh was closer to Dwaraka than Hastinapura. He had also written to Balarama, his Guru, for advice and eagerly awaited a reply from the Yadava leader.

A guard arrived and bowed to Suyodhana before handing over a sealed message. It was an invitation to the Princess of Panchala's *swayamvara*. Indifferently, he threw it onto the table after glancing at it, his thoughts returning to Subhadra. What did her silence mean? He had to go to Dwaraka and see her. Perhaps things would turn out right if he formally asked for her hand. Yes, that was it. She was shunning him because he had not taken the initiative to take the relationship further. Excited, he went to his writing desk and wrote a letter to Balarama, asking for Subhadra's hand in marriage. He despatched it with his personal courier to Dwaraka, and felt happy and relieved.

Suyodhana casually re-read the invitation to Draupadi's *swayamvara*. It required the suitors to shoot a metal fish revolving high in the air, by looking at its reflection in a small pool of water. He smiled at the ridiculous ways people chose to select grooms for their daughters. Was Draupadi a trophy to be won in a competition? He remembered the beautiful Princess and thought her too spirited and intelligent to be auctioned off to the most skilled archer. Was there no place for love in her life? Karna. It came to him in a flash. Suyodhana slapped his forehead. What sort of a friend was he if he was capable of forgetting the night they had spent in Panchala and the look of love and longing in both Karna and Draupadi's eyes? Shaking off his lethargy, he called for Aswathama and Sushasana, and paced the room, waiting in growing excitement. When they came, he showed them the invitation and waited.

"It is bad news for our friend," Aswathama said.

"What do you mean, Aswathama?" Suyodhana clicked his tongue irritably. "Do you know any archer other than Karna, who can win this competition? The only person who can give him some competition is you."

"I have no intention of getting beaten up by Karna. The issue is, did he even get an invitation?"

"Why should he not get an invitation? He is the King of Anga, do you mean to say the Panchalas will not invite him because of his caste?"

Aswathama gazed at his friend in silence, watching Suyodhana grow angrier by the minute.

"Sushasana, get our troops ready. We are going to Draupadi's *swayamvara*, and we are taking Karna with us. Send a message to him to join us on the way. Send another to Jayadratha. If anybody dares to insult Karna, we will teach them a lesson they will never forget."

By that evening, the arrangements had been made and Suyodhana and his friends started out with a large number of troops for Panchala. When Karna joined them on the way, they were relieved to find Aswathama's fears were unfounded. Karna showed them his invitation from the Panchala King. The five friends spent some of their happiest moments together, on this journey, racing each other on their horses, tasting the finest wines, talking to people, visiting remote villages and hermitages, hunting game in the forest, and singing and dancing under the skies. Karna was teased repeatedly and Sushasana and Aswathama's raunchy comments often led to fights. Their morning practice sessions were riotous, with Aswathama matching Karna's skill in archery and threatening to steal the bride. Jayadratha wanted to say something to Suyodhana about Subhadra, but the thought better of it. They were all having such a good time that he did not want to spoil the Prince's fun.

When they entered Kampilya, Panchala's capital city was in a festive mood. Marigolds hung from ropes tied across the streets and the buildings had been freshly painted. The streets shone after being scrupulously washed and thousands of people milled about in festive attire. Hawkers, peddlers and vendors added to the gaiety with their cries, while street magicians and snake charmers entertained the crowds. The gold-plated chariots of various Princes sped by, and the rulers of various kingdoms paraded majestically atop their elephants. Groups of Brahmins walked about singing devotional songs. It was a grand event.

As they neared the palace, a long procession overtook Suyodhana's group. Sitting majestically in his *howdah* was a noble-looking old man. He smiled at the Crown Prince when their eyes met. The Prince and his friends bowed respectfully. Behind the elephant, a large, middle-aged, black man, rode a beautiful white horse. Holding his head proudly, he looked straight ahead. He nodded curtly to the Crown Prince of Hastinapura and resumed his stone like posture.

"Who was that?" Karna asked Suyodhana.

"Jarasandha, King of Magadha. He is a great man and one of our best administrators. Bhishma has a lot of respect for him. He often says that with Balarama in the West, and Jarasandha in the East, the Southern Confederate can never take over all of India and impose Parashurama's agenda on the country. The black man riding behind him is Hiranyadhanus, Commander-in-Chief of the Magadha armies. He is a Nishada, and one of the finest generals in India. Jarasandha defied all caste rules in elevating him to such an important post. When Parashurama chided him for the gross violation of caste rules, he replied that he ran his country on merit, not by outdated scriptures. Angered, Parashurama ordered Kalinga to mount an attack on Magadha, but the Nishada general routed the Kalinga army, proving Jarasandha's faith in him to have been right."

Karna looked at the passing procession with new eyes. He was not, after all, the first person to have broken the caste ranks. Someone had done it from an even lowlier position. And Suyodhana had not been the first Prince to defy the strict caste rules. But the mention of Parashurama touched a painful chord in the Suta's heart.

"Hey, do you know the Nishada General has a son whom he left behind with his brother when he went off in pursuit of his ambitions?" Jayadratha asked his friends.

"I have heard so. It is also rumoured that he is the same boy my father ordered to sacrifice his thumb for Arjuna's sake. Ekalavya... yes, that was the name. Even now I cannot get over the gross injustice my father did to that poor boy," Aswathama said.

The others looked away embarrassed, not knowing how to react. When they entered the huge hall where the event was to take place, they saw Balarama talking to Jarasandha. Suyodhana went towards his mentor and Guru and touched his feet. One by one, his friends did the same. Balarama introduced them to the King of Magadha and his faithful Nishada General. Jarasandha then took his leave and went to his allotted seat with his General.

"I received your letter Suyodhana, and I am happy for both of you. We shall have the engagement after the monsoon. I was afraid you would never ask and leave my sister broken hearted. I shall drop in at Hastinapura and seek the permission of His Highness Dhritarashtra, and the Grand Regent, so that we can formally settle the alliance," Balarama said to an ecstatic Suyodhana, while Jayadratha twitched his fingers uneasily. "Ah, King of Anga... I am proud of you, Karna. You have proved that talent knows no barriers." The Yadava leader clasped Karna by the shoulders.

Karna swallowed the lump in his throat and smiled at the man who had inspired him to surmount all odds. He looked around and saw a bejewelled Draupadi seated on the dais. Their eyes met and his heart leapt in his chest. She smiled at him and Karna thought he would collapse and die. He looked away, trying to listen to what Balarama was saying to him.

"This is an uncivilised way of arranging a match. It insults the dignity of a woman. I came here to ensure no Yadava Prince participates. Either the man and woman fall in love and get married or the elders arrange a suitable match."

Engrossed in Balarama's tirade against the barbarian custom of the modern *swayamvara*, Karna and his friends did not see Krishna move towards Draupadi. Shikandi and Prince Dhristadyumna were with him, as was the Chief Priest of Panchala. Had they looked at the dais, they would have seen Krishna gently chiding the Panchala Princess, and the dismay on her face. But they did not see Krishna pointing to Karna and saying something. Her brother too whispered in her ear. Draupadi turned away, trying to control the tears brimming in her eyes. Then Krishna pointed towards a group of Brahmins. She looked up to see five tall men standing amongst them. Somehow, they looked like warriors rather than Priests. One amongst them stood staring at her. When their eyes met, he looked away, as if ashamed. Before she could say anything, the bugle announcing the arrival of her father sounded and the assembly rose as Dhrupada, King of Panchala, walked in with his Queen. The murmuring died away as everyone waited for him to speak.

"Honourable Kings and Princes of India, Panchala humbly acknowledges your esteemed presence. From the moment a girl is born, her parents wait for this auspicious day. Today, my precious daughter will find her life partner. All the Princes assembled here today are fine warriors, yet there is no limit to a father's greed when it comes to the good of his daughter. I want only the very best to win her hand, by mesmerising us with his skill. My Minister will explain the rules of the contest." The King sat down with a happy smile and the assembly of nobles resumed their seats.

Animated chatter broke out among the nobles and stopped only when the Prime Minister of Panchala announced the rules. He drew their attention to a metallic fish rotating on the ceiling at blazing speed. A huge copper vessel, filled to the brim with water, was placed directly below it on the floor. A slightly wavy reflection of the rotating fish could be seen in the water. Each contestant had to pick up the bow placed over the vessel and string it. Then, looking only at the reflection of the fish, he had to shoot the metal fish in the eye. Each contestant had two minutes to make the attempt.

The task seemed ridiculously simple compared to the rules at other *swayamvaras* they had attended. One Prince related how he had fought a tiger to win his present wife. Compared to that, this challenge seemed silly. Karna looked at the faces around him and smiled. He had correctly judged the difficulty of the task. His eyes locked on Draupadi, his heart pounding. Why was she not looking at him? Karna was desperate to catch a glimpse of those lovely eyes, but the Princess kept staring at her toes.

When Balarama rose to speak, there was angry murmuring among the contestants. "Your Highness, forgive me if I sound impudent. But I think your daughter deserves better than this. She is not a prize horse to be auctioned. It is time we stop this custom. In ancient times, the *swayamvara* had no contest. The maiden chose her husband from many suitors, by placing a garland upon him. Only the woman's choice mattered. This game of showmanship is disrespectful towards the woman, making her a commodity to be bartered, sold, won, or lost, like cows and sheep. Let the Princess Draupadi chose her husband and let there be no unseemly contest for her hand."

"Sir, with all due respect, this is my daughter's future. What is wrong with a father wishing only the best warrior to wed his daughter? She is young and cannot be expected to make a rational decision. She might just choose the most handsome man, as young girls are wont to do. I want only the best for my daughter and as a Kshatriya; I prefer her husband be a great warrior." The Panchala King spoke politely to Balarama, but the Yadava leader did not miss the underlying contempt in his host's voice.

"Your Highness, she is like a daughter to me too, but the best warrior need not be the best husband. I too, am concerned for her future. If the Princess does not have freedom of choice, why call this a *swayamvara*? But I will not waste everyone's time. Perhaps I am old-fashioned and unable to keep up with these modern trends. But as the leader of the Yadavas, I can speak for my people. We are against this custom and I order that no Yadava take part in this contest." Balarama sat down, his face carved in stone. A groan rose from the ranks of the young Yadavas. Their leader was becoming crankier by the day.

Karna did not hear half his mentor's words. Suyodhana said something to him but that too went over the Suta's head. His lips had gone dry. He prayed she would look at him just once more. When the gong sounded, marking the beginning of the contest, he was startled and averted his gaze from her. His eyes met those of Krishna. He smiled at the Yadava and Krishna smiled back. 'Perhaps he no longer hates so much,' Karna thought, relieved at the apparent cordiality of his old foe.

The contest began in earnest. Lots were drawn and the first few Princes soon found the task was not as easy as it looked. The bow was very heavy and if a contestant managed to lift it, ripples disturbed the faint reflection in the water and they could no longer see their target. One by one, each one failed. There were angry murmurs and protests that the time stipulated was too short. As the day wore on, there were many sulky faces. A few were able to lift the bow, but their aim left them embarrassed. Jarasandha, King of Magadha, almost got it but his arrow missed the fish's eye by a fraction. From his smile it was evident he did not wish to win, and winked at Balarama as he passed him.

"You are old enough to be her father, Your Highness," Balarama said to his old friend as the Magadha King returned to his seat.

"I am here merely to do my duty by my kingdom, not to win," said the King.

Karna's turn came. He did not hear Aswathama wishing him good luck. He felt Suyodhana's hand on his shoulder. Like a man in trance, he walked towards the bow. 'One glance from her, oh God,' he prayed. But Draupadi sat like a statue, her head bowed. The gong sounded again. The warrior in Karna pushed away the lover. He took his time to walk around the bow, judging its weight by its appearance. Then he looked at the revolving fish. Finally, he stood at an angle to the bow and lifted it easily, without causing any ripples in the water. The assembly of nobles waited anxiously as Karna strung the bow and raised it above his head. He picked up the arrow and drew the bowstring taut, his eyes never leaving the reflection of the target in the water.

"I will not marry a Suta." The soft whisper came from Draupadi. It sounded like a thunderclap in the silent and expectant hall.

There was a stunned silence. But Karna did not hear. Every cell of his being was concentrated on the target. He shot the arrow and hit the eye of the revolving fish with a clang. A roar of applause shattered the silence as Karna looked triumphantly at Draupadi. But she did not raise her head. Prince Dhristadyumna went up to Karna and asked him to return to his seat. Karna looked perplexed. Had he not hit the target after all?

A Priest shouted angrily, "Did not you hear, Suta? The Princess does not wish to marry a low caste. Go back to driving your chariot."

Karna looked at Draupadi's bent head, rage and shame burning in his brown eyes. 'How dare you insult me like this? I was invited to come and I won fairly,' he wanted to shout. Then he saw her lift her head and gaze at him. He saw a sadness that was even deeper than his own, reflected in those dark eyes. Near her, Krishna stood wearing his characteristic smile. Karna knew he had lost.

Suyodhana and Aswathama rushed into the middle of the assembly, their swords drawn. Jayadratha and Sushasana followed close behind. Shikandi and Dhristadyumna ran to stop them and soon many of the Princes present were running into the middle and taking sides randomly. It became a bloody riot, with the elders screaming at the hot-blooded young men to stay calm. Finally, Balarama, Jarasandha and General Hiranyadhanus, boldly ran into the middle and prised apart the fighting warriors. When the combatants had calmed down, there were many people writhing on the floor with grave injuries and a few who were dead. No one saw a dejected Karna leave the assembly.

Karna's world had come crashing down. He jumped into his chariot, whipping the horses. The chariot rushed through the busy streets of Kampilya and people moved aside in fear. The son of the charioteer sat grim faced, anger and hate welling up in his heart. 'Nothing but caste matters here,' he thought bitterly. 'What have I done to deserve this?' As he sped towards Hastinapura, Karna vented his anger on the poor horses. He drove dangerously fast along the highway, when suddenly a beggar and a dog appeared on the road. Karna cursed and pulled urgently at the reins. The chariot stopped perilously close to the beggar and his dog. With one look at the beggar the curse on Karna's lips died. It was the same beggar who had saved his life.

"Swami, do you remember me? You fed me when I was small. Jara... I am Jara.... Do you remember? See how my Krishna has blessed you. You are a King now. The good Prince Suyodhana is your friend. I saw you riding in his chariot the day of the graduation, when we last met. Do you remember, Swami?"

Karna looked at Jara's happy face and the dog's wagging tail. All his anger melted away. The beggar was not speaking of his own role in saving his life; he was not talking about the beatings he had received while Karna, Parashurama's disciple, the great *Dharmaveera*, had been hiding like a coward in a tree. Instead, the beggar was grateful for the cup of rice Karna's mother had served him years before

"Why are you sad, Swami? You have become a King. But still you are so sad?"

"Jara, take me somewhere where I can find your God. I have lost the meaning of my life." Karna reached out his hand to the beggar.

"Come with me," Jara said, and started running along the road.

Karna shouted at him to get into the chariot, but Jara kept running, his dog in tow. Karna followed in the chariot and soon found himself in a colony of lepers and sick people. Everything became clear to him. Balarama's words about what he owed each blade of grass in this country, came rushing back to him. He saw Jara giving away the little he had earned that day to people still more unfortunate than himself. Karna was stricken with guilt. 'I am a mere Suta yet my friend made me a King. The best Gurus trained me. I have everything, yet I am bitter because a woman, who cannot think beyond caste, did not want me.'

Impulsively, Karna began giving away his ornaments. Then he stripped his chariot of its golden stripes and gave them away as well. Soon he was mobbed by people asking for more and more. He gave away almost everything he had with him. Jara sat in a corner and sang about the love of Krishna. As dusk fell, more and more people arrived to accept the Suta's charity. His friends arrived, and Aswathama tried to drag Karna away, telling him to fight and regain Draupadi. But Karna refused to move. Suyodhana understood his friend. Silencing Aswathama and gesturing for him to follow, he quietly went to join Karna.

When Karna was left with only his armour, earrings, and the clothes he wore, Suyodhana silently began unclasping his priceless necklaces and handing them over to his friend, who promptly gave them away. Jara was singing about Radha's lost love, Krishna. Despite himself, the bitter echo of Draupadi's words, 'I will not marry a Suta', refused to leave Karna's wounded heart.

***

When the guards had removed the dead and injured, Balarama stood up to address the Panchala King. "Your Highness, such a fracas is to be deplored. You have insulted the King of Anga, a valiant young man, without cause. If you did not wish him to marry your daughter because of his caste, you should not have invited him at all."

Krishna stood up and said with a soothing smile, "Brother, the King has not spoken a word against Karna or his caste. The Princess herself expressed her unwillingness to marry a person of low caste. A few minutes ago, you were telling us that women should have the freedom to choose their husbands. Why should we then deny the Panchala Princess that freedom?"

Balarama glared at his brother in fury. He knew Krishna had tied him in knots using his own words. How clever!

Jarasandha touched his friend's shoulder to pacify him, whispering into his ear, "Leave it, Balarama". The Yadava looked into his friend's eyes for a moment and then shook his head sadly. Jarasandha squeezed his shoulder, forcing him to sit down. Krishna smiled at Dhristadyumna.

All the Princes present had tried their luck, but there was no winner. As the day wore on without any conclusion, the King of Panchala grew more and more anxious. On the advice of Krishna, Draupadi had rejected the only archer to have won her fairly, because of his caste, and now, none of the Kshatriyas was able to even lift the bow, let alone shoot the target. The Panchala King looked pleadingly at Krishna, who smiled, gesturing for him to stay calm. Finally, when there was no Prince left, a tall and muscular Brahmin stepped forward and bowed to the King. There was a smattering of applause from the ranks of the Priests, but everyone else looked at the young Brahmin indifferently. The dejected King nodded his approval for the young Brahmin to try his luck. The Brahmin looked at Krishna for reassurance and Krishna put his clenched fist to his heart and nodded his head.

The Brahmin went up to the bow and studied it. Mimicking the Suta who had won the competition a few hours ago, he lifted it gracefully. The murmurs in the assembly suddenly died away. A few people stood up to get a better look. The air was tense with anticipation. Would this Brahmin win the contest when all the great Princes of India had failed? The drummer, who counted out the seconds with a rhythmic beat of his drum, reached the last three beats. The spectators sat frozen with tension. The Brahmin stood, every inch of his body alert, his mind seeing only the target. A fraction of a second before the last drumbeat, the arrow flew towards the revolving fish. It hit the target precisely as the timekeeper struck his last beat. The assembly was shocked. The Brahmin had done the impossible.

Krishna rushed into the middle and hugged the winner. He turned to the King and announced proudly, "Behold Arjuna, Pandava Prince, and the only man worthy of being Draupadi's husband."

There was a stunned silence at the announcement. The Pandavas were supposed to have perished in the fire at Varanavata. One by one, Arjuna's brothers embraced him and then Krishna. They stood together as Krishna addressed the shocked and silent crowd.

"As you see, the Pandavas did not perish in the fire set by the malicious Duryodhana and his companions. They escaped unscathed since they are no ordinary mortals but of divine origin. Here is Yudhishtra, the epitome of *dharma* and the son of the Lord of Death. Here is Bhima; he is none other than the son of God Vayu, Lord of the Winds. Arjuna is the son of Lord Indra, King of the Gods. And Nakula and Sahadeva, are the sons of the divine Aswhini brothers." Krishna paused to gauge the reaction of the assembly. He avoided looking at his brother. He knew Balarama loved him irrespective of their differences of opinion and power struggles. The Yadava leader was naïve and soft of heart. Krishna knew he had all the time in the world to pacify him later. But the derisive smile on Jarasandha's lips and the piercing eyes of the Nishada General Hiranyadhanus worried him. The others looked receptive enough and he was confident of his oratory and powers of persuasion.

Krishna continued, "Do not be swayed by the arguments of evil men like the Kauravas, that the Pandavas do not have any claim to Hastinapura as they are not the real sons of Pandu. The Kauravas claim Pandu was impotent. There can be no greater untruth. Pandu insulted a Brahmin in his youthful folly and the holy man cursed him saying he would die if he attempted physical intimacy with a woman. That is the truth and every learned man in this country knows it. As per our scriptures, with the husband's permission, wives can have sons by any Brahmin or God. We consider such women chaste. Learned men also say that the Brahmins or Gods, who thus bless these fortunate women with sons, do not have any responsibility or claim on their progeny. The husband is blessed and the sons born of such divine relationships are considered his progeny alone. Duryodhana wishes to propagate the scandal that the Pandavas are bastards. Greed for power has made him blind to the truth that Yudhishtra is the rightful Crown Prince and not him. He is blinded by arrogance and does not respect *dharma*.

"My brothers and sisters, *dharma* is withering under the onslaught of such evil men. Duryodhana has made a Suta the King of Anga. We have to nip such actions in the bud, for such naked transgression of our traditions will only lead to the destruction of our great civilization. That son of the charioteer got lucky with his shot and hit the target. I was tense for a moment but am happy that better sense prevailed and Draupadi put him in his place. I applaud the courage she has shown in not letting her heart win over her head. It is easy to be impressed by Karna. He is handsome and arguably has some skill with the bow. Know that the little knowledge he has, was gained by cheating the great Guru Parashurama. Know that the person who looks so heroic is nothing but a low class imposter, who lied to a great man. The Guru loved this pretender like his own son, thinking him to be a Brahmin. When he learned the truth, he lost consciousness and is even now struggling for life. The powerful Kings of the Southern Confederate are on the lookout for this charlatan."

Krishna paused, happy to have destroyed any lingering sympathy towards the Suta. Before Jarasandha or Balarama could say anything to the contrary, he moved to where the Panchala Princess sat with her eyes cast down, all youthful gaiety erased from her face. "Princess Draupadi, we are proud of you. A better man could not have gained your hand. May you always be happy and have a hundred sons."

Jarasandha looked at the smiling Krishna and chuckled. He said to Balarama in a low voice, "I cannot stand this farce any longer and am now leaving." He clasped his friend's hands and held them close to his heart. Then he walked out of the assembly with his faithful General in tow. Balarama stood up and followed him out. As the venerable King of Magadha was mounting his elephant, Balarama caught up with him. The elderly King said, "This country is going to the dogs Balarama, and I truly pity your clever brother."

They could hear the chanting of the Priests from the *sabha* as Draupadi was duly married to Arjuna, according to traditional rites and rituals.

"His views are conservative and he thinks people have deviated from the path of *dharma*. He has taken upon himself the task of saving the world from people who think differently. That is all. He says he has come to earth to restore *dharma*," Balarama said to the older man, unwilling to let him leave with a poor opinion of his brother.

"I hope he will not become dangerous and is just a closet fanatic, as you want me to believe. But I fear his passion will divide people into two opposing groups. If he does not acquire the wisdom that there is nothing like absolute *dharma*, be assured there will be a terrible war and the whole of India will be sucked into the vortex. In such a conflict, there will be no winners except a handful of Priests, who will survive and flourish," Jarasandha said sadly, suppressing the urge to be more harsh on Krishna, in the face of Balarama's obvious love for his charming brother.

"I will try to make Krishna understand. But as you say, times are unsettled and there are many people willing to believe that you are in fact one of the evil Kings of India. Be careful of misguided young men like the Nagas, who would be happy to endanger you," Balarama told his friend, eyeing the haughty Nishada General.

"Balarama, I have not lived my seventy years as a coward and I am sure it is not Takshaka who wants to finish me. Do not worry. As long as I have faithful men like General Hiranyadhanus here, I fear neither the Nagas nor the netherworld, or *avatar*s who walk this poor earth for our salvation. Farewell Balarama, do come to visit us sometime soon." With these words, the King of Magadha gave the order to his *mahout* and the elephant lumbered forward. General Hiranyadhanus bowed to Balarama. The Yadava leader bowed back with equal deference.

With a man like the Nishada General as his aide, Jarasandha had nothing to fear, thought Balarama, as he watched the entourage leaving Panchala. There was a time when Jarasandha had been Balarama's greatest enemy.

Soon after Krishna and Balarama had assassinated their uncle Kamsa, then King of Mathura, Jarasandha, his brother-in-law, had laid siege to the city, bent on revenge. Those had been difficult days. Balarama had been young and impulsive. Jarasandha and his Nishada General had attacked Mathura and ransacked the capital seventeen times. Krishna wished to finish off Jarasandha somehow, and the chance came as an invitation to peace talks at Pataliputra, the capital of Magadha. Krishna planned to assassinate the usurper during their visit, and included Balarama in the conspiracy. However, what he saw at Magadha changed Balarama's perspective and his life. He arrived in Pataliputra with his mind filled with hatred, and came away with immense respect for Jarasandha. He vetoed Krishna's plan, leaving his brother furious, and decided to move the Yadava people to the West coast of India, to build a dream city – Dwaraka. Jarasandha became a dear friend.

***

Soon, a delirious crowd carried the newlyweds seated in a palanquin, to the home of the Pandavas. They swarmed round the couple with loud celebrations and wild dancing. Balarama saw the sadness in Draupadi's eyes. 'Daughter, you do not know what you have missed by rejecting Karna because of his caste. May Arjuna keep you happy,' he prayed as he watched the palanquin moving away quickly. He did not know then that Kunti would take a momentous decision when the bridal procession reached her door. It would alter the course of history forever.

22 MARRIAGE

KUNTI STOOD SHOCKED INTO IMMOBILITY as the bridal procession reached the Pandavas' humble hut. The dwelling was small and neat, set in a sylvan hermitage where similar huts were inhabited by Brahmins and holy men. The Pandava brothers patiently waited for their mother to open the door and welcome them in. A woman's instinct made Draupadi uneasy as she stood, shaking a little with nervousness. Arjuna's four brothers stood behind her. She could feel the heat from their eyes on her back as well as their jealousy towards their successful brother.

"Mother, Arjuna has brought you a present," Yudhishtra called out.

Draupadi could see two eyes boring into her through the crack in the door. Finally, Kunti spoke from the darkness within. "Whatever you have brought, Arjuna, share it with your brothers."

Had she heard correctly? 'Share it with your brothers! *It*?' Draupadi's quick temper flared at her mother-in-law's instruction to her son. Each of Kunti's words was like a needle piercing her soul. In the years to follow, she would often remember the chill of those words and recall the lust in the eyes of the Pandavas as she stood trembling; and her warrior-husband's helplessness – that supreme archer who had won her.

"Is that the right thing to do, mother?" asked Arjuna, sounding like a peeved child who had lost his favourite toy to his siblings.

Draupadi burned with indignation. They were discussing her yet she had no voice in deciding her own future. She was just 'it', a thing without heart and feelings; to be bartered, shared, fought over, and pawned when its use was over. But she held back her tears, remembering she was first of all a Princess of Panchala and the daughter of a King.

"Krishna," Kunti opened the door and addressed their guest. "Explain to Arjuna what *karma* and *dharma* are. Why is he angry? Does he not know they must all stand together to defeat Duryodhana? I do not wish them to fight over this girl. She should be proud that each of my five incomparable sons will share her. I too, have done that in my time, as did my husband's second wife, Madri. That is how all five of them were born."

"Am I a prostitute to share the bed of all your sons?" Draupadi exploded in rage, no longer able to remain silent in the face of such humiliation. "Why are you silent, Arjuna? You won me and I am your wife. Do you want me to share a bed with your brothers? Why do you remain silent? Are you not a Kshatriya?"

Krishna came forward. "Aunt, allow me to mediate." He took Draupadi's hand and led her apart. Arjuna followed them.

Yudhishtra placed a mat on the floor, sat down, and closed his eyes, at peace with himself. Bhima vanished into the kitchen to forage for food, and the twins stood gaping at Draupadi. Kunti looked at the serene face of her eldest son. She had taken a gamble and hoped Krishna would be able to convince this spirited girl. Gandhari's sons were strong because of their unity. This girl was so beautiful she could create trouble and frustration if she lived in this house with five young men, all of whom secretly coveted her.

When Krishna came back, it looked like he had managed to sort things out. Draupadi kept her eyes lowered and Kunti could not decide whether she was petulant or merely shy. Anyhow, she looked resigned to her future, in the best tradition of Indian wives. Arjuna looked away, not prepared to face his mother, brothers, or wife. Yudhishtra came out of his meditation when Krishna patted his shoulder. Addressing Kunti, Krishna said in the voice of reason, "She understands. I have explained everything, including the scriptural authority for this. She asked Arjuna whether he agreed, and Arjuna replied that he would follow whatever I decide. So I have told him what is right. Everything is settled. Yudhishtra will have her for one year, then Bhima for the next year. Arjuna, being third, will have her for the third year, and the fourth and fifth are for the twins. The cycle will continue in the same way, with a month between each new cycle, and Draupadi will be the wife of all five brothers."

Yudhishtra quickly cast down his eyes to hide his elation. As the eldest, he would be first. He then looked at his mother. "The power of meditation and prayer is more powerful than skill with arms, mother. Arjuna won her, but he knows his duty – that whatever we win has to be shared." He walked over to Draupadi. "Do not worry anymore. The wedding rites will be performed immediately to marry you to each of us. You are ours now and we will protect you until death claims us all."

"But my husband is Arjuna, your own brother..." Draupadi turned imploringly towards Arjuna, willing him to speak. But Arjuna, the mighty warrior, would not meet her eyes and turned away, his heart unaccountably filled with shame. But was he not following *dharma*?

Draupadi looked at her mother-in-law. "Mother, I hope these are all the sons you have."

"Why... why do you ask, daughter?" Kunti's voice had lost all its usual authority. She averted her gaze from the young Princess standing so proudly before her.

"So I do not wake one day to find myself wife to half a dozen men. I am sure there are enough scriptural authorities to prove that too, would be my *dharma*."

Yudhishtra did not wait for his mother's answer. Sahadeva ran to fetch the Priests who would conduct the marriages as per Vedic rituals. The others followed Yudhishtra into the house. Only Arjuna remained standing outside. The closing door sounded as final as death.

***

Later, as Draupadi lay on her bed like deadwood, she did not think about Arjuna, the great archer who had won her, or Yudhishtra, lying asleep beside her. Her eyes were filled with the image of a man slipping away like a chastised dog from her father's splendid Court. Her mind and body felt violated, defeated and numb. Her own words, 'I will not marry a Suta,' screamed back at her endlessly in the deafening silence.

***

Arjuna sat grim and silent, looking at the fireflies dancing around. The hermitage was abuzz with activity as preparations were being made to feed a hundred Brahmins to celebrate the Pandavas' marriages. Krishna came to sit beside his friend. He took out his flute and began playing. Soon a magical world enveloped them. The mesmerising music caressed Arjuna's bruised soul. A crescent moon peeped from behind dark clouds and poured molten silver onto the still earth. From somewhere in the shadows of the swaying trees, the sweet song of a nightingale accompanied Krishna's enchanting melody. Arjuna closed his eyes and lost himself in the music.

"There is somebody waiting for you... who loves you. We can leave for Dwaraka tonight." Krishna said softly to his friend as the music faded away, dissolving into the surrounding mist. Arjuna slowly came out of his trance and looked at Krishna, his eyebrows lifted in a question. "Forget Draupadi, Arjuna. You married her for political reasons. By marrying the Panchala Princess, the Pandavas have become strong enough to challenge Duryodhana. Now it is time for love. Come with me to Dwaraka. I have a much more beautiful Princess waiting for you. Arjuna, follow me and you can steal my sister Subhadra's heart."

"Subhadra? But isn't she betrothed to my cousin Suyodhana? How can I do such a dishonourable thing?" Arjuna asked, confused.

"I know my sister better than anyone else. She no longer loves Duryodhana. She adores you. Remember the day Duryodhana insulted you by elevating the charioteer's son? Everybody's eyes were on the upstart Karna, except for my sister's. She alone felt for you. Noble Prince, the Suta stole your thunder that day, but you gained something more precious – my sister's heart. Do you think I would allow her to marry Duryodhana, my friend?"

"How can I do something so dishonourable? She is promised..." Arjuna paused and looked at Krishna's smiling face. Rage struck him with the force of a thunderbolt. To hell with honour! His own brother had stolen his bride from him in the name of *dharma*. If Yudhishtra could do that to him, why could he not do the same to Duryodhana? Arjuna smiled at his friend and clasped his hand.

***

The chariot carrying Krishna and Arjuna sped towards Dwaraka. On the way, they stopped at a tavern to feed the horses and refresh themselves. A group of travellers were sitting around a fire. The two friends were about to resume their journey when Arjuna was attracted by the beauty of a voice singing a devotional song. He moved towards the fire to listen while Krishna waited impatiently near the chariot, his dark body merging with the shadows and making him almost invisible.

A beggar with a horribly scarred face was dancing near the fire, his hands rhythmically clapping to his song. A dog lay nearby, its tail wagging to the rhythm of the song while it gazed at the star-sprayed sky with unseeing eyes. The man sang rapturously about the love of God for all creation, and lamented Man's ingratitude for the blessing of life. Every moment was a cause for celebration, every breath a joyful melody, every act a prayer, and every thought an offering at Krishna's divine feet. Arjuna did not know why the poor beggar's song affected him so much. He felt he was doing something sinful and wrong. A group of young men came out of the tavern with food and began serving everyone. Most of the people being served were poor Untouchables. When the fire flared in the breeze, Arjuna suddenly saw one of the faces clearly, and was shocked. It was Karna! He also recognised the man playing with the blind dog. It was Aswathama. The three others distributing food were Suyodhana, Sushasana and Jayadratha.

Arjuna suddenly felt ashamed. This was supposed to be his wedding night. How could he explain his presence here? He hurried back to the chariot and seated himself. When Krishna whipped the horses, Arjuna said, "That beggar was singing about you. Are you really a God to inspire so much faith in such poor creatures?"

Krishna smiled as the chariot lurched forward, carrying away the Prince who kept wondering about the people who were said to be evil but who were spending the night with the poor; and his elder brother, who was the epitome of *dharma*, but was spending the night with the woman he had stolen. Only a God could explain such mysteries to him. The beggar's song and the scene he had just witnessed continued to haunt Arjuna's disturbed mind as they travelled through the night.

***

Suyodhana impatiently awaited the arrival of the wedding procession bringing his bride to Hastinapura. The joy in his face gave the lie to his studied nonchalance. The palace buzzed with activity as there were just three days left for the Crown Prince's marriage to Princess Subhadra of Dwaraka. If this was not reason enough for Hastinapura to celebrate, the Princess Sushala's marriage to King Jayadratha of Sindh was to take place at the same time and venue.

Almost a year had passed since Arjuna had won Draupadi at the *swayamvara*. The news that all the Pandava brothers were sharing Arjuna's bride, had shocked everyone. But gradually it became just a matter of ridicule. Six months before, Balarama had arrived in Hastinapura to arrange his sister's marriage to Suyodhana. Krishna had not accompanied him. Suyodhana was disappointed Subhadra had chosen not to come either. But he had been happy at the turn of events. Jayadratha had warned him that her feelings had warmed towards Arjuna, but he refused to believe it. Nevertheless, he set his spies to check on the whereabouts of Arjuna. They informed him that Arjuna had been missing from the day of his marriage, and that Draupadi was serving her term as Yudhishtra's wife, with Bhima eagerly counting the days for his turn as Draupadi's husband. There was a rumour that someone had seen Arjuna and Krishna travelling towards Dwaraka in Krishna's chariot. But Krishna had arrived at the Dwaraka palace alone. Nobody had seen Arjuna. That eased Suyodhana's mind. Jayadratha had it all wrong.

Once the Grand Regent and King Dhritarashtra had given their approval to the alliance with the Yadava Princess, Suyodhana had spoken to Balarama about fixing a day for the ceremony. If he felt any unease at

Jayadratha's warning words, he buried it in his mind. His sister's alliance with one of his closest friends added to his joy. It had been Suyodhana's idea to have both ceremonies performed together. The wedding party from Sindh had already arrived, adding to the festivities. It was difficult to walk around the palace without bumping into someone.

Aswathama burst into Suyodhana's room and grabbed him by the shoulders. "Prince, what is your opinion about true love? Love that is written in your heart *blah blah blah...*"

Suyodhana saw Karna's embarrassed face behind the impish Brahmin and was amused. "What has happened? Has Draupadi agreed to take Karna as her sixth husband?" Suyodhana saw Karna's face turn grim and immediately regretted his insensitive comment. Poor man! He had not forgotten the fiasco at Kampilya the previous year.

Aswathama laughed and said, "Oh no! That disaster has not yet happened, though I am sure our friend here would be more than willing to be Draupadi's sixth husband. This is a different love story. The hero in this tale becomes a saint following his love's betrayal. Remember the day we stormed out of Dhrupada's palace in search of Karna, after Draupadi refused to marry him? And where did we find him?"

"She insulted me in front of everyone. Living with five men is better than marrying me? I feel nothing but disgust for her now. But where you found me that night has nothing to do with it. I was genuinely moved by the plight of those people. I am no different from them after all," said Karna, looking away.

"Yes, yes, it was a spontaneous reaction. Of course we believe you," agreed Aswathama grinning and infuriating Karna further. But before Karna could respond, the Brahmin turned towards Suyodhana. "Prince, remember the scene that day? We found him among some beggars. He was spending money like a crazy drunk, buying every delicacy available and feeding them. When we wanted to go back to Dhrupada's palace and snatch Draupadi by force, he refused to come! You remember that night.

That beggar with the dog kept singing the praises of Krishna. Except for his armour and earrings, Karna gave away everything he had brought from Anga. After a while it was not only the beggars but the Brahmins too, who queued up to partake of Karna's generosity. Hell, he forced us to do the same as him. I was as poor as those lepers by the time this idiot got over his madness. We thought then that it was just an odd reaction to the day's happenings. But this madman has now made a habit of it."

"You fools! How many times do I have to tell you that my actions have nothing to do with what I felt for Draupadi? In fact, she opened my eyes that day. I *am* a Suta. I was pretending to be a Kshatriya. If not for the generosity of Prince Suyodhana, I would have remained a charioteer. Her rejection reminded me of who I am. When I came out of that assembly and saw the group of beggars, I felt I had been ungrateful for the blessings I have received. If the Prince could risk his entire kingdom and make powerful enemies for my sake, the least I could do was share my fortune with the less fortunate. I cannot explain what I feel when I give to those unfortunate people." Karna looked away from his friends, afraid of his own emotions.

"Aswathama, he is trying to divert us. Tell Suyodhana what you came to tell him in the first place." Sushasana walked in and sat down near his brother.

"Well, Saint Karna has found a new love and is waiting for your wedding to be over before announcing his own," Aswathama said with a wide grin.

Suyodhana rushed to Karna and embraced him. "Tell me my friend, which Princess is the lucky girl?"

Karna looked into his friend's eyes. "She is not a Princess but a Suta called Vrishali. I met her during one of the routine trips I undertake in disguise on most nights I am in Anga. Fate willed we meet. She lives with her mother. Her father died in service. She was running from pillar to post to get the compensation due to her. But you know what our bureaucracy is. I got her the money and punished a few corrupt officials in the process.

We fell in love. Even now, she does not know I am the King of Anga. She thinks I am a horse trader with some influence in the bureaucracy because of my business. I would have brought her to meet you, but she would be bashful about coming into the presence of the Crown Prince of Hastinapura. Even though I have told her many times that you are my best friend, she refuses to believe it and thinks I am just bragging to impress her."

Everyone burst into laughter. Aswathama pranced around the room crying hoarsely, "I am waiting to meet her, Karna. Then I will tell her some stories... like Draupadi's Well near Kampilya... and the feast for beggars, hosted by the King of Anga on the day she ditched him... as well as other revelries when he proved himself to be as big an ass as he looks... *ouch!*"

Karna had shoved the Guru's son to the floor. Soon the others pounced on the poor Brahmin and began pummelling him. There was a knock on the door and they hurriedly got up, adjusting their clothing and hair to look as respectable as possible. Vidhura entered. They all bowed in deference. The Prime Minister looked at the mess the room was in and ignored the sheepish smiles of the young men. He turned to Suyodhana and said gravely that the Grand Regent wished to see him at once.

Suyodhana was immediately alert to the tone in Vidhura's voice. Unless it was important, his uncle would not have come himself. Suyodhana grew tense, fearing something had happened to someone he held dear. Vidhura did not utter another word till they reached the *sabha*. Then he gave Suyodhana's shoulder a squeeze and went to take up his usual position near Bhishma. As Suyodhana's eyes adjusted to the brightly lit room, he saw his father and mother were seated next to the Grand Regent. A familiar figure stood in the shadows, but he could not quite identify him until the man moved towards him. Balarama! The Yadava leader was looking so distraught that it took Suyodhana a moment to recognize him. Balarama had aged since Suyodhana had last seen him. The Yadava leader fell to his knees and would have touched Suyodhana's feet had the shocked Prince not caught him by his shoulders. "Sir, what are you doing?" Suyodhana pulled up the older man and then bent to touch his Guru's feet.

"Forgive me, Prince. I have failed you. I have brought shame upon you and your kingdom. Punish me in whichever way you wish," the Yadava leader said.

Suyodhana looked around in confusion. The silence was disturbed only by Balarama's attempts to catch his breath. A worm of doubt began gnawing at Suyodhana's heart.

"Suyodhana." Bhishma's heavy voice pierced the uneasy silence and Suyodhana almost knew what was coming. "Balarama has come here to announce the marriage of his sister Subhadra with your cousin, Arjuna, and to ask for our blessings. A few months ago, he came here to finalise an alliance between his sister and you. Knowing your wishes in the matter, we agreed. Now it seems there is a change of plan on the Yadava side. His sister has eloped with Arjuna, from the palace in Dwaraka, with the assistance of Krishna."

"I am sorry, Suyodhana... I did not know..." Balarama said, the lines deepening on his forehead.

The world came crashing down upon the Crown Prince. Anger rose in every cell of his body. He felt feverish. How could Arjuna, the bastard son of Kunti, dare touch his girl?

"Suyodhana, there is no doubt this is a great insult to Hastinapura. We hold the leadership of India, north of the Vindhyas, and a vassal kingdom has dared to humiliate us. Not even our sworn enemies, the Southern Confederate, have stooped to this level. I certainly never expected this from a man I considered my own brother. Suyodhana, you have a choice now – to either ransack their puny kingdom and teach the Yadavas a lesson or fight Arjuna to win back your woman. I wish to discuss this with you." Bhishma's voice trailed away when Suyodhana slowly shook his head.

The Crown Prince did not speak for some time but kept looking at his mentor. The Yadava leader finally averted his eyes, unable to hold the

Prince's gaze. Finally Suyodhana said, "Guru, please tell me who drove the chariot they eloped in. Was it my cousin Arjuna or…"

It was painful for Balarama to say it. He loved his sister like a father and she had repaid his love by insulting him. Swallowing hard, he looked into the eyes of his disciple. "Son, it was not your cousin; it was Subhadra who drove the chariot."

Suyodhana bowed to the assembly and began walking away.

Bhishma stood up. "Suyodhana! Give me a reply. If you wish to fight and win back your woman, the entire army of Hastinapura is at your disposal. Do not run away from your duty as a Kshatriya. Fight for your woman, your kingdom, your honour."

Suyodhana stopped and turned. "*Pitamaha*, It is evident Princess Subhadra has chosen my cousin, Arjuna. I do not wish to fight her or use my kingdom's resources to settle a purely personal matter."

"You will be the butt of ridicule and will be accused of cowardice," Bhishma told him sternly, not mincing his words.

"I wish my cousin and Princess Subhadra happiness. Do not let my personal issues affect the policies of our kingdom. I respect my Guru Balarama all the more for having had the courage to come here and tell us the news personally. Let not the relations with Dwaraka suffer because of this small incident." Suyodhana walked towards the door, which just then looked like a million leagues away.

"Suyodhana!" Something in Bhishma's voice made the Prince stop and turn. He saw the glitter of tears in Bhishma's deep eyes and waited for the Grand Regent to speak. "Son, I am proud of you."

Suyodhana bowed again and left the hall as hurriedly as he could. He did not forget to return the bows of the guards at the door but as soon as he had moved sufficiently away from the *sabha* and found a quiet and shadowed corner, he pressed his face to the cold marble of the wall. The emotions he had kept damned, burst, and he wept shamelessly. He tried to curb the hatred he felt towards his cousin but Subhadra's lovely face jeered at him, mocking his naivety and foolishness. He could almost hear Arjuna's laughter at his plight. He knew the Priests would enjoy his loss of face. He felt worthless and used. 'Son of blind parents, I too, did not have the vision to see Subhadra was making a mockery of my love. I have been blind,' he thought, pressing his burning face to the cold stone.

An hour later, Aswathama found him in the same posture. Initially, the Prince refused to tell his friend the cause of his distress. Later, when he finally related what had happened, and that Subhadra was already married to his cousin, his friends were outraged. It took Jayadratha and Karna's combined strength to stop Aswathama rushing out in search of Arjuna. The son of Drona vowed revenge on Arjuna for stealing the brides of two of his friends, first Draupadi, and now Subhadra. Meanwhile, a drunken Sushasana slipped out to shower abuse on Balarama. The Yadava leader bore his insults without lifting his head, until someone informed the Grand Regent. Bhishma promptly placed Sushasana under house arrest until the morning of Princess Sushala's wedding. It was left to Vidhura to apologize profusely to Balarama on behalf of Hastinapura.

***

Princess Sushala's wedding day witnessed curious events. Learned men said that such things did not augur well for the ancient kingdom or Indian civilization as a whole. 'The Gods have shown Duryodhana his place by making him the fool who lost his bride to his cousin,' the Priests whispered to each other. Yet the arrogant man refused to learn. What angered Dhaumya most was the audacity of the Crown Prince in conducting the marriage of two Sutas at the very venue he himself was supposed to have been married. The Priests under Dhaumya refused to solemnize Karna and Vrishali's marriage, but Aswathama and Kripa stepped forward to do so. They were thus married beside the King of Sindh and Princess Sushala. The renowned generosity of the Suta further angered Dhaumya, when he discovered that many of his followers had secretly blessed the couple and accepted gifts from Karna. He could not understand why the Gods allowed such evil men to flourish in this holy land. Perhaps it was the advent of

Kali, the age of *adharma*. Dhaumya assembled the Priests in his house and prayed sincerely for deliverance from sinful men like Suyodhana and his friends. Has not the Lord delivered them from demons like Ravana and Mahabali before? What was important was keeping faith in His divine wisdom, Dhaumya told his dejected followers. As they did not have anything other than the words of the Chief Priest to cling to, the holy men waited for the Gods to take care of Suyodhana and his friends.

***

Ekalavya sat with his friend Aswasena, discussing the impending attack by Takshaka on Hastinapura. Around them, the tall trees of the Khandivaprastha forest stood like sentries. It was almost a year since Ekalavya had returned. He had been welcomed like a hero by Takshaka and given command of a platoon of guerrilla fighters. However, the old King Vasuki kept telling Ekalavya that he had made a mistake in returning and that he should escape from the insane world Takshaka was creating.

Except for the singing of the birds and the occasional rustling of dry leaves in a reluctant breeze, it was frighteningly silent. The sky was pregnant with rain and the forest waited in anticipation of deliverance from the grip of the scorching summer. Mayasura, a young Asura architect in his early twenties, sat with them, quietly drawing pictures of fantastic palaces and temples in the sand. Mayasura had learned his trade at the great Asura School of architecture. The school, which had flourished on the southeastern coast of India, had lost its charm after the collapse of the last Asura Emperor, Ravana. But its traditions secretly continued. Many of the students only built clay models since there was no longer a demand for the palaces and temples the Mayan school of architecture and science had been famous for. Theirs was a dying art. The practitioners became destitute, pushed into the ranks of the Untouchables or Pariahs, as the Vishwakarma School gained prominence. Mayasura was a victim of this social change and was one of the many new recruits into Takshaka's rebel army.

The secret Naga camp in the Khandiva forest was teeming with desperate men and women, who lived in a forgotten India. The forests covered the ancient city from where the first King of the Indras had ruled India, thousands of years before. Later, when power moved into the hands of the

Brahmins, ancient ruling clans like the Indras went into decline. The incumbent Indra was a broken old man, living in the ruins of his crumbling palace deep in the jungle. It was rumoured that he had fathered Arjuna, and had come back with a few copper coins for the service rendered to Kunti. Bitter and mean, he had allied himself with the Nagas in the hope that he would regain some of the lost prestige of his illustrious ancestors. Takshaka had tactfully taken advantage of this and moved his army into the dark forests ruled by Indra. From Khandiva, it was only a couple of day's journey to Hastinapura. The jungle was ideal for Takshaka's kind of warfare.

Now, Takshaka and Kaliya walked across to where Ekalavya sat. The young man stood up respectfully before the Supreme Leader of the Revolutionary Army. Takshaka was displaying an increasing penchant for referring to himself by pretentious names. This mouthful was the latest. He hugged Ekalavya. "I knew you would bring us luck. We were desperate for a powerful ally and we now have none other than General Hiranyadhanus's son with us."

"Why are you looking so confused, Ekalavya?" Kaliya asked, hiding a smile. "The great General of Magadha has sent the Supreme Leader this letter. Read it."

Ekalavya took the palm leaf from Kaliya with trembling hands. The revelation that his father was alive shocked him. He eagerly scanned the letter with the Royal seal of Magadha. It was addressed simply to Shri Takshaka. General Hiranyadhanus explicitly stated that Ekalavya was his long-lost son and wished Takshaka to return him safely to Magadha.

Takshaka handed over another message to Ekalavya as well. It was a personal letter to Ekalavya, in which the General sought his son's forgiveness for having abandoned him as a child. The General had gone in search of his fortune, leaving his infant son with his brother, following his wife's demise. He had become an exceptional warrior. Due to his good fortune, he had met a King who thought merit was more important than caste, and placed trust in him. In time, he had risen to become Commander-in-Chief of the Magadha army. He had tried to contact

Ekalavya many times but he had always been unsuccessful. The General had heard about the horrible fate of his sister-in-law and his five nephews, and rumours that Ekalavya was alive and had joined Takshaka's forces. He wanted to meet his son and requested him to come to Pataliputra, the capital of Magadha.

Ekalavya threw away the letter in disgust and anger. Where had this man been when he had been struggling to keep body and soul together? Memories of his poverty, the struggle to learn something worthwhile, the insults, the way his people were treated, and the death of his aunt and cousins, all came rushing back. He turned away, retching into the bushes.

"I have no father. To hell with this great man..." He turned and ran towards the river. The Yamuna seemed to beckon the Nishada into its dark depths. The sudden shock of knowing his father was alive was too much for his bruised mind to bear.

Takshaka followed and touched his shoulder, but Ekalavya did not respond. He stood perilously close to the raging river, his hands covering his dark face. The Naga leader saw it was best to leave him alone to find his own tortured peace. Later, Takshaka and Vasuki both tried to persuade him to go and meet his father, who was a powerful man. The revolution needed such friends. The attack on Hastinapura was imminent. The General was a downtrodden Untouchable who had risen to great heights through his own efforts. Even if Ekalavya did not need a father, the revolution needed the General. Takshaka used his persuasive powers and even threatened Ekalavya with dire consequences if he acted against the interests of the revolutionary army. But Ekalavya refused to budge. Takshaka turned away angrily, hinting at action against those who betrayed the revolutionary cause.

Finally, the old man Vasuki succeeded in thawing Ekalavya's frozen heart. His anger slowly gave way to curiosity and then pride. The Nishada decided to make the fateful journey to meet his illustrious father. On the day Hastinapura was celebrating Karna's marriage, Ekalavya started towards the Eastern kingdom of Magadha, where a King who did not care for social rules reigned and an Untouchable commanded her formidable army. Ekalavya was warming up to the idea of meeting his father. The young architect Mayasura asked if he could accompany Ekalavya on his journey. He wished to see the famed city of Pataliputra. But Ekalavya only said, "Some other time, Mayan." Ekalavya was unsure of how he would react on meeting his father in the flesh and did not want witnesses.

As the horse carrying the dark form of the Nishada vanished into the horizon, the architect sighed in disappointment. He had only learnt architecture theory and had never even seen a major city, let alone designed or built one. As an Untouchable, he was not allowed to walk near any of the palaces or temples. He yearned to see great buildings, touch the stones and sculptures with his own hands, and walk through the paved streets. In his heart of hearts, he nurtured a secret ambition, which was far more than a mere wish. One beautiful thought robbed him of sleep; one dream recurred every night; and one prayer rose to his lips. It was beautiful because it was impossible. Mayasura, whose ancestors had designed the great temples of India thousands of years ago, now fell to his knees and folded his hands: "Oh Mahadeva, forgive my impudence in asking for something I do not deserve. Oh compassionate one, grant me this one boon. Let me build the most beautiful city in the world. Let my city live forever and... be the heart of my holy motherland."

In answer, the skies erupted angrily in loud claps of thunder. A bolt of lightning struck a tree near the kneeling Mayasura and sent it up in flames. The young architect looked fearfully at the dark sky, where clouds jostled each other and clashed in flashes of lightning. It was as if the Gods in the high heavens were angered by the grandiose dreams of this puny little man. Mayasura ran towards his hut, his hands clutching the tiny Shiva *linga* he wore on a string round his neck, and closed the rickety door to shut out the fury of nature. It took a long time for the anger of the heavens to subside.

"WE HAVE NO CHOICE, VIDHURA. Make arrangements to hand over the governance of Khandiva to the Pandavas," Bhishma said to his Prime Minister.

"Sir, the district is jungle for the most part. The river is unpredictable there and often floods the plains, even in summer. Moreover, reports indicate rebels under Takshaka are camped in the forest." Vidhura was uneasy about the Grand Regent's decision.

"Do you have a better suggestion, Vidhura? Kunti has come back to the palace with her sons and daughter-in-law, now that it is known they did not perish in the fire at Varanavata. The caucus around her is busy spreading rumours that she is being discriminated against by the King. I dislike the cold war between Gandhari and Kunti. Moreover, if the reports about Takshaka being in Khandiva are true, I would like to see how the Pandavas handle him. We will not always be around to help them. Let us see how the new generation copes with these problems. They need experience in governance and it will be good for everyone if the Pandavas make their headquarters at Khandiva, and rule half the kingdom from there. I sounded Suyodhana on the idea and he does not perceive any problem. The boy has yet to come out of his depression over losing his girl to Arjuna, but I think he is mature enough not to mix personal issues with the public good."

"I am not sure about Suyodhana's intentions. The house of lac in Varanavata..."

Bhishma did not allow Vidhura to complete his sentence. "The less we talk about Varanavata the better. You personally investigated the matter and should know better. The only thing that points to a conspiracy is that the house was built with highly inflammable materials. Purochana, the person who built it, also perished in the unfortunate accident. Initially we thought the Pandavas had died in the fire, but your investigations revealed that the poor Nishada woman and her five innocent sons were the victims. Who is responsible for their murder? Suyodhana or the Pandavas? We thought of Purochana as a corrupt man, but when we visited his house after his demise, it did not look prosperous at all. His widow is living on the small pension I have sanctioned. Why did such a man give his life attempting to save an Untouchable? If there was a conspiracy to finish off Kunti and her sons, I am sure Suyodhana was not responsible for it. Have we forgotten the farce when Kunti accused the Crown Prince of murdering Bhima and we wasted Court time conducting a trial?"

"Very well Sir, I will make the arrangements. Another important issue is that Krishna has taken Bhima and Arjuna to Magadha. I do not know why." Vidhura felt awkward about raising the matter with the Grand Regent, given his opinion on the Varanavata case.

"I know," Bhishma responded. "I do not know what Krishna is up to this time. Last time he took Arjuna with him, we know what happened with Subhadra. I do not know what his agenda is. Bhima has sired a boy with an Asura tribal woman, hasn't he?"

"Yes, her name is Hidumbi. Bhima killed her brother in a drunken brawl. Since Draupadi was with Yudhishtra for a year at the time, Kunti allowed Bhima to marry her. They have a son called Khatotkacha," Vidhura said flatly.

"Sometimes I am embarrassed by the doings of Kunti and her sons. I do not know which book they refer to on morals and *dharma*. Let us hope Bhima and Arjuna's visit to Magadha with Krishna, is for some good reason. Convey the decision about Khandiva to the King, and request his official sanction. Let us hope everything turns out well," Bhishma said with a weary sigh. He was getting tired of running the country. The idea of leaving everything behind and going to live in the Himalayas, in search of peace and God, was most appealing.

Vidhura bowed and left to speak with King Dhritarashtra about the arrangements.

**

"Khandiva! Who wants that hell? Mother, we have been duped again." Nakula was furious when he read the order from the King.

"It is all swamp and jungle and infested with wild beasts and guerrillas," cried his twin Sahadeva, in annoyance.

"Do not get agitated. Let us wait until Krishna returns from Magadha. He will know what to do." Yudhishtra returned to his meditation.

So the three brothers, an indifferent wife, and an anxious mother, awaited Arjuna and Bhima's return from their mission. They had an empire to build.

**

Meanwhile, Krishna, Arjuna and Bhima had reached Magadha. They arrived at the city gates and requested permission to see King Jarasandha. They did not have to wait for long. Krishna was surprised at the warm hospitality extended to them by the King of Magadha, who was a great devotee of Lord Shiva. He arranged a dinner in honour of Krishna, in the courtyard of the gigantic Shiva temple. Krishna looked around. He needed a provocation for his plan to work. Arjuna was engrossed in polite conversation with Jarasandha. Krishna's eyes stopped at General Hiranyadhanus, sitting beside Bhima, quietly eating. Nowhere in India, other than in Jarasandha's Magadha, would an Untouchable have sat with the King and eaten as an equal. Unmindful of the illustrious General beside him, Bhima was gobbling the food as if he had not eaten for days. It took Krishna some time to catch his eye. He gestured to him to topple over the tumbler of water, placed as per custom to the left of his plantain leaf, onto the leaf of the General. Bhima did not understand this strange request, but he was never troubled by reasons and doubt. What Krishna asked, he always obeyed without hesitation. He toppled the glass of water as if by accident, and the water flowed onto the General's leaf. Reacting quickly, the General tried to push the water away and a few droplets fell on Bhima.

"Hey, this is a slight!" Krishna cried jumping up. Everyone looked up from their plates in surprise.

Bhima picked up his cue. "How dare you to throw dirty water onto a Kshatriya, you Untouchable?" Bhima slammed his fist on the table with great force.

No one dared talk to the General that way and Jarasandha stood up angrily. "Prince Bhima, please apologize to General Hiranyadhanus immediately. There are limits to even my hospitality. You cannot come to my palace and insult my friend and Commander-in-Chief, and hope to get away with it."

"Your Highness, it is nothing," Hiranyadhanus said to the enraged King, with quiet dignity. Turning to Bhima, he said, "Sir, it was my fault! Please accept my apologies."

"You have insulted a Kshatriya and will know the wrath of a warrior. I challenge you to a duel." Bhima stamped the ground in a great show of anger.

Hiranyadhanus hesitated, surprised by the Pandava's words.

"No Bhima, leave it. It seems the General is not willing to accept your challenge. He is but a prop in the King's Court and holds his office because Jarasandha has made an undeserving man his Commander-in-Chief," Krishna said, the smile never leaving his lips.

The General had no choice. The eyes of his subordinate officers and soldiers were upon him. If he backed away from Bhima's challenge, he would lose their respect. He had lived honourably all his life, served his master and country well, and wished to die with his head held high. Though he knew he was no match for the young Pandava, thirty years younger than him, he accepted the challenge and walked away to wash his hands. He bowed before the small niche holding a Shiva *linga*. Touching his forehead and chest in surrender to the will of God, he said his final prayers calmly. Lord Shiva had been kind to him. He had reached a position which no low caste could dream of. His only regret was that he would not see his son, Ekalavya. "Lord, take care of my son," he prayed before straightening up and walking towards Jarasandha.

The General looked at the man who had stood staunchly beside him, braving orthodoxy and entrusting the army to him. Jarasandha hugged the General, whispering into his ear, "We have been trapped Hiranya. None of them will leave Magadha alive. If anything happens to you, I will kill them with my bare hands."

The General nodded and said, "Farewell Your Highness. My heart remains at your feet forever."

When the duel started, Bhima thought he would finish off the older man in minutes. However, the Pandava soon realized the veteran General was no walkover. With grit and determination, he fought Bhima, matching the sheer size of his opponent with his experience and skill. Two hours later, the duel was still on, going nowhere. The General had Bhima flat on the ground twice, but respecting the code of warriors; he patiently waited for him to get up on both occasions. But age had its disadvantages and as time progressed, the General began showing signs of fatigue. Bhima, sensing his opponent was tiring, got his chance when the General slipped and fell. Bhima had been taught no code of honour was applicable when doing one's *karma*, so he pounced on the fallen man, pinning him to the ground. In one swift movement, he broke the neck of the first Nishada General of India.

Seeing his dear friend die, Jarasandha lost his cool and jumped into the fray, roaring with rage and indignation. Krishna smiled at the reaction of the Magadha King. It was precisely what he had expected. He always advised anyone willing to listen, that attachment was the root of all misery and unhappiness. Equanimity is the virtue leading to *moksha*. But the foolish monarch had lost his composure on seeing his friend die. Jarasandha was thus an ignorant man, lost in the world of illusion. Attached to his dead friend, he did not have the wisdom to know that the soul did not perish and death was but an illusion. He did not know that his friend had merely changed garb and his soul had gone in search of another body to inhabit. Bhima had not killed the General's soul, so the General had not died at Bhima's hands. All this was but *maya*.

Bhima looked at the body of his seventy-year-old opponent and laughed aloud. He kicked the corpse to one side and rushed to grab Jarasandha in his huge arms. The King deftly moved aside and caught Bhima's neck in the crook of his left arm. With his powerful right hand, he began beating the life out of the lout. Bhima struggled in vain, looking pleadingly at his saviour. He received a message from Krishna's eyes and delivered a punch to Jarasandha's groin, which freed him from the death grip. The King doubled over in pain and anger, and spat at his opponent. Not even common soldiers hit below the belt in battle. But Bhima, unquestioning as always, was simply following the instructions of his Lord. He rushed towards his opponent and shoved him to the ground. He tried jumping onto Jarasandha's chest as he had done with the General, but the elderly King still had a few tricks and rolled away at the last moment. Bhima fell flat. Jarasandha was atop him in a flash. He tried wringing Bhima's neck, but the Pandava managed to wriggle away. Jarasandha knew his time was running out. In a prolonged duel, he was sure he would meet the same fate as his friend.

Krishna watched the contest with interest. True to his philosophy, he did not have any attachment towards Bhima or any of the Pandavas, all of whom were willing to live and die for him. He was too wise for that. If a Bhima or Arjuna died, there were hundreds to take their place. Yet, Jarasandha's victory would go against everything he believed and lived for. Bhima was more useful than even Arjuna, who had the habit of asking uncomfortable questions. The giant Bhima just obeyed. He had larger plans and uses for Bhima, whereas Jarasandha was just a pawn on his chessboard. He could not afford to risk his rook for a pawn. Krishna brought out a betel leaf and waited for Bhima to look at him. When Bhima caught his eye, he tore the leaf into two, throwing the halves to either side of him. Bhima nodded his understanding.

When Jarasandha fell again, he expected Bhima to rush for his neck and was ready. Surprising him, the Pandava caught his right leg and pinned

Jarasandha to the ground by placing his huge feet on the fallen King's left leg. Then, using his massive strength, he started tearing Jarasandha in two, from the groin. Jarasandha screamed in agony as inch by inch, Bhima tore him apart. The great Jarasandha, the man who had attacked Mathura seventeen times and caused Krishna and Balarama to flee to Dwaraka, the man who had dared challenge orthodoxy and the holy *smritis* by building and running a kingdom based on merit and not caste, died slowly and painfully for all his sins.

Bhima celebrated his victory by beating his fists on his broad chest. Krishna knew better. He had seen the unrest in the soldiers' ranks at the death of their General and then their King. The last thing he wanted was a riot. He ran to where he knew the city prison was located. Sensing danger, Bhima followed him. Krishna asked Arjuna to keep the agitated soldiers at bay somehow, and ran on. His spies in Jarasandha's palace joined him as per plan. His aim was to free the ninety-five vassal Kings imprisoned by Jarasandha for disobeying him years ago. Most of them had rebelled against his liberal policies at one time or another. Among them was Sudeva, Jarasandha's son, who had attempted a coup when his father had made an Untouchable the Commander-in-Chief.

Krishna opened the doors and freed the prisoners quickly. They ran to where Arjuna and a few of his newfound supporters were trying to pacify the agitated soldiers. The sight of the Crown Prince of Magadha calmed the situation a little. Krishna addressed the soldiers saying the General and King had both fought and died as Kshatriyas. It was the *dharma* of a Kshatriya to fight and they had achieved *moksha* by doing their *karma*. With silver-tongued oratory, Krishna pacified the soldiers. Sudeva, the darling of the conservatives, became the new King of Magadha before the embers of his father and the General's funeral pyres had cooled.

When Krishna and his friends finally left Magadha, a small section of the Magadha army, who were loyal to the dead King and Commander, broke away and fled towards the vassal kingdom of Chedi, to seek asylum. The ruler of Chedi was Shishupala, an old friend of Jarasandha. On the way, the soldiers met the son of the slain General Hiranyadhanus. Ekalavya was devastated when he heard the news of his father's death. He had longed to meet him.

On their way back to Hastinapura, Krishna heard about the rebels. It was a minor problem and he would deal with it when the time came. It proved to be a costly mistake for the master strategist.

**

"Think of it not as a problem but an opportunity," Krishna told Yudhishtra, smiling.

"But Khandiva is an impenetrable forest and is said to be infested with all sorts of beasts and fierce tribes. How am I to build a city there? My uncle Dhritarashtra has done this to spite us." Yudhishtra was trying to keep calm, but the more he thought about the injustice of it, the angrier he became.

"Why are you worried when I am here, my friend? I think Arjuna and I will take one more journey, this time to Khandiva." Krishna smiled at Arjuna and the great warrior smiled back uncertainly.

Within a week, Krishna and Arjuna, moved towards Khandiva forest with their army. On the way, Krishna told Arjuna the pathetic story of the last Indra, to whom the forest actually belonged. When they neared the low hills of Khandiva, Krishna said something that almost made the Pandava fall from his saddle.

"What do you mean? You are confirming my worst suspicions. You mean my cousin Suyodhana was always right in calling us bastards? I thought the story of us being the sons of Gods was just propaganda. Now you are saying my father lives and is a Prince of the fallen Deva dynasty?" a shocked Arjuna asked Krishna, trembling with anger.

His friend smiled enigmatically. "It does not matter. Ask your mother. Or if you meet Indra, ask him. You are the last Indra's son, Arjuna. Be proud of it. The present Indra might be an incompetent man, but the blood of illustrious ancestors flows in your veins."

"But that means we do not have any right to the crown of Hastinapura. It means Suyodhana should inherit the kingdom. We are mere bastards and he the firstborn of the incumbent King. More than that, my uncle Dhritarashtra is the elder son and rightful heir, and my father Pandu... he had no claim to the throne. What is the point, Krishna? Why are you making me do all this?" Arjuna looked at his friend in confusion.

"Arjuna my dear friend... do not worry over such minor matters. Your brother Yudhishtra is the only person who can save our country from *adharma*. Duryodhana becoming King will spell disaster for this holy land. Just look at whom he befriends – Karna the Suta, Aswathama the fallen Brahmin, Kripa the mad man, Carvaka the atheist, and the list goes on. Imagine him ruling. Imagine what would happen to the system our ancestors built with so much thought. What would happen to our social order? His being the firstborn of the King is a mere technicality. Do not bother about such things. When the time comes, we will see. Now, do your duty as a Kshatriya. Your focus should only be to destroy Khandiva. From its ashes, a new city will rise and from that city, India will be ruled."

Krishna saw doubt in the eyes of the young warrior. "Arjuna, one day I will explain all these things to you. Let the time come and I will clear all your doubts. I will teach you what your *karma* and *dharma* are. For now, let us focus on the task ahead. You Pandavas need your own kingdom to take on the might of Duryodhana. Do you wish to keep your wives in a hut forever? Do the Princesses not deserve better? For the sake of your mother and your brothers, fight!"

Krishna's words struck a chord within Arjuna. His mother and brothers deserved better. Draupadi, the Princess he had won with his skill, and Subhadra, whom he loved more than his own life, deserved better. Krishna was showing him the path of progress and civilization. A forest was nothing but some trees and shrubs. It housed birds and beasts. It was home to a few uncivilized tribes. It was his duty to show them the light. Krishna was right. The forest needed to be gutted. In its place, a city would come up. Where hills stood, towers of progress would rise. The tall trees should give way to shops. Where tigers roamed, chariots would speed, and where mountain streams flowed, sewers would run.

Arjuna looked at the vast expanse of green hills to the East. The river Yamuna snaked her way through the forest, playing hide-and-seek among the woods, her dark waters contrasting with the lush greenery on either bank. A flock of birds swooped though the sky and vanished into the canopy of trees with poignant cries. The air was rich with the aroma of flowers, and butterflies of many colours fluttered around him. There was a promise of rain in the air. Somewhere in the womb of the jungle, a peacock cried in anticipation of love. A moist breeze rustled the leaves and tugged at Arjuna's clothes, caressing his handsome face, and then leaving with a sigh. It started drizzling and a rainbow arched over the green forest. The croaking of frogs kept time to the symphony of crickets as the rain fell gently on the earth. The great warrior went soft at the knees. His strong hands holding his bow trembled. "Krishna..." he pleaded.

But Krishna's face remained impassive. When the sky had dried its tears, the man who believed he was God, steadied the warrior's hands and commanded in a calm voice, "Fire!"

A flame-tipped arrow arched over the treetops and plunged into the heart of the forest. The warriors with Arjuna began decimating the forest with enthusiasm. Soon the hungry God of Fire began devouring the forest with gusto. The army encircled the forest and stood in strategic positions to prevent the escape of any human or beast attempting to flee the flames. When the first deer darted out of the jungle in panic, Krishna cried to Arjuna, "There!" The warrior shot an arrow through its heart. It fell, quivering for a few minutes and then dying without a sound, its glassy gaze fixed on Arjuna. The Pandava read accusation in those gentle eyes and a strange fear gripped him.

"You are doing your duty, Arjuna. You have freed the poor animal from the infinite cycle of suffering through numerous births and deaths. I have given it *moksha*. Do not hesitate... there... see those birds... shoot!" Krishna cried, and the warrior obeyed.

The creatures of the forest began fleeing the raging fire in panic. Arjuna and his warriors cut them down mercilessly. If they missed anything, the Lord pointed it out and the men obeyed. "Not a single living thing should escape. Show no mercy. We will build a great city here and a proper cleansing is required before we begin something new. Shoot down everything moving, flying or crawling." Krishna encouraged the men with his words.

Soon the ground was littered with the corpses of animals, birds, and reptiles. Sensing danger, some ran back into the fire, expecting more mercy from the flames than from Man. The fire welcomed them, granting them *moksha* from this worthless life. The air was heavy with the stench of burning bodies.

Inside the forest, there were over 2000 Nagas in the rebel camp. They were mostly old men, women, and children, as Takshaka had taken most of his warriors to Dandakaranya in the South. The rebel army was penetrating the South and Takshaka had thought it prudent to meet the leaders of the southern Nagas to prepare them for the impending revolution. He had not expected an attack on Khandiva and had left security in the hands of young Aswasena.

When the first arrow landed on his thatched roof with a hiss, Mayasura the architect was sitting in the small veranda of his hut, enjoying the beautiful sight of the rainbow. He looked up in surprise as scores of flame-tipped arrows hissed over his head. A few of the other men came out of their huts and stood looking at the skies in surprise and shock. Before they could react, their huts began going up in flames. The panicked screams of women and children rose in a macabre chorus.

"What are you gaping at, you fools? Get the women and children out!" Vasuki shouted over the din.

Mayasura ran towards the old man. A few of the younger Nagas had gathered around the erstwhile leader and the old man was directing them in the rescue operations. As Mayasura reached him, he saw an angry

Aswasena arguing with the old man, who yelled, "This is no time for disagreement. Maybe you are right and the fire was started by the Prince of Hastinapura. We can discuss that once we have saved ourselves. Get all the able bodied men to put down the fire and rescue the weak."

"You old fool! There is no point in fighting the fire. See how we are being showered with flame-tipped arrows. We have to take them head on. If we do not save our horses and arms, there will be hell to pay when the Great Leader returns," Aswasena shouted back as another hut crumbled beside him.

The tall trees around them had caught fire and the heat was becoming unbearable. Mayasura's first instinct was to run but Vasuki's calm courage held him back. The screams of women and children dying in the flames were unbearable.

As the inferno raged all around, Aswasena and Vasuki glared at each other. "You go and fight your fool's war, son. My first duty is to save my people, rather than a few horses and swords," Vasuki spat on the ground and turned away.

Aswasena shrugged. "Rot in hell," the young man, yelled as he ran towards the stables. The horses were whining in fear as the fire raced towards them. Most of the young men abandoned Vasuki and followed Aswasena. Mayasura watched in horror as hundreds of men entered the burning stables.

"What are you gaping at? Go and save your mothers and sisters," Vasuki barked at the young architect.

Mayasura ran towards the huts. A few men followed him. The blast of heat was intense. The fire had swallowed many of the huts near the edge of the clearing. The smell of burning flesh was overwhelming. Mayasura saw a group of women and children huddled in the south corner of a clearing but wildfire was steadily engulfing them. He ran towards the jungle, trying to circumvent the fire. If he could reach the central ring of huts before the flames did, he might be able to save those people. As he ran towards the forest, the Naga cavalry galloped past. His eyes briefly met those of Aswasena, and the Naga captain looked at him in utter contempt as they rushed past. As far as Aswasena was concerned, men like Mayasura were cowards who hid behind their books, despising action. He did not have time to waste on such effeminate bastards. He wanted a chance to take revenge on Arjuna and earn the respect of his Great Leader.

Mayasura watched them vanish behind the burning trees and thick columns of smoke. They were rushing to take on Arjuna's mighty army head on. The ear-splitting sound of a huge tree crashing jolted him from his stupor and he jumped back. The men with him watched the disappearing column of Aswasena's cavalry. Mayasura shouted to them to follow him. They ran diagonally to the group of women and children, curving away from the raging fire. Fingers of flames came perilously close, trying to grab them. Mayasura thought his eyeballs would burn in their sockets from the blazing heat. As the flames danced in the changing breeze and smoke curled towards heaven, he could see the frightened faces of the children, crying in fear. Mayasura leapt across the flames and ran towards the huts standing between the group and the advancing inferno. The men followed. Some of them emerged on the other side, choking and coughing smoke, beating the flames from their clothes. They were shocked to find Mayasura torching the huts. A few screamed that he was mad. Unmindful of their protests, Mayasura kept throwing flaming faggots onto the thatched roofs of the remaining huts. A few understood what the architect was trying to do. He was creating a firebreak by burning down the huts in the path of the advancing fire. They hurried to help him and a gap quickly appeared in the path of the licking flames. The women and children were safe for now. Though the fire raged all around, Mayasura had managed to create an island of safety.

Vasuki walked towards them, leaping over the slowly dying fire with an ease that belied his age. He sought out Mayasura and hugged him. A ragged cheer rose from the crowd of survivors. The soft spoken and unassuming architect had saved their lives.

However, Vasuki raised his staff and shouted for silence. Then they heard it. They could feel the earth rumbling beneath their feet. They were children of the forest and knew what the sound meant. A despairing wail rose from the group of women and the children clung to their mothers in fright.

"Move to either side of me... NOW!" Vasuki shouted at the top of his lungs. The crowd parted in two.

Mayasura, who had lived in the outskirts of southern cities most of his life, did not understand what the sounds heralded and wondered why the forest dwellers were panicking when he had saved them from the fire. He soon understood. The charred trees began trembling. Mayasura could feel the earth shaking more and more vigorously. Suddenly, a herd of elephants broke from the jungle and stampeded towards the group of humans. In the distance, flames were rushing for them. They waited anxiously as the herd trumpeted past; smashing everything in its way, overturning the half-burnt trees and following the path Aswasena's cavalry had taken. Bison, rhinoceros, gaur, and other beasts of the jungle, followed the elephants. Occasionally, tigers and lions raced by, creating panic. Exotic birds screeched high in the sky. The sight of the stampeding animals froze the humans with fear.

When the last of the beasts had passed, Vasuki cried aloud, "Follow them now. They know the path to get out of the forest fire."

Without waiting for further instructions, the Nagas joined the fleeing beasts. They thought they were escaping the cruel fire, but at the other end, the greatest warrior in the world and his divine friend waited for them. They had a city to build and the forest had to be cleared. The fire advanced rapidly, trying to grab the fleeing humans and animals. As the stampede neared the edge of the forest, arrows fell on them thick and fast, creating further panic and pandemonium. Elephants, bison and rhinoceros began running amok, some turning back towards the advancing flames and colliding violently with the oncoming stampede. Some managed to pass through the thick column of animals fleeing in the opposite direction and reach the Nagas running behind. Women and children scattered in fear. Many were trampled under the feet of the frightened elephants. When the beasts encountered the advancing fire, they once again turned and ran back through the crowd of Nagas, leaving another trail of death. A few of the huge beasts attacked Arjuna's men, causing many deaths in their ranks, but the soldiers soon cut them down with swords, spears and poison arrows.

"There! There!" Krishna kept pointing and Arjuna shot his victims down with unfailing accuracy.

When the surviving Nagas managed to reach the edge of the forest, the innumerable corpses of animals and humans littering the ground shocked them. As they fled over the dead and dying, a few slipping and falling in the mess of blood and flesh, Mayasura realised the brave Aswasena and his band of soldiers were no longer alive. He did not know how many had died in his own group. Death danced around them. Many of the Nagas stood frozen in fear, not knowing what to do until death caught up with them. Mayasura was sure his own death was imminent. He saw Vasuki trying to control the people's panic. The sight of him standing with unflinching courage amidst the fearsome bloodbath was awe-inspiring.

"Mayasura… save the Deva King…" Vasuki shouted at him.

Mayasura looked to where Vasuki pointed and saw an enraged elephant charging at Indra. The old Deva King stood staring at certain death. Mayasura ran towards him, trying not to think about the arrows flying perilously close. The elephant had knocked down Indra with its trunk and raised a foot to crush the old man's head. Without thinking, Mayasura dived, grabbed Indra, and rolled to his left. The elephant's heavy foot descended with juddering force. Another two inches and the old King would have been pulp. The elephant lumbered away while Mayasura helped the trembling Indra stand up. His heart leapt with joy when he saw Vasuki's curt nod of appreciation. He had never suspected he possessed so much courage. For a moment, he forgot where he was and felt proud of himself.

Indra's grip tightened painfully on Mayasura's wrist and shook him out of his self-congratulatory reflections. He saw the resigned look on the old man's face and turned to see what had created so much fear. What he saw chilled his blood. All his courage oozed away. The elephant was returning for its kill, rushing toward them at great speed. The young Asura and the fallen Deva King, stood immobile, hands clasped, fascinated by the sight of approaching death. They could faintly hear Vasuki screaming at them to move out of the elephant's path, but their limbs refused to move. They could see the elephant's eyes as the huge shaking form approached them in a cloud of dust. They closed their eyes when the elephant was barely six feet away. Its trunk almost scraped Mayasura's waist before collapsing with an earth-shaking thud. When the dust settled and their heartbeats returned to normal, they saw an arrow had pierced almost three feet into the brain of the beast. The elephant quivered for a few seconds and died.

Mayasura looked back to trace the flight path of the arrow and saw Arjuna standing tall, aiming at his throat. Petrified, he pulled his wrist from Indra's grip and ran. The arrow hummed past his right ear. On an impulse, he turned and ran towards Arjuna, both hands raised high above his head in the universal gesture of surrender. "Swami... Swami..." he cried, trying to be heard above the din.

Krishna saw him and pointed him out to the great Warrior to pick him off. Arjuna aimed his arrow at Mayasura but something in the young man's eyes made him hesitate. Mayasura stumbled and fell as he neared Arjuna, but got up and ran on. He fell at Arjuna's feet, pleading for the life of his people. "Swami... Swami... have mercy on us," he begged. "We shall be your slaves for life. There are only small children and helpless women here. All the warriors are dead. Please forgive us for what we have done..." He was sobbing hysterically.

Arjuna looked at his Lord for advice. "*Hmmm*... maybe they can be of some use," Krishna said. "Ask him what he can do."

Mayasura's sobbing suddenly stopped. He was an architect, a sculptor, an engineer, and now he was a slave. He felt reticent to declare his talent before these great men, but stood up slowly. He needed some wet sand to say it with his fingers. Mere words would not suffice. He found what he was looking for and began moulding it with his fingers. It did not matter that the blood of his people and many mute beasts had wet the sand. He was indifferent to the dead bodies around him. He did not hear the sound of humans and beasts dying. He did not think about his almost certain death a few minutes before. He had become one with his creation. He went into a trance as his fingers caressed and slapped the red mud. From it, a city began rising like magic.

Arjuna watched fascinated. He ordered his soldiers to stop the massacre. They too, crowded around to watch the Asura building his city of sand. Half the Nagas had perished in the carnage and the forest of Khandiva was history. A few animals managed to scurry away as the men stood watching a dream unfolding. The surviving women and children joined the crowd around Mayasura. The young architect was unaware of his surroundings, nor did not know his skill had saved the lives of his people yet again. From his fingers a model city rose. He built palaces and fashioned ornate temple pagodas that reached towards the skies. They watched him create city streets, fountains, walkways, gardens, market places, and beautiful lakes.

When he finished, Arjuna forgot himself and hugged the Untouchable. "Can you build this in stone for us?" the great warrior asked the little man.

Mayasura fell to the ground, kissing Arjuna's feet in gratitude. A cheer rose from the crowd. Mayasura had been granted his dream.

24 A City Cursed

SUYODHANA TRIED BLOTTING OUT the misery of losing Subhadra by working with even more passion. He was being trained to rule the kingdom by Bhishma. But with the Pandavas back in the palace, he was afraid of meeting Subhadra somewhere with her husband, and he tried staying away from Hastinapura as much as possible, travelling to the remote areas of the kingdom and visiting nondescript villages and distant border towns. Aswathama was his constant companion on these journeys. Suyodhana also accompanied Vidhura on his official tours. His admiration for the Prime Minister increased with every trip. Sometimes he found time to visit his sister Sushala in Sindh. Then Karna would travel there too, and the friends would meet. On some of the trips to Sindh, they would impulsively travel on to Dwaraka, to see Balarama. They avoided the days they knew Krishna would be present. It helped that Krishna was often with the Pandavas in Khandiva, where their new city was coming up. The relationship between Subhadra and Balarama was no longer what it had been before her marriage to Arjuna and she was now closer to her other brother, Krishna.

On one such trip, Balarama proposed a pilgrimage to Kashi. Since everyone lauded the idea of travelling together, it was agreed. Under Balarama's direction, a large entourage started towards the ancient city. Jayadratha and Sushala joined them. They wished to pray at Lord Vishwanatha's shrine, as they remained childless after two years of marriage. Karna rushed back to Anga to bring his family along. They joined the others at Kashi. Karna now had an infant son and was a proud father.

On the way to Kashi, they received another pleasant surprise. Vidhura brought Dhritarashtra and Gandhari to join the pilgrimage. His own family also accompanied him. It became a standing joke in the group that Vidhura had manipulated the King and Queen in order to get a well-deserved break for himself. Vidhura denied any such thing but it was evident he was enjoying his vacation.

The moment the Royal group entered the ancient city, news spread like wildfire that the Kings of Hastinapura, Dwaraka, Anga, and Sindh, had arrived on a pilgrimage. Touts and Priests surrounded them. These were neither thinkers nor philosophers, but petty traders who sold their God for money. They stopped Vidhura and Karna from entering the sanctum sanctorum, saying they were Shudras. But having received their pieces of silver, they moved aside. They chanted *mantras* without knowing what they meant and invented extempore stories, attributing them to the *Puranas* to justify what they did. They were obsessed with ritual purity and their own superiority, yet the city and river was littered with filth. They thrived on death like vultures. They fattened themselves on the guilt of those who had lost their loved ones. They threw half-burned bodies into the Ganga to save firewood and maximize profit. Death was a thriving industry in the holiest city of India. No enemy of the country could have treated the holy river worse, even though its waters were sacred to all races and castes from the Himalayas to the southern seas. Yet they considered themselves pious and treated others with contempt.

The vassal King of Kashi came to pay his respects to Dhritarashtra, who accepted his invitation to stay at the palace. As they waited near the river, hundreds of women came down the steps with oil lamps in their hands. When the waters of the Ganga turned saffron in the evening sun, they began singing hymns that were as old as humanity. They created golden arcs in the air as they moved the oil lamps in a circle and Suyodhana, who was seeing the famed evening Ganga *aarti* for the first time, stood spellbound. The hymns were the humble tribute of an ancient civilization to a great river. The Ganga flowed silently, caressing the land with her holy waters. From the icy glaciers of Gangotri to the warm seas of Vanga, she accepted the prayers and abuse of her children with equanimity. She took death and gave back life to India.

As the Royal group watched mesmerised, the worshippers floated the lamps onto the water, creating tiny islands of light in the vast darkness.

The last song was a prayer of thanks to all the holy rivers of India – Ganga, Sindhu, Yamuna, Brahmaputra, Saraswati, Narmada and Kaveri – for their munificence. Suyodhana wondered how a culture that revered rivers, could abuse them so heartlessly.

Servants supplied oil lamps to the Royal group and Suyodhana slowly walked down the steps of the *ghat* to the river, trying to keep the flickering lamp alight in the playful breeze. As he was about to put his feet into the water, he heard a soft voice behind him say, "No, do not touch the Holy Mother with your feet first. It is a great sin." Suyodhana turned in surprise and his heart skipped a beat. He was afraid that if he did not avert his eyes from what he saw, he would lose his heart, yet again. The wounds Subhadra had inflicted had yet to heal and he was afraid of love. So he looked into the distance, towards the distant bend in the river, where a few funeral pyres were still burning. He could see a Priest gesturing to a *chandala* to topple a half-burnt corpse into the river. He imagined he could hear the hiss as it fell into the water, disturbing the floating lamps.

Without turning, Suyodhana said, "Devi, you say the river is so holy that one should not put one's feet into her first. Can you not see the half-burned corpses floating in the water, and the filth and garbage?" He knew what he said was provocative and hoped she would either argue or go away. He did not want to look into the depths of her dark eyes or see her lovely lips reflecting the golden light of the lamp she held. He turned away, not expecting a reply.

When he heard the rustling of her skirts, he turned to see her leaning towards the water, scooping some into her cupped hands. The lamp she had floated swirled away in circles, starting its journey towards the distant sea. Her eyes were closed in meditation as the river water seeped through her long fingers. He could not look away. Unexpectedly, she opened her eyes and caught him staring at her. She smiled at his embarrassment.

He knelt beside her and gently placed his own lamp upon the water. They watched it float away together. Suyodhana asked, "Devi, may I have the honour of knowing your name?" He tried to suppress the butterflies fluttering in his stomach. His mouth went dry when she did not respond immediately.

Finally, she said, "Bhanumati, daughter of King Bhagadatha of Pragjyothisha."

"I am Suyodhana, firstborn of King Dhritarashtra."

"I know. I have heard about you."

"I hope they were only good things," said Suyodhana smiling.

"Not always." A mischievous smile played on Bhanumati's lips.

"Will you marry me?" asked the Prince, astonishing himself. He regretted the words as soon as he had uttered them.

"Is it not preposterous to ask me like this?" Bhanumati turned away her blushing face.

Suyodhana flushed too. He did not know how to handle the situation he found himself in. 'Was there ever a fool like me? What possessed me?' he wondered. His heart hammered in his chest.

"But I like preposterous things. My father is in the temple." Hiding a smile, Bhanumati lightly ran back up the steps of the *ghat*. She almost collided with Vidhura, standing a few steps above them. She murmured an apology and vanished into the crowd of her ladies.

It took a while for Suyodhana to comprehend she had accepted his fantastic proposal. He did not know why he had proposed like that to a girl he had just met. Was his love for Subhadra so shallow?

Vidhura came up to him and asked with a gleam in his eyes, "Would you like me to speak to her father?" Suyodhana flushed seeing the mischievous smile in Vidhura's eyes.

"Please do so Sir, before he does something rash," a voice cried out from the darkness.

Suyodhana wanted to bang his head on the stone steps of the *ghat* when he heard it. He had completely forgotten his friend Aswathama's presence. He would certainly enact the whole scene to the others. The rascal was supposed to be meditating.

Aswathama came up to them. "Will you marry me?" he said, imitating Suyodhana's deep voice perfectly. Suyodhana aimed a punch at the mischievous Brahmin's face, but Aswathama ducked and continued in a feminine voice, "Is it not preposterous to ask me like this? But I like preposterous things…" Suyodhana pounced on him, stopping him from saying anything further. But his friend slipped from his hands and ran off shouting, "Karna… Karna… do you want to hear something preposterous? Will you marry me?"

Suyodhana chased after Aswathama as his friend ducked and weaved through the crowd. People were staring at them. Suyodhana knew they were behaving like idiots. Their gaiety and laughter was sure to look like a mockery of tradition and custom to pious believers. People came to Kashi from all over India to die, and here they were brimming with life and laughter. It was not going to do his already stained reputation any good. But his immediate priority was to stop Aswathama telling Karna. He did not want to spend the night as the subject of their amusement.

"Shall I take it as a yes?" Vidhura called from the *ghat* to Suyodhana's disappearing form, but did not get a reply.

***

They were married in the temple of Kashi Vishwanatha in a simple ceremony, fourteen days after they had met. Karna fed the entire city and gave gifts to everyone, regardless of caste, colour or language, adding to his reputation for philanthropy. Suyodhana was glad not to have won his wife in a contest like a trophy or a prize cow. When they reached Hastinapura, the Grand Regent invited the nobles and the vassal Kings to a grand celebration. Invitations also went to the kingdoms of the

Southern Confederate. It was a State occasion and the marriage of the Crown Prince was celebrated with great pomp and splendour, unlike the simple ceremony at Kashi. Among the people who attended was Krishna, who came to bless the couple. The Pandavas too, came to celebrate the occasion with their cousins. The two powerful women of the Kuru clan stood next to each other receiving their guests. Seeing all the Kurus together, the ambassadors of the Southern Confederate wondered whether the news of a schism in the Kuru clan was merely an exaggerated tale carried by their spies to please them.

"Things did not quite turn out as you wished, Gandhari," Kunti whispered, not letting the smile leave her lips.

"I do not understand what you mean, Kunti." Gandhari could sense the glee in Kunti's words and prayed Dhritarashtra would not overhear and make any nasty comments.

"We survived Varanavata, and my sons won the hand of the Panchala Princess, despite the best efforts of your son."

"Suyodhana was not involved. Why do you always suspect him?"

"Suspect! I am sure of it. Ask him why he built the house of lac for us. Or was it your husband who did that?"

"This is a happy occasion. Do not ruin it with these thoughts, Kunti. Whoever made the house of lac; it was a poor Nishada woman and her children who perished in it, not you or your sons."

"You would have preferred it to be us?" Kunti asked as she folded her hands in welcome to a minor Prince from the east coast of India.

Gandhari did not reply. She felt uneasy about the way misunderstandings and hatred were growing within the family. "We will talk about it later, Kunti. Today is an auspicious day; the Crown Prince is getting married."

"Crown Prince! Where do you get such ideas, Gandhari? Yudhishtra was married long ago."

"You won't leave it alone will you? Suyodhana is the firstborn of the reigning King. That is it."

"We will see who sits on the throne of Hastinapura finally, Gandhari. We are no pushovers."

Gandhari turned towards Kunti, a deadly smile on her face. "We will see, Kunti. Since Suyodhana is my legitimate son, he will rule this country."

Before Kunti could retort, the Pandavas and Draupadi came. "Seek the blessing of your aunt and uncle," Kunti said, all emotion gone from her voice. Draupadi and her five husbands bowed to touch Dhritarashtra and Gandhari's feet. Gandhari reached out to touch Draupadi. Her proud and erect posture surprised Gandhari. There was nothing bashful about this young woman, the Queen thought. What did she look like? She had heard Draupadi was very beautiful. But why had such a bold and lovely Princess agreed to be the wife of five men? The question nagged at Gandhari. Later, she had the opportunity to ask the Panchala Princess herself as they sat together.

"Aunt, you of all people should not ask me that question. Why did you choose blindness when Lord Bhishma brought you here?" Draupadi said. "Perhaps my mother-in-law feared her sons would fight over me. She wants them to be united," she added to diffuse the sharpness of her earlier remark.

"Daughter, I have a hundred sons but they do not need to marry the same woman to remain united. Has Kunti brought up her sons with so little self-control that they would fight over their brother's wife?" Dhritarashtra asked, as he joined them.

Draupadi hid her embarrassment by bowing low to the King. Gandhari bit her lip, fearing Kunti would overhear her husband's insensitive comments.

What she feared happened within seconds. She heard Kunti's sharp voice say to her daughter-in-law, "Yudhishtra is looking for you. What are you doing here?"

She heard Draupadi walking away. She heard her husband coughing in embarrassment. The poor man had not known that Kunti was sitting nearby. Fortunately, for him, Vidhura came to say some of the vassal Kings were waiting to greet him. She heard him walk away, chatting animatedly to his Prime Minister about irrelevant things to shut out any possibility of Kunti reacting to him. Kunti would not react to him, Gandhari knew. She braced herself for what was coming.

"You leave no opportunity to insult me or my children, Gandhari," Kunti hissed into the Queen's ear. Gandhari did not offer any reply or apology. She stood up in haughty silence, ignoring Kunti and her words. Kunti walked away, trembling with anger, leaving Gandhari to feel sad for the young girl who had to share her bed with five men so that her mother-in-law could play her political game. 'Draupadi is almost like me,' Gandhari thought. 'In this country, every woman is a tool to further the interests of men.'

***

What Suyodhana had dreaded occurred the morning after the grand feast. He came face to face with Subhadra for the first time after her marriage to Arjuna. She accompanied Bhanumati. Subhadra carried her baby son. She quietly put him into Suyodhana's arms. As her fingers brushed his, Suyodhana averted his eyes from her lovely face. The baby gave a toothless smile and cooed and the Crown Prince of Hastinapura melted. He stood tongue-tied as the baby played with the long string of pearls he was wearing. The woman he had once loved madly, chatted with his newly wedded wife as though they were long-lost friends. How could they be so nonchalant? 'Did my love mean nothing to Subhadra?' he wondered.

When the baby wet him and began crying, the women turned towards Suyodhana, laughing. Subhadra took the baby from his hands, talking to it in the language only women and babies understand. The infant stopped crying and smiled. "Does he not look like his father?" Subhadra asked Suyodhana. She did not notice the pain on his face as she cooed to her son.

The baby reached towards Suyodhana. He picked up the child and then took off the lustrous string of pearls from his neck. Folding it into four loops, he placed the necklace over the infant's head, lost in the innocent smile.

Arjuna walked into the room and stopped, seeing them all together. Subhadra ran to her husband. "Suyodhana gave this to him." She proudly displayed the valuable gift Suyodhana had bestowed on their son.

Arjuna bent to touch his cousin and Bhanumati's feet. After all, they were elder. For a while, they spoke of the celebrations and seeing so many familiar faces. Then, as Arjuna and his wife turned to leave, Suyodhana called after him, "What is his name, cousin?"

But it was Subhadra who answered. "Abhimanyu."

That night, as they lay in the massive four-poster bed, which had been a gift to them from her father, Bhanumati kissed her husband's lips and whispered, "Subhadra is a lucky woman. I wish I had a son like Abhimanyu."

Suyodhana ran his fingers through her hair, not saying anything. He was trying hard to love the woman he was holding in his arms with the same passion he had once felt for Subhadra.

***

Meanwhile, on the charred banks of the Yamuna, where once the impenetrable forests of Khandiva stood, a great city was rising. Those three years were the best of Mayasura's life. He was a perfectionist and a tough taskmaster. The surviving Naga women and children formed the workforce for building the great city. In the searing heat of summer, the pounding rain of the monsoon, and the freezing cold of winter, Mayasura toiled, along with the frail Naga women and their emaciated children, to build his beautiful city for the Pandavas. Just for food and a humble dwelling, the coolies worked to erect the magnificent palace where Yudhishtra and his brothers would live and rule. Under the relentless drive of the young Asura, the Nagas built market places, paved roads, created gardens, and built homes. Stone by stone, they created the greatest city

India had ever seen. Bigger than Dwaraka, more meticulously planned and executed than Hastinapura, lacking the urban chaos of Heheya or Muzaris, it was a blend of various styles of architecture. Mayasura experimented with different schools and fashioned temples like those of the Asuras; the musical halls with their perfect acoustics, were derived from Gandharva; the Western coastal city of Heheya inspired the markets; the inns and travellers' rest houses resembled those in Muzaris, while the sculptures were fashioned in the style of Gandhara. Mayasura created a masterpiece that somehow captured the soul of India. Its fame spread far and wide, much before it was finished.

The Pandavas camped on the banks of the Yamuna to oversee the construction. When they ran out of funds for their luxurious city, they raised the taxes or raided the countryside. They watched the magnificent city rise with pride and satisfaction and revelled in the paeans being sung in its praise. The Gods were kind to them but they were not surprised by this benevolence. Had they not always followed the word of the Lord and walked the path of *dharma*? It was nothing less than what they deserved. As the city neared completion, their Priest and Counsellor, Dhaumya, arrived from Hastinapura with his disciples, to ensure Yudhishtra kept treading the path of righteousness.

A few days after Mayasura had laid the first stone for the new city; Vasuki left it with some men of his choosing. He did not try to dissuade Mayasura, for he knew nothing could tear the possessed man from the city he was yearning to build. But Vasuki had an urgent mission. After the carnage at Khandiva, Takshaka had tried to take revenge on Hastinapura by mounting a series of terrorist attacks. Bhishma had ruthlessly put down the rebellion. The current whereabouts of Takshaka was unknown. His hold on the poorer sections of Hastinapura had weakened considerably after Vidhura had smashed Durjaya's network. Vasuki felt uneasy about their unethical liaison with elements like Durjaya. He also suspected a ruthless and powerful person was manipulating them from the shadows and rejoicing in the chaos, which ensued. From experience, he knew nothing good could from this unholy alliance.

Vasuki had heard the rumours about General Hiranyadhanus and Emperor Jarasandha's death. He had to find Ekalavya before he did something rash. He was the last of hope for his blighted people. Vasuki was growing old and his time was running out. If he could just manage to make Ekalavya or himself the leader of the Nagas, instead of the arrogant and power hungry Takshaka, perhaps there would be some hope. Deeply worried, the old man left Mayasura and went in search of Ekalavya.

The other old man in the gang chose to stay with Mayasura. He had nothing in common with the Nagas and his alliance was due to the pitiful straits he had fallen into. In another era, he would have been sitting on the throne of India, lording over inferior men like Takshaka, or even Bhishma. The contrast between the first Indra, who had smashed the old Asura kingdoms ruthlessly and established Deva rule and their dynasty, and the present one who scurried about like a mouse, living on the tid-bits thrown by men like Takshaka, was stark and pitiful. In his youth, Indra had dreamt of regaining his empire but as he grew older, the dream turned sour and left him an embittered old man.

The highpoint of his life had been when Kunti had invited him to her bed for a few weeks. He had left his ruined palace in the Khandiva forest and walked all the way to Hastinapura. He had waited anxiously, like a common villager, at the entrance of her comfortable dwelling on the outskirts of the forest. When she finally granted him admittance, he could feel the cold contempt in her eyes. Dhaumya the Priest was there too and it was evident it was he who had persuaded the Princess and her impotent husband to invite him. As he bore the indignity of the rituals and *mantras*, he wondered about his fate. He was about to share the bed of another man's wife. She already had two sons whom her husband had not fathered. Indra felt like a prize bull, brought in to impregnate the Royal womb. Had he not needed the money desperately, he would have cursed them all and stormed out.

While the Priests discussed philosophy outside, he had fumbled with Kunti inside the stuffy room, fuming at her contemptuous smile. For the first two days, he had burned with shame at his own impotency. When he finally succeeded in his task, he felt more relief than pleasure. Collecting his money and gifts, he had felt like a prostitute. He wondered about this strange world and its morality until genteel poverty reasserted itself and blotted out such meaningless thoughts.

Indra had taken shelter in Mayasura's hut but he was irritated by the very sight of the dreamy architect. The thought that the last Indra owed his life to this effeminate Asura, made him bitter. He expressed his frustration by abusing the young man whenever he got the chance. Mayasura, lost in his own dream world, ignored the rantings of the old man. It was easy to do as his work kept him more than occupied. He made sure he left the hut before Indra woke and returned only after he was asleep. Occasionally, however, arguments broke out between them and Mayasura's amused smile would drive Indra almost mad. During one such argument, Indra blurted out that Arjuna was, in fact, his son. Mayasura rolled on the floor with laughter at the preposterous thought. Indra stormed out of the hut, abusing the Untouchable, and walked to the camp of the Pandavas. As he neared, his bravado vanished. He stood outside the camp and would have turned back had the hawk-eyed Dhaumya not seen him. He said something to Krishna, who had come to visit his friends, and before Indra knew it, all of them were walking towards him.

Krishna bowed and smiled. "Your Highness, welcome to the humble abode of the Pandavas."

Yudhishtra then came forward and touched his feet. Indra was taken aback, both by the form of address and by the gesture of respect from the eldest Pandava. It had been a long time since he had heard anyone address him as 'Highness' and it sounded strange to his ears. He searched for any trace of scorn in their smiles but they stood bowing respectfully, as though Indra was sitting on the throne of India as its rightful Emperor.

"Here is your son, your Highness." Krishna pushed forward the reluctant Arjuna.

Indra was overwhelmed with emotion. Being introduced to his grown-up son suddenly brought back all the dark memories. It reminded the last

Indra of the harsh reality – that he was a failure in life. When he lifted up his son, who had stooped to touch his feet, he could not control himself and broke into sobs. The Indra dynasty would not end with him, it would continue through this Pandava. The old King felt his life finally had some meaning and purpose. "My son... my son..." he kept mumbling through his tears as he caressed the stiff warrior.

They showed Indra around the wonderful city they were building and he felt more elated with every passing sight. Krishna asked him whether he realised it had been Arjuna who had saved his life by killing the charging elephant the day Khandiva burned down. Indra looked at his son with pride. It was a relief to know he was not indebted to that Asura after all. It was his son who had saved him, not the Untouchable. The hatred he felt for Mayasura dissolved with that knowledge. He no longer felt indebted. Instead, Indra told them about Mayasura's many gifts, heaping praise on the architect. But Mayasura's patrons, the Pandavas, remained indifferent to Indra's words. Krishna smiled at the erstwhile King and said the Asura was just doing his duty, there was nothing extraordinary in that. He too, owed his life to Arjuna, and he was merely repaying his debt.

Krishna's words silenced Indra. He did not wish to argue with the powerful man and destroy the happiness he had finally found. To change the subject, he asked the Pandavas whether they had thought of a name for their new city

"Sir, the name honours you," the eldest Pandava said. A smile broke the usual calm placidity of his face. Indra's heart skipped a beat. "It will be called..." Yudhishtra looked around at his beaming brothers. "Arjuna, why don't you tell His Highness what has been decided?"

Arjuna nodded. "Indraprastha – City of Indra." He said it so quietly that the others had to strain to hear.

The last Indra's ecstasy knew no bounds. Tears filled his eyes. In the autumn of his years, he finally knew the Gods had not forgotten him. The greatest city of India would be named after him. His son would continue his lineage. He had not lived in vain. Indra stood in complete silence. His joy was too great to bear.

"We have named the city in honour of the first Indra, Purendra," said Krishna.

The words brought the old man back to earth with a thud. It was cruel of them to remind him. He was just a broken old man who had only the glory of his ancestors to call his own. Mortification filled his soul as he turned away.

"Sir, we mean no offence. In fact, we are all proud that the blood of the great Purendra Indra flows in the veins of my brother Arjuna, through you," Yudhishtra said to Indra.

But Indra's mind had returned to a place of darkness. The new palace and the city no longer looked beautiful in his eyes. He wanted to get away and hide in his hut. The bitterness he had felt towards Mayasura, for being indebted to him for his life, now turned towards Arjuna. 'God willing, I will repay the debt to my son,' the last Indra vowed. He knew how to do it. He had heard rumours about a great Suta warrior named Karna, who was becoming a threat to Arjuna. He had heard Karna wore a breastplate that could not be penetrated by ordinary arrows. Indra still remembered the secret formula used to forge an unbreakable iron arrow with a diamond tip. It could penetrate anything, even the armour fashioned by the sun-worshippers of the Eastern coast. The weapon had been developed by the first Indra, and was called Vajra, the Diamond. The secret had been passed from father to son in the Indra clan, but the ironsmiths who could make it had long vanished.

Perhaps Mayasura could reinvent the technique, Indra thought in growing excitement. 'I will bestow the Vajra on my son, to take on the mighty Karna and thus repay my debt and become free. Until then, I will not step into his palace or face him. The world will then know, the last Indra was not a complete failure.' Indra hurriedly said his farewells to Krishna and the Pandavas. It gave him pleasure to refuse their invitation to remain. But when Yudhishtra offered to convey him to his door, he did not decline. He wanted his neighbours in the coolie line to see him getting down from the Royal chariot. But more than that, he wanted Mayasura to witness his triumph.

***

Mayasura came home early. He was perplexed to see his master's chariot stopping at his gate and rushed out to pay his respects. He was shocked to see old Indra getting down from the chariot, wearing a smug smile. Yudhishtra warned the Asura to treat Arjuna's father with all due respect. He explained, that as an ascetic, Indra did not care for material comforts; hence, he preferred to reside in the hut rather than in the palace. The young architect bowed in silence.

Returning to the Pandava camp after depositing the cranky old man at the Untouchable's hut, Yudhishtra shook his head in disgust. He hated going to the stinking coolie colony. He would now have to take a bath. Nor did he look forward to the session with Guru Dhaumya, where he would certainly be lectured on the necessity of keeping the body and spirit pure. A few gifts to the Brahmins would absolve him of this particular sin, but the palace was grander than he had ever imagined and the coffers were almost empty. He would be forced to raise the taxes again.

For a moment, Yudhishtra envied his cousin Duryodhana, who had the courage to stand up against the likes of Dhaumya. 'Duryodhana! Why does he always make me look like a weak fool?' wondered his cousin. The path of *dharma* was difficult. He trod every step in fear, lest he commit a sin that would earn him the wrath of the Brahmins and damnation from the Gods. When he was alone in his chamber, free of the heavy cloak of righteousness he painfully wore, he was afraid to look in the mirror and see himself. His entire life was a lie. He lived in fear. Deep in his heart, he knew he had no claim to the throne of Hastinapura. He needed the support of the obscure *smritis* and the fanciful interpretations by amoral scholars, to justify his claims. But he had no choice. He needed men like Dhaumya as much as they needed him.

Yudhishtra entered the camp and went to take a bath, ignoring both his wife and mother. He could endure anything but not Draupadi's scornful smile. His greatest fear was not having to confront Duryodhana or Karna in the battlefield one day, but facing his wife in the privacy of their chamber. He suspected she knew him better than he knew himself. He was afraid she had already found the turbulent darkness that hid under the surface of his vaunted uprightness. He did not wish to look into her lovely eyes and see his reflection in those dark depths.

***

The relationship between Indra and Mayasura changed after that day. The old man was less harsh in his criticism and the younger man showed more respect to the deposed Deva King. The city project was in its final stages. More and more people began arriving from Hastinapura and other parts of the country. Mayasura heard the complaints about the higher castes imposing restrictions on the movements of the Nagas in various places, but obsessed with the completion of the temple; he did not heed the early warning signs.

Things soon turned for the worse. Returning from work one day, he found many people crowded at the gates of the slums. It was nearly midnight. It was unusual for so many women to be on the road at that time of night. Trying to suppress the nameless fear that bubbled in his mind, he walked quickly towards his hut. A few men stared at him in accusation as he passed but refused to answer his frantic questions. Some of the women were frantically arranging their meagre household possessions, getting ready to move out. He saw Indra sitting dejectedly in the veranda and rushed to him.

"The King's men have announced they will be demolishing this colony. They have asked everyone to move to the other side of the Yamuna, to the place reserved for Untouchables and low castes. They want to create a public park here."

Mayasura sat down on the mud steps of his hut and covered his face with his calloused hands. He waited for the tears to come, but they had dried long ago. He waited for anger, but that too had vanished. When dawn began encroaching into the night sky, the elephants came and began demolishing the huts. Silently, the people walked towards the river and waited for the ferry. The city no longer needed them. They were once again unwanted. The old Deva King and the young Asura sat together without exchanging a word. When the elephants came to demolish their humble hut, they just stood up and walked to the edge of the clearing, and watched them pulling down their home.

Day broke with light showers falling on the desolation of the coolie camp. The *mahout*s had taken the elephants away after the demolition was completed. The place where the Nagas had spent three years was just a pile of rubble now. The alleys that had buzzed with life and the laughter of children just the previous night had vanished without a trace. It was as if the Government had wiped out three years of their lives.

The last Indra leaned on Mayasura's shoulder, watching the frogs jumping in and out of the puddles. He asked in a soft voice, "Does God not see this injustice?"

It was a lament more than a question, but it shook Mayasura from his stupor. "Oh my god, how could I forget?" he cried aloud. Dropping Indra's arm, he ran towards the temple, leaving the old man perplexed.

Puffing and panting, Indra followed the Asura towards the Royal highway, where a grand procession inched along. Both sides of the street were decorated with marigolds and jasmine. The rhythmic chanting of *mantra*s rose into the sky along with the auspicious sound of conch shells and brass bells. At a distance, the tall spires of the new temple sparkled in the sun. The procession was more than a mile long. Young men and women walked along gaily. When they saw Mayasura running towards the temple, they were surprised. 'He is an Untouchable. Stop him before he defiles everything that is holy,' someone cried. The crowd parted in horror as if the Asura architect carried a contagious disease.

Mayasura reached the head of the procession where Yudhishtra was sitting in a slowly moving chariot, with his wife. His brothers stood behind, proudly viewing the grand city they had created. Krishna sat nearby. The Asura ran beside the chariot, screaming as loudly as he could. Yudhishtra ordered the driver to stop. The music and chanting trailed into silence.

Dhaumya and Kunti, who were in the chariot behind, got down to enquire about the sudden halt. The Priest saw Mayasura standing near the Royal chariot and immediately shouted, "Do not touch and pollute us, you filthy pig."

Mayasura jumped back in horror. His courage fled as words failed him. He caught Arjuna's eye and thought he saw a hint of compassion. He looked at the great warrior who had spared his life three years before and said, "Forgive me, Swami. Their eyes are closed. Please allow me to open them." He pointed to the massive stone idol of Lord Shiva and his consort, Parvati, which he had sculpted in the temple. They were beautiful works of art, perfect in each detail, except for their eyes. It was as if the God and Goddess had closed their eyes, unable to bear the doings of Man. Mayasura walked towards the idols to complete his work.

"Stop!" Dhaumya cried. Two guards immediately blocked the path of the architect.

Indra had managed to reach the Royal chariot and saw Mayasura trying to get past the guards. He was aghast at what was unfolding.

"Let me open their eyes... please let me open their eyes..." Mayasura cried, struggling to get to the holy idols.

"Take him away before he pollutes anything else," Dhaumya ordered.

The guards looked at Yudhishtra for confirmation. He nodded, and they dragged the struggling and pleading Mayasura from the temple he had toiled three years to build. They dragged him over the steps he had so lovingly polished. When he tried to grab the pillars he had carved with his own hands, they kicked them away so he would not defile them. The temple had been consecrated. It had no use for the man who had built it. The Gods had gone to new owners and people like Mayasura had no place in their abode.

"Brother, is it not inauspicious for the idols to be blind?" Arjuna asked Yudhishtra.

"Arjuna, once you grow wiser, you will understand that temples are not required for enlightened men. They are just props for the common people, steeped in the world of illusion. Do not worry about that Asura. You spared his life in exchange for his skills. You have both done your duty and acted as per *dharma*."

Arjuna saw Indra standing near the chariot. He climbed down and invited his father to be his guest. Indra gave a derisive laugh and walked away without a word. Arjuna watched him follow the guards pushing Mayasura. The repeated cries of the Asura, 'Their eyes are closed... let me give them eyes... the Gods are blind... let me open their eyes,' created a strange dread in his heart. He could feel Krishna's eyes on him and turned back. His friend reached down a hand to pull him into the chariot. The procession went on its way.

***

The guards dumped Mayasura on the riverbank. They proceeded to bathe, to wash away the pollution caused by touching him. Indra sat down near the architect, gently touching his dark head. The young man was burning with fever and he was delirious. The wind carried the holy chants from the temple along with the faint odour of camphor and incense. Indra dipped his *uttariya* in the river and wiped Mayasura's forehead. A few miles away, holy men were inaugurating India's greatest city, but the man whose name it bore continued sitting with the man who had built it. No one cared about either of them. As Indraprastha came officially into existence and the Priests predicted it would one day become the capital of India, the last Deva King sat wiping the forehead of an Asura, son of a race his illustrious ancestor had vanquished long ago. Indra heard the dark waters of the Yamuna gurgling at the irony of it and he laughed along with her. Mayasura had stopped mumbling. He was asleep with his head on the old man's lap. Indra did not dare move lest he wake him. The world could wait.

When dusk came creeping on long shadowy limbs and spread her cloak over the earth, Mayasura awoke. His hands involuntarily searched for his tools. He was afraid he had overslept and was late for work. Then cold reality grabbed hold of him. He was no longer allowed to set eyes on what he had created. He could no longer whisper his secrets and dreams to the sculptures he had chiselled. He would never again caress the smooth limbs of his Shiva. The God was no longer his. He belonged to the rich and privileged, jailed in a temple with fat Priests as his guards. His God was blind! With a vehemence, he had never suspected he possessed, he jumped up and looked at the distant city, glistening in all its glory. He spat on the ground. Then the Asura cursed his creation with so deep a hatred that Indra feared the city would carry the curse as long as it existed. The terrible words were uttered from the heart of a man who had lost the meaning of life. With every sentence he spoke, the Asura slapped the earth with both palms.

"Blind Gods! Hear my words. If there is truth in my art, let what I say be true eternally. The sweat and blood of Naga women built this city, but you banished them. From today, may no woman feel safe in this city. May corrupt and evil people forever rule this wretched place. May every man be possessed with lust – for woman, money, position, prestige, and power. May each man fight another. May brothers butcher brothers and rape their own sisters. Every time a woman steps outside her home, may she feel the fear of violation. Let this be the asylum of evil men and woman. May the high and mighty ever fear for their lives and live in self-imposed jails for security. May the ruled despise their rulers and may the rulers fear the ruled. May this be a city of graveyards. May invaders from across the borders ransack the city repeatedly, changing the roles of oppressor and oppressed without end. May invaders plunder the city of her wealth again and again. May this be a city without trust, a city of anger and violent passions. May the blood of holy men fall here. May her citizens pollute this sacred river, making it into a sewer. May the air be poisonous and the streets filthy and crowded. May this city be damned forever."

Mayasura broke into wrenching sobs. He lay down on the wet ground, grabbing the mud between his fingers. Much later, when Indra had managed to calm him, the architect repented his harsh words about the city he had built. Indra said curses were just words. It was mere superstition to believe in them. That put the Asura's mind at ease. Indra spoke to him about developing the Vajra. Gradually, the Asura's attention shifted to what the Deva King was saying. He promised to build the secret weapon.

The guard who had gone to ensure they took the ferry across the water, rushed to report Mayasura's curse to Yudhishtra. Terror gripped his soul. He did not wait to hear about the plans to build a secret weapon. When the guard finally managed to get out his frantic words, Yudhishtra's eyes clouded with worry.

"Why are you so concerned over any man's curse Yudhishtra?" Krishna asked. "I promise you that no other city in the world will match the glory of Indraprastha. Her rulers will live in splendour and luxury. Officials, relatives and friends, will have security guards to protect their wealth, power and prestige. While the rulers make the rules, as is their duty, they will break them when required, as is their privilege. The rulers may be cursed in private but in public, they will always be respected, envied and feared. The Gods will shower every blessing on the rulers of this city. This is my promise to you."

Yudhishtra breathed in relief at Krishna's words. But Arjuna, with his knack of asking uncomfortable questions at inappropriate moments, said, "You have only spoken about the rulers, Krishna. What about the common man? Will the curse affect the ruled?"

Krishna did not answer as he stood looking at the long queue of migrants at the city gates. Officials were issuing the necessary copper tokens for identification. He saw a beggar sitting a little away from the entrance with a black dog. People had gathered to listen to his singing. The breeze carried the faint notes of his song to Krishna, who felt an irresistible urge to play an accompaniment to the melody. He pulled out his flute and began playing the song the beggar was singing in the street. Enraptured by the divine music they created together, everyone forgot Arjuna's doubts. Some questions are better left unanswered.

25 RAJASUYA

THE BREAKAWAY LOYAL FACTION of Jarasandha's army, which was fleeing towards Chedi, met Ekalavya on the outskirts of Mathura. Initially they took him to be just another Nishada travelling to Magadha in search of a position in the army. They told him the days Nishadas could gain employment as warriors had vanished with Krishna and his henchman killing King Jarasandha and General Hiranyadhanus. Ekalavya was devastated to learn of his father's death. He had been looking forward to meeting the father he did not remember. In his mind, he had woven dreams of being together with the man who had grown to be a legend in his own lifetime. He was distressed that now he would never see his father or the great King Jarasandha. The thought that he was an orphan, left to fight his lonely war for survival yet again, made him feel bitter.

Seeing the young man's evident distress, the leader of the troop enquired of the reason. When he learnt Ekalavya was General Hiranyadhanus's son, a thrill passed through the ranks. The soldiers animatedly began discussing the news. The leader went up to Ekalavya once again and said, "Sir, we are happy to meet the great General's son. I am Shalva, once a vassal King of Jarasandha, and now Krishna's sworn enemy. Like you, we want the man dead at any cost. He is the nemesis of our country. He may not be a powerful King, but he is an expert in deceit and cunning. He has fooled many common people into thinking he is an *avatar* of Lord Vishnu, come to earth to protect *dharma*. His *dharma*, that is. He is the antithesis of whatever our King stood for. The other man who claims to be an *avatar* of Lord Vishnu, Parashurama, has already made the life of the common people a hell in the kingdoms south of the Narmada River. Between them, Krishna and Parashurama will ensure that all of India comes under their sway. We have to stop it at any cost. The majority of the Magadha army have deserted us for petty rewards and money and have chosen to support the new King, but we have refused to accept Krishna's puppet as the King of Magadha. Fortunately, we are not alone in our war against the unscrupulous Yadava. There are Dhantavakra and Shishupala, two powerful monarchs, who can lend us a hand. We are going to Chedi to meet King Shishupala now and seek his help. Do you care to join us?"

Ekalavya looked at the hundreds of men eyeing him curiously, trying to judge what he was really like. Ekalavya had planned to sneak into Indraprastha or Dwaraka and kill the hated man, but Shalva was offering him a better plan. Ekalavya burned with hatred against Krishna and his friend Arjuna. He would do anything to see them dead. "Sir, I am honoured to be a part of your army." Ekalavya bowed to Shalva as the soldiers cheered.

***

They raced to Chedi. On the way, Ekalavya learnt that, true to Jarasandha's principles, all the soldiers and captains were selected on merit and that no position was inherited. There were Brahmins, Nishadas, Mlechas, Chandalas, Asuras, Nagas, Vaishyas, Kshatriyas and many other castes in the army, but their positions had no connection to caste hierarchy. There were Brahmin captains reporting to Nishada Majors and vice versa. Shalva explained that in Magadha, all positions had been based on merit alone and the selection process was one of the toughest in the entire country, whether for Government administrators' posts or officers in the army. Ekalavya understood why Jarasandha had been successful in sacking Mathura seventeen times before the Yadavas fled to Dwaraka. He had a professional army that fought well.

Just before they entered Chedi, they met Vasuki and his men. The old Naga King told them of the carnage Arjuna and Krishna had unleashed in Khandiva. He also narrated the story of the new city they were building on the ashes of the forest. That added fuel to the fire and many wanted to take on Arjuna and Krishna immediately. However, Vasuki advised caution. It would be suicidal to take on a powerful enemy without proper preparation.

When they met King Shishupala, he was enraged by their description of the manner in which Krishna had instigated Bhima to kill Jarasandha. It was decided to seek King Dhantavakra's opinion on the best course of action. It took a month for Dhantavakra to arrive at Chedi. He was of the same opinion as Vasuki. Soon, under Shishupala, Dhantavakra, Shalva, and Ekalavya, the army began training and practising for the big battle against Krishna and his friends. The Generals often differed on strategy and there were intense arguments between them. Minor chieftains from various parts of the country, who did not agree with Krishna and his methods, soon began declaring their allegiance to Shishupala. Others wavered, unable to take a decision. The Priests created fear among the petty nobility by talking about Krishna's divinity. Among the common people, a cult of worshipping him as an *avatar* of Lord Vishnu, was taking root.

When the invitation to Yudhishtra's *rajasuya* arrived, Krishna's enemies were still undecided on how to take him and the Pandavas on. By conducting a *rajasuya*, Yudhishtra was challenging them to either accept his suzerainty or fight him. Vasuki warned them against accepting Yudhishtra's invitation, suspecting a trap. But no self-respecting King could walk away from such an open challenge. Shishupala decided to take Ekalavya to Indraprastha with him, leaving the other two on standby on the outskirts of the city with their armies. His decision to take Ekalavya to Yudhishtra's court was deliberate and provocative. He wished to see how the orthodox Priests and the Pandavas would react to the presence of a Nishada in the august assembly.

***

The year before, Bhanumati had given birth to twins, a son and a daughter. She soon discovered Suyodhana was a doting father. She often found him playing with the infants or watching them contentedly while they slept. Whenever Subhadra visited, she brought her son Abhimanyu with her, and the little boy developed a deep bond with his uncle. He often sat near Suyodhana, observing the twins lying on their father's lap. Abhimanyu asked his uncle why he had named the boy Lakshmanakumara and the girl Lakshmana, but Suyodhana never gave him a clear answer. Every time he invented a new story for the similar names and invariably those stories involved ghouls, spirits, angels, *gandharva*s and animals. Bhanumati loved seeing her growing twins smile at Suyodhana and try to follow Abhimanyu with their tottering steps.

Bhanumati developed a deep friendship with Subhadra, despite knowing she had been Suyodhana's first love. She trusted her husband completely and knew he would never stray. He was so unlike the other Princes and Kings she knew, who competed with each other in filling their harem with gorgeous girls. Suyodhana was the butt of jokes for remaining faithful to his wife in a culture that adored Krishna for his harem of 16,008 'wives'. Bhanumati cherished the serene quality of their marital relationship. She shared Suyodhana's love for nature, the arts, and music; she loved him for his kindness towards common people, as well as for his arrogance towards those whom he despised, and his blunt way of speaking the truth. She loved him for his skill with the mace and for his pride and honesty. She loved him in a thousand ways, but more than anything, she loved him for the deep trust he had in his friends.

Bhanumati suspected Suyodhana loved his friends more than they loved him back. He was the Crown Prince and he would inherit a vast kingdom. He had nothing to gain by befriending a chariot driver or a poor Brahmin, whereas they stood to gain much. Yet nobody could have been more loyal than Suyodhana towards them. Bhanumati adored him for his courage and conviction in making Karna a vassal King, despite his lineage; yet a seed of jealousy started sprouting in her mind. She respected Karna for his achievement in becoming the most credible challenger to Prince Arjuna in archery. It was a remarkable feat for someone born a poor Suta. She had no doubt that Karna was noble at heart and her husband's faithful friend. His charitable actions were spreading his fame throughout India. Yet, Bhanumati harboured the niggling doubt that whereas her husband would not hesitate in choosing the welfare of his friends over glory, Karna would take glory and fame over friendship if such a choice ever arose. Perhaps it had something to do with an incident that happened early in their marriage.

Bhanumati, pregnant with the twins, was experiencing a bout of mild depression when Karna dropped in unexpectedly. She invited him to join her at a board game while he waited for Suyodhana to return from a meeting with the Grand Regent. Karna happily obliged. Thinking he would be a pushover, considering his childhood as a Suta, she was surprised see how well he played a game that was the preserve of Princes and Kings. She soon saw he was as formidable an opponent in the game as he was in battle. Bhanumati hated losing. With a playful and naughty smile aimed at distracting Karna, she stole one of his winning pieces. He smiled back at her and asked her to put it back. She became angry that he had caught her, and pouted, pushing the board away and trying to leave the game.

Karna also played to win. In the heat of the moment, he grabbed her wrist and pushed her back into her seat. She wriggled away from his grasp and tried running from the room. He jumped up and grabbed her by her waist. At that moment, Suyodhana arrived. For a few seconds, they stood in a frozen tableau, the Prince gazing at his wife being handled by his best friend. Bhanumati recovered first and tried to free herself from Karna. But his strong hands did not release their vice-like grip on her still slim waist. She tried pushing him away. Suddenly, he freed her. The string of pearls she was wearing at her waist broke and hundreds of pearls began bouncing around them, accentuating the silence in the room.

"Do you want me to find these pearls alone or will you come out of your daze and give me a helping hand?" Suyodhana asked his friend and wife with an amused smile, as he knelt to catch the pearls running away from them to hide under the furniture. Bhanumati sat down on the bed, covered her face with her long fingers, and broke into sobs. Karna knelt to help his friend gather the pearls.

"What is this? Are you two so drunk that you are crawling on the floor?" Aswathama came into the room and as usual, made them laugh. He too joined in the pearl fishing. Soon the three friends left the room, having put back the string of pearls they had carefully threaded. When their laughter faded away, Bhanumati slowly stood up. She was afraid Suyodhana would take up the matter when they were alone. She spent the whole day worrying about her future. When he was late in reaching their chamber that night, she fretted, thinking he was punishing her for her indiscretion. When he finally arrived, he quietly kissed her on the lips and lay down on the bed without saying a word. Fearfully, Bhanumati put her hands on his broad chest. She could feel his breathing change. She wished he would say something about the incident that morning and was even ready for his abuse. But Suyodhana quietly caressed her hair in silence. When she thought she would burst, she said to him softly, "It was not what you may suspect..." She stopped in mid-sentence, realizing the oddness of her statement.

"There was nothing to suspect," he whispered into her ear and her heart leapt with joy. She kissed him passionately. When she pulled away to get her breath back, he said something she would never forget until the day she died. "I have complete faith in Karna. He would never do anything dishonourable."

Bhanumati went stiff when she heard it. She wished he had not spoken those words. It meant he trusted Karna more than he did her. The flame of passion that was rising between them died away. Suyodhana sensed it in the coldness of her movements. He tried to make amends by whispering his love for her, but the damage was done. Later, while he slept, she lay looking at his face for a long time, wondering whether he was doing the right thing by trusting his friends so naively. She put her arms around him protectively. Moonlight peeping in through the window lit his handsome face as he smiled in his sleep. Bhanumati's heart dissolved in love. She hugged him close, trying hard to suppress the fearful premonitions that filled her mind.

When the invitation for the *rajasuya* arrived, Bhanumati did not want Suyodhana to go. She feared Krishna and Yudhishtra. She was sure they would lay a trap for her husband. She tried to dissuade him. But he said he did not have a choice as the Crown Prince of Hastinapura. Karna came to Hastinapura, eager to go. Jayadratha came from Sindh. He was of the opinion that Suyodhana should go. Only Aswathama sided with Bhanumati, arguing that the *rajasuya yajna* was a trap and it was better to ignore it. Finally, Uncle Shakuni persuaded Suyodhana to go, arguing that it would be cowardly not to accept the invitation and would be conduct unbefitting a Kshatriya. How Bhanumati hated that Gandhara Prince! But left with no option, she accompanied them to the temple at the Ganga *ghat*, from where they would leave for Indraprastha.

When they emerged from the temple, Kripa was sitting in his usual place under the Banyan tree. Suyodhana went up to him to seek his blessings. As the Prince turned to leave, Kripa said, "Suyodhana, do not get provoked at any cost."

Shakuni sniggered. Suyodhana hesitated a moment. Bhanumati shuddered at the words. They echoed her own fears and she tightened her grip on her husband's arm. Thousands of people had gathered to see their Prince leave for Indraprastha. As they hailed him, he gently loosened his wife's grip and smiled at her. Then he said goodbye to the twins and the procession started towards the Pandava capital.

Aswathama looked back and met Bhanumati's eyes. He nodded, gesturing he would be there with his friend. She walked back slowly to the waiting palanquin with her twins and collapsed into its soft luxury. She tried playing with the children to forget the fear that tugged at her heart. Kripa's words of warning kept returning like a bad rash. She thought she could hear the distant rumblings of a bloody battle and hugged her children in fear.

***

The Brahmins were furious about the hideous looking beggar and his blind dog. How dared he defile the holy place of *yajna* with his presence, they asked each other? Yudhishtra stirred uneasily. He had just completed gifting immense wealth, clothing, and cows to the Brahmins and had been basking in their praises when the ugly Untouchable entered the holy venue and began singing. Yudhishtra would have ordered his death, but the beggar was singing about the love of his God Krishna. Except for the Priests around Dhaumya, the others stood around enthralled. Yudhishtra wished Krishna and Arjuna would arrive before he had to take a decision. The Priests with Dhaumya started shouting to him to throw the unclean man out, or better still, kill him. Yudhishtra looked at the beggar who was dark on one side and a dirty golden on the other. With his protruding teeth and burn marks, he looked like a mongoose. The mangy dog with him kept wagging its tail in time to the beggar's rapturous song.

A sudden roar from Dhaumya made Yudhishtra stand up. "Your Highness, kill this rascal! Can you not hear what he is singing?"

Yudhishtra listened more intently to the beggar's song and the colour drained from his face. The song insulted him, the learned Priests, and even the *Veda*s that sanctioned the great sacrifice he was conducting. The beggar sang that learning was useless if there was no love; that sacrifices were meaningless without purity of heart; and gifts worthless if bestowed on the undeserving. He sang that this *rajasuya* sacrifice was a charade to gain fame and not a sacrifice at all; that real sacrifices happen unknown and unheard, by people expecting nothing in return – neither fame, nor wealth, heaven nor salvation. Those sacrifices had God's blessings.

Yudhishtra trembled in anger. The audacity of the Untouchable not only to pollute the *yajna* venue but also to insult the King and the learned Brahmins, enraged him. "Arrest him!" he commanded. Soldiers rushed towards the beggar.

"What has happened, brother? Why has the singing stopped? I came to listen. That man has magic in his voice." Yudhishtra turned at the question and saw Arjuna. Draupadi suppressed a giggle from behind him. Yudhishtra turned towards her in irritation. "He was insulting all that we hold sacred and you are laughing?" he asked angrily.

"No normal person would dare come here and insult you. Either he is mad or a saint. Why don't we ask him why he was singing what he was?" Arjuna said, trying to pacify his enraged brother.

Draupadi looked at Arjuna and smiled in approval. Yudhishtra raised his hand and ordered, "Free him. Let us hear what he has to say."

The soldiers jumped back, relieved that the command had come before they touched the beggar and polluted themselves. A susurrus of 'Sin… sin…' came from the ranks of the Priests. The beggar looked around. When he understood no one was going to arrest him, he resumed his song. This time he sang about the night he had entered a poor Brahmin's hut with the intention of robbing him; what he had seen there, and how the Brahmin had sacrificed his family, home, and life, so a poor Untouchable like him could eat. The sacrifice of a man, who had nothing, for a man who was nothing, was a real sacrifice. Such places were holy, not this place of *rajasuya*, where greed and avarice ruled. The hut was where his Krishna resided; and only the pure of heart could hear the divine music of His flute. Finally, he said, "To hear that music oh King, silence the croaking of the Priests; burn their *smritis*; and free yourself from the tangle of meaningless rituals and tradition."

There was uproar from Dhaumya and his Priests.

Draupadi asked, "Who are you?"

"I am nobody," the beggar replied. "But I visit everyone whether they like me or not. I am Jara, and this is my dog. It reminds me to feel grateful for my life and its blessings. We live in the streets, chased away from the temples and mansions, yet we live happily and rejoice in the blessing called Life. We lack nothing and thank God every day for His grace."

Arjuna became uneasy. Memories of the day he had blinded a puppy with his arrow came rushing back. Moreover, the image of the severed thumb of a Nishada lying in the mud while Guru Drona stood with an impassive face, clawed furrows in his conscience. He had an irrational urge to know the name of the dog he had blinded and asked, "What is your dog called?"

Jara looked at the furious faces of the Priests. His eyes met those of Dhaumya. The Chief Priest looked away, as if afraid of the Untouchable's eyes. "Dharma," Jara said and the blind dog wagged its tail.

There was a stunned silence before the Priests erupted in anger. 'Sin... sin... calling a dog Dharma! He is insulting our religion and Holy Scriptures. Kill him! Kill him!' they screamed, falling silent only when Yudhishtra took his sword from its sheath.

"Let him be. He is a saint," Draupadi said, holding onto her husband's hand.

Seeing Yudhishtra hesitate, Dhaumya yelled out in an authoritative voice,

"Do not stop a King from doing his *dharma*. Nothing can be a greater sin and you will pay for it."

Yudhishtra looked into Draupadi's eyes. All his fears came rushing back. He felt naked before her gaze and his sword fell to the ground.

Fearing the arrogant beggar would walk away free, Dhaumya shouted, "Yudhishtra, you have forsaken your *dharma* and the same *dharma* will forsake you. You will pay for it. You have allowed an Untouchable to insult Brahmins and the *Veda*s."

Krishna, walking into the commotion, saved Yudhishtra any further insult. Jara saw his living God standing before him, and rushed forward, sobbing in joy and ecstasy. Dharma followed him. However, a huge crowd of Priests mobbed Krishna, complaining about the way Yudhishtra and his wife were treating them. Krishna smiled at them and said it was good to listen to new ideas once in a while. Yudhishtra was relieved that Krishna took the incident lightly and did not censure him. But Dhaumya looked peeved.

Jara waited, but the crowd around Krishna kept thickening. "He has become a prisoner of the Priests," Jara said to Dharma. The dog licked his hand. Jara slowly walked away. As he was turning into a side street, a troop of cavalry galloped by. It was Ekalavya and Shishupala, rushing towards Yudhishtra's *rajasuya*.

When Shishupala and Ekalavya entered the venue, the commotion created by Jara had died down. Shishupala boldly walked to the seat nearest the sacrificial altar and invited Ekalavya to sit beside him. Angry murmurs rose from the crowd at this provocative act. The King of Chedi was throwing an open challenge to Yudhishtra and the Priests by having a Nishada sit so close to the holy altar. Yudhishtra rose, but Krishna restrained him. The ceremony resumed.

Shishupala and Ekalavya watched the proceedings with unconcealed hostility. When Dhaumya announced Krishna as the Guest of Honour, there was a splattering of polite applause. Murmurings arose from the assembled Kings and Princes but the Yadava walked with confident steps to the special seat reserved for him.

"Stop!" Shishupala was standing with his sword drawn, every eye upon him.

He turned to the assembled Kings and noblemen of India and addressed them. "Respected Kings, this is a great insult to us. The King of Indraprastha has chosen a common cowherd over a Kshatriya as his Chief Guest. What is it that he has done to deserve this honour? He is a thief and a scoundrel. We have heard enough stories about this cowherd and none can be repeated in decent company. Is there any crime he has not committed? We have lost count of the number of people he has murdered on the sly. He never fights like a man. He killed his uncle by deceit; he has come here after murdering one of the greatest Kings our land has ever seen. He was afraid of Jarasandha, knowing he was no match for the great man. He trapped him and used Bhima to get rid of his enemy – an enemy who had defeated him seventeen times. He arranged for the murder of General Hiranyadhanus, the father of this young man sitting here." Shishupala paused to gauge the reaction of the crowd.

The Priests were shouting, but he knew that he held the attention of the Kings and Princes. Confident of his audience, the King of Chedi pressed on. "Why should this man be given the honour of being Chief Guest? King Yudhishtra, if you wish to honour a man for his steadfastness in *dharma*, chose the great Bhishma instead. If you want a great warrior, chose Drona. If you want to elect a man of wisdom, choose Vidhura. And if you want a man of compassion and righteousness, chose your cousin Suyodhana. If you want a man of intellect, choose Kripa; or if you want a man of reason, choose Carvaka. If you want a man of unflinching loyalty, chose Aswathama. If you want to honour a man who has struggled against the odds and emerged victorious, it will be a difficult choice for you, for both Karna, the large-hearted King of Anga, and this brave young man, Ekalavya, fit that description. If you want a man who transcends all these qualities, choose the sage Veda Vyasa. But for the sake of humanity, do not choose the icon of *adharma*."

Krishna walked towards Shishupala and bowed to him reverently. "May I know why you call me amoral, Your Highness?" he asked, the mocking smile never leaving his lips.

Ekalavya tensed in his chair but Shishupala gazed straight into the eyes of his foe. They stared at each other for a moment before Shishupala turned to the assembly and said in a clear voice, "I am reluctant to speak of the exploits of our Chief Guest in this august company of Kings, but he leaves me no choice. Please forgive my harsh words but this is the most dangerous man to have walked our land. He is leading us along the path to disaster and war. He wishes to preserve a social order that grants privileges to a few and hell to the rest. No wonder people like Dhaumya support his claim of being an *avatar* of Vishnu. The Priests actively propagate his divinity, for they will be the benefactors of his philosophy. Unfortunately, the poor have begun believing it.

"What are these divine acts? His trail of murders began at the age of eight. He stole from the cowherds he lived among, in his village. He drove away Nagas like Kaliya, and took away their land. He murdered his uncle. He has even stolen women's clothing while they were bathing and then paraded them naked before him. He jilted his lover, Radha, when he ran away to Dwaraka, for fear of Jarasandha. Wise men thought he would mellow with age. But he has no morality. He keeps a harem of 16,008 girls but Radha has no place in it. Yet he claims he is an *avatar* of Vishnu. He wishes to share the mantle of none other than Lord Rama, who was steadfast in his love towards his wife Sita, and who fought a war with the demon King Ravana for her sake. Can there be a greater irony?"

"*Noooo...*!" Ekalavya screamed as he saw King Shishupala collapse onto the ground, blood spurting from his throat. The King of Chedi went into death spasms.

Krishna picked up his *chakra*, a small disc with very sharp edges, from the throat of his enemy and wiped off the blood.

'It is cold blooded murder,' someone shouted. A few Kings rushed to attack

Krishna with their swords drawn. The Pandavas sprang up to defend their friend and guide. The *rajasuya* venue turned into a battleground. Ekalavya's first reaction was to fight Shishupala's murderer, but prudence overcame instinct. He knew Krishna's supporters outnumbered those of the slain King. Krishna and the Pandavas were cutting down their detractors mercilessly. Shalva and Dhantavakra were waiting with an army on the outskirts of Indraprastha. If he could reach them somehow, he could turn the tables. Ekalavya ran from the venue, cutting down the soldiers who tried to stop him, without breaking stride. More and more soldiers were rushing to join the fight. The Brahmins were quietly slipping away as Ekalavya mounted his horse and galloped towards his friends through the streets of Indraprastha, cleaving through the sea of people running about like panicked chickens. He kicked a beggar out of his way and saw him lurch and fall, face down on the pavement. An angry dog chased his horse for a while but then returned to its master, who was writhing in pain. Ekalavya cursed them both silently as he sped through the dusty streets of the great city. How he hated the lazy men who stood in the way of others.

When he reached Dhantavakra and Shalva, he was panting with excitement and anger. Somehow, he managed to tell them Krishna had murdered Shishupala and they had to take revenge. His furious friends cursed the Yadava. They ordered their army to race into the city. But as the ranks lurched forward, Vasuki stood in their way. The old Naga leader raised his staff and ordered everyone to calm down. The column stopped in confusion, the horses neighing in fright and irritation at the sharply pulled reins.

"Move, you old fool, or you will become the dust under the hoofs of our horses," Dhantavakra cried.

Vasuki looked at him with a contemptuous smile but addressed Ekalavya. "Indraprastha is too strong to be taken by this small army. Besides, any attack on Indraprastha will turn the anger of Bhishma upon us and the Hastinapura army will finish us off in no time. We need money to raise a proper army and we need a fortified city from which we can operate. Krishna is playing games here. We will turn the tables on him. He has left

Dwaraka to a pacifist, his brother Balarama. We will storm their city and throw out the Yadavas. Once Dwaraka falls, we can control both the Southern Confederate and Hastinapura. We can choke the trade routes by land and sea, between the major empires. Dwaraka is far from here, but Ekalavya, you know the way through the desert and forests. Let us rush to take the city of Krishna. I will somehow reach Takshaka. If Krishna follows you to save his city, we will prepare an ambush for him. Go to Dwaraka... now!" Vasuki stood waving his crooked staff.

Ekalavya and Shalva looked at each other in astonishment. The old man's strategy was risky but brilliant. Balarama was a pacifist and he would not fight. They could easily take Krishna's city from him. Dhantavakra blew his conch and the army turned towards the southwest and thundered past Vasuki as he watched with a satisfied smile. Once they succeeded in taking Dwaraka, the leadership of the Nagas and the revolution would be back with him instead of that upstart Takshaka. Nevertheless, he had to find the Naga leader in order to ambush Krishna. He walked as fast as he could towards the forest, in search of Takshaka.

***

Suyodhana and his troops were nearing the ridge over the Yamuna when Aswathama drew their attention to the rising column of dust on the southwestern horizon. They could see the vanishing end of a cavalry column, racing towards the desert.

"Who is that?" Suyodhana asked in surprise.

Suddenly, from the rear, more cavalry appeared and galloped past at a furious pace. At their head rode Krishna, his face grim and anxious. Sushasana leaned from his saddle and pulled at the reins of a passing soldier. The horse swerved, neighing in fear. Other riders jumped over the struggling horse without slowing. Sushasana dragged the fallen man from the path of the pounding hoofs. When they had seen the tail of the last horse disappear, they asked the captured man the reason for the commotion. He told them the story of Shishupala's murder and the news of Dhantavakra and a Nishada leading an army to attack Dwaraka, to avenge the death of their friend.

Shakuni, who had accompanied his nephew to the *rajasuya*, heard the news of Krishna leaving Indraprastha and fondly caressed the dice lying hidden in the folds of his dress. The game was getting exciting. This was the beginning of the end of India, he told himself. He could not help laughing. As suddenly as it had appeared, the glee in the Gandhara Prince's face vanished. The master of dice had planned his next move.

26 THE FALL

"IT IS BREATH-TAKING!" SUYODHANA exclaimed as they neared the city gates.

Aswathama and Karna were gazing at the golden spires of the palace, glistening in the late afternoon sun. "I wonder how much they spent in creating such a marvel," Aswathama said and whistled softly, taking in the beautiful gardens. They moved slowly through the broad avenues of Indraprastha, exclaiming at each new wonder, pointing at the sculptures and fountains that lined every junction, excited to be nearing the palace itself.

"I wonder how Yudhishtra succeeded in solving the greatest problem that plagues our country. Do you see there are no poor people in the streets? The place looks rich and prosperous," Suyodhana said, trying to control his pangs of jealousy.

"Suyodhana," Karna moved his horse forward to keep pace with the Crown Prince. "Do you notice something strange? There are only a few people in the streets and they all look important. Why does the city look so deserted of common folk? A city this size should be buzzing with activity, especially since the *rajasuya* is going on. "

"It does not look like there has been a battle or riot in the city streets. Everything is in order. Perhaps all the citizens are at the *rajasuya* venue," Suyodhana said calmly, though he too had begun to worry about the uncanny silence that pervaded this place. They could hear the bells of police chariots on patrol, but they only amplified the edgy silence that cloaked the sombre city.

"Hey, look!" Karna shouted suddenly and jumped down from his horse. Suyodhana saw him run to the pavement and lean over a bundle of rags lying at the door of a closed shop. A dog barked suddenly and shot towards Karna, its teeth snapping viciously.

The bundle stirred. Suyodhana exclaimed, "It is a man and he is alive!" He dismounted hurriedly and ran to Karna.

Aswathama followed his friends. The dog tried keeping them at bay. A tattered blanket moved and the man moaned for water. Karna took another step forward but the dog jumped at him. He moved quickly away and the dog fell with a yelp.

"The dog is blind," Aswathama said, carefully placing his hand on the animal's head. When it tried to snap, he began gently caressing it with soothing strokes while speaking gently. The dog calmed down and put its paws on the Brahmin's shoulders. Aswathama submitted to its licks with a smile. A funny thought entered his head: he wished his father could see him now, accepting the devotion of a street dog. When he was barely six years old, he had once dragged a puppy home. It had made his father blind with rage. Drona had beaten Aswathama until the cane broke, saying it was a sin for a Brahmin to have a dog as a pet. Dogs were dirty animals, and represented all that was considered sinful in the Brahminical world: dogs were attached to their masters; they guarded territory and fought for it; they were emotional and loved life too much. A dog was the symbol of man's attachment to this illusory world, whereas a cow was holy because it was unattached to its master and went through life with equanimity. For Aswathama, the reasons his father had enumerated were the very ones that drew his love and respect. He hugged the blind dog and it continued licking his face with a love no human was capable of.

Karna carefully moved away the tattered covering and Suyodhana turned his face away in horror. There were deep blue bruises on the man's scarred face and the blanket was wet with blood. Karna shouted for water. Immediately, a soldier came running with a water pot. He poured water into the beggar's mouth and the man gulped it down greedily. Shivering, he painfully tried to get up, but collapsed back onto the ground.

Suyodhana reached out and lifted him up. "What happened to you?"

"Someone who was in a hurry to reach my Lord's abode pushed me out of his way. Later I became my Lord's pathway and I was run over by him," the beggar answered enigmatically.

"What is he blabbering about?" asked Aswathama.

"It seems that first Ekalavya's army knocked him down and then Krishna's army rode over him in their pursuit of Ekalavya's men," Suyodhana said.

The beggar cried, "Krishna! Blessed am I that I could offer my body for you to tread upon. Blessed is Jara, for even in your hurry you thought about this poor devotee and touched me with your horse's hoofs. Your *leela* is unfathomable, your love immeasurable, my Lord."

"Well Suyodhana, one answer to your question stands before you. Here is a poor man in Indraprastha," Karna said. 'Why do you come to break my heart always Jara?' he thought to himself.

"I know this person…"

Before Suyodhana could complete his words, Jara said to him, "You want to see the poor of this city? Come with me. The poor are the blessed for they are the true devotees of my Lord. When someone loves my Lord sincerely, the Lord loves him back manifold. The first thing He does is take away wealth. He gives his devotees unhappiness and suffering, for He knows that only in suffering can we remember His glory. If we have wealth and happiness, we will not think about Him and will thus remain immersed in worldly pleasures. He gives us misfortunes so that we hate the illusory world and strive for *moksha*. He is compassionate. Come and see His people, my Hari's people, my Krishna's people, and you will know what heaven is."

"Whoever his Lord is, he seems to be an insecure person, obsessed with everyone singing his glory and praises," Aswathama quipped. Everyone except Jara and Suyodhana laughed.

"Krishna, Krishna…" Jara ran towards the river, crying his Lord's name in ecstasy.

Dharma freed himself from Aswathama's grasp and ran after his master. Suyodhana and his friends followed. When they reached the *ghat*, they saw Jara pleading with the boatman to take them to the opposite bank. The boatman looked annoyed, but when he saw Suyodhana and his companions, his attitude changed suddenly. He was all obsequious eagerness as he ran to free his boat.

They left their army on the city shore and travelled with the beggar and his dog to the other side of the Yamuna. As the boat moved toward the colony of the poor and Untouchables, the sun slowly dissolved in the purple waters of the river. The horizon was peppered with birds hurrying home. Crows lamented the dying of the day. Jara began singing his Lord's praises. The men sat mesmerized by the beauty of the river. They forgot everything but the rich voice of the beggar, the sound of the paddle hitting the water in time to his poignant song, and the river caressing their boat and flowing away. As they approached the opposite *ghat*, a silver crescent moon in the eastern sky found reflection in the water before it broke into a million ripples.

When they stepped onto the *ghat*, a dark man jumped in front of them. Suyodhana was stunned by his sudden appearance and his hand went to his sword. But the man caught hold of Suyodhana's wrist blabbering, "Are you a Prince? Yes, you look rich. But why should a Prince come to visit us? We are Untouchables. No one comes here, at least not anyone like you. You will become polluted and fall from your exalted caste. Maybe you have come in search of me? Do you want an architect to build a city in your kingdom? I can do it. Take me with you and I will build a city that will make this cursed place look like a child's sandcastle. I built that city for them and then they banished me from it. If I build a city for you, you must allow us a corner… a little space for me and my people. I promise we will not pollute you. Just a little space… that is all we ask… a little respect… a little consideration. We too are human and it is not our fault that we were born with dark skins. I promise to build a great city for you. Have you seen

Indraprastha? I built it... we all built it... in the sun... in the rain... the women and children of this village built that glistening city of gold... I sculpted the God in the temple... but he is blind... they did not allow me to complete my work. If I build you a bigger temple, will you allow me to give eyes to the Gods?"

Suyodhana gripped Aswathama's hands for support and Karna gritted his teeth. They understood who the babbling lunatic was. It was Mayasura, the legendary architect. The Pandavas had banished the likes of Mayasura to the grim world beyond the Yamuna, far away from their great city, to the land of the poor and destitute. The stink of urine and excrement hit them like a body blow. When their eyes adjusted to the dim light, they could see league upon league of shanties. Small oil lamps flickered here and there and they could hear the noise of drunken brawls and screaming. There was enough misery here for everyone to hate their lives and pray for *moksha*. The Lord's compassion was overwhelming.

"Mayasura, what are you doing?" An old man came and grabbed the architect by the hand. But he fell silent when he saw Karna. His eyes wandered over Karna's armour. When he saw the warrior's dark eyes staring back at him, he turned away saying, "He is not keeping well. Sometimes, when he is not working, he loses his senses and blabbers like this. He is not mad as you may think. In fact, he is a genius."

When Mayasura noticed Karna's armour, he exclaimed, "Father, is our armour as strong as this man's? We may have to change the design."

The old man's face turned pale with fear as he tried dragging Mayasura away before he could say something to endanger them both. Some of the onlookers who had gathered to watch the scene, began making loud comments questioning Mayasura's sanity.

As they disappeared into the darkness, Aswathama shouted after them, "What about Karna's armour, Mayasura?"

The architect paused and shouted back, "We are designing a weapon that can pierce Karna's armour. Have you heard of Karna? He is Arjuna's greatest enemy and Arjuna is my father's son. My father is Indra, King of the Devas. But he loves me more than he loves his real son, so he lives with me. We are going to present the arrow to Arjuna so he can kill Karna. That will please the Prince and he may allow me to complete my sculpture of Lord Shiva and open his eyes." His voice faded away in the din from the slums as Indra dragged Mayasura away. He was afraid that Karna or Suyodhana would come after him.

"That old man looks oddly familiar," Karna said, staring at the vanishing duo.

"He is Indra, the fallen King of the Devas. He looks familiar because he is the real father of Arjuna," Suyodhana told his friend.

"That explains why he is after me," Karna said with a crooked smile.

Before the others could react, Jara called to them to tour the slum with him and see the people who lived here. The deeper they moved into the hellhole, the more depressing it became. Shakuni, who had come with them but remained silently in the background, was bubbling with joy. These foolish Indians and their Gods and god men were making his task easier by the day. Yudhishtra had created a huge opportunity for Takshaka to recruit people into his revolutionary army. 'I should bring this to the attention of Durjaya too,' thought the Gandhara Prince. How long could India resist her enemies, with such a heartless caste system, useless rituals, corrupt rulers, irresponsible citizens, and a religion that denied the real world for the sake of imaginary happiness? 'You are bleeding from a thousand cuts and your downfall is imminent,' the foreigner thought with malice. A war, a bloody, all-consuming, all-destroying war, was coming, when all the Indian kingdoms would clash and destroy each other. Shakuni could smell the blood; he could feel death in the air. The end was coming. The sound of war drums was deafening.

"I cannot stand this anymore. What sort of world has Yudhishtra created? This is a cursed city. The Pandavas have built a city on the carnage of thousands of men and beasts. They destroyed Khandiva forest and killed everything in it. They are treating the majority of their people like worms in order to please a few Priests! Come, let us go to Yudhishtra's fine palace and ask the Son of Dharma a few pertinent questions," said Suyodhana, his mind and heart sickened by what he had seen.

Suyodhana rushed back to the *ghat* and ordered the boatman to row them back to the city. His friends followed. Jara accompanied them to the riverbank. No one spoke. Though the Crown Prince kept a level head most of the time, his anger was legendry once aroused. Now he said in a voice in which rage had overcome caution, "First they murdered a Nishada woman and her five children in Varanavata. Then Krishna and Arjuna executed the great massacre of Khandiva. Then King Jarasandha and his Nishada General were killed by trickery and Shishupala murdered in cold blood. How many more must die for their ambition? How many will they kill in the name *dharma*? Murder, arson, rape, everything is explained away or justified by a few Priests. This hypocrisy is galling. See how they have treated Mayasura. In any other kingdom, they would be erecting statues honouring him and Kings would be competing for his talent. Here, he is banished to the stinking outer city because he was born an *avarna* and Untouchable. So many people are living there like pigs, in abject poverty, and those bastard Pandavas are taking pride in building a city of riches. Such acts have given birth to Takshaka and Durjaya. I fear for people like that beggar Jara, blind in their faith and innocent at heart. They are fodder for the raging ambition of men like Yudhishtra."

His friends heard him out patiently. He was echoing their thoughts. Shakuni, immersed in deep reflection, kept clicking his dice together in his right hand and running the fingers of his left hand through his salt-and-pepper beard. The sight of the palace bathed in golden light and the contrast it presented with the darkness on the other side of the Yamuna, added flame to Suyodhana's anger. The breeze carried the faint notes of Jara's song from across the river. To him, his song was an act of piety and prayer; for the Prince and his friends, it sounded more like the lament of a broken people clinging to the feeble straw of faith to stay alive in this turbulent world.

***

When Suyodhana and his friends stormed into the palace, the King of Indraprastha was enjoying an evening of music and dance. The *sabha* was filled with courtesans, nobles, Priests, as well as the Kings and Princes who had accepted Yudhishtra's suzerainty. Many warriors and Princes had died in the scuffle following the murder of Shishupala, but that did not dampen the festivities. Yudhishtra's brothers and Draupadi sat near him, as did the Priests. When Suyodhana strode into the hall, the *sabha* fell silent and every head turned towards him. He stood contemptuously viewing the luxury everywhere. Behind him stood Karna, Sushasana, and Aswathama, matching the Crown Prince's look of disdain. Shakuni stood with a smile playing on his lips. Suyodhana fixed his gaze on Yudhishtra.

"Welcome, Suyodhana," Yudhishtra said, getting up to greet his cousin.

"So, this is the palace built over dead bodies and the place where the King of Chedi was murdered in cold blood. Yudhishtra, you have banished half the population from your city. You should hang your head in shame at the way you have treated the people who built Indraprastha."

"Enough, Duryodhana!" Dhaumya interrupted. "This model state will always be ruled by the holy *smritis*. How dare you come here and insult the epitome of *dharma*? What do you know about *dharma*? You are the one who should be ashamed for befriending a lowly Suta and making him a King; you are the one who should hang your head in shame for having Aswathama, who is a disgrace to all Brahmins, as a friend. You are trying to destroy our society. But you will never succeed as long as I live." He stopped his tirade when he saw Suyodhana rushing towards him with sword drawn. His disciples scrambled to get out of the way. Dhaumya shouted, "*Ma... Ma...* he is going to murder me! Is there no protection for a poor Brahmin in this kingdom? Arjuna, Bhima, help me..."

Before the Pandavas could make sense of what was happening, Suyodhana had reached the group of Priests who were running like mice before a cat. Dhaumya ran towards Yudhishtra as Suyodhana chased him, pushing people away as he ran after the Chief Priest. His friends tried to stop the Crown Prince, but it was impossible for anyone to swerve Suyodhana from his purpose once he was angered. However, fate often intervenes in curious ways. In his blind anger, Suyodhana did not notice the sunken pool in the floor. It was a foot deep and three feet wide, but it ran from one wall of the *sabha* to the other. Except for the darker shade of tiles, it merged with the floor of the *sabha* and could not be easily distinguished, as the polished floor reflected as much light as did the water in the pool. Dhaumya instinctively jumped over the narrow pool, but Suyodhana stepped into the water unknowingly and fell flat on his face. The impact threw his sword from his hand and it clanged onto the floor near Yudhishtra's feet.

For a moment, there was perfect silence. His friends rushed to Suyodhana's rescue. But he stood up before they could reach him. His *dhoti* slipped from his waist and lay limp in the water. Everyone watched the unfolding drama with shocked faces. The Crown Prince of Hastinapura stood ridiculously exposed, wincing in pain and anger, naked except for a loincloth, in front of the grand assembly. No one dared utter a word.

Karna leaned down to pick up Suyodhana's *dhoti* from the water. As he did so, laughter echoed though the hall.

"*Andha*! Blind, just like his father." It was Draupadi. She bit her lip pointing to the naked Suyodhana, no longer able to control her mirth.

Laughter filled the hall and became a roar. The whole assembly shook with amusement. Suyodhana stood naked in the middle of the Court, laughter and ridicule burning his ears, shamed and insulted beyond imagination, as the Priests who had run away in fear a few moments before, came back boldly and began showering abuse on him. Suyodhana refused to take his *dhoti* from his friend's hand or come out of the pool that barely wet his ankles. He stood there defiantly while insults and ridicule showered on him from all sides.

"Serves you right, you son of a blind man," Dhaumya shouted at Suyodhana. Gazing at the assembly of nobles and vassal Kings, he said, "All Kings and Kshatriyas present here, behold this scene. It is a lesson to all. This is the penalty for insulting a Brahmin. God has willed it to happen.

This is the price for elevating a Suta to kingship; this is the cost of speaking against our holy *smritis*. But it is just the beginning. This evil man will pay dearly for his sins. See how he stands naked, like any ordinary slave."

"*Andha, Andha...*" the Priests took up the chorus amidst catcalls and whistles. Only Arjuna stood grim-faced, his head bowed and arms crossed. Draupadi made no attempt to hide her amusement. Her eyes met those of Karna, fuming with rage at what was happening to his friend. At the sight of the man she secretly loved, the shame of sharing her bed with five men came rushing back to fill her aching heart. With a viciousness that only a woman trying to hide her own yearning can show, she said to Karna, "Suta, drive your friend away in your chariot before he loses his loincloth too."

Karna's sword was out in a flash, but Aswathama held him back.

"The Suta thinks he can fight Arjuna? What a joke!" Dhaumya cried as the hall reverberated with more laughter and whistles.

Shakuni looked at the fools laughing around him and thanked his stars. They were laughing at the Crown Prince of the most powerful empire in India because a potbellied Priest did not like him. They were insulting the best archer in India because he was born in a low caste. The Gandhara Prince wanted to fall on his knees, face West towards Gandhara, and thank God for the windfall. But as he stood watching his nephew being ridiculed, all traces of the elation he felt were hidden behind the grim expression on his face.

Suyodhana raised his head and brushed back the dark wavy hair that had fallen into his eyes. He shook his head to free it of water. Then he glared at Yudhishtra. The King of Indraprastha took a quick breath. Suyodhana turned to gaze at Draupadi, and her laughter trailed into silence. She looked down at her toes, not wanting to face the Crown Prince. Suyodhana took a step out of the pool. Dhaumya backed away and vanished behind the group of Priests. Aswathama handed him the *dhoti*, but Suyodhana refused to take it, flicking it away with one hand. The hall grew silent again. Without saying a word, without attempting to cover his nakedness, the Crown Prince of Hastinapura walked out of the hall with his friends in tow. As he walked amidst them in a loincloth, his head held high, the Kings and Princes bowed in fear and respect. They were ashamed of their conduct, but the urge to laugh at the fall of an important man had taken possession of them for a moment. He acknowledged their bows with curt nods and walked out into the darkness, his eyes looking straight ahead. The silence of the tomb descended on Yudhishtra's palace.

***

Aswathama, Karna, and Sushasana, were urging Suyodhana to declare war on Indraprastha. It was mid-afternoon, three days after the incident and they were in the Prince's chambers. No man ought to swallow an insult like that. Indraprastha ought to be called upon to pay the price of her indiscretion. They were sure they could convince the Grand Regent about the justice of their cause. How long could a puny little kingdom like Indraprastha last before the might of Hastinapura? Besides, Krishna was away, fighting the Nishada, if the Yadava had managed to reach Dwaraka at all. The Southern Confederate was in shambles without the leadership of Parashurama, who still lay in a coma. This was the right time to finish off the Pandavas and impose more humane laws that were not based on any scriptures, respected all faiths, had no caste-based privileges, and treated everyone the same. This was the moment to save the country from the anarchy Takshaka envisaged or the theocracy of Dhaumya and Parashurama.

Suyodhana hesitated. He too wanted to do what his friends suggested. He found it difficult to swallow the insult or forgive and forget. 'I am a Kshatriya, not a saint,' he kept telling himself. Yet, every time he thought of war, the image of the slums he had visited came to mind. The face of Jara and his blind dog danced before his eyes. The thought of Mayasura and the women and children who had toiled to build that beautiful city, pulled him back from the brink. In the greater order of things, it did not matter that he had been insulted. How many lives were to be lost for the sake of his honour? The poor would pay the price. That thought made him weak. However, Draupadi's laughter still rang in his ears. 'How could they insult me like that?' He burned with shame whenever he remembered standing naked in the middle of Yudhishtra's *sabha*. Was there a way to make the Pandavas pay, yet avoid war?

Shakuni was watching Suyodhana closely. His initial reaction to the incident in Indraprastha had been glee. He looked forward to the impending war and destruction of his enemies, but the intervening three days had caused him to look at the situation with more logic. He feared that after the initial scuffle, Bhishma would intervene and arrange a patch up between the cousins, and his dreams of an apocalyptic war would fade away. Besides, Krishna was away. If there was anyone who wanted a war as much as he did, it was Krishna. The participation of the Southern Confederate was doubtful, and Dwaraka was fighting its own battles. 'No, a war at this time would not suit my purposes,' he thought. What he needed was a conflict involving all the kingdoms – from Pragjyothisha, Anga, Vanga, etc. in the East, to Dwaraka, Sind, Gandhara, etc. in the West – a grand war that included the mountain kingdoms of the Himalayas to the Asura kingdoms of the South, like Chera and Pandya. The armageddon could not spare a single kingdom of India. He yearned for the total destruction of this cursed land and its misery.

"Prince, there is another way to exact revenge and conquer, without firing a single arrow or spilling a drop of blood," Shakuni said, as if reading Suyodhana's mind. They all turned to look at the foreigner with interest. "It is sanctioned by all your... I mean our... holy scriptures. A King can conquer another kingdom by marriage, war, payment, or dice. Why don't we invite Yudhishtra to a game of dice?" Shakuni said with a smile.

They looked at each other. Then Aswathama said, "A game of dice is a game of chance. What is the guarantee that Yudhishtra will not win?"

Shakuni took out the dice from the folds of his *dhoti* and said a silent prayer. With his eyes closed, he cried, "Twelve".

Suyodhana and his friends watched anxiously as the dice spun on the floor, hit each other in fury, reversed the direction of spin for a moment, and finally came to rest. Both showed six – a perfect twelve!

"Eight," the Gandhara Prince cried and threw the dice again. They rolled to form eight. "Six," called Shakuni, and the dice obeyed. He threw the dice a hundred times. Each time the dice came up correctly.

Taking up the challenge, Karna, Suyodhana, Sushasana, and Aswathama, each took turns to cry out numbers. With the practised ease of three decades, the foreigner rolled the dice.

When the show was over and the showman had bowed to his admiring fans, Suyodhana stood up. "Yes, we can roll the dice. We will send the Son of Dharma an invitation he cannot refuse. We will tie him in the knots of his own *dharma*. We too can play games."

A cheer rose from his friends as they hugged each other. Shakuni watched the scene with amusement. He rolled the dice for the hundred and first time and cried twelve. That roll was a challenge, a dare to the fools that ruled India, from a tiny mountain kingdom on the outskirts of her ancient civilization. The Indians, who kept fighting each other for language, caste, religion, race, and petty egos, did not see, hear or feel the dice rolling over their holy land. The dice obeyed the foreign hand as usual.

27 ROLL OF THE DICE

"I HEAR YOU HAVE INVITED YUDHISHTRA to a game of dice." Bhanumati gently broached the subject to a moody Suyodhana. He merely grunted. When she asked him again, he left the room in silence. She knew he was hurt, but did not want the hurt to fester into a wound. There was enough hatred around them. She rarely got to see him as he spent most of his time with Uncle Shakuni. Her heart ached seeing her husband filled with anger and bitterness. She yearned to have her generous-hearted husband back.

A few days before the game of dice with his cousin, Bhanumati waited to confront him in the privacy of their chamber. By the time he came in, the twins were sound asleep. He hesitated a moment at the entrance and she could see him checking to see whether the children were asleep. She too, feigned sleep. She heard him blow out the lamp, and felt the mattress sink under his weight. Then she turned and gently touched his shoulder. Immediately, she felt him stiffen. She was afraid but determined. She could no longer hold herself back. "Do we need to make it such a big issue?"

There was no reaction. Softly she said, "It was just an accident..."

"Stay out of this, Bhanu!" Suyodhana jumped from the bed, toppling over a stool. "This is not just about me and my cousin. It is about this country and the future of its people. You have not seen Indraprastha. You have not seen how the poor live in the model city of the Pandavas. You have not seen..."

"Keep your lectures for your friends. Those things may have contributed to your anger, but this game of dice has more to do with your ego than..."

"It is not only me they insulted. They insulted Karna too. Draupadi asked him to drive me in his chariot..."

"So if this is not about you, it is about your friend Karna."

"Enough!" Suyodhana's voice had an edge Bhanumati had never heard before. "Yes, it is my ego. I was insulted. And you expect me to take such insults lying down? I am a Kshatriya. I am the grandnephew of Bhishma. You expect me to grin and bear it? You expect me to keep quiet when they treat men like Mayasura worse than a worm?"

"Then fight but do not trick them." Bhanumati was trembling.

"And be responsible for thousands of deaths? Be the reason for a devastating war after which nothing will be left? This way, I avoid bloodshed."

"That is not the Suyodhana I know. That is not my husband speaking, but the Prince of Gandhara."

"You think I am a puppet in his hands? That I cannot think for myself?"

In the dim light that filtered through the silk curtains, Bhanumati saw Suyodhana's eyes glittering with insanity and hatred. She felt afraid. Bhanumati quickly moved towards her daughter who stirred and gently patted her back to sleep. She tried to control her tears. Without facing her husband, she said, "The path you are choosing will lead us all to disaster. Forgive Draupadi her thoughtless remarks, and her foolish husbands. You have the generosity to forgive the mistakes of lesser men."

When she turned, she saw only the curtains swaying in the wind. Suyodhana had walked into the darkness. She hugged her children, trying to shut out the ominous hooting of an owl in the garden. At that moment, she hated Draupadi with all her heart.

***

"There she is!" Subhadra rushed in from the balcony. She had come to Hastinapura to visit Bhishma as the Grand Regent wished to see her son. He had written to invite her to Hastinapura. The conch sounded, announcing the arrival of Yudhishtra, King of Indraprastha, and his brothers. "I will go get her," Subhadra said as she went out with her young son, Abhimanyu, who ran ahead to greet his father.

Bhanumati sat glued to her seat. She heard the chariot carrying the Pandavas come to a halt on the gravelled driveway. She could hear Abhimanyu giggling as Arjuna threw him up into the air and caught him again. She heard her husband's voice welcoming his cousins. She heard little Abhimanyu jump from his father to his uncle, and the laughter that followed. She heard her husband joking with Abhimanyu, whom he regarded as another son. Subhadra joined in the laughter. Bhanumati heard Arjuna commenting that his son was fonder of Suyodhana than of him. She felt choked. Yudhishtra asked for her. Bhanumati kept watching the door, fear filling her heart. Any moment now, she would be face to face with the woman she hated.

"Bhanu, see who has come to see you." Subhadra's excited voice floated to her as the colour drained from her face. Subhadra stood at the door, her lovely smile lighting up the whole room. Behind her, Draupadi stood, gazing at her with a smile.

Bhanumati folded her hands stiffly in greeting and managed to utter, "Why do you stand at the door? Come in."

Draupadi hurried in and grasped Bhanumati's hands, pressing them, almost as if she would lose her courage if she let go. "I owe you and your husband an apology. What I did was wrong. But I never meant any harm. Bhanumati, forgive me. Suyodhana is like my brothers Dhristadyumna and Shikandi. I would often tease them but they always took it in their stride. What happened was like that."

Bhanumati's heart sank. It was not what she had expected. She had practiced harsh words and angry retorts to slight Draupadi, expecting her to behave in her characteristic haughty manner. But Draupadi had disarmed her with her apology.

Draupadi had not finished. "I know Suyodhana is a good man. If he had taken the incident to heart, he would not have invited us to this dice game. It shows he has forgiven us. He knows Yudhishtra likes nothing better than a game of dice. It is good of your husband to forgive his sister's mistake."

"I know who you were really laughing at, Draupadi," Subhadra said naughtily. Bhanumati saw a smile tug at Draupadi's beautiful mouth. "Does he still have a place in your heart? Do you really need to hurt him so much?" Subhadra asked, with a crooked smile.

Draupadi turned away. Her voice was flat when she answered. "I do not know which Suta you are talking about, Subhadra."

"I never spoke of a Suta at all," Subhadra said laughing.

Draupadi bit her lip as colour flooded her face. Then both women laughed. Looking at them, Bhanumati thought perhaps there was some hope after all. If Draupadi told Suyodhana even half of what she had said to her, everything would be fine. She prayed Suyodhana would come into the room.

Draupadi told the women she had not been feeling well due to a painful menstrual flow, but that Yudhishtra had insisted she accompany them to Hastinapura. It was an important day for him and she could not stay behind. Draupadi had agreed, thinking she could use the opportunity to make amends with Bhanumati and Suyodhana, for her indiscretion.

**

Yudhishtra looked around at the gathering of noblemen in the Hastinapura *sabha*. Arjuna had advised him to decline Suyodhana's invitation. His mother Kunti had warned him about the possibility of being ambushed on the way. Finally, he had gone to Dhaumya for advice. The Priest had deliberated with his disciples and other scholars and said it was a Kshatriya's *dharma* to play dice. That had made Yudhishtra smile, for he was an inveterate gambler. The dice game excited him as nothing else could. Furthermore, Suyodhana had promised to stake his position as Crown Prince, against Indraprastha, even though he would be represented in the game by his uncle, Shakuni, Prince of Gandhara.

A win would enable Yudhishtra to grab the mighty Hastinapura Empire. Given the support he already enjoyed with the Priestly class, the Southern Confederate could be persuaded to pay him homage, making him Emperor of India – from the Himalayas to the southern seas. Dhaumya predicted Yudhishtra would win easily, as he always followed *dharma*. As an additional guarantee, they met with an astrologer, who threw cowry shells on the ground, did some obscure calculations, moved a few shells from one box to another, and then predicted Yudhishtra's win as a foregone conclusion since all the planets favoured him. Finally, the Priests had given Yudhishtra an amulet to wear as a success charm. When he entered the Hastinapura palace, accompanied by his brothers, there was some gossip and comment about the amulet, prominent among the pearl and diamond jewellery he wore.

***

After the trial throws, with Yudhishtra winning most of the plays and Shakuni getting only a few points, the game began in earnest, based on throws and the movement of coins – calling for a mixture of skill and luck, rather like life itself.

"Your Highness, the game now begins. Let us set the wager," Shakuni said, looking blandly at Suyodhana.

"I place my pearl necklace," Yudhishtra said. Karna smirked, irritating the other Pandavas.

"I do the same," Suyodhana said calmly, unclasping his pearl necklace and placing it near the board.

The dice started rolling.

***

Dhritarashtra sat listening to the commentary from his scribe and secretary, Sanjaya. He wanted his son to win. He was relieved Gandhari had not appeared yet. She had always been set against the game. It was he who had encouraged his son to play, saying it was an accomplishment required of a Kshatriya. She had gone to the temple to feed the poor. Not to be outdone, Kunti had followed her. Let them remain there, the King thought

416

chuckling. The women had no business in the *sabha* after all. It was the realm of men. Bhishma and his new ideas!

"*Aha*, I win!" cried Shakuni with unconcealed glee as the crowd craned to see the result of the first throw.

Dhritarashtra smiled to himself. 'Gandhari, you were dead against dicing. Now see how easily our son is pulling the rug out from under Yudhishtra's feet.' Shakuni was a resourceful man, thought Dhritarashtra when more applause rippled through the *sabha* as the dice obeyed the foreigner again. He wondered for the thousandth time why his wife disliked her brother so much. He was handing the kingdom to Suyodhana on a platter. Men played to win while the women went to the temple to pray. Dhritarashtra sat in silence, willing the dice to roll in Shakuni's favour.

***

As a reluctant sun lazily rose over the mist-covered trees, a man galloped towards the capital of Sindh. He had ridden for two days almost without a break. His back was sore and his joints ached, but he knew he had to get his message to the King. When he reached the city gates, he slowed to a trot to appear inconspicuous. Then he dismounted and began weaving his way through the busy streets, leading his horse as he pushed forward to the palace. He wiped the perspiration from his face with the tail of his turban and looked longingly at the wayside inns where men were resting on charpoys, sipping cold milk or wine, under the shade of the trees. He was tired unto death and longed to sleep for a hundred years. But the information he carried was explosive enough to destroy the sleep of many important men across India.

When he reached the fort gate, the guards kept him waiting while they made various entries. They asked him irrelevant questions while his eyes scanned the palace courtyard. It seemed almost deserted. "Is His Highness not present?" he finally asked.

The guards lifted their heads and looked at each other. "Do you not know? King Jayadratha has gone to Hastinapura."

"Hastinapura! Why the hell…" he swallowed his words lest he say something insulting about his King.

"Who are we to question the King about his movements? I think he has gone to a dice game. If you have anything to convey to His Highness, you can give us the message and we will make sure he gets it once he is back. That will cost you two silver coins," the younger of the guards told him officiously. But the messenger shook his head and starting walking out.

"Hey you, you said you have a message for the King. I can pass it on for one coin," the guard cried out, but the messenger had already mounted his horse.

'Fool! Can I tell him Durjaya has slipped into Gandhara with hundreds of his men and is being trained to wreak havoc on our cities?' the spy thought as he turned north-east, towards Hastinapura. How typical! When the country was about to burn, the rulers were playing dice. To hell with being inconspicuous. He kicked his mount with a vengeance. The frothing horse, carrying the bitter and tired man, sent everyone in its path scurrying for safety as it galloped towards Hastinapura.

***

Yudhishtra touched his amulet. In the trial throws, the foreigner had not appeared to be a skilled player. Perhaps it was just beginner's luck, he thought a little uneasily. Lifting his head he said, "I wager all my golden chariots."

Shakuni rubbed the dice together. "Golden chariots, Your Highness? That would be somewhat unfair. Hastinapura has far more golden chariots than Indraprastha."

"I add my corps of trained elephants," Yudhishtra answered immediately. Nothing in his demeanour showed that his heart was thudding in his chest.

The dice rolled again.

"Bad luck, Your Highness! Your elephants and chariots are now Suyodhana's," Shakuni said with a smile.

Yudhishtra cursed under his breath. How was it possible? No one had ever worsted him in a game of dice. Arjuna whispered to his brother to stop. They had already lost a major part of their army. But Yudhishtra, stung by the smug look on the Kauravas' faces, lost his usual calm and staked his mansions, horses, gold, diamonds, treasury, cows, all the villages in his kingdom, his armoury and the wealth of his merchants.

The dice rolled again, sweeping everything from Yudhishtra's grasp in each of the next ten throws.

"Stake something worthwhile Prince, instead of a horse or a cow at a time. Then you can win big. Suyodhana is staking his position as Crown Prince. If he loses, you will be Crown Prince of Hastinapura, and King when the time comes. He will go away as a mendicant. Match that if you dare. Win and you gain an empire; if you lose...?"

Shakuni's smiling words provoked the gambler in Yudhishtra. He touched his amulet again and took a deep breath. "I wager my palace in Indraprastha."

The dice rolled for the eleventh time.

"Oh! It is not your day, Highness... you lose again!" Shakuni exclaimed in mock dismay.

Arjuna began to look grim. The smiles had vanished from the faces of Bhima, Nakula and Sahadeva. Yudhishtra sat pale and withdrawn. There was pindrop silence in the *sabha*. Suyodhana was overcome by sudden pity for his cousin. He had got his revenge. The Pandavas had nothing left. They would have to live on his charity. He had reduced his cousins to petty Royals without spilling a drop of blood. He stood up to end the game.

Shakuni saw it and tensed. The fool was going to spoil all his plans. But fortunately for the foreigner, Yudhishtra lifted his head and said clearly, "Cousin, do not insult me by stopping the game now. I am sure I will win in the end." The gambler in Yudhishtra had taken possession of him. Nothing mattered but the next roll of the dice. He knew with utter certainty that his luck would turn.

Suyodhana sat back, surprised by his cousin's uncharacteristic words and rashness. He knew there was no winning for the Pandavas that day, no matter how skilled a player his cousin was.

Sushasana whispered in his ear, "Why do you want to stop now? We are winning."

Suyodhana looked at his brother, who appeared almost drunk with vicarious pleasure. It was evident Sushasana had been pouring himself a drink every time he went out. "Go and sleep it off in your chamber and do not create a scene here," Suyodhana said quietly. But Sushasana only gave him a crooked grin in reply.

"I wager my brother, Nakula." Yudhishtra's voice shook.

There was a moment's stunned silence, and then the *sabha* erupted in talk and discussion. The dice rolled. Sushasana laughed openly when Yudhishtra lost again.

"One more throw and you could win back everything you have lost, as well as gain the throne of Hastinapura. But do you dare?" Shakuni asked Yudhishtra casually.

Arjuna placed a restraining hand on his brother's shoulder saying, "Enough! Let us go."

"No. How can I leave Nakula a slave to Duryodhana? We have to win him back," Yudhishtra replied, his eyes glittering with the fever of his addiction. He threw the dice with trembling hands. Nakula was lost. But Yudhishtra was beyond counsel now. He rolled the dice again saying, "I wager Sahadeva," and promptly lost him too.

"Fools! A foreigner is rolling the dice and you rulers of India are gambling away your country? Stop this nonsense!" Kripa, who was watching the game, could no longer control himself.

"There is nothing is wrong in gambling. Our scriptures permit it. It is the *dharma* of a King to play at dice." Dhaumya could not resist showing off his superior knowledge of the scriptures. Rarely did he get a chance to get back at Kripa. They glared at each other.

Kripa laughed. "Fools! Idiots!" he kept muttering as the dice rolled again and again... and Yudhishtra lost Arjuna, Bhima, and even himself. He had nothing left to wager. He and his brothers were now Suyodhana's slaves.

Shakuni turned to Dhaumya. "Tell me, great scholar, as per the *smritis*, does a master have the right to decide what costume his slaves should wear?"

Dhaumya squirmed, but he did not have a choice. "Whatever the master wishes, the slave must wear, but..."

"Thank you." Shakuni interrupted the Priest. He looked at Suyodhana in open invitation to take his revenge.

A few days before, Suyodhana had stood in Yudhishtra's *sabha* naked, while the whole world laughed at him. The wheel had turned full circle. The Pandavas had become his slaves and he could do anything with them. "Remove your clothes and stand there," he ordered his cousins while the assembly sat in stunned silence.

The Pandavas hesitated, but knew they had to obey. One by one, they took off their clothes and ornaments. Finally, they stood in their loincloths, shamed and humiliated. Karna and Aswathama's mocking laughter filled their ears, just as their mirth had burned in Suyodhana's. All the Kaurava brothers followed suit.

Shakuni was watching Suyodhana nervously. He feared his nephew would magnanimously return everything to his cousins now that his thirst for revenge had been satisfied. He quickly made his master move. "Would you like to wager anything on a last throw, Yudhishtra?"

The Pandava did not miss that the Gandhara Prince was now calling him by his name. He was a slave and people could call him anything they liked. How could astrology be so wrong? He had followed everything the Priests had said and still Suyodhana had won. "There is nothing left to wager," he said, his voice cracking with emotion.

"Have you forgotten your most prized possession, Yudhishtra?" Shakuni gazed at his opponent in surprise. "You could win back everything by staking her. She is your lucky charm, is she not? Your astrologers cannot be wrong. It is a science after all. So far luck has favoured me but one right throw and you could win back not only what you have lost, but gain the kingdom of Hastinapura too. Who can predict how the dice will roll the next time?"

"He is afraid, Uncle," Sushasana said, slurring his words. As an afterthought he added, "Poor slave".

Yudhishtra could bear the humiliation no longer. "I wager my wife," he said softly, his heart hammering in his chest. He had to try one more throw. Surely, the Gods would smile on his courage?

The words hit Arjuna like a punch in his face. How dared Yudhishtra do this? He wanted to scream that it was he who had won Draupadi with his skill and valour. His brother had merely followed their mother's wishes, justifying his action based on some obscure *smritis*. What right had he to gamble Draupadi and play his dangerous games? Yet, when he looked at the broken man before him, he could not bring himself to ask that cruel question.

"The wife who is common to all of you... am I right?" Shakuni asked, gently rubbing salt into their wounded hearts. Not one of the Pandavas replied.

Vidhura was unable to stand by in silence any longer. In desperation, he appealed to the Grand Regent. "Sir, stop this before it gets worse."

But Bhishma just shook his head and said, "If a man is a fool, not even God can save him. How can we entrust a kingdom to a gambler? Nobody forced him to play. He played because of greed and he is now paying the price. That is nature's way of eliminating the undeserving. Do not interfere."

"Guru," Shakuni addressed Dhaumya again, "this slave wants to wager his wife, who is also wife to all his brothers. Can a man wager his wife? What do your *smriti*s say?"

Dhaumya wished he could turn and flee the accursed place, but knew he had to answer the question or lose face. "Hmm... if a man is in distress, he may sell, pawn or stake his house, wife, children, and cows, in that order. A woman is essentially not entitled to freedom, as she is her husband's property. But that..."

"Thank you." Shakuni bowed to Dhaumya before he could go into an explanation to suit Yudhishtra.

But Dhaumya was not concerned about Yudhishtra losing his crown. It was a temporary setback. When one ruler went, another came to fill his place. Kings were merely puppets in the hands of the Priests. Now that this puppet had become unusable, it was time to find a new one to play the game. So he continued watching the unfolding drama with interest, hoping he would not be called upon to make any further statements. Silence would serve him best.

"We accept your wager," Shakuni said.

Kripa laughed again, irritating everyone. Truly, one cannot save a fool, he thought.

"Twelve!" cried Shakuni.

"Eight," Yudhishtra said in a shaking voice.

Yudhishtra said a fervent prayer as the dice spun viciously. The words were wasted. In the duel between a lucky amulet and the skill developed over three decades of dedicated practise, the latter won handsomely.

"Aha, Draupadi is ours," Shakuni said in triumph. Sushasana got up eagerly but rather unsteadily.

"Guru, what caste does a slave belongs to? Are they above Sutas?" Shakuni asked with a humble look, craving enlightenment.

Dhaumya looked at the Gandhara Prince and said weakly, "Slaves do not have any caste. They are Untouchables."

"Really!" exclaimed Shakuni unctuously. "So you say they are now Untouchables? That Arjuna is a slave? That big-bellied Bhima is a slave, as are the handsome twins? And, of course, this Son of Dharma is now an Untouchable too? Do you advise us to have the palace cleaned with cow dung? Now Karna will have to take a bath if he touches any of the Pandavas."

Expressing the hurt and bitterness only a man spurned by the woman he loves can feel, Karna said, "Bring out the woman who shares her bed with five men. Let us all see what our slave looks like." Draupadi's words, 'I will not marry a Suta' and her taunt to him to drive away the naked Suyodhana in his chariot, returned to sear Karna's mind.

Suyodhana looked at Karna in surprise. His heart went out to his friend. How deeply Karna must have suffered to be so uncharacteristically cruel. He caught Aswathama's eye. The Brahmin was shaking his head, trying to tell him they had gone too far.

"Have you forgotten her laughter, nephew? Have you forgotten the day you stood unclothed and ridiculed?" Shakuni whispered to Suyodhana.

His uncle's words poured oil on the embers of the fire in Suyodhana's mind. The flames leapt up again. "Bring Draupadi here," he commanded.

Vidhura pleaded again with Bhishma to stop the insanity. But the Grand Regent sat in unmoved silence.

***

"What is he doing, Sanjaya?" Dhritarashtra gripped his scribe's wrist.

"Your son wishes to drag your nephew's wife to the *sabha*, Your Highness," Sanjaya replied in his characteristic flat tone, not offering any opinion. His job was to describe what he saw to the blind King, not to comment on affairs of State and the actions of those more important than he.

The King's tortured thoughts roiled in his brain. Where had Gandhari gone? What was she doing in the temple when she was needed here? Why was Suyodhana doing this? Surely, it was because of the company he kept. He was doing it for that Suta, or perhaps that Brahmin boy. 'Should I stop this farce and risk losing everything Shakuni has won for my son?' he wondered frantically. Why was the wise, know-it-all Bhishma silent? The King tightened his grip on Sanjaya's wrist and gazed at the *sabha* with unseeing eyes.

***

"That boy has style. It is just a matter of time before Dwaraka falls," Takshaka said as he watched the vanishing column of dust from a rocky overhang in the jungle. Kaliya agreed with his leader as usual. The army led by Ekalavya, Shalva, and Dhantavakra, was rushing towards Dwaraka.

Vasuki, leaning on his crooked staff nearby, kept scanning the horizon with his shortsighted eyes, his hand lifted against the glare of the setting sun. The heat was oppressive and two channels of sweat ran down Vasuki's cragged face. "There they come!" he exclaimed suddenly. Takshaka and Kaliya turned towards the direction Vasuki pointed to.

"Krishna, your story ends today," Takshaka laughed.

Vasuki, gazing intently at the approaching column, did not join in the Naga leader's joy. The speck on the Eastern horizon soon grew into a column of galloping cavalry. Takshaka raised his sword high in the air. Its tip caught the red rays of the setting sun. His men, hidden in the bushes and rocks behind him, saw the signal and grew alert. He heard them getting ready. Takshaka stood unmoving, with his sword raised high. He knew his men were watching his every move. Vasuki and Kaliya clambered down from the rock.

"Remember Khandiva!" Takshaka shouted, pointing with his sword at the fast approaching cavalry. He smiled at the anger he knew he had aroused in the ranks. Dramatically, he raised both hands. "Success to the revolution!" he yelled. Hundreds of throats answered the war cry as Takshaka jumped down from the rock and rolled into his hiding place.

As darkness crept in, they waited with drawn bowstrings, for Krishna and his men to reach them.

***

Balarama sat cross-legged in his prayer room. His wife Revati stood outside the closed door, ignoring the bawling of the two-year-old Valsala. Where was Krishna? Had he been here, there would not have been any dilemma. She could hear the murmuring of members of the Yadava Council, outside the chamber. They had been waiting since morning for Balarama to make a decision. She knew the mental torture her husband was suffering. For a man who believed in non-violence and loved the people he ruled more than anything else in the world, it was a tough call.

Revati picked up little Valsala and tried to pacify her. On a normal day, she would have taken the child to the window and distracted her with the sights and sounds of the bustling city outside. But today was not a normal day. A sense of foreboding hung in the air. The usually busy streets were deserted. Dwaraka was under siege. Revati kissed her daughter, pulling the little fingers gently to make her giggle. An elephant trumpeted from the far end of the fort and the call was answered by another. Valsala tried to wriggle out of her mother's arms. She was fond of elephants. The *mahouts* would be preparing the war elephants, Revati thought, her heart sinking at the thought of war.

The door of the prayer room opened suddenly. Revati gasped at the sight of her husband standing with his mace over his shoulder. She rushed forward, tears blinding her. "You said you believed in non-violence. You said you would never touch any weapon again. Then why are you doing this?"

"What choice does a man of honour have, Revati?" he asked her as he put down the mace and picked up his daughter, kissing the child on both cheeks. The girl tugged at his earrings and smiled happily.

Revati took Valsala from her husband. He embraced her as she pressed her head to his broad chest, and stifled a sob. She knew there was no power in heaven that could turn him from his purpose.

"If I do not fight, they will destroy the city. I do not want a war, but as the leader of the Yadavas, I cannot leave my people to the mercy of the Nishada army. I detest war and violence, but I am not a coward. Non-violence has to be a position of strength. It cannot be a filthy cloth to cover the shame of cowardice. I will not indulge in peace talks until we are in a position to win. Non-violence is my personal belief. It should not stand in the way of what is good for my people. God protect us all, Revati."

She saw him walking away. Valsala wriggled down and ran behind her father. He stooped to caress her innocently smiling face.

"Then why are you not wearing your armour?" Revati cried. Her heart felt like a heavy stone in her chest.

"I do not believe in false protection. If I have ruled my country well, loved my people, and never done anything to earn the wrath of those men standing outside our fort gates and baying for our blood, I will return alive and victorious. Nothing will touch me."

Revati felt weak. Everything looked blurred through her tears. 'Krishna, where are you? Why have you left your brother alone when you are most needed?' she silently cried.

"Daughter, take care of your mother and your two naughty brothers," Revati heard Balarama tell Valsala. As her little daughter ran to her, she saw him vanish through the door. Revati entered the *puja* room where her husband had spent the whole morning and shut the door. Her daughter ran to play with the *puja* bell. Its tinkling sounded incongruous to her ears. She could hear cheering and war cries outside. Why had war come to Dwaraka? After they had left Vrindavan, life had been peaceful and good in this coastal city. Life had been idyllic in Vrindavan too, until her husband entered politics and became the leader of the Yadavas. When did he get the fancy idea that he was called to serve his country and build an ideal city? Why did men have such impossible dreams? Why could they not be happy with their families? Why did they play dangerous games and bring home misery and tears?

Revati prostrated herself on the floor, her forehead touching the ground. She did not want to look up and see the idol of Lord Rama and his consort Sita, for whose sake Rama and his brother had destroyed cities and slain thousands. The idol looked dangerously similar to her brother-in-law, Krishna. Why were the Nishadas attacking their city? If any ruler had shown concern for the plight of the Nishadas and other unfortunate people, it was Balarama. He was the only ruler who genuinely cared about them. Yet, now they were repaying his goodness with war. She felt bitter and cursed the Nishada leader who had brought bloodshed to her door. If Krishna did not come soon, everything would be lost.

As she heard the massive doors of the fort creaking open and the thunderous cries of *Har Har Mahadev* echoing from her husband's army, she shut her eyes and rested her cheek on the cold marble floor. Her daughter played on, jingling the bell innocently before the idols and throwing flowers in mock imitation of a *puja*. She was fascinated by the monkey god Hanuman and kept throwing the best flowers at his feet. The war cries outside the window rose to a crescendo and then gradually died away...

***

In the South, the Kings of the Southern Confederate stood around the bed of a frail, old man. Uthayan, Karna's old rival, was now the Chera King, and it was for his coronation that the powerful Asura Kings had assembled in Muzaris. Their Guru, Parashurama, had still to recover completely from his long coma, but when the physicians announced the Guru had awoken and was showing signs of life, the Kings of the Confederate had rushed to his bedside.

Guru Parashurama opened his eyes painfully and the Kings heaved a collective sigh of relief. Uthayan moved forward and the glassy eyes of the old man locked onto his face. Parashurama was trying to say something. The newly crowned King moved close to his Guru with joy in his heart. 'I am blessed,' he thought, 'for among all these Kings, he had chosen to speak to me first.' Uthayan strained to hear what the Guru was trying to say. But when he deciphered the whispered words, his face became as dark as midnight.

"Karna… where is my Karna? I want to see my Karna," the Guru kept mumbling.

The assembly of Kings became agitated. The greatest Kings of the South stood at his bedside and the Guru's first words were about that Suta, that cheat who had insulted them and escaped! It made them all look ridiculous. They walked out of the room, cursing the physicians who had made their Guru insane with their medicines.

"Perhaps the Guru meant we should bring Karna to him. That bloody Suta has to be taught a lesson," the King of Vatapi said.

The idea caught like wildfire. Yes, their Guru wanted revenge. They would drag the low caste imposter to the South and make an example of him. The old King of Kalinga advised caution, but there were too many young hot-bloods among the Southern Confederate rulers and no one wished to heed his unpalatable advice.

"Who is afraid of a Suta, his friend Duryodhana, or even that old man Bhishma?" asked Uthayan. That was enough to bolster the fragile egos of the proud Kings. There were angry murmurs in the *sabha*.

"Hastinapura is very far away. Are our coffers brimming with wealth that you wish to contemplate such an expedition?" the Kalinga King asked. Being the northernmost kingdom of the Confederate, his land and people would be the first to pay the price if something went wrong.

Uthayan understood the reasons for the King's caution. He moved closer and said, "Your Highness, this is why we have taxes. The people will willingly pay more in taxes for the sake of *dharma*. Do we not owe at least that to our Guru? It is a small price to pay to serve the man who taught us right from wrong. That Suta insulted all of us and we did nothing. Now, our Guru has asked for him. By Lord Vishnu, I swear we will get that arrogant Suta!"

The Kalinga King still hesitated. Uthayan stared at him intently. He could see the old man was worried about the armour he had bestowed upon Karna. Perhaps he was wondering if the Sun God had been wrong about Karna's worthiness? Uthayan sensed it was time to move or he would lose the chance to get even with the upstart Karna. The flame of revenge Karna had ignited years ago, still raged in Uthayan's mind.

"Bring the holy lamp from the temple of Lord Vamanamurthy," Uthayan commanded. Immediately, servants ran to fetch it. When it arrived, he placed it in the centre of the *sabha* and lit it.

As the Priests chanted holy *mantras*, the Kings of the Southern Confederate stepped forward one by one, and placing their palms over the flame, took a vow in the name of religion and *dharma*, to capture Karna and drag him to the feet of Guru Parashurama. As the *sabha* filled with the pungent smell of singeing flesh, riders set out, galloping towards the great cities of the Confederate. They carried only one message: *Guru Parashurama commands all the Kings of the Confederate to place their forces at the disposal of the Council of Kings. The mission before this special force is the invasion of Hastinapura; the crushing of the northern kingdoms; and the capture of the Suta, Karna, who will be dragged to meet his fate at the feet of the divine Guru.*

'Karna, where can you run to now?' Uthayan laughed to himself as he gazed at the warriors assembling near the Chera fort. The thunderous drumming of the *chendas* rolled around him, shaking the very ground he stood on. It was better his father had not lived to see this day. He too, would have talked like the old Kalinga King, advising restraint and caution, thought Uthayan. His time to take on the Suta was at hand and nothing was going to stop him.

***

Bhanumati sat in her chamber with Subhadra, Draupadi, and the children, trying to understand what was happening in the dice game below. The faint sounds of cheering, as well as despair, came to her ears. Oblivious to the drama unfolding below, Draupadi and Subhadra sat chatting. Bhanumati wondered how they could discuss the men they knew so casually. Draupadi was saying how boring Yudhishtra was, that she could make Bhima do her bidding every time, and how handsome Nakula and Sahadeva were. Karna too, came under their scrutiny and both women agreed he would have been their clear favourite if only he had been a Kshatriya. Judiciously, they avoided discussing Arjuna, their common husband. Bhanumati was surprised by the camaraderie between the two women who shared the same man. Even after so many years, even knowing her husband was faithful, Bhanumati still could not control her racing heart whenever Suyodhana stole a glance at Subhadra.

Why had the *sabha* gone so silent? Why was that mad Brahmin, Kripa, laughing so loudly? Then Bhanumati heard something that made her heart freeze. She looked in alarm at Draupadi, still chatting animatedly with Subhadra. She could clearly hear it now – the creaking of the wooden stairs. She could hear someone approaching. The footsteps stopped outside the door. Bhanumati was about to let out a sigh of relief when there was a soft knocking. She looked up in sudden fear. Her heart told her something terrible was about to happen. As the knocking grew louder and bolder, she closed her eyes, trying to keep the tears from escaping. The knocking turned into banging. A horse neighed in the street as the first tears fell into Bhanumati's lap.

***

Shakuni looked at the fool who had gambled and lost everything, including his wife. He looked at the Crown Prince sitting near him; his face pale and withdrawn. He looked at the Suta, paying back every insult he had faced, double fold. He looked at the Grand Regent wearing a stony expression, refusing to interfere. He looked at his mute brother-in-law, sitting on the throne of Hastinapura, pretending to rule India. The foreigner looked towards the door, expecting Sushasana to enter at any moment, dragging a screaming Draupadi by her hair. He wanted to laugh aloud at the five impotent husbands who sat like statues, waiting for their common wife to be stripped in public. He looked at the Priests busy debating, always debating, the rights and wrongs of what was happening.

'Father, it is done.' Shakuni smiled smugly. The dice, chiselled from the bones of a long-dead King of Gandhara, was not going to stop rolling any time soon. He could visualize clearly the apocalypse that was fast approaching; he could smell blood and see death and destruction. The Great War was near! It would consume everything. Shakuni rubbed his hands in glee.

The *sabha* was as silent as death. Except for the irritating howling of a street dog somewhere outside the palace, and the faint singing of that ugly beggar lamenting the fate of the country, there was no other sound. Everything looked perfect to the Gandhara Prince. This land was finished. Shakuni could almost hear the voices of his slain people, echoing around him. He wanted to cheer with them. But this was not the time for triumphant displays. There was still work to be done. He waited for the inevitable.

The dice had fallen.

***

To be continued in
AJAYA, Book II, *Rise of Kali*

POLYANDRY IN ANCIENT INDIA

One of the first instances of polyandry occurs in the *Rig Veda*. Surya, also known as Ushas, is wooed and married by the Aswini brothers – the Gods of Dawn and Dusk. The Vedic poet wonders about their journey through the sky in a three-seated chariot, with their bride Surya (not to be confused with Surya, the Sun God). Surya has another husband – none other than Soma, the Moon. The *Rig Veda* also mentions Rodasi (Lightning), common wife of the Maruts – the Gods of Clouds and Storms. Another example is Sage Vasista, said to have been the son of both Mitra and Varuna, from Urvashi. It is easy to dismiss these mentions as poetic license; however, the truth remains that all writers use imagery that is accepted and understood by contemporary society. These examples serve to tell us that polyandry, though not a dominant practice, was never shunned in the pre-epic period – an age which appears, even to our modern eyes, to have been both liberal and inclusive.

In the *Mahabharata* era, the practise of polyandry was more the exception than the rule. The explanations and justifications given for Draupadi's marriage to the five Pandava brothers show the changing social values of the period. The arguments seem somewhat contrived and lack the confident assertions of most Vedic writing. The *Mahabharata* says that all five Pandava brothers married her, according to Vedic rituals (*Agnisakshi* and *Saptapada*), and hence it was not just a case of cohabitation, as is sometimes opined by critics. The arguments regarding the propriety of a woman marrying five men go back and forth in the epic. There is mention that according to tradition, a woman could marry only four men at the same time, any more would make her a prostitute. This statement is particularly intriguing in the case of Draupadi.

Kunti is also aware of this. But who is to be left out from the five Pandavas, if such a rule was to be applied in case of Draupadi, is the great dilemma she faces. Yudhishtra rescues everyone by justifying polyandry by citing the examples of Marisa, the tree spirit's marriage to ten sages; and that of Vrakasi to the ten Practesa brothers. However, later in the *Mahabharata*,

Karna uses the argument that any woman who marries more than four men is considered a prostitute, hence stripping Draupadi in public takes on another dimension. Karna refers to existing norms rather than those of the Vedic period.

Marriage was considered valid only after the performance of the Vedic rituals. Though Arjuna wins Draupadi at the *swayamvara*, in order to obtain the sanction of society, all five brothers are married to her as per Vedic rituals according to their seniority. The rules of sharing are also laid down by Kunti, and each brother has Draupadi for one year. The text is ambiguous about the sharing arrangements during pregnancy, but we can assume that Draupadi remained with the father of the unborn child until its birth and the stipulated time thereafter for maternal rituals to be completed, before the rotation began again. Also, it is likely that one menstrual cycle elapsed between the end of one husband's time and the beginning of the next. These rules were applied to prevent confusion regarding who was the father of the child.

Kunti justifies the marriage of her five sons to one woman using the concept of *niyoga*. This is explained in various texts in different ways. It was a very flexible idea. In an era prior to the time of the epic, younger brothers had rights over their sister-in-law (the firstborn's wife), though not the other way round. Later, as the social norms changed *niyoga* was permitted only in exceptional circumstances. It originally meant that a woman whose husband was either incapable of fathering children or had died childless, could appoint a man to be the father of her child – rather similar to the modern concept of sperm donation. *Niyoga* also had societal sanction if a younger sister-in-law became a widow without having any sons. That particular rule is quoted by Bhishma in the cases of Ambika and Ambalika; hence, Vedavyasa becomes the natural father of Dhritarashtra, Pandu and Vidhura. In a sense, this is also polyandry. *Niyoga* also came to mean that with the husband's consent, the wife could bear sons from men of any of the three castes; or according to some schools of thought, only by *sapinda* (brothers/those who shared the same *pinda*). Kunti and Madri's polyandrous relationships with various gods had the consent of their husband, Pandu.

But Kunti having children using *niyoga*, may have had more to do with politics than custom. She does not disclose the identity of her illegitimate son until the very end; nor does she ask for her brother-in-law's help in procreation, as per custom. According to the *Manusmriti*, *niyoga* can be performed only if there are no male heirs and hence the lineage is on the verge of extinction. That was not the case in the Kuru ruling house. If Pandu was impotent, Dhritarashtra was still able to father children, and did. But Kunti wished her own son to succeed to the throne of Hastinapura and not Gandhari's. Hence, in Kunti's *niyoga*, it was not a brother-in-law or even a mortal who takes part, but the Gods themselves. The Pandavas thus become known as divine progeny and the sons of Gods. From this seed sprouts the conflict portrayed in the *Mahabharata*. Yudhishtra's claim to the throne is justified by the rule that sons born of a *niyoga* relationship are considered the husband's sons. The logic for this was that if a neighbour planted seeds in another's land, when they sprouted the plants became the property of the owner and not the one who planted them. But these ideas are pushed even further in the case of the Pandavas. One may wonder what could be a modern explanation for impregnation by various Gods?

Pandu and his two wives chose to retire to the forest to undertake *niyoga*. The clandestine nature of this act stands in stark contrast to a similar situation in the previous generation, when Satyavathi called upon her ascetic son, Vyasa, born before her marriage, to be the *niyoga* partner for her widowed daughters-in-law. Vyasa then lived in the palace and did as his mother asked, in an open manner. Society accepted both the Dowager-Queen's illegitimate son (Vyasa) and his *niyoga*. Pandu himself was a product of this. Possibly, Kunti and Pandu thought that children born in the usual *niyoga* norms would not gain the support of the people; hence, the sons of Dhritarashtra and Gandhari would then have the only legitimate claim on the throne of Hastinapura.

Most probably, the *niyoga* of both Kunti and Madri was with forest dwellers or travelling ascetics. Yudhishtra could have been of Brahmin origin. It may be noted that there were, and still are, Brahmins who aid in Hindu funeral rituals. One of the three Brahmins, who partake in the *pinda*, is designated Yama, or the God of Death, for the duration of the ritual. As per custom, the three Brahmins need to be men learned in the scriptures and respected for their knowledge. Yudhishtra's father could very well have been one such scholar. Bhima's lineage could be that of a forest dweller. The fact that Kunti permits only Bhima to marry a *rakshasi*, Hidumbi, may bear on this possibility. Bhima has a violent nature and there are a few occasions when he drinks the blood of his enemies. Arjuna, of course, is the son of the Deva King, Indra. The *Mahabharata* shows Indra dwelt in Khandivaprastha, and was a friend of Takshaka. Whatever may be the truth, in an era when people believed in Gods coming down from heaven and bestowing children upon mortals, the propaganda that the Pandavas were the sons of Gods was a political masterstroke by Kunti and her strategists.

Another curious nugget in the *Mahabharata* is the fact that Vidhura's two sons shared one wife, though Vidhura himself advises against polyandry. While reading the *Mahabharata*, one cannot but wonder at the openness of society then, and how effectively the great epic captured the changing social norms of what was acceptable and what was taboo.

DHRITARASHTRA-GANDHARI'S 100 SONS & ONE DAUGHTER
Pandu retired to the forest with Kunti and Madri. The news that Kunti had become pregnant with a divine child, made Gandhari impatient and insecure. She wanted 100 sons. Vyasa had granted her a boon saying she would have them. However, she did not bear a son, even after a pregnancy lasting two years. When she heard the news about Kunti, Gandhari hit her own stomach in frustration and delivered a lump of flesh. Vyasa divided this lump into 101 pieces and sealed them in mud containers, where they developed to become 100 boys and one girl. Gandhari delivered the lump of flesh nine months before Yudhishtra's birth; but the 100 boys and the lone girl, were born a day after Yudhishtra was born. Hence, Suyodhana was part of the lump Gandhari delivered long before Yudhishtra; but he was born a day after Yudhishtra. Which of the Princes was the eldest was thus a perplexing question and it forms the root cause of the *Mahabharata* war.

Being the rebel I am, I have tried to find a logical explanation for the seemingly absurd situation of a couple having 101 children. What does this mean to the modern mind? A human pregnancy cannot last two years. Just as Kunti was in the race to produce the firstborn in the family, Dhritarashtra and Gandhari must also have been desperate to produce the firstborn son. It could be that Gandhari miscarried and the story of her two-year pregnancy and the lump of flesh being divided was an excuse to hide the fact that her son was younger than Yudhishtra. Or did Gandhari perhaps miscarry and Vyasa give her a concoction, leading to the multiple births the following year? The remaining Kaurava siblings could have been the children of concubines. This theory has the merit of plausibility. More fantastic theories suggest the ancients knew about test tube babies and cloning; however, a more rational explanation is that while all the Kauravas may have been Dhritarashtra's children, they were not essentially Gandhari's, as they are often referred to as 'Dhartarashtras', in the epic. Suyodhana refuses to acknowledge the Pandavas lineage and claim on the throne by always referring them as Kaunteyas, or the sons of Kunti, but not Pandu, whereas he is called Dhartarashtra, son of Dhritarashtra. It is also pertinent that, except for Suyodhana and Sushasana, none of the other Kauravas is referred to as sons of Gandhari, but only as Kauravas or Dhartarashtras. While the other Kauravas could have been the sons of Dhritarashtra's concubines, perhaps the role of Vyasa was to legitimize the 'containers' or wombs of these other woman who carried Dhritarashtra's seed. Obviously, in the race to produce the firstborn, neither Pandu nor Dhritarashtra were taking any chances.

When I had raised the question with my late father, L. Neelakantan, he proffered a simple but beautiful explanation. His advice was not to approach the *Mahabharata* just as a story, for it contains hidden symbolism: the 100 Kauravas represent the Desires and follies of the mind. Hundred is just a number used to represent 'numerous', and should not be taken literally. Dhritarashtra represents Ego, which is blind and produces numerous Desires. Some are good and others bad. The Kaurava names have both the positive suffix *Su* and the negative prefix *Du*. Gandhari represents the Mind and blind maternal Love. Hence, the Desires are sons of blind parents – Mind and Ego.

On another plane, the Pandavas represent the five Senses. They are all married to Draupadi, also called Krishna (black). Black represents Anger. The marriage of the five Senses to Anger, has catastrophic results when fighting the Desires – such as when the Pandavas visit the Kaurava *sabha* for the game of dice. Believing in Fate, not action, they gamble with the Desires, and lose everything. Anger is shamed and disrobed by the Desires and Fate. The Pandavas also represent the five Virtues: Yudhishtra represents Wisdom, as the son of Time (*Kala*). Bhima portrays Strength, as the son of Vayu (*Prana*). Arjuna represents Willpower, as the son of Indra. Nakula and Sahadeva stand for Beauty and Knowledge, as sons of the Aswinis, the Gods of Dawn/Beginnings. It is Krishna who brings the Pandavas and the Desires together at Kurukshetra. He is the Universal Soul (*Paramatma*). Black represents vastness/depth here. The Virtues are fated to lose without this aid. Kurukshetra represents the Soul. With the aid of Universal Consciousness, the Virtues triumph over desires.

This was my father's explanation of the underlying significance of the *Mahabharata*. However, his rebel son's take on the great epic is *Ajaya*.

SUGGESTED READING

1. Sarva Daman Singh. *Polyandry in Ancient India*. Motilal Banarsidass New Delhi, 1988

2. John Dowson. *Classical History of Hindu Myth and Religion*. Munshiram Manoharlal Publishers, New Delhi, 2000

3. A.L. Ahuja. *Women in Indian Mythology*. Rupa & Co. New Delhi, 2011

4. Ram Sharan Sharma. *Aspects of Political Ideas and Institutions in Ancient India*. Motilal Banarsidass, New Delhi, 2012

5. Vettam Mani. *Puranic Encyclopedia*. Motilal Banarsidass, New Delhi 2010; Malayalam ed: DC Books, Kottayam 2013 [Ed: Perhaps the most comprehensive book on various Puranic characters; written as short notes, alphabetically arranged. A good reference source for anyone interested in Hindu mythology.]

SELECT GLOSSARY

Aarti – Worship with lamps

Acharya – Guru, teacher

Achuyuta – Another name for Krishna

Aghoris – Ascetic worshippers of Shiva who do not believe in caste or the taboos of Hinduism; known for extreme and even outlandish penances

Ajaya – Unconquerable

Andha – Blind

Anga – Ancient Indian kingdom; present-day Eastern Bihar and parts of Bengal

Angavasthra – Shawl worn by nobles

Ashwini Twins – Gods of sunrise and sunset

Astra – Arrow/shaft; described by the epics as having divine powers

Asura – Hindu mythology portrays Asuras as demons of darkness – the antithesis to Devas, the Gods; here, they are one among many tribes

Atharva – The fourth *Veda*, which speaks of magic, spells, etc.

Atma – Soul

Avarna – A person who does not belong to the first three castes; literally one without colour (*varna*); opposite of *savarna* (person with a good colour)

Ayurveda – Ancient Indian system of medicine

Bindi – Red dot worn on the forehead by Hindu women

Brahmacharya – Self-imposed vow of celibacy; a period of life as a student when a man observes *brahmacharya*; to seek or follow God

Brahman – The Supreme Power responsible for Creation and the Universe

Brahmin – The highest Hindu caste and *varna* – Priests and scholars; Hindu society was divided into four *varnas* (refer Varna for details), and further sub-divided into *jatis* (castes); these varied from region to region (eg. a Brahmin from Kashmir in the north and one from Andhra in the south, belonged to the same *varna* but did not intermarry as they belonged to different castes)

Chaitra – Indian calendar month when spring begins

Chandagyo – One of the most important of the *Upanishads*

Chandalas – One of the lowest of the Untouchable castes; keepers of graveyards; those who carried the dead

Chaturvarnas – The four *varna*s (refer Varna for details)

Chenda – A south Indian drum beaten with a curved stick; known even today as the *Asura Vadhya* or 'musical instrument of the Asuras' and used during festivals in Kerala and parts of south Karnataka and Tamil Nadu

Chera – Ancient kingdom in south India, with Muzaris as its capital

Chettis – Merchant caste of south India (corruption of the term *shresti*)

Crore – One hundred lakhs; ten million

Dakshinajanapada – Land south of the Vindhyas; south India

Darshan – Literally 'view'; it was customary for Indian monarchs to appear at a balcony and hear petitions from their subjects

Dasa – Servant or slave

Dasi – Female servant/slave

Dhanurveda – Science of arms and weapon-making

Dharma – Rough translation: duty, righteousness etc; but *dharma* encompasses more – it is the code of life; antonym: *adharma*

Dharmaveera – Warrior or hero of *dharma*

Dharmayudha – Ancient code of battle

Dhoti – Traditional lower garment for men, made from an unstitched length of cloth; also worn in different styles by lower-class women in ancient India

Gandhara – Present-day Kandahar in Afghanistan

Gandharvas – Singers in the courts of the Gods; considered to be supernatural beings pining for love; messengers between the Gods and men; here, they are simply another aboriginal tribe

Ganga – Ganges

Gangotri – Glacier from where the Ganga originates

Gayatri – Sacred Hindu *mantra* from the *Rig Veda*; when the caste system was at its zenith, many texts forbade Shudras from even listening to it; some texts advocated pouring molten lead into the ears of Shudras who heard the *Gayatri* even accidently – though it is doubtful if it was really practised

Ghat – A broad flight of steps leading down to a river

Gobar – Cow dung

Har Har Mahadev – Hail Shiva, the Greatest God

Hari – Another name for Lord Vishnu

Hastinapura – City of Elephants, capital of the Kuru kingdom

Indra – King of the Gods; used here as a generic name of the tribe who are the nominal rulers of the Devas; Indra, their last King, lives in penury; he is also the biological father of Arjuna

Indraprastha – Ancient capital of the Pandavas; present-day Delhi

Jambu Dweepa – Ancient Indian name for Asia

Jaya – Victory

Kala – Time; also God of Time and Death, commonly known as Yama (derived from the unit for measuring time – *yamam*)

Kalaripayattu – Traditional martial art form of Kerala

Kalinga – Present-day Odisha (roughly)

Kaliya Mardana – Kaliya: a poisonous snake (*naga*), in the original *Mahabharata;* Mardana: punishment, suppression, etc. Kaliya Mardana is one telling of the legend of Lord Krishna punishing the *naga* for his evil deeds

Kamarupa – Ancient name for present-day Assam

Karma – Action or deed

Kashi – Another name for the holy city of Varanasi or Benaras

Kauravas – Scions of the Kuru dynasty

Khandiva – Present-day Delhi

Kingara – Servants; soldier-slaves

Kinnaras – In Hindu mythology, these are celestial musicians, half-horse and half-human; here, they are treated as just another tribe

Kirata – A wild tribe

Kshatriyas – The warrior caste; often kings and rulers

Kuravan, Malayans, Vannans, Velans – Tribes from the Western Ghats (Sahyas) of India. They were Priests before the Brahmins became prominent; even today, many rituals in the Malabar region are conducted by these people

Kurta – Indian shirt

Lakh – One hundred thousand

Lathi – Staff, usually used by police to control crowds

Leela – Divine play or drama

Lord Vishwanatha – Lord of the Universe; another name for Shiva

Ma – Mother

Madhava – Another name for Krishna

Mahadeva – Great God; another name for Shiva

Maheswara – Great God; another name for Shiva

Mahout – Elephant handler

Mata – Mother

Maya – Illusion

Mela – Gathering

Milavu, Timila, Maddallam & Mrudangam – Percussion instruments

Mlecha – Barbaric/uncivilized people; term usually used for foreigners like the Greeks or Chinese, in ancient India

Moksha – Salvation; *nirvana* in Buddhism

Muzaris – Ancient port city on the South-Western coast of India, 50 kms north of modern-day Cochin, in Kerala

Nagas – An ancient tribe; literally 'serpents'; here they represent a warring tribe who rises against caste oppression

Namaskara – 'I bow to the goodness in thee' – a form of greeting; also *Namaste*

Nishada – A hunter tribe

Onam – The only Indian festival celebrated in honour of an Asura King – Mahabali; State festival of Kerala; people still believe the reign of this Asura King (cheated of his kingdom by Lord Vishnu in his Vamana *avatar*), is the ideal; and every human being was considered equal under his rule.

Pallavas – Ancient south-Indian kingdom; its capital was Kanchipuram/Kanchi

Pallu – The loose end of a sari worn

Panchayat – Indian village Council, usually with 5 members

Pandavas – Sons of Pandu

Pandya – Ancient kingdom in south India with Madurai as its capital

Parameswara – Literally 'Supreme God'; another name for Shiva, one of the Trinity of Hindu Gods (the other two being Brahma and Vishnu)

Parashuramakshetra – Place of Parashurama – the ancient kingdom of Cheras (Gokurna to Kanyakumari, between the Sahyas and the sea). It is believed Parashurama reclaimed this land from the sea and gifted it to the Brahmins

Pariah – Lowest caste, and the most discriminated against

Parvati – Lord Shiva's consort

Pasupathi – Literally 'Lord of the Beasts'; usually applied to Shiva

Patala – Netherworld; here, capital of the Asuras in exile

Poorna – River in Kerala; also known as Periyar

Prabhasa – A city in present-day Gujarat

Prabhu – Sir, an honorific; also used to mean a rich man

Puja – Religious ritual

Purendra – Indra, King of the Gods; also known as 'destroyer of cities'

Ragas – Scales in Indian classical music

Raja Dharma – Code of ethics for rulers

Rajasuya – Sacrifice performed by Indian Kings in ancient times, who considered themselves powerful enough to be Emperors

Rakshasa – Mythological evil being

Sabha – Court or assembly

Sahya – Mountains running parallel to the Western seaboard of India

Samhita – A collection of holy hymns/science/knowledge

Sanathana – Eternal; Hinduism is often considered an eternal religion without beginning or end

Sari – Traditional attire of Indian women, made from 6 yards of unstitched cloth

Sarpanch – Village Chief/Head of the Panchayat

Sarswati – A mighty river which once flowed between the Indus and Ganges, which has now vanished

Shastras – Rules, codes, tradition, science, specialized knowledge

Shiva – The Destroyer, one of the Hindu Trinity of Gods who at the end of each eon, destroys the Universe, after which Brahma the Creator, recreates it

Shivalinga – Phallic symbol of Lord Shiva

Shravan – Fifth month of the Hindu calendar; considered a holy month

Shri – Honorific for gentlemen; equivalent to Mister; also spelt *Sri, Shree*, etc.

Shudra – Lowest of the four Varnas, the other three being (in order of precedence): Brahmana, Khshatriya, and Vaishya

Sindhu – River Indus; also the land around it; here, Indus is ruled by Jayadratha, Duryodhana's brother-in-law

Smritis – 'That which is remembered'; Hindu laws written by different sages; including *Manu Smriti*, the code for society in ancient India

Soma – Important ritual drink during Vedic times; also the moon

Somanatha – Celebrated temple of Lord Shiva – Lord of Somas (life energy)

Suta – Charioteer caste; also famous as storytellers. Kings often used them to propagate tales of their valour in battle

Swami – Sir, an honorific used to address a social superior

Swayamvara – Ancient Indian custom wherein a girl chose her groom from a gathering of suitors, sometimes through a competition

Tapsya – Penance

Timila – Percussion instrument of Asura origin

Trimurti – Trinity of Gods: Brahma the Creator, Vishnu the Preserver; and Shiva the Destroyer

Tulsi – Holy Basil; a plant revered in Hinduism, especially in the worship of Krishna or Vishnu

Upanishads – Collection of holy books; along with the commentaries (called *Brahmanas*), which form the basis of Indian philosophical thought

Urumi – Sinuous, belt-like sword used in Kalaripayattu, an ancient marital art form of south India

Uttariya – Shawl, worn as a shoulder cloth

Vaikunta – Abode of Lord Vishnu and the heaven reserved for his devotees

Vaishya – Merchant caste

Vana – Grove or forest

Vanara – Monkey; here they are a tribe of mixed descent, living in southern India

Vanga – Present-day Bengal, including Bangladesh

Varna – Literally 'colour'; also meaning 'social groups'; Hindu society was divided into 4 basic *varna*s: Brahmana or Brahmins (Priests and teachers), at the top; Kshatriyas or warriors second; Vaishya or merchants third; and Shudras (farmers, craftsmen, foot soldiers, petty traders, dancers, musicians, etc.) at the bottom of the caste hierarchy; below these were the poorest of the poor, the Untouchables

Varnashrama – In the ancient Hindu way of life, the ideal lifespan of an individual maintaining *dharma*, was divided into 4 stages: student, householder, retiree; and renunciation

Vatapi – Present-day Badami, a city in north-central Karnataka

Vayu – God of Winds

Vedas – The four holy books (*Rig*, *Yajur*, *Sama* and *Atharva*), of the Hindus; considered to possess all the wisdom of the world

Vijaya – Victory

Vindhyas – Mountain ranges which separate northern and southern India

Vishnu – The Preserver, second of the Hindu Trinity of Gods, who protects the rhythm of the Universe

Yadava – Tribe of cowherds

Yajna – Ritual sacrifice of herbal preparations into the fire with Vedic *mantras*

Yaksha – Supernatural beings; sometimes the patron gods of trees and forests in Hindu mythology; believed to guard hidden treasures; the female of the species (Yakshi), are notorious for charming unsuspecting travellers into the forest and drinking their blood or eating them; here, they are simply a tribe

Yavana Desa – Greece

Yavana – Greek

ACKNOWLEDGEMENTS

My thanks go to my readers, without whose support, encouragement and criticism of my debut novel, *Asura, Tale of the Vanquished*, I would not have toiled to write about the other great 'villain' of our epics, within the span of a year. I thank each of my readers who was kind enough to write to me with his/her feedback.

To Swarup Nanda, for being my friend and guide, both for *Asura* and *Ajaya*.

To my Editor, Chandralekha Maitra, for guiding me in making my writing better while giving me enough creative freedom, and then suffering my draft manuscripts with patience.

To my Publisher, Leadstart Publishing, for showing confidence in me by publishing my second book, *Ajaya*. As also to the other team members: Pretti, Iftikar, Rajesh, Ramu, Salim and many others, who have worked with dedication to make the first book a success and showing the same enthusiasm for my second.

To my father, the Late L. Neelakantan, and mother, Chellamal, for introducing me to the world of mythology.

To my Aparna, for your unstinting support in my endeavours and for the love I often wonder whether I deserve.

To my daughter Ananya and son Abhinav, for keeping the storyteller in me alive by demanding more and more stories every night and being the critics any author dreads.

To my sister Chandrika and brother-in-law Parameswaran, my brother Lokanathan, Rajendran and my sisters-in-law, Meena and Radhika. Also my nephew Dileep, and nieces Rakhi and Deepa, as well as my extended family members, for all those wonderful days.

To my pet Jacky, the blackie, who keeps me glued to my laptop by barking at the slightest show of laziness and demanding I take him for a walk as punishment the moment I lift my fingers from the keyboard.

To Santosh Prabhu, Sujith Krishnan, and Rajesh Rajan, for the evenings spent together discussing Indian philosophy and the *Mahabharata*, years ago, which sowed the seed of this novel in me. To Rajiv Prakash and Shevlin Sebastin, for their frequent mails that have sparked my creativity. To Premjeet, for his maverick ideas. To GMP Nayak for his insights. To (Essarpee) S.R. Prasanth Kumar, for his great support.

To my country and my people, for tolerating different points of view and for the richness of our history and mythology.

To the rich traditions of my hometown, Thripoonithura, and the history of Cochin.

To Vedavyasa, the patron of all Indian writers; the greatest writer to have walked this earth.

To the masters of writing in all our Indian languages, with sincere apologies for daring to attempt something that has already been so skilfully essayed by you over the centuries.

I owe much to all of you, as well as to many others who I may have forgotten to name here.

AJAYA
Epic of the Kaurava Clan
BOOK II

RISE OF KALI

"Beware!" the young captain shouted and Aswathama pulled on the reins of his horse in the nick of time. A massive boulder missed him by inches and crashed onto the narrow path with a thud. It bounced down the cliff face and disappeared into the river deep below, felling a few trees on its way. When the dust cleared, Aswathama was still trying to steady his panicked horse. One misstep and he knew he would follow the path made by the boulder and splatter like an eggshell, a thousand feet below. The splash of the boulder hitting the water sounded unusually loud.

Aswathama's heart pounded in his chest. Had the boulder been an accident or was someone following them? He looked around; the place looked desolate and forlorn. Nothing stirred. Far below, the Deodar trees in the valley had turned white with snow. The eerie silence when the wind stopped howling, was frightening. The mountain crouched painfully, like a wounded beast. He had undertaken this mission thinking it would be an adventure. He had always longed to see the ivory-tipped peaks of the Himalayas. It had been so inviting and he had jumped at the opportunity.

Far away, he could see the mountain ranges dissolving into the sky. He wanted to rub his hands to get the circulation back, but was afraid to let go of the reins. It was freezing cold. The chill pierced his skin and gnawed at his bones. But more than the elements, it was the inaction and boredom that was killing him. "Where are the bastards hiding?" Aswathama asked, more of himself than the captain.

"Sir, I think we have lost our way again." He heard the pain and frustration in the captain's voice and his anger returned in a flood.

"No, we have not!" He watched the words escaping his mouth in white puffs. An argument would have been welcome, but his captain refused to oblige.

When silence crawled back, Aswathama loosened the reins and the horse started walking forward. His army of twenty men dragged themselves behind him, through the treacherous mountain path. It had started snowing again.

Boom! A scream followed the crash and Aswathama almost fell from his saddle. They had been hit. In that instant he knew, the first boulder had been no accident and that more were on the way. The second one hit the rear of the column and carried away two men, along with their horses. Aswathama knew that all his arrogance about being a great archer was futile in this battle. He was not fighting on the vast and dusty plains of India. This was Gandhara and the country had the reputation of teaching reigning superpowers and empires hard and unforgettable lessons. The next boulder crashed down just behind him, hitting the captain and his horse. He saw them topple over the cliff and vanish into the depths below. The agonized screams of the man and his beast echoed around them, making the survivors edgy. He could sense the fear of his companions. He had to do something.

What was that moving there? Rather, who was it? Aswathama peered painfully towards the top of the mountain, shading his red-rimmed eyes with his right hand while the left gripped the reins convulsively. He had seen someone moving. Or was the snow playing its usual games of illusion? As he kept staring at the point high above, a silent scream began rising from his belly. The warrior in him sensed it long before his eyes could see. The enemy had waited until they reached this narrow path, with the towering mountain on one side and the deep abyss on the other – the perfect ambush spot for the Gandharans.

Carefully, Aswathama's right hand went to his sword. At that moment, the entire mountain began to reverberate as mounted warriors began descending on them at great speed. "Forward!" he shouted, galloping like a mad possessed. He had to get off the narrow path. It was now or never. The mountainside began exploding behind them as the Brahmin warrior and his daredevil companions rushed across the perilously narrow mountain path. Boulders rolled down, frightening the horses and threatening to dash them all into the waters far below. Behind, men, their faces masked with their turbans, were chasing them towards their deaths.

"Either we get that bastard Durjaya today or we all perish. We owe ourselves at least a warrior's death in service of Suyodhana and our country." Aswathama shouted over the din, trying to motivate his companions. He could not be sure they heard. But his next action inspired them to follow suit. It was one of reckless courage, yet the very insanity of it made them delirious. Aswathama let go the reins and stood up in his saddle, facing the Gandharans, his back to his galloping horse. Balancing perilously, he drew his bowstring. His men did the same. His first arrow pierced the throat of the man leading the attack, while those of his companions took out others.

"Shoot to kill… shoot… shoot!" Aswathama yelled as he showered lethal arrows on his foes. They had slowed down their pursuers but Aswathama knew they could not continue holding them off. A mis-step by one of the horses or a hit by any of the boulders falling around them would finish everything.

And then he saw him and he almost slipped from his saddle. It was just for a moment, as the cloth covering the face of one of the pursuers slipped. Yet there was no mistaking that face…

ASURA

TALE OF THE VANQUISHED
The Story of Ravana and His People

ANAND NEELAKANTAN

Tomorrow is my funeral. I do not know if they will bury me like a mangy dog or whether I will get a funeral fit for an Emperor – an erstwhile Emperor. But it does not really matter. I can hear the scuffing sounds made by the jackals. They are busy eating my friends and family. Something scurried over my feet. What was it? I haven't the strength to raise my head. Bandicoots. Big, dark, hairy rats. They conquer the battlefields after foolish men have finished their business of killing each other. It is a feast day for them today, just as it has been for the past eleven days. The stench is overpowering with the stink of putrefying flesh, pus, blood, urine and death. The enemy's and our's. It does not matter. Nothing matters now. I will pass out soon. The pain is excruciating. His fatal arrow struck my lower abdomen. But I am not afraid of death. I have been thinking of it for some time now. Thousands have been slain over the last few days.

Somewhere in the depths of the sea, my brother Kumbha lies dead, half-eaten by sharks. I lit my son Meghanada's funeral pyre yesterday. Or was it the day before? I've lost all sense of time. I have lost the sense of many things. A lonely star is shimmering in the depths of the universe. Like the eye of God. Very much like the third eye of Shiva, an all-consuming, all-destroying third eye. My beloved Lanka is being destroyed. I can still see the dying embers in what was once a fine city. My capital Trikota was the greatest city in the world. That was before the monkey-man came and set it on fire. Trikota burned for days. Shops, homes, palaces, men, women, and babies, everything burned. But we restored it. Almost every able man joined in rebuilding Trikota. Then the monkey-men came with their masters and destroyed everything again. Hanuman did that to us. The monkey-man brought us death, destruction and defeat.

I do not want to dwell on that. I should have killed him when my son captured him. Instead, I listened to my younger brother, who then plotted against me. But treason and betrayal is nothing new to the Asuras. I was naïve. I foolishly believed I would always be loved by my brothers and my people. I never imagined I would be betrayed. I feel like laughing now. But it is not easy to laugh when one's guts lie spread around like a wreath. Sounds of joy float down to me from my city. The enemy is celebrating their victory. The monkey-men will be busy plundering Trikota. My temples will be looted; the granaries torched, and schools and hospitals burnt. That is how victory parties are. We have done the same and worse to many Deva villages, when the Goddess of victory was my consort. Some ugly monkeys must have entered my harem. I hope my Queen has the sense to jump from a cliff before anything happens. I cannot control anything now. I can feel the hot breath of death on my face.

The jackals have come. Which part of my body will they eat first? Perhaps my guts, as they are still bleeding. What if a part of my breastplate chokes a jackal? I chuckle at the thought. A jackal sinks his teeth into my cheek and rips off a chunk of flesh. That is it. I've lost that bet too. They have started on my face. Rats are nibbling my toes. I, Ravana, have come a long way. Now I do not have anything left to fight for, except this battle with the jackals. Tomorrow, there will be a procession through the streets. They will raise my head on a pole and parade it through the same roads that saw me racing by in my royal chariot. My people will throng to watch the spectacle with horror and perverse pleasure. I know my people well. It will be a big show.

I do not understand why Rama came and stood over me when I fell. He stood there as if bestowing his blessings on me. He said to his brother that I was the most learned man in the world and a great King, and one could learn the art of governance from me. I almost laughed out loud. I had governed so well that my empire lay shattered all around me. I could smell the burning corpses of my soldiers. I could feel my Meghanada's cold and lifeless body in my arms even now. The acrid air of a smouldering Trikota smothered my senses. I could not save my people from these two warriors and their monkey-men. And he was saying I was a great ruler? I could appreciate the irony of it. I wanted to laugh at my enemy; laugh at the foolish men who trusted me, who were now lying all around, headless, limbless and lifeless. I wanted to laugh at the utopian dreams of equality for all men on which I had built an empire. It was laughable indeed. But laughing was no way for an Emperor to die. I have worked hard and fought with the gods and their chosen men. I doubt if heaven has a place for people who die of laughter.

Then just as suddenly as it had started, the rats and jackals scurried away. A shadow, darker than the dark night, fell upon me. A dark head with curly hair blocked the lonely star from my view. *Is it Kala, the God of Death, who has come to take me away?* I struggled to open my eyes wider. But dried blood held my eyelids together. *Is it one of Rama's lowly servants come to severe my head and take it back as a trophy?* I want to look him in the face. I want to look into his eyes, unwavering and unflinching in my last moments. Something about that head and curly hair reminded me of my past. *Do I know him?* He leaned down to look at my face.

Ah! It is Bhadra. My friend, perhaps the only friend left, but I do not know if I can call him my friend. He was my servant, a foot soldier to start with. Then he got lost somewhere along the way. He strolled in and out of my life, was sometimes missing for years together. Bhadra had access to my private camp when I was the head of a troop that resembled a wayside gang of robbers rather than a revolutionary army. Then, he had had access to my private chambers when I was the King of a small island. Finally, he had access to my bedroom when I was ruling India. More than that, Bhadra had access to the dark corners of my mind, a part that I hid from my brothers, my wife, my lover, my people, and even from myself.

What is Bhadra doing here? But why am I surprised? This is just the place for people like him, who move about in the shadows. I can hear him sobbing. Bhadra getting emotional? He was never angry, sad or happy. He acted as if he was very emotional now. But I knew he had no emotions. And Bhadra was aware I knew. *Bhadra, carry me away from here. Take me away to…* My strength fails me. I do not know whether the words were spoken or died a silent death somewhere in my throat. Bhadra shakes his head. I am cold, extremely cold. My life is ebbing out of me. Then Bhadra hugs my head to his bosom. I can smell his sweat. Pain shoots through me from every angle and spreads its poisonous tentacles into my veins. I groan. Bhadra lays me back on the wet earth – wet from my blood, the blood of my people, the blood of my dreams, and the blood of my life. It is over. A sense of sadness and emptiness descends upon me.

"I will complete your work, Your Highness. Go in peace. I will do it for our race. My methods may be different, even ignoble, compared to your's. I too was once a warrior but I have grown old. Arms frighten me now. I am terrified of war. I cannot even hurt a child. Nevertheless, my methods are deadly. I will avenge you, me, and our blighted race. Rama will not go free for what he has done to us. Believe me and go in peace."

I did not hear most of what Bhadra said. Strangely however, I was soothed and slipped away from this foul-smelling Asura and drifted back to my childhood. A thousand images rushed to me. My early struggles, the pangs of love and abandonment, separation, battles and wars, music and art, they flashed through my mind in no particular order, making no sense. Meaningless, like life itself.

I sensed Bhadra bowing down to touch my feet, then walking away. I wanted him to call him back and take me to a doctor who would put my intestines back, fit my dangling left eye back into its socket and somehow blow life into my body. I wanted to withdraw to the Sahyas forests in the mainland and start a guerilla war, as Mahabali had done years ago. I wanted to start again. I wanted to make the same mistakes, love the same people, fight the same enemies, befriend the same friends, marry the same wives and sire the same sons. I wanted to live the same life again. I did not want the seat Rama has reserved for me in his heaven. I only wanted this beautiful earth.

I knew it was not going to happen. I was sixty, not sixteen. If I lived, I would be a one-eyed, dirty, old beggar in some wayside temple, wearing stinking and tattered clothes – a long way from what I once was. I wanted to die now. I wanted this to end. I wanted to go away. Let the burning cities take care of themselves. Let the Asuras fight their own wars and be damned along with the Devas. I only wanted to return to my childhood and start over again, every single damn thing, again and again, and again...

Wish To Publish With Us?

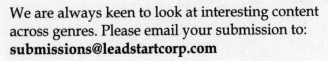

We are always keen to look at interesting content across genres. Please email your submission to: **submissions@leadstartcorp.com**

The submission should include the following:

1. Synopsis

A summary of the book in 500 – 1000 words. Please mention the word count of the manuscript.

2. Sample chapters

Two chapters, not necessarily in order; just send the two best.

3. A Note About The Author

An interesting note about yourself (about 200 words).

4. Additional Information

- Target audience,
- Unique selling points
- List of illustrative content (if any)
- Other comparative titles
- Your thoughts on marketing the book.